BOOKS BY RACHEL BRANTON

Lily's House
House Without Lies
Tell Me No Lies
Your Eyes Don't Lie
Hearts Never Lie
Broken Lies
No Secrets and Lies
Cowboys Can't Lie

Finding Home
Take Me Home
All That I Love
Then I Found You

Other Books
How Far
Royal Quest

UNDER THE NAME TEYLA BRANTON

Unbounded Series
The Change
The Cure
The Escape
The Reckoning
The Takeover

Unbounded Novellas
Ava's Revenge
Mortal Brother
Lethal Engagement
Set Ablaze

Imprints
First Touch
Touch of Rain
On the Hunt
Upstaged
Under Fire
Blinded

Colony Six
Insight
Sketches
Visions

RACHEL BRANTON

WHITE
STAR
PRESS

This is a work of fiction, and the views expressed herein are the sole responsibility of the author. Likewise, certain characters, places, and incidents are the product of the author's imagination, and any resemblance to actual persons, living or dead, or actual events or locales, is entirely coincidental.

How Far

Previously published as *Saving Madeline* by the author under another pen name.

Published by White Star Press
P.O. Box 353
American Fork, Utah 84003

Printed in the United States of America
ISBN: 978-1-948982-09-2
Year of first printing: 2019

To the many young children in the world
who don't have anyone to fight for them.
I hope this book can be your voice.

Chapter 1

Parker Hathaway walked slowly, almost casually, to the front door of the house in South Salt Lake, not crouching or darting, yet keeping to the shadows made by the huge walnut tree in the front yard. The back door would have been a better choice for staying out of view, but it was too close to the neighbor's dog kennel. If the child's mother awoke, she'd call the police.

Or maybe not. Given her current circumstances, Dakota Allen was more likely to call the hulking, balding boyfriend who'd been hanging around almost constantly during the past week, though Parker had made sure his battered car wasn't in the driveway tonight. Of course, Dakota might still be awake. He didn't know anything about her sleeping habits these days. Did she drop off the moment her head touched the pillow? Or maybe she lay awake nights like he did, thinking of how he had to do something—anything—to prevent the disaster he knew was imminent.

It didn't matter. He hadn't come for her. When he was through here, she'd hate him with a murderous passion that might barely begin to approach the feelings he harbored for her.

He shivered in the cold, and thoughts of the small whisky bottle he'd once kept in the cab of his truck made him ache with longing. But that was a place he would never go again. He forced his thoughts back to the task at hand. Two more minutes, maybe three tops, if all went well. He slipped the credit card into the crack between the door frame and the faceplate of the lock mechanism. Good, the dead bolt hadn't been engaged. He'd hoped for that. Maybe she'd been too tired. Or maybe she simply didn't care. Women like Dakota didn't. Not about the things that most people considered important. They were too busy using others to expect to be victims themselves.

Even if she'd thrown the dead bolt, he'd come prepared with the glass cutter in the truck, but this was better, cleaner. Less evidence that he'd been inside the house. What he planned to do there could land him behind bars. Deep behind bars.

Far more easily than Parker had dared hope, the card released the latch. He eased the door open, and only as he went inside did he allow his gaze to scan the neighborhood. Not furtively but carelessly, as though he belonged. Indeed, he had belonged to a neighborhood exactly like this one for as long as he'd been able to bear it. A neighborhood like this and all it entailed was what had driven him near the edge of sanity.

No one was in sight, and even if someone was looking out a window at that moment, they might assume he was the husband coming home after a night shift. They were used to having people come and go at all hours here. Three o'clock on a weekday morning, the time he'd chosen, was when they had the least traffic. He'd watched for three nights to be sure, eating up tankfuls of gasoline in the car he'd borrowed for the purpose.

He took a step inside, shut the door quietly, and then took another step as his eyes strained to be sure the tiny living room was empty. The furnishings were plain and mismatched, with a tattered brown couch, a blue love seat, and a white coffee table that had seen better days. The floor was clean. This surprised him, and he felt his first tremor of doubt.

No. Doubts were fatal. He had no choice but to continue. Desperation drove Parker onward. Another step and the floorboards creaked. He froze, listened for a full minute, and then continued when only silence met his ears. Moonlight filtered in from the kitchen window between sheer curtains that even in the dim light appeared tired and desolate. The counters were clear, though dishes were piled high in the sink, some with globs of food stuck to them. Turning his head, he slid down the dark hallway, a step at a time, stopping to listen between each movement.

Two rooms were at the end, both doors closed. What mother closed her bedroom door in the middle of the night with a helpless child sleeping nearby? How would she hear its cry? He took the left door, the front bedroom. He'd seen Madison in the window and knew it was hers.

Carefully, he twisted the doorknob and pushed open the door. There was the faintest of creaks but not loud enough for alarm. The bedroom was not as plain as the living room. Here, colorful posters lined the walls, numerous stuffed animals filled a book shelf or lay scattered over the floor and bed, and an easel for drawing stood in one corner. All the furniture was made of light oak and definitely on the new side.

His breath caught in his throat as he saw Madison lying in her bed beneath the window, a smile curving the edges of her button lips. Moonlight spilled onto her outstretched hand, a hand that beckoned to him. His heart constricted as it always did at seeing her face.

No doubts here. They belonged together. *I'm here, sweetheart.* In three steps he was kneeling at her bed, his hands reaching toward her.

A sound made his hands jerk to a stop—a soft murmur that came not from the bed but from the crib against the wall. Curious, he stood and peeked inside. Another child lay there, dressed in a blue, short-sleeved T-shirt, his mud-colored hair curling softly at his nape. He was huddled face down with his hands and feet tucked under his small body, as if trying to protect himself from the cold. Parker hadn't realized this child would be here tonight. Scrubbing a hand over the week-old growth on his face, he considered the boy. He wished he could take them both.

Better stick to the plan, he thought. Where he was going with Madison, he couldn't take the boy. He would only be a liability. Jaw clenched, Parker grabbed the furry blanket near the boy's feet and pulled it up to his neck.

Resolutely, he turned his back on the crib, kneeling again near the bed. He pulled down her blanket, scooting one hand under her warm body. She wore a thin nightgown with cap sleeves, completely inappropriate for the November night, even in a heated house. With his other hand, he grabbed the princess lap blanket folded at the bottom of the bed and pulled it up to her neck, tucking the furry warmth around her body as he drew her toward him.

She stirred as Parker rose to his feet and folded her tightly against his chest. He rocked her until she buried her face in his shirt and was still. *It'll all be over soon,* he promised. Turning, he tripped over a jumble of stuffed animals on the floor, but he caught himself in time. The dresser was open, and clothes peeked out this way and that. She wouldn't need them.

He was nearing the bedroom door when footsteps made him freeze. There was no time to hide before the other bedroom door was flung open. Dakota, most likely. He stood motionless in the darkness as she stumbled to the bathroom down the hall, not shutting the door behind her. The sound of urination filled the quiet of the house.

Parker swore under his breath. The closet—he should hide there. But if she were to check on the children, the missing girl would be noticed immediately. Then he'd have to do something to prevent the mother from calling anyone.

Or he could put Madison back in her bed.

Swiftly, he crossed the room and laid the child down, pulling the larger blanket over her to hide the furry one. Then he sprinted to the closet.

He needn't have worried because the woman didn't come into the children's bedroom. Yet she didn't shut her door, either. He waited for her to fall asleep again, though he knew every minute put him closer to discovery.

After fifteen minutes, he could wait no longer. Again, Parker knelt by the bed and scooped up the little girl. This time she didn't react but slept on like an angel. Down the dark hallway he went, shuffling slowly to be sure he didn't trip over anything. Then he was at the front door, shutting it behind him and stepping quietly over crunchy mounds of snow. His blue truck was parked between this house and the neighbor's. He climbed inside and, still holding the child, started the engine.

The cab was cold—he hadn't planned for the wait inside the house—but he'd brought blankets. Headlights appeared ahead, and he stiffened until a car passed, the lights fading behind him. He should have borrowed his friend's car again instead of using his own truck, but that hadn't been possible tonight, and he couldn't afford to wait. The cost might be too high.

Two blocks away, he stopped and settled Madison on the seat next to him, tucking blankets around her to help her feel secure.

The faint red lights from the dashboard barely illuminated her baby face, but he could see that her eyes had opened, small slits in her chubby roundness. "Daddy? Is that you?"

The light made it difficult for her to really see much of anything, and her apparent trust made the ache in his chest intensify. Parker swallowed, the dryness hurting his throat. "It's okay, sweetheart," he murmured. "Sleep, now. That's my girl."

Obediently, she shut her eyes and was lost again in her dreams.

He drove to I-15, heading south. What he wouldn't give for a drink. Just a sip to burn a little warmth down his throat. He knew it was a battle he'd fight for the rest of his life, but no way would he let that vice steal what he had worked so hard to achieve. His entire life and future were tied up in that little girl lying there so peacefully on the seat. He must arrive at his destination. Then he could decide what to do next.

Chapter 2

Public defender Caitlin McLoughlin rolled onto her back and opened her eyes, staring at the dark ceiling of her bedroom in her West Valley home, lit only faintly by light from the street lamp that filtered through her blinds. How she could work all day and feel so exhausted and yet still not sleep didn't make any sense, but here she was again—rehashing the past and worrying her choices would take everything from her.

Tomorrow deputy district attorney Mace Keeley would finish presenting his evidence, and she'd have to begin her defense. The problem was that her client was guilty. Thoroughly and utterly guilty. In a vicious and premeditated attack two and a half years earlier, Chet Belstead had pushed his former girlfriend down in the grass at a local park and raped her. There were also five deep stab wounds, with jagged lines connecting them across the woman's back like a contorted dot-to-dot picture. It was a miracle she'd survived.

When she'd first been assigned the case, Caitlin had hoped Belstead was innocent. It happened now and again, in her work as a public defender, that her client was mistakenly accused or simply in the wrong place at the wrong time. But those cases were few and far between these days, or perhaps they were assigned to attorneys who weren't as experienced or as good as Caitlin. These days she almost always got the dirty ones.

She'd known Belstead was guilty from the moment she walked into the room at the county jail where they'd met for the first time. He'd been far too slow to bring his hazel eyes to meet hers, dragging up her body as if caressing every curve. When his eyes finally did lock onto hers, a lazy, annoyingly confident smile slashed across his plain face, as if daring her to mention his behavior. She understood at once that underneath his apparent normalcy was a monster that existed only to gratify himself.

Instead of calling him out, she'd begun firing questions at him, willing her pale, freckled cheeks not to flush with frustration. She'd acquired those telltale cheeks from her Irish father, along with her copper-colored hair, but from her English mother she'd inherited a stiff backbone and the famous English aplomb that served her well as a defense attorney. She'd had to draw a lot on that backbone during her initial meeting with Belstead—and in all the meetings after. For two and a half years, she'd soldiered on. It was almost over now.

Belstead had faked innocence in the beginning. They all did, so he wasn't too different from her other guilty clients. She hadn't been fooled. He was easier than most to figure out. She'd once made the mistake of taking off her jacket in his presence, when the heat of the holding cell had become unbearable. Though her blouse was more than modest, his stare made her feel dirty. That was when he'd casually mentioned the knife, wrapped in his thin jacket and thrown away in an unused trash can. Perhaps he thought the danger the knife represented made him more attractive to her.

After a few more weeks of subtle prodding, she learned the route he'd taken home from the park that night, and that information allowed her to determine the most obvious place he might have deposited the knife. He'd believed she would never manage to connect the bits of information he'd given her—and even if she did, so what? She was bound by ethics as his legal counsel to keep her mouth shut and let him go free. In his mind there was no possible way he could be convicted.

He was almost right. He had worn a mask, and there was no physical evidence to connect him with the crime. Nothing except the lack of an alibi and the fact that he'd threatened his ex with violence after she began dating another man. That he'd been seen loitering near the grocery store where she worked on the night of the attack wasn't exactly solid proof.

Enough evidence for a trial but never for a conviction. Caitlin was good at her job, and she had known Belstead would walk away free—until she made sure he wouldn't.

She'd made a call to Kenny Pratt, a local private investigator she sometimes used and asked him to canvas the area to find out if any of the nearby residents had seen something unusual. She told him she had a robbery case she was working on. That was it, nothing more. Nothing about Belstead or about rape and attempted murder.

He'd called her back two weeks later. "I found a teenager," Kenny had told Caitlin. "Says he was in his car with his girl-friend in the driveway of her parent's house and he saw a guy run by, looking real nervous. There's a streetlight right outside, and he claims the man had a big stain on his shirt. Something dark. And before you ask, he couldn't tell if it was blood. It was too dark. The girl didn't see anything. But both of them heard a banging at the abandoned house next door. Maybe a garbage can lid. I checked out the house, and it still looks abandoned. The garbage can is sitting in the carport near the back door. It's about half full. I didn't go through it. Anyway, it wasn't on the night you were asking about. It was two days before. They knew the date because they'd been to a school football game."

Two days before the date she'd given Kenny landed the event squarely on the night of Belstead's attack. She'd known Kenny would report anything he discovered—anything near the date in question. She forced her voice to be calm. "Not something I can use, but you might encourage the boy to call the police. Whatever the man dumped might still be there. Maybe it connects to something else they're working on. That's a scary neighborhood down there."

"I'll do that. You want me to keep poking around? I covered the whole block, but I might have missed someone."

"No. I think it's a dead end. It tells me what I needed to know."

"Okay. It's your call."

"Send me a bill."

He laughed. "I always do."

The police had taken a day to find the knife and another two to connect it to the rape. That was fast, considering the four months that had passed since the crime. Simple. No real connection to her at all.

I shouldn't have done it, she thought, still staring at the ceiling. Despite her continuous rationalization over the past months, she'd been wrong to go that far. She had put herself at risk—and that meant putting Amy at risk.

The thought of Amy made her stomach ache. Amy was in the next room sleeping even now, tucked in with her dolls and stuffed animals. Sweet Amy, who knew only the world of a child and would never have to make the decisions Caitlin did.

Feeling for her phone, Caitlin turned it on. Four o'clock already, which meant two hours before she had to be in the shower. Sighing, she dropped it back onto her nightstand, closed her eyes, and tried to sleep.

Chapter 3

Parker reached Mt. Pleasant in two hours. Normally, he could have shaved off twenty minutes or more of the journey, but he didn't want to attract any unwanted attention. Not that there were too many policemen on patrol at this time. He was, however, starting to pass people driving north or south to their jobs in bigger neighboring towns. There wasn't much to do by way of work in Mt. Pleasant, unless you happened to work at the gas station or grocery store.

He passed the family-owned Kathy's Herb Shoppe on Main Street and turned the corner to his mother's house, pulling up in the driveway and jumping out to punch in the code on the side of the garage. Normally, he'd park outside if he came so early, but today he didn't want to risk his truck being seen. The stop was necessary in his mind, though, because he needed to talk to his mother, to prepare her for what was going to happen. He was all Norma Hathaway had left.

She was waiting by the kitchen door when he entered

with his key. In one hand she held the telephone, in the other a can of pepper spray. When she saw him, the anxious look on her tired face vanished, and she stepped toward the door, rapidly punching in the code for the alarm he had installed last year when there had been a rash of burglaries in the neighborhood. Petty things like small TVs and thin gold bands had gone missing, but worse was the violation people had felt. They didn't have a lot in this town, and Parker had wondered why anyone would target them—until a gang of teenagers had been arrested. Biggest news of the city in the past decade. At least before today. By evening, his mother would be the recipient of many meals and desserts from the neighbors, outpourings of their love and sympathy over her loss.

"Have you been drinking?" she asked, studying him carefully.

He shook his head, irritated but not angry. "No."

She had a right to suspect him, though he hadn't let her down in a long time. She would probably always wonder if he would fail, and her constant worry and fear alone were enough to keep him sober—even if he hadn't already decided that he would never return to his old ways.

One thing both of them would agree upon: his actions of this night were not a failure. Though his mother hadn't known of his plan, she would be happy he'd succeeded. She knew what was at stake every bit as much as he did.

"Look," Parker said, speaking urgently. "I'm only here for a few minutes. I have to work this morning." He was employed at a construction site in Manti, a good half hour's drive from Mt. Pleasant.

"Why are you here then?" Her hands were on her sturdy hips, and her brown eyes that matched the shoulder-length hair were intense. "Did something happen?"

In answer, Parker took her hand and led her out to the garage. She hesitated when one of her slippers fell off, and he impatiently waited for her to put it back on. "People are going to be coming around asking questions," he said. "I didn't want you to worry."

They stood on the passenger side of his truck now, and he gestured toward the window. His mother was short and had to stand on tiptoe to see inside. It always amused people that Norma could be so short while Parker and his brother had been such tall, strapping boys. Like their father. But he didn't want to think about his father or his brother. There had been no love lost between them during his growing up years, and he still paid the price for that every day of his life.

"Madison," Norma breathed. She stepped back, flung open the door, and reached for the child.

"No." Parker held her back. "Don't wake her. I've got to get her to Manti before I go to work."

"But who'll watch her?"

"I have someone."

Norma's brow wrinkled. "Someone she knows?"

Parker shook his head. "She's used to strangers."

"Let me come with you." Her brown eyes were ringed in small wrinkles, really the only place that showed her fifty-seven years. Wrinkles born of great suffering.

"I don't want you involved. People are going to be asking questions. I only came here so you'd know she's okay when the questions come. But I can't tell you where I'm taking her, and you can't admit to anyone that I was even here."

"You're going away. I'll never see you again." Panic laced Norma's voice.

"No." He shook his head. "If it comes to that, we'll go together."

"It will come to that. Dakota won't let it rest."

"Maybe she will."

"Then the law won't."

"I can't let her hurt Madison!" Desperation tightened his chest. "I have to protect her."

"I know." His mother's arms went around him, as comforting as they had been when he was a child. "I'll get my stuff taken care of," she whispered. "Don't you worry. I'll sell the house, cash out everything. We'll disappear."

He knew how much it cost her to say that. This was her home. She'd come here as a young bride, raised two sons, and become a widow. She was offering to leave all her friends and extended family.

"It might not be necessary."

"It will. You can't hide her here that long."

"Maybe I can—at least for long enough. Maybe the authorities will investigate Dakota."

"Maybe."

Parker drew back and shut the truck door. "You call and let me know where she is," his mother said.

He shook his head. "I'll be here sometime during the weekend, same as always. This time without Madison." That was a given because his daughter would have to remain in hiding, but he wanted his mother prepared. She lived for Madison's visits.

"I love you, Parker. Don't you forget that."

"I love you, too, Mom."

"Grandma?" Madison pushed herself to a seated position, rubbing her eyes.

This wasn't going at all as Parker had planned. He shouldn't have stopped. Now if the authorities caught him, Madison would remember that she'd seen her grandmother.

Norma opened the truck door and gathered the little girl into a hug. "Oh, baby. It's so good to see you. But you have to lie down now and go back to sleep. You and your daddy are taking a little trip."

Madison grinned. "I like trips with Daddy." She yawned. "Is it my birthday again?" For her fourth birthday two months ago, he had taken her to Disneyland.

"Not yet," Parker told her. "And we're not going to Disneyland, but we'll have fun anyway."

"That's right." Norma patted the seat. "You're tired, sweetie. Lay your head right there and take a little nap."

Madison yawned again. "Okay, Grandma."

Parker exchanged a meaningful look with his mother. "I'd better get going."

"Yes. You'd better."

He hugged his mother and whispered in her ear, "I'm sorry. Sorry for all of this. I'm sorry it's going to be so awful for you." Answering questions, lying for him and Madison—who knew what she might be forced to do? He knew his mother well enough to understand that a little part of her would die every time she took a step closer to the wrong side of the law. That he felt the same showed he'd come a long way.

"I'm stronger than you think," she said. "I'll manage. You just keep her safe."

He drove to Manti, not to the small apartment he shared with two guys from work but to a small, run-down house on the edge of town that he'd rented fully furnished for less than he'd expected. There was still time to change Madison's hair color and her clothes before the local girl he'd hired came to babysit, a girl who barely spoke English, and whose family had reasons of their own not to contact authorities. Then he'd drive his truck back to his apartment and climb in his window in time to "wake up" with the other guys.

He'd tried to think of everything, but what if he'd missed something important? His heart banged in his chest with a fierceness he hadn't felt since that first time Dakota had left him and taken Madison, and he'd realized he had no way to protect his daughter.

For now, at least, Madison was safe.

As he carried her inside, her arms went up around his neck. "I'm glad you came and got me, Daddy. I missed you."

Tears gathered in his eyes. "We're together now. And I'm not ever letting you go again."

Chapter 4

Wednesday dragged by slowly, long and grueling—and not just because Caitlin had spent so much time staring at her ceiling the night before. Listening to deputy district attorney Mace Keeley address the jury in their Salt Lake City courtroom, Caitlin wondered for the millionth time what she was even doing there. When she'd started law school, she'd never dreamed she'd end up defending a creep like Belstead.

"After a search revealed this knife in a trash can at an abandoned house two blocks north of the defendant's apartment," Mace said, "we took it into evidence and had our forensic team test it. The knife has traces of the victim's blood." He paused dramatically as he always did before going in for the kill, a flair Caitlin both hated and admired. That he was drop-dead gorgeous didn't help matters—at least for her client. The jurors seemed to hang on his every word. "The knife also contains two of the defendant's fingerprints."

Caitlin didn't meet her client's gaze as the state prosecutor's words hung heavily in the courthouse. Normally, she hated the moment in the trial when the prosecutor presented seemingly irrefutable evidence, but today she felt only triumph. After the first shock of silence, murmurs burst like a wave from the spectators. The jury stared accusingly at the defendant, and the faces of the victim's family showed terrible triumph. Caitlin kept her own expression stoic, not feigning outrage or protesting in her client's defense, as some might have done in her position. Doing so would only make it worse for him.

Mace nodded toward the judge. "The prosecution rests our case, Your Honor."

Judge Harper inclined his gray head and glanced at his wristwatch. "Very well. As I mentioned when we got started this morning, I have an unforeseen conflict in my schedule later this afternoon, so I think this is a good place to conclude for the day. That will also give both parties time to consider options before we continue on . . ." He paused and consulted briefly with his clerk. "Since this trial has taken longer than expected and both the prosecutor and the defense are scheduled for separate trials tomorrow, apparently, we'll reconvene these proceedings on Friday. But I want any new motions, if applicable, on my desk by close tomorrow. Defendant is remanded to custody. Court is now adjourned."

Caitlin stood with the others as the judge rose and left the room. She could tell by the rigid lines of the judge's weathered face that Belstead was as good as on his way to prison. *Chalk one up for the good guys,* she thought. Beneath her outward calm, Caitlin allowed herself to feel the slightest bit of satisfaction.

Yet as much as Belstead deserved to rot in prison for the full length of time the crime required, the blatant attitude change in the courtroom now demanded that she attempt to arrange a plea deal for him. Hopefully he'd be too stubborn to accept, as he had been during the prosecutors' stab at summary judgment. The prosecutors might also be too sure of their evidence at this point to offer him anything worthwhile.

Caitlin's thoughts fled as Belstead turned and pushed close to her, ignoring the guard who stood ready to escort him back to his cell. "I thought you said I'd get off!" he said in a harsh whisper, his hazel eyes level with hers. "You said they didn't have enough proof!"

Caitlin studied him, taking in the desperate, wild look that no longer matched the closely cropped sandy hair and shaved face. He was pleasant-looking in an ordinary way, but there was nothing to set him apart from dozens of other ordinary, middle-aged men. Except perhaps his clothes. These had obviously been chosen with great care, as though he was trying to impress someone. Women, most likely. Young ones who would be enthralled by a wolf in sheep's clothing.

She had told him in the beginning that the prosecution didn't have enough proof, but that was long before they'd found the knife. "You knew they were going to bring up the knife," Caitlin said coolly. "We talked about it in discovery. We'll still have our chance to discount the evidence. Now keep your voice down. You don't want to make a scene in front of the jury."

Belstead's nostrils widened and his face flushed a deep red. Nevertheless, he waited until the jury disappeared through a door in the back of the jury box before continuing. "And how did they get that so-called evidence?" he sneered. "We never talked about that, did we?" Abruptly his voice became a deadly whisper close to her cheek. "You told them! You must have. No one else knew." Swearing viciously, he made a move toward her, but the guard grabbed his arms and pulled him back.

Caitlin made her voice icy hard. "You're not helping your

case. Word of this tantrum will get back to the judge. Now calm down. I'll do everything I can to negate the effects of this evidence." And she would, even if she didn't want to.

Her words had the desired soothing effect. "See that you do," he muttered, his narrow shoulders slumping. "Or else."

"Or else what?" She lifted her chin as she met his gaze.

"Nothin'." His eyes were full of hatred as the guard led him from the room.

The threat was probably just talk, but she was glad she would be able to sleep that night, knowing there was no chance he would be anywhere near her house. As a flight risk, he hadn't been permitted bail. She suspected at this point he'd prefer another attorney, which would be a relief after the past years of contact, but unfortunately for her, he didn't have the money to hire one on his own. Working full time at a local hamburger joint before his incarceration hadn't exactly resulted in a savings account large enough to pay high-class attorney wages, and any savings that hadn't been eaten by his recent bills had probably gone toward clothing. She could, of course, recuse herself from the case, but that wouldn't be looked on favorably by her boss. It would also be giving in to her fear.

Caitlin swallowed with difficulty and closed her burning eyes.

"You know your client's guilty," said a mocking voice beside her.

Caitlin opened her eyes to see deputy district attorney Mace Keeley and his co-counsel, Wyman Russell. "I guess that's for the jury to decide," Caitlin muttered, her stomach tightening as it always did in Mace's presence.

He laughed. "Public defending is the worst, isn't it?" Though in his late thirties, he could be the posterchild for West Coast surfing ads—blond hair, blue eyes, and a build that made women drool. Most women, anyway, though Caitlin tried not to be one of his groupies. The aloof manner she strove for at work protected her most days, but every now and then when she least expected it, a little scene of the two of them alone on a beach somewhere stole into her daydreams.

"Well, there is a good side to your losing," said his co-counsel. Wyman Russell was also a deputy district attorney, or DDA, and the attorney who had originally been assigned to prosecute the case. Sometime after the knife evidence had been discovered, Mace had taken over as lead counsel. Caitlin had never received any explanation as to why there had been a change.

"And what's that?" Caitlin forced herself to respond politely to the shorter man. Though he was reasonably handsome and his voice pleasant, she didn't like Wyman. Not because of his thinning brown hair and flabby body, or even because two years ago he'd been chosen for the job that should have been hers, but because of the calculating jabs he always took at her. The feeling had been bad enough before, but since they'd become opposing counsel on this case, he seemed to find altogether too many opportunities to unnerve Caitlin with his annoying comments. Either he had the hots for her, was trying to throw her off her game, or was just particularly weird. She was leaning toward the latter.

Wyman grinned. "Chet Belstead is going to jail for a long time. That's worth a loss in my book."

He won't be going away for long enough, Caitlin thought as the two men chuckled.

"Don't be jealous of our mad prosecuting skills," Wyman added.

Mad prosecuting skills? Had he really just said that? The truth was that Wyman was a terrible prosecutor, and in the past she'd defended against him successfully in several cases he should have won—cases she'd hoped he'd win, given her clients' obvious guilt. Perhaps that was why Mace had been called in to help with this case, to be sure Wyman didn't mess up again. The family of the victim was working the media hard, and a loss by the DA's office would not be taken lightly. Mace or no Mace, Caitlin would have won this case too—if she hadn't helped things along.

"It's not over yet," she forced herself to say. Mechanically, she began picking up her papers and storing them in her brown leather briefcase, too aware of Mace and the fact that he was still watching her. Her nerves tingled.

Wyman stepped around Mace, coming uncomfortably close to Caitlin. "You still think you're going to get him off? How? His fingerprints were found on the weapon, and the victim is ready to swear it was his voice she heard in the park that night. They dated for six months. She should know."

The arrogance in his voice stung her into replying. "I'm sorry, but I refuse to discuss this further unless you have something official to convey. Otherwise, you'd better get back to examining the knife and the jacket and hope you have enough evidence to convince Belstead to cut a deal."

Mace laughed. "She has a point. I for one am interested to see what she comes up with during her defense." He smiled at Caitlin and she grinned, swaying toward him slightly before pulling herself back. It had been far too long since she'd been in a relationship with a man as attractive as Mace. Or any man, for that matter. "See you later, Caitlin," he said with another stunning smile. She watched him walk away for several long seconds before she realized Wyman hadn't followed him.

"Why did you say there was a jacket with the knife?" Wyman asked.

Caitlin froze. Hadn't Mace mentioned it during the trial? She went over the scene in her mind. No, he hadn't. And now that she thought about it, she couldn't remember seeing mention of the jacket in the lengthy discovery documents, either. Which meant she had made a serious error, one that could not be excused by her double caseload. No jacket meant the knife had not been wrapped up as Belstead had told her, or maybe someone had removed it from the loaded trash container before the police found the knife. Given the part of town where the knife had been found, that might have happened. It was also possible the police had withheld that tidbit for reasons unknown, though that shouldn't be the case this far into a trial.

"I misspoke," she said. "I must be mixing it up with another case. I got less than four hours of sleep last night. You know how it is."

"Oh yeah?" He tilted his head to the side. "Funny thing is, the blood on the knife was consistent with being wrapped, but the police didn't find anything else, or we would have included it in discovery and in our evidence list." He paused for a moment before rushing on, a mad sort of glee coming into his eyes. "Wait. He told you, didn't he? That idiot told you what he did."

"I shouldn't have to remind you that what my client tells me is privileged information." Though she spoke calmly, a tremor of fear shuddered up Caitlin's spine. What if they found the boy who had made the anonymous call and traced him back to her? That had been her fear from the moment she'd told Kenny to ask the witness to call the police. If anyone accused her of a breach of ethics and they found evidence, she could be disbarred.

Caitlin searched the room, searching for an easy excuse to extricate herself. But the courtroom was clear now except for the two of them and Jodi Rivers, a paralegal from the Legal Defenders Association, who was standing near the door waiting for Caitlin.

Wyman reached out and briefly touched Caitlin's arm. "We have more in common than you think, Caitlin." The arrogance was gone from his voice.

"What are you saying?"

"We both want the bad guys to go to prison."

She studied his oblong face, noting the deep line in his forehead between his eyes. She'd heard he and his wife had separated, and she wondered if that was what had marked him or if the line had come from years of concentrating on his cases.

"Maybe so," she said, feeling inexplicably sorry for him, "but we both know my real *job* is to get as many clients through the system as quickly as possible—period. Even if they get off. You're the one who's supposed to send them to prison." She didn't add that he wasn't very good at it. She didn't have to; his record spoke for itself.

"We could be on the same team," he said lightly. "Think about it."

"I tried to join the DA, but you took my spot. Remember?"

His face split into a surprisingly compelling smile. "You still holding a grudge? Did you ever think that it might be for the best? Sometimes you can accomplish more working outside the DA's office."

Two days ago, she wouldn't have hesitated to slam his slightly veiled suggestion of cooperation back in his face as a blatant breach of ethics. But doing so now might make him more eager to open an investigation into the anonymous caller, and the caller would eventually lead to Kenny Pratt, her private detective.

Kenny would never volunteer the information that he'd

been making inquiries on her behalf, but she employed him often enough for the DA's office to make a connection. At least she hadn't told Kenny her true reason for sending him to the street where the knife had been found. That was something.

Wyman left her then, but she knew it wasn't over. She began gathering her papers and files, her mind racing.

"Are you okay?"

Caitlin looked around at Jodi, surprised to see the younger woman still waiting for her. "Yeah, I'm fine." But she sank back into the black, high-backed chair behind the defendant's table.

"Too bad about the knife."

She sighed. Jodi Rivers was a good paralegal, so good that in some cases, Caitlin sent her to do the preliminary work with the clients so that Caitlin would only need to meet with them personally once before a hearing or trial. That left her free to spend her time on the most difficult or disturbing cases. Like Chet Belstead's. In fact, if she had still been working misdemeanor cases as she had at the beginning of her career, she'd only see her clients at the trial itself, never actually talking to them alone, instead relying on Jodi and others like her to take care of the legwork.

Yet for all her experience, Jodi was still young and too idealistic to understand that because of Caitlin, many really bad guys walked free to harm others again. Jodi still believed in second chances while Caitlin had seen repeated offenders too often to subscribe to that vein of thought.

Jodi sat down next to Caitlin in Belstead's vacated chair, her long, dark hair falling over her shoulders nearly to her slender waist. Caitlin envied that waist, not to mention the hair and flawless complexion. Jodi tapped a French-manicured finger on the file she held in her hands. "I saw him staring at you. I think he likes you."

Caitlin sat up straighter. "You do?"

"Yes, and he's cute. I mean, he could be a little taller, but he's taller than you, at least. I hear he and his wife are getting a divorce."

Wife? Mace Keeley didn't have a wife. He was rumored to be in a long-distance romance with an attorney in California, though if they didn't love each other enough to be together, Caitlin didn't think there was much hope for the relationship.

That could only mean Jodi wasn't talking about Mace. She groaned. "Uh, if you're talking about Wyman Russell, then eewww." The dragged-out word said it all.

Jodi shrugged. "He's not bad looking."

"He's a terrible prosecutor! You saw how he brought Mace Keeley in to help this case." Since there was so much damning evidence, she was surprised Wyman hadn't continued the case on his own. He'd naturally want the glory of the win for himself.

Jodi grinned. "I see your point. A woman can overlook a lot of things in a man but not stinking at his job. But speaking of Mace Keeley, that's one guy I'd go out with in a heartbeat."

"You and most of the other women around here."

Jodi shrugged. "Lucky for him, I guess." She clapped her hands on her knees, just visible beneath her tight skirt, and leaned forward. "Well, I'm heading back to the office. Can I help you with anything this afternoon?"

"I wish. But it's stuff I have to deal with personally. I need to chat with another client so we're ready for trial tomorrow morning." A typical busy Wednesday for her. Even though the judge had ended their court time earlier than expected, the few extra hours only meant that she'd be slightly less behind.

"You mean the arsonist?"

"That's the one." As luck would have it, Wyman was the prosecutor on the case. The defendant had purposefully set a fire that had killed an old man, so Wyman had gone after him with a murder one charge, but there was enough doubt in Caitlin's mind about the defendant's intentions that she was giving the case her full attention. Since she was up against Wyman again, she would probably save her client from life imprisonment. Unfortunately.

Nodding, Jodi arose. "Well, give me a holler if you need some help with visual aids for the arson trial."

"I thought you had a brief to write for Sampson."

"I do, but it's boring." Jodi laughed and started down the aisle.

"In that case, I'll take you up on the visual aids. There's a file on my desk that has them outlined. Top one. Red folder, I think. And, Jodi, thanks."

"No problem."

Caitlin watched her leave. Thinking of Amy, who was probably waiting for her even now, playing with dolls or maybe coloring a picture, a fresh load a guilt assailed her. *I shouldn't have done it,* she thought. *She's my responsibility. I should have let Belstead walk.*

All Wednesday morning, Parker had been tense as he waited to hear from Dakota. It had been all he could do to drive to work at eight and pretend everything was fine. Construction in winter wasn't always pleasant, but they'd finished framing the office building yesterday and had draped plastic to keep out the snow. As long as he wore a heavy jacket, the portable heater did a halfway decent job of making the air tolerable.

Nine o'clock had crept by and then ten and eleven. Still nothing. It was after the noon break before Dakota finally called him in tears. "Madison's gone," she said without preamble. "Just gone. I've searched the whole house."

"She'd better not be," he retorted, ducking under the plastic and moving away from the others so he wouldn't be overheard. "And this better not be a way to get more money from me."

"It's not!" The panic in her voice sounded real. "I've

searched everywhere, like I said. I thought she was watching TV, or maybe playing outside."

"She's four!" he nearly yelled. "How could she be outside without you knowing?" But he knew how, and so did she. "How long has she been gone? When was the last time you saw her?"

"When I put her to bed last night."

"Last night?" His outrage wasn't fake. How could she have not noticed Madison was missing all morning? Probably Dakota had just dragged herself from bed. "What kind of mother are you?"

"Will you shut up?" she screamed. "Madison is missing. That's the important thing. You need to come find her." A cry began in the background. Must be the little boy he'd seen last night.

So his ex-wife apparently thought he'd drop everything and go running up to Salt Lake. And she would have been right, if Madison had really been missing. "You find her," he growled. The screaming kid in the background grew louder, and he had to raise his voice again to hear his next words. "This is exactly why I want custody. You just don't remember where you left her. Were you shooting up again last night?"

"No! I wasn't, and you're a jerk even to say it."

Parker held the phone away from his ear as Dakota let out a stream of curses. When it was quiet, he put the phone back and said calmly, "If she really is missing, call the police. Right now. Right this minute. Do it, Dakota. This is our baby we're talking about. You need to find her." This was part of his plan, that she'd call the police and they would find evidence to convict her.

The child's cry in the background had cut off during his

plea, so either Dakota had picked him up or she'd gone into another room. "Right," she gave a big sniff. "I will."

"I'll call you later then. But let me know when you find her."

"Okay."

He pocketed the phone and went back to work. His mind was only half on what he was doing, but his body knew what to do. So he worked. And waited.

He didn't receive a call from the police until nearly three hours later, and that told him Dakota had cleaned up the house before officially reporting Madison's absence, or at least made sure there was nothing lying around that would reflect badly upon her. The police had apparently searched the house from top to bottom. Nothing. Officers were beginning to comb the neighborhood and gather volunteers to form search parties. Since Parker hadn't deigned to show up, the female detective who called was coming to him. He'd have to explain himself somehow. He hoped it would be enough, because he wasn't leaving town. Not unless they made him.

The female detective arrived at the construction site just before quitting time at five. She wore an ordinary suit on her large frame and drove an unmarked car. She was alone, which he thought odd, but perhaps that meant they didn't really consider him a suspect.

One could hope.

She stopped and talked to the foreman, who pointed him out. Parker ignored them and kept working, using his crane to lift timbers to the men up on the scaffolding, where they were beginning to frame the roof. The building was coming along nicely, even in the cold, though they needed to get the roof on before the next heavy storm. At least inside the cab of the crane, it was almost toasty, though he'd have to trade one of the others before long.

"Mr. Hathaway?" she called up to him over the roar of the engine and through the glass of the window.

He held up a finger without looking down at her, then finished positioning his load and cut the motor. He opened the door and climbed down from the cab. "I'm Parker Hathaway."

"I'm Detective Sally Crumb. We spoke on the phone." Her warm breath billowed in the cold. She was six feet tall, at least, barely an inch or two shorter than Parker. If the weight she carried had been on a man's frame, she would have been on the slender side, but on her, the wide shoulders and hips lent an impressive air of solid authority. Yet Sally was all woman, and a pretty one at that, from her large-sized boots to her expressive, wide-set brown eyes.

"You find my daughter? Is she okay?" He felt his heart rate increase, as he worried about her seeing through this misdirection.

"No. I'm sorry. I do need to ask you some questions, and I think it's only fair to tell you we have a squad car at your apartment right now. The building manager let them in."

He shrugged. "I have nothing to hide. But you're barking up the wrong tree. Madison was with her mother last night, and I was at my apartment. My roommates can attest to that. I went to bed when they did and one of them was still there when I got up this morning."

"Yes, we know." She gave him a flat smile that did little to lighten the somber expression on her attractive face. She had blond hair much like Madison's had been before his color job this morning, though the detective's locks were shorter and probably equally as dyed. Her soft-looking skin was reddened with cold.

At a gesture from his foreman, Parker led her to the trailer they used as the office and break room. "I don't understand," he said, unzipping his coat before sitting on the worn loveseat against the wall. "Shouldn't you be out there searching for my daughter? I mean, if she really is missing?"

"Oh, she's missing all right." She pulled the chair in front of the desk around to face him and sat. "What makes you think she isn't?"

Parker scratched his unshaven face. "What time did Dakota call you?" he countered.

"About two-thirty this afternoon."

He nodded, his lips tightening. "Well, she called me just after noon. And she told me she hadn't seen Madison since she put her to bed last night. Now I ask you, if she's really worried about Madison, why did she wait so long?"

Detective Crumb's brown eyes narrowed. "What are you saying?"

"That her mother has problems with drugs. That she got rid of the evidence before she called you. Frankly, I've been worried for years that something would happen to my daughter."

"And you did nothing to stop it?"

Parker gaped at her, his frustration real. "Everything I could. I've kept every single weekend visit with my daughter since the divorce—except for the few months right after Dakota left me and I didn't know where she was staying. I also call Madison every day, usually after work, but sometimes at lunch too. Check the phone records, if you don't believe me." He let the venom he felt leak into his voice. "And while you're at it, why don't you tell me what else I can do when the law says my daughter has to live with a drug addict?"

Detective Crumb tilted her head to study him, her pen tapping on the notebook in her lap. "You've been divorced for a year. Our records show that your ex-wife was the one who filed."

"We'd still be married if she hadn't."

"You still love her?"

Likely the detective thought love was a motive for kidnapping, and she was right. But it hadn't been for love of Dakota. "Dakota and I didn't have a marriage since before Madison was born, and the only reason I stayed at all was for Madison. That's the truth." Parker stood. "Look, if you're going to charge me with something, then do it. Otherwise, I'm going back to work."

"You're not joining the search for your daughter?" Surprise registered in the detective's eyes.

He stared at her, knowing he had to make this good.

"Madison isn't lost. Dakota's just stashed her somewhere—probably to punish me for not giving her more money than I already do. She disappeared with her once before, you know. For months after Dakota left me, I didn't know where my daughter was. Dakota's the one who needs to be investigated. Find her friends, and I'll bet one of them has Madison. She probably left her there before shooting up. That's Dakota's idea of responsible. Meanwhile, I have to work to make sure that when you do find my daughter, she'll have food to put in her stomach and a roof over her head."

Detective Crumb arose, extending her notebook and pen to him. "Can you give me a list of Dakota's friends?"

He strode to the desk, leaning over it, and began scribbling names. "These are the friends she used to have when I knew her. Like I said, even when we were together, we had separate lives. I might still have some of their numbers in my phone, if I ever had them." His script was large and deep and angry, but he'd let her draw what conclusions she wanted from that.

The detective stood mutely near him as he wrote, and when

he was finished and returned the notebook, she asked quietly, "What happened between you and your ex-wife? If you don't mind my asking."

Parker did mind, but this was also part of the plan. "I was tired of living that life. I want what every other normal man wants—the American Dream. But Dakota wasn't ready to grow up. I don't think she ever will be. Look, Detective, when I went to pick up my daughter last month, I saw a plastic bag of drugs sitting within easy reach on the couch. If my daughter had gotten hold of that . . ." He shook his head. "That's what I'm up against."

"Why didn't you call the police?"

"At first, I was too stunned, I guess. Then she threatened to not let me see Madison. She promised me she wasn't using anymore, but I've cursed myself every day since then for not calling." The reality was far worse than the words. Every night he'd awoken in a sweat, fearing that day would be the one he'd get the call telling him that his precious daughter had paid the price for his past.

Detective Crumb nodded, something akin to pity crossing her broad face. "Thank you, Mr. Hathaway. We'll keep in touch."

He nodded and watched her leave the trailer. If he'd played his cards right, she wouldn't suspect him for not jumping into his truck and driving to Salt Lake.

Or maybe she could see right through him.

He sat back down in the chair the detective had vacated, feeling as though he hadn't slept in weeks. Leaning forward, he propped his elbows on his knees and let his head fall into his hands.

Bob Jenkins, the muscled foreman, entered the trailer. "Everything all right?" he asked.

Parker shook his head. "My daughter's missing."

Bob's jaw dropped. "You're kidding. That's terrible!" He looked over his shoulder and only then did Parker notice that Jason Rosen, the thin, gray-haired contractor who employed them both, had come in after Bob.

Rosen took a few steps toward Parker. "When did it happen?"

"Last night. They're not sure."

"Geez, I don't know what to say," muttered Bob. Parker wondered if he was thinking about his own five daughters, all of them under ten years old.

"We can help search the area," Rosen said. "Pull in hundreds of people within the hour."

Parker felt a stab of guilt, though he wasn't surprised at the offer. From what he'd observed of Rosen, he was always ready to help, and he certainly had connections. "I don't know what the police want in that respect. They don't seem to think she just wandered off."

"I'll follow up with them," Rosen said, and Parker admired how sure he was.

There was an uncomfortable silence and then Rosen spoke again. "I know this is a bad time, but actually I came here to offer you a job as a foreman on a new office complex I'm building in Salt Lake."

Once he would have been thrilled to be closer to Madison, but Salt Lake now meant leaving her. He shook his head. "I appreciate the offer, I really do, but with all that's happened, I can't take it on right now. I wouldn't want to do any less than my best."

"I understand." The look in Rosen's eyes told him he respected Parker for rejecting the offer on those grounds. Parker felt ill at the deception.

"Do you need time off?" Bob asked.

"No. The police are doing everything they can. I have to believe that's enough. In fact, I really believe she's not missing at all, that this is just one more trick up my ex-wife's sleeve to get more money."

The men alternately nodded and shook their heads. Parker didn't think either man really understood. They had never seen their wives strung out on meth. Or on a cocaine high. They probably thought he was a negligent father for not running up to Salt Lake. He should have thought this through better.

"I would like a few minutes to stop by my mother's," he said. "She's got to be worried." The detective would probably visit her as well, and Parker hoped she was up to it.

"Sure, it's quitting time anyway," Bob said. "And if it turns out you need time off, just let me know. Or I'll know if you don't show up."

"Let us know if we can help," Rosen added.

Parker nodded and murmured his thanks, though neither of the men could hold his gaze for long. No doubt they were remembering the child who had been found murdered only weeks ago in a Salt Lake neighborhood.

Madison wouldn't be a statistic. He'd made sure of that. Now if only he could manage to keep her safe until enough evidence was found to make sure she'd be safe forever.

Chapter 6

S ally Crumb drove away from the construction site, all
her nerves humming with warning. Parker Hathaway
was lying. For a man to hold on to a loveless marriage
for years to protect a young child was believable, but to think
that same man would remain at work after his daughter went
missing wasn't. The situation reeked of deception.

Still, there was something inherently endearing about the
man, and she had the feeling he might be a person one would
be lucky to call a friend. Loyal to the extreme. Of course, that
didn't mean he wasn't responsible for his daughter's disappearance. In fact, it could mean he was very much involved.

The accusations about his ex-wife would have to be checked
out. Both the drug allegation and Hathaway's assertion that
Dakota Allen had waited hours to report Madison's disappearance. Sally had already requested phone records before driving
to Manti, and they should be waiting for her by the time she
got back to Salt Lake. Of course, if there had been a delay,

Allen could have been calling friends and driving around the neighborhood.

Maybe.

She shook her head and called the team who was at Parker's apartment with the local authorities. "Find anything?"

"Nothing. No sign of the little girl or anything belonging to her. Just a few pictures. We've been very thorough. Roommates say they only saw the child once a few months ago."

That was odd. Hathaway said he never missed a weekend. Was that part of the lie? "Talk to the neighbors," she said, "and then head on back."

So did not missing a weekend visit mean Hathaway had gone to see Madison, or that she'd spent several days with him elsewhere? Had he taken her to a hotel in Salt Lake? To his mother's? The more she thought about it, the more likely this last idea seemed. A responsible man would want his daughter to spend time with her grandmother, and a normal home environment would be a better choice than an apartment with single men whose lives might not be conducive to the needs of a small child.

Pulling over to the side of the road, Sally thumbed through the file she'd begun gathering on the kidnapping. It was less than half an inch thick so far, but that would quadruple before the day was over and all the requests she had out came pouring in. There it was. Norma Hathaway lived in Mt. Pleasant. Sally had called the woman this afternoon, but no one answered, and she'd yet to receive a report by the local police who had talked with Norma Hathaway earlier this afternoon. It certainly wouldn't hurt to have a chat with the woman personally since it was on her way home.

As she drove, Sally entertained herself with visions of miraculously finding Madison at her grandmother's. Maybe the whole thing was a mistake. Maybe tonight Sally could go to sleep without nightmares of the scene Salt Lake police had found two weeks ago: a strangled seven-year-old whose body showed obvious signs of sexual violation.

Yet the very intuition that made her a good detective also made it impossible for her to believe in this fantasy. Something was wrong. Everything in her gut screamed it. From her initial negative impression of the child's mother to the certainty that Parker Hathaway was lying. Where did Madison fit into all this?

Maybe the grandmother would be the key to unraveling the puzzle.

Norma Hathaway turned out to be a short, sturdy, neatly dressed woman with stylish brown hair. She looked at Sally's badge with brown eyes that were red from crying, her expression solemn and unsurprised.

"I'm Detective Crumb," Sally said. "Your son might have called to let you know I was in town. Could I come in for a few minutes?"

Neither confirming nor denying the phone call, Norma opened the screen door to let her in. "I've already talked to the police." She led the way to the living room, seating herself in an armchair while indicating that Sally should take the couch.

"I know you've talked to local authorities, but I have a few more questions. I just came from talking to your son."

"He hasn't done anything wrong. He's a good dad."

"As opposed to Madison's mother?"

Norma lifted her shoulders. "Dakota's always been a self-centered woman. I know she's using drugs, and that means she's not good for Madison."

"Apparently the custody judge didn't agree."

Norma opened her mouth as though to protest, then changed her mind. "Look, shouldn't you be out there trying to find my granddaughter?"

"We have a great many people working on a physical search. But in every kidnapping case, talking to relatives is vital. Most children are taken by relatives or someone familiar to them."

Norma nodded. "What do you want to know?"

"Do you see your granddaughter a lot?"

"Every other weekend. And on holidays. She's the light of my life." For the first time, a faint smile touched her lips. "Parker and I try to make things good for her when she's here, so she can see what a regular life is like."

Sally felt some satisfaction knowing her hunch had been correct.

"At her mother's, everything is always fluid," Norma continued. "Dakota doesn't have a steady job, and Madison is shuffled around a lot to neighbors and friends. Parker volunteers to take her, but Dakota's afraid she'll lose child support if she lets him take her too much. Dakota has another child too. A little boy about a year or so. He spends most of his time with his dad's relatives."

"You obviously have no love for your ex-daughter-in-law."

"Not one bit. She was a horrible wife, and she nearly destroyed my son. She was six months pregnant with another man's child before she even left him. Her son was born before their divorce was final."

"Can you think of anyone who would take Madison?"

A flash sparked in Norma's eyes, but she shook her head, her lips pursed tightly, and Sally knew she wouldn't be able to get anything more from the woman. Yet Sally could tell Norma felt deeply guilty about something, and that told her far more than the woman herself would.

"I would like your permission to send a team here to your house," Norma said.

"My house? Why?"

"Since Madison stayed here so much, there might be clues."

"She was taken from her mother's, not from here."

"We've been through Ms. Allen's house very thoroughly, I assure you. But you wouldn't want us to overlook anything. Would it be all right?"

Only a slight hesitation before the old woman nodded. "Yes. Of course. If it might help."

"Thank you, Mrs. Hathaway," Sally said, rising. At the door, Sally turned to her. "I have just one more question. Do you know where your granddaughter is?"

Norma blinked in surprise at her question, and there was a ring of sincerity when she responded. "I don't know where my granddaughter is right now, but I can say with all truthfulness that even if she was home with her mother, she'd still be in terrible danger. Dakota's the one you need to look into, Detective Crumb."

"That may be so, Mrs. Hathaway. Let's just hope Madison is safe, or all the looking in the world won't make a difference." Turning on her heel, Sally stalked to her unmarked squad car.

She didn't leave right away but grabbed her cell phone. "I want a team at Norma Hathaway's house," she barked. "She's agreed to let us in. And I've changed my mind about sending you home. I want surveillance on both Parker and Norma Hathaway. I'll coordinate things with the local authorities. Call it a gut feeling, or whatever, but I think the Hathaways are hiding something."

Clicking the phone off, she looked up at the small, well-kept rambler for several minutes before driving away. She wished she could stake out the home herself, but there was more information she needed to sift through. Better let the others take care of it. Once in a while, even she was wrong.

Chapter 7

After an unproductive chat with the arsonist at the county jail, Caitlin finally headed through the snow-lined streets to her home in West Valley. A stack of files she would work on later filled her briefcase. Though it was only six-thirty, her eyes ached and her head screamed for sleep. All she wanted was to crash on her bed and never wake up. Instead, she made the usual detour two streets over from her house to pick up Amy at the sitter's. Caitlin had looked for several months to find a woman who could handle Amy, and the white-haired Sarah Burnside, a sixty-eight-year-old grandmother of thirty, had been a real find.

Sarah's husband, Kyle, let her in, and Caitlin found Amy sitting on a stool in the kitchen with Sarah, kneading saltwater dough on the countertop. "I'm helping," Amy announced. Her short red hair, a shade darker than Caitlin's, framed her round, grinning face. Any time flour and water were involved, Amy was content.

"I see," Caitlin said. "That's very nice."

At the sink, Sarah rinsed a final dish before drying her big hands on a dish towel. "You can take that home, Amy."

"Oh, thank you! You're so nice, Sarah." Amy began rolling the dough in a ball with plump fingers. "Can I have a sack?"

"Of course, dear." Sarah moved her bulky form to a cupboard over the refrigerator and brought down a box of plastic zip bags from the top shelf.

Leaving Sarah to store the dough, Amy slid off her stool and hugged Caitlin, nearly overpowering her with exuberance. Amy didn't realize how strong she was, which was why it was important that her sitter be sturdy, both in body and in temperament. "I missed you so much," she gushed. "Did you miss me?"

Caitlin looked up into her younger sister's eyes, as green as her own were blue. "I did miss you." And it was true. With Amy things were always simpler. She was twenty-seven, but intellectually she would always remain five or six. Their parents had married late, having Caitlin when their mother was forty-three, and Amy surprised them five years later. There wasn't a time when Caitlin hadn't been involved in taking care of her sister, and now that their parents were gone, the burdens and the joys rested solely on her shoulders.

Amy didn't look any different from other women her age, and sometimes that was the most difficult thing for Caitlin. Sometimes she almost forgot that she could never share her life with Amy the way most sisters could. Amy would never be able to counsel her about a boyfriend or buy her that sweater she had her eye on. Or even fix dinner on the nights Caitlin was too exhausted to stand. But these were selfish thoughts, and for the most part Caitlin was happy that her little sister would never know all the pain the world carried.

On the drive home, Amy began her usual babble about the day's events. Caitlin only half-listened, nodding at all the appropriate times. Most of it was a repeat of the day before. In fact, Amy often got events from past weeks mixed up. It didn't really matter. But suddenly her words grabbed Caitlin's attention.

"Caitlin, are you ever going to have a baby?"

Caitlin glanced over at the passenger seat to see Amy staring at her earnestly. "Why do you ask that?"

"I think you should. If you had a baby, I could watch it. I would be a good babysitter."

"I'm sure you would, but having a baby is kind of complicated." Caitlin didn't know how to explain reproduction to her sister, much less falling in love and making a permanent commitment. "Remember our gerbils and how they won't have any more babies since they don't have a husband?"

"That's because we gave all the husbands away. I liked having the babies. They were cute."

"We couldn't keep so many in the cage. They wouldn't be happy."

"But you wouldn't have tons of babies. Just one." Amy tilted her head in a pleading gesture. "Please, Caitlin. Sarah's daughter had a baby, and I got to hold him today. I was very careful. He smiled at me."

"I bet that was a lot of fun."

"So will you have a baby? Pretty please with sugar on top?"

Caitlin stifled a sigh. "I don't even have time to meet a man, much less marry one. Besides, I don't know that we want a guy hanging around all the time. I sort of like having you all to myself."

Amy giggled. "Me too."

Hoping that was the end of the conversation, Caitlin pulled

into the driveway of their modest home. The garage could hold two cars, though they didn't need the space. Amy would never drive. While Amy ran to play with the gerbils they kept in a corner of their kitchen, Caitlin rummaged in the outside freezer for a bagged pasta meal she'd bought at Costco. Amy loved the curly noodles and the meat, and usually even ate a carrot or two, though she wouldn't touch the broccoli. The calories in the meal were outrageous—probably one of the reasons Caitlin had put on a few pounds lately, but at least it cooked quickly and tasted decent.

Amy talked to the gerbils, repeating everything she'd already told Caitlin about her day, her big hands gentle with the creatures. She'd had twenty-seven years to learn to be five.

"Why don't you go wash up?" Caitlin suggested. "It's almost ready."

From her seated position by the gerbil cage, Amy's face lifted toward Caitlin, her childlike sweetness shining through. "Can we have ice cream after?"

"Why not?" There was really no point in denying Amy the treat. It wasn't as if she would have to fit into a prom dress any time soon. A sudden burst of sorrow came with the thought, but it was immediately erased by Amy's gleeful cheer.

"I love you so much, Caitlin. You're the best sister ever!" She jumped up and gave Caitlin a powerful hug.

Forty minutes later, Caitlin was washing their dinner dishes when her cell phone rang. "I'll get it!" Amy left her bowl of Neapolitan ice cream and raced over to Caitlin's purse on the counter, delivering the phone to Caitlin's damp hand.

"Hello?"

"Caitlin, it's Wyman."

She stifled a sigh. "Hi, Wyman. What's up?"

"It's about the Belstead trial."

She sighed. "You're offering a plea deal?"

"Maybe. I thought it wouldn't hurt to stop by and chat. But I wanted to make sure you were home before I knocked."

"You're at my house?" Caitlin strode to the front door, pulling it open. Sure enough, Wyman was climbing from a sleek gray car, careful not to put his feet in the mound of snow the plow had left next to the curb. She shut her phone and watched him walk slowly up her icy drive to the porch. The house had been built on a postage stamp-sized lot, like all the other houses in the subdivision, so it didn't take him long to reach her.

"If you're offering a deal," she said, flipping on the porch light. "I want it in writing."

"That's not exactly why I'm here. I mean, it is related to the case, but not in the way you might think."

"Then what is it?" Her voice sounded odd, even to her. Would he catch the undercurrent of nervousness?

He glanced around, his breath making white clouds in the cold November air. "I'd rather discuss this in a more relaxed situation. Can I come in?"

"Not tonight. I have too much work to do." And she already felt like dropping, but she wasn't going to let him know that.

"Right, and you didn't get much sleep last night," he remembered. "You mentioned that at the courthouse. Then how about discussing it over dinner this weekend?"

"I'm sorry. I don't feel it will be beneficial to my client to socialize with the opposing counsel. You know as well as I do that we have a fine line to walk."

"It's just dinner. Between friends."

They weren't friends, and she wasn't going to waste her few weekend hours off in the company of a man who definitely didn't interest her. Besides, the less contact she had with him the better. She didn't want him nosing into how the knife came to light. "I could meet with you Saturday morning, if you don't mind meeting me at my office."

His light blue eyes narrowed, turning icy. "Look, here's the thing. A little while ago, I had a chat with the teenager who made the anonymous call to the police about your client's knife. He said the only reason he came forward in the first place was because a man came around asking about anything odd happening in the area. The man was probably a private detective, and some of us in the DA's office find it strange that a private detective would just happen to be snooping around in that area."

"What does that have to do with me?" Caitlin said coldly.

"That's part of what I want to find out."

"And you'll find nothing. The way I see it, you should be grateful for any break in the case. You and I both know I would have won without the evidence of the knife."

Wyman studied her, an unperturbed smile on his face. Caitlin felt ill. He knew something. Or suspected.

"Who is it?" Amy said from behind Caitlin. She peered eagerly around Caitlin, pushing her to the side in her enthusiasm. Ice cream smeared her chin, which told Caitlin she'd been licking her bowl again. Amy had once asked why Caitlin washed the bowl afterward, since it was already so clean.

"A man from work," Caitlin said, automatically shifting to the softer voice she reserved for Amy.

"Hi." Amy grinned and lifted a hand in greeting. "I'm Caitlin's sister."

Wyman looked back and forth between them, apparently noting the similarities—the freckles, the hair, even the build, though Amy was heavier and taller than Caitlin.

Amy wiped her chin on her sleeve and said to Caitlin, "I like my new ice cream better than the kind with those yucky nuts. Can we always buy this kind?"

"Yes. Now why don't you go get your pajamas on?"

Amy clapped her hands. "I'll get the book!" She glanced at Wyman. "Bye!"

Realization slid over Wyman's face, followed by a fleeting expression of what Caitlin was sure was revulsion. Then Wyman smiled. "I didn't know you had a sister."

Caitlin didn't respond.

"Well, think about what I said. We can talk later." With a wink, he turned and sauntered down her drive.

Caitlin's thoughts careened through her head. If she agreed to have dinner with Wyman, maybe she could distract him long enough to get him off the trail. After all, her client would go to prison and Wyman would get credit for his conviction. What did it matter how it came about? In fact, if she managed to go out with Wyman a time or two—as friends, of course— she might stall him long enough that the point would be moot.

But what if it wasn't enough? She shivered. He might be handsome in Jodi's eyes, but right now everything about him repulsed her. The idea of going out with him alone wasn't her idea of fun, even if it had been two years since she'd dated anyone seriously.

"Okay," she called, raising her voice to be heard. "Dinner."

He stopped and turned, a slow smile coming over his face. "I'm glad you changed your mind. We'll make plans tomorrow then, after the arson trial."

Caitlin nodded, already wishing she hadn't agreed. But for Amy's sake, she had to protect her career, and for now that meant playing Wyman's game.

Chapter 8

On Thursday shortly after noon, Caitlin met police detective Sally Crumb at the Judge Café on Broadway that served only breakfast and lunch until three in the afternoon. They both enjoyed the food and the ambience—along with dozens of other downtown workers, many of them attorneys—so it was a frequent choice for their weekly lunches together. That it was within walking distance of the courthouse made it an extra plus for Caitlin. She detested fighting the busy traffic.

When Caitlin arrived, her cheeks tingling with cold from her brisk walk, Sally was already waiting in one of the many niches the restaurant owners had carved out when remodeling the historic building. Pictures of old Salt Lake stretched over the dark wood of the bar, and the architectural features of the walls were accented by the paint's subdued yellow tone.

"How is the arson trial going?" Sally asked as Caitlin set down her briefcase and shrugged off her full-length gray wool coat.

"Horrendous. I mean, we're not contesting the fact that my client started the fire, so why bring in so much evidence? We would have finished last week if not for all of that, instead of dragging it on another day." She rubbed her fingers to warm them. "They won't be able to convict him of first-degree murder, though."

"But he intentionally lit the fire that caused a death, so it should still be murder one." Sally tucked the strands of her short, bleached hair behind her ears, making it look even shorter.

Caitlin sighed. "He didn't intend to burn the building down exactly. At least so he claims, and he has a lot of friends who support that claim."

"So what's the catch?" Sally arched a thin brow.

"After the testimony this morning, the prosecutor offered a plea deal. Arson and manslaughter. I'm urging my client to take it, and I'm sure he will."

"Even though he might not be as guilty as the prosecutor thinks?"

"Oh, he's guilty. I just don't know exactly how guilty." Caitlin propped her elbows unabashedly on the table and let her chin drop into her hands. "I'm tired, Sally. I'm tired of defending these people. Sometimes I want to lock them all up without even listening to them."

Sally chuckled. "I know how you feel. But someone's got to do it."

"Maybe it's time I got out."

"What, and make it so the guys don't have anything to rib me about down at the precinct?" Sally's colleagues held no love for the Legal Defenders Association, and their mistrust of Sally's friendship with Caitlin was nothing new. But Sally and Caitlin had been friends from the minute they'd met during a DUI case that had turned out to be caused by prescription medication rather than alcohol. It was one of the few good cases Caitlin could remember in the past three years.

"Ah, here comes the food," Sally added. "I ordered you a grilled nectarine and chicken salad. Dressing on the side. Hope that's okay."

"Whatever you got is fine." They were always in such a hurry at lunch that their standing rule was that the first to arrive would order for both. Only once had Caitlin been held up long enough to make Sally take the extra lunch home for her dinner. And they knew each other well enough that Caitlin had never been forced to eat something she absolutely detested.

"So how's Amy?" Sally asked as the waitress set down her plate. She was having the Judge's Favorite, a healthy serving of hearty meat loaf with mashed potatoes, gravy, summer squash, and mushrooms.

"The same. She never really changes."

One side of Sally's mouth lifted in a lopsided smile. "Some mothers would love their children to never grow up."

Caitlin considered the statement as she moved her chicken and nectarines around on their bed of romaine lettuce. She'd never held any hope of Amy growing up, except in disjointed dreams that didn't make any sense. "Maybe they wouldn't mind so much if they knew the alternative."

"Probably. Still, sometimes I'd give anything to have Randi younger again. Fifth grade is tough."

"Is she doing better at the new school?"

"Yes. She's finally found some friends."

"Good." Unlike Randi, Amy had a lot of friends because she loved everyone and never took offense. Unfortunately, she could never play without supervision because she was often too rough on her younger playmates.

As though reading her thoughts, Sally stopped eating and reached into the inner pocket of her suit coat, bringing out a folded paper. "There are much worse things in life." She opened the paper to reveal a photocopied picture of a little girl. The child stared up at them, her eyes bright, her round face grinning. Her hair was so blond that it looked almost as white as the page, framing her face like a halo.

"She went missing from her bedroom yesterday," Sally said. "The mother has no idea when it might have happened. The girl was there at ten or so when she put the children to bed on Tuesday night, and then when the little brother started crying the next day, the mother discovered she was missing. We've canvassed the neighborhood, put out an Amber Alert, interviewed all the relatives and many of the friends. So far, we've come up dry."

"Poor thing." Caitlin set down her fork and reached for the picture. The child was beautiful and so young. "Who could have taken her?"

"Like I said, we don't have any leads. We're interviewing more of the friends today. The father was at work in Manti when I interviewed him, but the only thing he could do was point fingers at the mother. He accused her of drug addiction."

"I take it he and the mother are divorced?"

"About a year now."

"Is he your best suspect?"

"So far everyone's a suspect. A high percentage of children are taken by family members, but there are still far too many stranger abductions to count that out. It'd be a lot easier for us if the mother could pinpoint the time of disappearance a little better. The father says she told him when she called at noon that she hadn't seen the girl since she put her to bed, but we didn't get a call from the mother until two-thirty in the afternoon. She's claiming she searched for hours before she called us."

Caitlin set down the picture, but the little girl's trusting eyes still danced before her. "Claims?"

Sally snorted. "In this business I don't trust anyone. The mother supposedly took a sleep aid and slept late. She has a history of drug arrests but no convictions on her adult record, and nothing within the past three years, so she's either cleaned up or—"

"Hasn't been caught." Caitlin sipped her glass of water. "It's a sad world when a child can't sleep safely in her own bed."

"Sad indeed."

They were silent a moment as they both took another bite of their food, Caitlin washing hers down with water, and Sally with her usual diet Dr. Pepper.

"I heard about the reaction to the knife evidence yesterday in your other trial," Sally said. "Tough luck for your client."

Caitlin shrugged. "The DA offered a plea deal this morning on that case too. Twenty years with the possibility of parole if he'll admit to attempted murder and aggravated assault. Apparently, they fear I'll drag the case on for weeks." Which she refused to do because it wouldn't change the outcome, but she couldn't tell Sally that, no matter how good of friends they were. "My client has until three o'clock this afternoon to agree. Or his trial will resume tomorrow as originally scheduled." Against her gut feeling that wanted him to remain in prison for life, she'd advised Belstead to take the deal. Of the twenty, he'd likely serve only ten, if he was a model prisoner.

"And if he doesn't take it?"

"He'll serve twenty-five to life instead. If convicted, of course." Which he would be, but that was something else Caitlin wouldn't voice.

"I know what you hope he'll do." Sally gave her another lopsided smile.

"Either way, the trial will be over tomorrow, and I'll never have to see that creep again. Well, except at the sentencing." Caitlin massaged her temple where she had the beginnings of a terrible headache.

"You know what you need?" Sally asked. "A man. Preferably one with a little muscle. Dating does wonders for stress."

Caitlin choked on her water, sending it spraying over the table. "You'd know." Sally's husband, Tony, was a building contractor who had more muscles in one arm than most men possessed in their entire bodies. His animal magnetism was palpable.

"Oh, yeah, I know." Sally grinned. "So, anyone interesting on the horizon?" She looked around the restaurant, as though scoping out potential dates. Her voice lowered. "What about the infamous DDA with the girlfriend in California? Any news on that front?"

Caitlin groaned. "I can't believe I told you about him."

"We all have weak moments. And he's worth having one over. I got a glimpse of him this week when he came to the precinct. He is something else. Hot."

"And as untouchable as ever," Caitlin said. "But I do have a date for Saturday." Better to change the subject before Mace's name slipped from Sally's lips. It was bound to get back to the circles Caitlin traveled in if she wasn't careful.

"Who?" Sally leaned toward her. "Tell me right now, or I'm going to arrest you."

Caitlin laughed and held out her wrists. "Take me away. I need a break."

"If sitting in jail with a bunch of drunks and druggies sounds restful, I know you're overworked."

"Really, it's nothing. Just another DDA." After the arson trial dismissed for lunch, Caitlin and Wyman had agreed on Saturday night. He'd wanted Friday, but Caitlin liked to keep Friday night clear so she didn't spend the entire day away from Amy. She worked late far too many nights as it was. Saturday also delayed whatever it was Wyman was aiming for.

"Good-looking?" Sally prompted. She scooped up a fork of mashed potatoes, eating them with undisguised relish.

Caitlin rolled her eyes. "Look, this guy is handsome, sort of, but it's not like that between us." She didn't want to admit she suspected Wyman's motive was blackmail. That would get Sally's investigative nose going overtime, and Sally was one woman she didn't want on the case. "He's separated from his wife, maybe even filed for divorce already, but I don't plan to get involved until I make sure where he stands. It's more of a business dinner than anything." Actually, she didn't plan on getting involved at all, but she didn't want Sally digging around or feeling sorry for her.

"Let me know if you need me to order a background check."

"What?" Another laugh burst from Caitlin. "I can't believe you just said that."

"Hey, it's for a good cause." Sally shoveled in a few more bites as they waited for their check. "I'd better get on my way to Manti. I'll drop you somewhere if you'd like."

"The courthouse. My arson client should be ready to tell me if he's taking the plea deal."

"No problem."

A few minutes later, Sally pulled to the curb to let Caitlin out at the tall white building with its many windows that reflected the weak afternoon sun. "See you next week," Caitlin told her. "Good luck finding that little girl."

"If she's still alive." Sally's reply was grim, and Caitlin knew she was thinking about the other little girl who'd gone missing in Salt Lake two weeks before. The seven-year-old had been raped and killed within an hour of leaving her home, her body found days later in the basement of a neighboring apartment. Vicious, violent crimes that targeted the most helpless were what Sally dealt with on a regular basis. Most people had no idea.

Sally lifted her chin. "I'll find the guy who did this, and when I do, you'd better not get him off."

"Wouldn't dream of it." Caitlin watched her drive away, feeling a sense of something she couldn't put her finger on.

Across the street stood the county building, looking old and picturesque, peeking behind the bare trees. She liked the view better in the summer when green leaves filled the trees and the blue sky overhead held nothing but warmth.

"Caitlin!"

She lowered her gaze from the building and saw Mace Keeley coming across the street toward her, grinning widely. When he motioned for her to wait, she checked her watch surreptitiously before nodding, pleased to see she had plenty of time for a short chat.

"Needed some records," he said casually, tossing his head in the direction of the county building.

"Convenient, isn't it?" She herself had gone across the street more times than she could count to confer with one county employee or another.

"I heard you gave Wyman a run for his money this morning."

She grinned. "He offered a deal. Arson and manslaughter." Mace whistled. "Your client is lucky."

"Maybe. There isn't a lot of proof."

"He going to take it?"

"I'll find out within the hour. But I'm fairly certain."

"Good. One more client through the system."

"Yep." They stood silently for brief seconds, their breath making white puffs in the cold air. Caitlin's heart was thudding so furiously, she thought it a miracle he couldn't hear the barrage.

Be calm, she told herself. She angled toward the courthouse and he turned with her. Together they started up the stairs, joining the half-dozen other people who were heading inside. Mace held the door open for her, and she passed close enough to feel the warmth emanating from him and to smell the faint aroma of his aftershave.

In the building, he touched her arm, guiding her to the side so they wouldn't be overheard by the passersby. Even separated by the sleeve of her suit coat, his hand felt hot on her skin. "I was wondering if you'd like to have dinner with me sometime."

Caitlin was grateful she'd inherited a poker face from her mother and that at work, the English side of her was more prominent than the more abandoned Irish side. At least so far. Yet inside, the Irish in her was wildly shouting, *Yes, yes! I'll go out to dinner with you. Kiss me now!*

"Well, that depends," she said casually.

"Depends on what?" He gave her a lazy smile, completely confident of his charms. Her insides responded with a rush of warmth.

Concentrate, she told herself. "Well, rumor has it that you might be moving to California. It's very hard to commute to a dinner so far away." And she didn't have time to waste on someone who wasn't sticking around. Especially not someone seriously dating a woman in another state.

"Ah, I see." He regarded her quietly a moment, his blue eyes glinting with amusement. "Well, I'm sorry to have to quell that particular rumor, but between you and me, I'm not planning on moving."

Caitlin hoped he meant what she thought he did. At the very least, she'd let him know she was going into their dinner with open eyes. "In that case, dinner sounds fun."

"What about Saturday? I'd say Friday, but I have a case that's going to keep me late."

She opened her mouth to agree but then remembered her plans with Wyman. "Oh, I can't Saturday." She let a hint of disappointment tinge her voice. "I have plans already." She wished she hadn't relented with Wyman, but she couldn't change that now.

"Maybe another time."

"If you get off early Friday, call me. I'll be working late myself." *Did I just say that?* she thought. She hoped it sounded natural. Only thirty-two years old, and she'd been out of the game too long.

"I'll do that." He seemed sincere enough that she wondered fleetingly how she would explain it to Amy if he followed through. Maybe Sally would agree to let her go over for the evening to play with Randi.

With a nod and another breathtaking smile, Mace started away from her, and though she needed to go that same way, she busied herself by walking in the opposite direction to give him a head start. No sense in starting the rumors flying already. She'd worked hard to keep her professional life separate from her personal, and she wasn't about to give that up just because Mace made her pulse race. She might be secretly wishing she had a man in her life, but chasing off all the womanizing young attorneys who thought nothing of working their way through any and all willing females was not on her list of things she most wanted to do. Better to let them think her a hard woman with no interest in relationships.

Reaching the end of the hall, she checked her watch once

again, turned, and headed toward the courtroom where she was meeting her client.

"Hey, Caitlin."

She'd been so intent on her thoughts that she hadn't noticed Wyman before she nearly ran into him. "Oh, hi."

"Did you talk to your arsonist about the deal?"

"He's considering. I'm going to talk to him now. You'll have your answer soon."

"I'll let you go then." He reached out and touched her arm in a gesture that seemed too intimate. "I'm really looking forward to Saturday night. I think you'll find we have a lot in common."

Inwardly, Caitlin shuddered. "I'm sure it'll be interesting." She glanced at her watch pointedly. "Oops, gotta run. Don't want to keep the client waiting." She moved around him and continued on, aware of his eyes following her down the hall.

Chapter 9

For three days now, Parker Hathaway had been forced to sneak out of his own apartment through a window under the cover of darkness and use a fire escape to get to the ground. Then he'd jogged five miles to the rented house on the edge of town. He didn't know why the police had staked out his truck and apartment, but he couldn't risk leading them to Madison.

When he arrived at the rental house on Friday night, Madison was waiting for him in the front room. He could see her framed in the light from the window as she watched for him. "Daddy," she called faintly through the closed window. Faster than he could climb the four cement steps framed by a wobbling wrought iron railing, she was out the door and jumping into his arms.

"Careful, babe. I'm a little sweaty."

"Why?"

"Cuz I just ran all the way here." He'd showered off all the dirt from the construction site at the apartment, but now he'd have to shower again.

"Did your truck break?" she asked with concern.

"Something like that. Where's Carla?"

"She's making dinner."

"Did you have fun with her today?"

Madison nodded eagerly, her now-brown locks flowing in stray wisps around her face. "We played hide and seek, and she helped me build a tent, and she was teaching me Spanish. I can say table and chair and a whole bunch of other stuff." She demonstrated as they walked inside, and Parker was impressed.

"That's great! Just so you don't forget how to speak English. I don't know Spanish."

Madison giggled. "That would be funny if I was saying stuff and if you didn't know what I was saying. And then I would have to tell you and you would say, 'Oh, that's what Madison is saying.'"

Parker laughed. Madison always made up imaginary scenarios that amused both of them.

Carla had paused in the kitchen as they came in. She smiled. "I weel feeneesh deener for Madeeson. Then I go."

"Thank you," he said, marveling at how quickly Carla was learning English. He'd been in Mexico once for a week and hadn't understood a thing. Apparently, Carla was more adaptable. He'd felt from first meeting her that she was intelligent, and it was one of the reasons he'd hired her. That and he knew she wasn't likely to run to the police. "Is there anything I should know about? Did everything go okay?"

Carla nodded. "Ees fine. She ees a good girl."

"I'm glad. You can always call me if you need something." The owner of the house had agreed to install a phone and add it to the rent, so Carla and Madison had access to a phone. He'd given them the number of the new burner phone he'd recently bought. It was possible the police had some way of hearing or tracing his conversations on his regular phone, so he didn't dare use it to communicate with them.

Carla nodded, but Parker suspected that her limited English would prevent her from ever calling. He'd have to teach Madison how to dial tonight in case she needed him. He went into the bathroom and removed his shirt.

"Are you going to take a bath?" Madison asked, watching him from the doorway with interest. He could tell she was disappointed.

"Nope. Just cleaning up a bit." He leaned over the sink, splashing water on his face, over his head, neck, and under his arms. Then he rubbed himself dry with a towel, pulling on a new shirt from the backpack he'd carried through the streets. After Madison was in bed, he'd shower properly and this time he'd leave the dirty clothes here for a spare, since Carla had agreed to do the laundry. That beat jogging over here carrying an extra set of clothes.

He hadn't found time to shave in nearly a week, and he stared into the mirror at a face he barely recognized. How long would he be able to keep up this duplicity? Though tomorrow was Saturday, he still had to work, and that meant another five-mile jog back to his apartment in the morning after Carla arrived, and another five miles after a grueling day at work. Yet he couldn't afford to quit working. Two months earlier he'd opened his apartment to roommates to lower the costs he'd known were pending, but he still had his child care payments to Dakota, this rental house payment, the truck payment, and the rent on the house for Dakota and Madison, with only a few thousand in savings to tide him over.

How long before he made a serious mistake? How long

before the police figured out what he'd done? They would have followed him here already if Donald, one of his roommates, hadn't recognized the officers in the unmarked car in front of their apartment Wednesday evening. Fortunately for Parker they were the same officers who'd interviewed Donald, and he had noticed them shortly before Parker had come home from work after a quick stop at his mother's. Tonight it was a different car and different people, but he knew they were cops.

Worry bit at Parker's mind. What if the police couldn't find anything on Dakota? What if they didn't even try? What if they stayed on his tail for a month? A year? More? How could he give Madison any semblance of a normal life?

"Daddy?"

Parker was startled from his thoughts by Madison's voice. He took his unseeing gaze from the mirror. "All finished, honey. Let's get some dinner, and then we'll play. I missed you so much today."

"Can we go outside?" Madison asked. "Carla said no."

Parker smiled past his exhaustion. "If we bundle you up really well, we can go outside in the back yard for a bit. But Carla was right about not going outside during the day."

"Why?"

"It's not safe here unless I'm home."

She nodded solemnly, easily accepting his explanation. "Can we make a snowman? A really big one?"

"The snow's too old and crunchy to pack, but as soon as it snows again, we'll make the biggest and bestest snowman ever."

Madison hugged him. "Yay!"

He lifted her into his arms and started for the door. "Daddy?" she asked. "When am I going back to Mommy's?"

"Do you miss her?"

She shook her head and held up three fingers as she counted

them. "I've been here only one, two, three days. I don't want to leave. Carla makes really good pancakes."

"Okay. Then you stay."

She put her arms around his neck, squeezing him tightly and bringing tears to his eyes. "I wish Ricky was here," she whispered in her ear. "He would like to have fun with you, too."

Ricky, the little boy who'd been in the crib—Madison's half brother—was now in as much danger as Madison had been. "I wish he could be here too," Parker said, a pit of cold settling in his stomach. "But maybe he's playing with his daddy." From what Madison had told him, Ricky spent a lot of time with his father. With any luck, Dakota would allow the man to take custody while the police investigated Madison's disappearance.

"Come on," he said, moving Madison around to his back. "I'll give you a horsey ride to the kitchen."

Madison's laughter filled the tiny house.

Chapter 10

At eight o'clock on Friday night, Caitlin was lying in bed in her pajamas watching TV, Amy sprawled next to her. There were dolls and stuffed animals and an array of picture books as well, since Amy always liked to stave off boredom.

The day had been long and torturous. Unlike her arson client who'd jumped at the prosecutor's deal, Chet Belstead had refused his offered plea deal and they had continued the trial. Wyman hadn't retaken lead for the prosecutor's case, though, as Caitlin had expected. In fact, he hadn't even shown up in court. Only Mace Keeley was present, as smooth-talking and flamboyant as ever. And as gorgeous. The jury loved him. Caitlin didn't have much left to present in Belstead's defense, but she did her best. After final arguments, the jury was out less than an hour before Belstead was found guilty. He went crazy at the verdict, cursing the jurors and judge, and finally lunging for Caitlin, but the bailiff, Mace, and several other men in the courtroom had managed to drag him out before there was any damage. Caitlin knew his final sentence would likely be a lot stiffer for his stupidity. She told herself that was a good thing, but losing a case, even one she'd wanted to lose, did nothing to help her feel better about the day.

She hadn't seen Mace after he'd left with the bailiff and her client, but now as her cell phone rang, she couldn't stop her hopes from rising. Her exhaustion vanished when she saw it was Mace.

Her hands fumbled as she swept up the phone to answer. "Hello?" She hoped she didn't sound as eager and breathless as she felt.

"Hi, Caitlin. It's Mace. I think I'm going to be finished early after all. You still up for dinner in, say, an hour?"

An hour gave her thirty-five minutes to change, throw on a bit of makeup, and find a sitter for Amy, and then twenty-five more minutes to make the restaurant and find parking. In attorney time, that was eons. "Sure. But I've got a few things to wrap up myself. Can we meet somewhere?"

"How about at Caffe Molise?" He obviously assumed she was still at her office. "They're open at least until ten, I believe."

"I'll be there." Caffe Molise was a popular Italian restaurant, and to get a reservation this quickly in the winter when there wasn't outdoor dining was no small feat. Mace must know someone to have organized this date so quickly—unless he'd anticipated that he would be able to get free and had made reservations earlier, just in case. Or maybe working late had been a lie all along, and instead he'd had a date that evening who'd canceled on him, leaving Caitlin his second choice.

Sometimes she hated being so analytical.

"I'm looking forward to seeing you." His voice was casual, but she sensed innuendo beneath the words, and her thoughts scattered. Who cared how she ended up at dinner with Mace Keeley? Just so she did.

"Me too." Caitlin hung up the phone and kicked into high gear. She began dialing a telephone number as she shrugged off her pajamas and stared into her closet, wondering what to wear. Something attractive that wouldn't show too much bare skin, as it was cold outside and she was supposedly coming from work. She chose a sheer red top with her fitted black suit coat and skirt. After she lost the jacket, the top would be dressy and the skirt just tight enough and short enough to emphasize her legs, which she considered her best feature.

Sally wasn't answering her home or cell phone, and neither were either of Caitlin's next-door neighbors or Amy's babysitter. Caitlin put a dab of perfume behind her ears and on her neck, beginning to feel a touch of despair. Her demanding job hadn't left her time for many friends, and that meant she didn't have a lot of people she could call on for help. Wait, she did have a cousin who lived in Salt Lake, who had offered to sit with Amy last year. Where was the number? She found it at last, only to learn the number had been disconnected.

"Now who?" she muttered, glancing at Amy, who was still sprawled on the bed, thumbing through her picture books. If only their parents were alive. If only Amy was normal. Sighing in disgust at her own thoughts, Caitlin slumped on the bed.

"Are you okay?" Amy asked. "You look mad. Did I do something?"

"No, sweetie. You didn't do anything."

Caitlin searched through the phone numbers on her cell phone again. Jodi. Maybe the paralegal would be willing. At least she knew about Amy.

"Hello?"

"Hi, it's Caitlin. Look, are you busy right now? I've had

something important come up, and I need someone to stay with my sister."

"I'm just heading to a movie," Jodi said. "I'd volunteer to take her with me, but"—her voice lowered—"I'm with this really hot guy I met in court yesterday. Sorry."

"That's okay. Thanks anyway."

Caitlin spied Sally's husband on her list of contacts. He'd at least know where her friend was.

"Hello?" Tony answered on the second ring.

"Hi, it's Caitlin. I'm looking for Sally."

"She's on a stakeout. She should be home, but she's got some hunch about this kidnapping, and she's pulling overtime. I decided to take Randi to visit my parents."

"You're clear up in Logan?"

"Yep. I thought I might as well drive up, since Sally's down in Manti."

"I see."

"You can call her on her cell."

"She's not answering."

"I'm sorry. Was it very important?"

Only my future with Mace Keeley. "Nothing that can't wait," she said aloud.

When Caitlin hung up the phone, she saw that all of her minutes were gone. *So much for eons of time,* she thought with despair.

Could she take Amy on her date? She let herself hope a few minutes longer. Amy might behave. She might actually eat the food she was given without complaint. Maybe she would be too tired to talk incessantly. She might not ask Mace to father Caitlin's children.

No. Taking Amy would be a disaster. Especially when Mace was only expecting her. And how romantic would it be anyway, with Amy watching their every move? Caitlin had no choice but to call Mace back and cancel.

"Hi," he said, sounding happy to hear from her.

She took a deep breath. "Hi, Mace. Look, I'm sorry, but I'm going to have to cancel. I thought I had everything taken care of, but there's something else I have to do. I'm really sorry. How about a rain check?"

"If you want I could stop by with some take-out." His voice sounded strangely compelling.

"I can't. I won't be alone. I was looking forward to it, but—"

"No problem," he said quickly. "I know how it is. We'll do something another day."

Caitlin stared at the phone in her hand for long minutes after their conversation. She knew she might never have another opportunity with him. She wished she didn't care so much.

Amy's arms went around her. "Caitlin, why are you sad?" Caitlin returned Amy's hug, blinking back tears.

They settled back on her pillows before Caitlin answered. "Well, there's a guy I kind of like, and I was going to see him tonight, but it didn't work out."

"Because of me." Amy frowned. "I could stay by myself."

"No, you can't."

"If I was smarter, I could."

Her tone made Caitlin feel worse. Though Amy had enough intelligence to understand that something was different about her, they didn't usually discuss it.

"Oh, Amy." Caitlin pulled her sister closer, gazing into her eyes. "I love you exactly the way you are."

Amy's lip curved in her sweet smile. "I love you too. More than anyone in the whole world." She laid her head on Caitlin's shoulder.

They were quiet a long moment as Caitlin pondered her

life. Any man she became involved with would have to know about and accept Amy. Because no matter what, she would never, ever leave Amy behind.

"Is he cute?" Amy asked suddenly.

Caitlin laughed. "Very cute."

"Would he make good babies?"

"I'm sure he'd make incredible babies." Though thoughts of a future with Mace was not something Caitlin was going to torture herself with tonight.

"Good." Amy was quiet for a moment and then abruptly her eyes closed. Like many young children, for Amy the difference between wakefulness and sleep was only a matter of seconds.

Caitlin eased her arm out from under her sister and went to change back into her pajamas. She was reaching for the remote and getting ready to numb her brain into thoughtlessness by watching whatever was on TV when Sally called.

"Hi, it's me," Sally said. "Need something?"

"You're on a stakeout?"

"I'm keeping an eye on the father of that kidnapped girl I told you about. I had some of my guys here last night, but I've got a feeling about this, so I wanted to be here tonight. I was chatting with some of his neighbors when you called before."

"I saw a clip about the kidnapping on the news."

"Yeah. Hopefully it'll bring in more tips."

"So, is there more evidence the father did it?"

"I don't know, but he's lying about something. But it's odd. He's my most likely suspect, but I kind of like him."

"Why?"

"I don't know. Maybe I'm partial to men in construction."

"Ah. Does he look like Tony?"

"Not at all. But he's not bad. If I weren't married . . ."

Caitlin ignored that. Both of them knew Sally was wildly crazy about Tony.

"So why did you call?" Sally asked into the silence.

"I wanted to see if I could drop Amy at your place for the night. I had the chance to go out to dinner with Mace Keeley."

"Ah, the handsome DDA you're crushing on. Apparently all that drooling over him this past year hasn't been in vain."

"I have not been drooling over him."

"Yes, you have."

"Well, so what?"

"That's the spirit. Nothing wrong at all with drooling, as long as it's over barbecue ribs or a good-looking man. What I want to know is why you didn't tell me before. I could have assigned this evening's stakeout to someone else."

"It wasn't planned. He was working late and managed to get off early. When he called, we decided to have dinner. But I couldn't take Amy, so I ended up canceling."

"Next time give me some notice. Randi would love to have Amy over."

"I'm not so sure there'll be a next time."

Sally was quiet a long moment. "You're selling yourself short, you know. You're the hottest lawyer babe I know. And don't compare yourself with that toothpick, pasty-faced paralegal you work with, either. You're a woman, not a little girl."

Caitlin sighed. She knew Sally meant well, but she wasn't helping.

"Well, at least you have tomorrow night," Sally added. Caitlin made a face but managed not to groan. With the excitement and subsequent disappointment of Mace's invitation, she'd forgotten all about her dinner with Wyman. What if he tried to blackmail her into giving him more information on other cases? Or used his knowledge to try to force her into a dating relationship?

He doesn't have proof, she thought.

Yet.

"Oh, yes. Can't forget tomorrow," Caitlin said with false gaiety. "And I guess I'd better hang up and let you go get the bad guys."

"I'm not so sure he is the bad guy, but I'm doing everything I can to bring that little girl home to her mother—whether the woman deserves it or not."

Caitlin hung up and watched TV until she fell asleep. Instead of dreaming about Mace Keeley, she dreamed of Wyman Russell running after her with the bloody knife he carried wrapped in a dark blue jacket.

Chapter 11

O n Saturday morning, clanging pans in the kitchen brought Parker to consciousness with a start. From the angle of light spilling in from the gauzy green curtains, he knew he was late. His head felt full of sand, and his muscles protested the slightest move. Apparently working construction used different muscles than jogging and playing half the night with a four-year-old.

There was something heavy on his chest, and he looked down to see Madison's head there, her feet splayed toward the side of the bed. Seeing her cleared the fog from his brain and sent him into action. This innocent, precious child was the reason he was going to such great effort, the reason he had to make it all work. Gently, he eased out from under Madison, leaning over to place a kiss on the small mole on her right cheek.

Hopefully, she'd sleep a good portion of the day so she wouldn't have as much time to get bored without him. He should probably think about finding her a preschool eventually. He doubted Carla would be able to teach her to read English.

Quickly, he changed from his pajama bottoms into his extra pair of jeans, having tossed the other pair into the dirty laundry the night before. He'd showered last night and his shirt was still fairly clean, so he was good to go.

Carla was in the kitchen, and her pretty brown face lit up at seeing him. "Good morning," she said. Her long hair was secured in the back with a clip the way Dakota had sometimes worn hers. For some reason it made him feel sad.

"Good morning." He ran a hand through his hair. "I'm late, so I have to get going. She stayed up pretty late. It's probably best to let her sleep."

Carla nodded. "She sleep. I bring book to read."

"Okay. Thanks."

"Want to eat?" Carla said, motioning to the stove where she was already cooking something he thought might be Madison's lunch. Their deal was that she'd buy food and make all the meals for Madison, and enough dinner for him as well. "I make eggs, eef you like. Or pancakes."

"No, thanks. I'll get something later. I'm really late." He pulled his sweatshirt over his head, wishing it wasn't so cold outside and that he didn't have five miles to run before he could get his truck.

"Daddy?" Madison was in the doorway, rubbing her eyes. "Why are you leaving?" Her lips drew into a pout.

"I have to work. But remember we'll spend the whole day together tomorrow."

"Can we see Grandma?"

He thought about it. "Maybe. I'll try to make it work." He bent down and held out his arms, and Madison ran into them. "Be a good girl for Carla today, okay? If you need me, call the phone like we practiced last night. But only if it's really important, okay? Otherwise, I'll call you at lunchtime again."

"Okay, Daddy, but it's kind of boring here."

"I'll bring you some games."

"Can I watch TV?"

"Yes." He hadn't figured on her being bored. Usually when they were together, they had so much planned they couldn't squeeze all the activities into the two short days they had been allotted for his visitation. "I'll be back soon, sweetie. I love you."

She squeezed his neck with mock ferociousness. "I love you too, Daddy. You're my bestest, bestest daddy ever."

"And you're my bestest girl."

After cautioning her to stay inside the house, Parker left for the long run to his apartment. The cold morning air seared the inside of his nose and throat as he ran. Since he worked outside most days, he'd learned to deal with the cold, but he still hated it with a passion. When it was hot he could dunk his head and gulp down water to chase away the heat from inside. The cold was another story. It seeped between the layers of clothing, crawled into his pores and mouth and nose, lodging in his bones and making him feel stiff and old. Maybe he should take that job as a foreman. He'd worked hard for the opportunity and it wasn't really a surprise to have it offered. Of course, even if he could move Madison, it was already too late for that opportunity.

As he ran, the weight of what he was trying to do threatened to crush him. The police were following him, not checking out Dakota as he'd hoped. For all he knew, Dakota was playing the poster mother for all lost children. Dakota, who'd thought nothing of letting her daughter live in a meth house, or who had locked Madison in her room so she could be alone with her friends to do a little recreational crack.

He made it back to his apartment and in through the window, changing quickly into a long-sleeved work shirt and his heavy coat. The unmarked car was still outside the apartment, and he stifled the urge to wave to the officers. No use letting them know he knew they were there. They might make their surveillance more subtle and somehow track him to Madison.

Driving to work, the realization hit him. *I can't keep this up.* The police weren't going to stop any time soon, and hiding inside all day was no life for a child—or for him. In that moment, Parker decided to tell his boss that he needed to quit so he could head up north and search for Madison. In reality, he'd be putting as much space between this state and Madison as possible.

His mother was right. They would have to disappear.

Chapter 12

As Caitlin readied for her Saturday night dinner, Amy was more excited than Caitlin. In fact, Caitlin dreaded the evening with Wyman. He was picking her up at six—a time she insisted on so they wouldn't be too late getting home. Gloria, her neighbor on the left, had agreed to watch Amy, but Caitlin had promised to pick her up before ten. Nine preferably. Or maybe eight? Would Wyman believe that?

She grimaced into the mirror. Oddly enough, she looked really good, even if she did say so herself. Her unruly copper hair often waved or curled out of control, usually in a half-and-half mixture that looked rather uneven and that almost always prompted Caitlin to pin her hair up for work, but today the hair was being remarkably well-behaved. A little gel had helped even out the waves and curls, and air drying helped tamed the frizz. Her makeup had gone on well, and the fitted blue blouse she'd chosen to wear over black slacks made her eyes even bluer.

She'd chosen these clothes because she didn't know where they were going and didn't really care about making an impression, but even she had to admit that she looked, well, hot.

"You look so beautiful," Amy said with a sigh. "Like a princess." She whirled around the bathroom, looking rather incongruous and awkward given her height and bulk.

Caitlin hugged her. "Thank you, Amy."

"I know you don't like him a real lot, but I think he's nice." Amy obviously hadn't noticed the momentary revulsion on Wyman's face when he'd first seen her, and Caitlin was glad. There were distinct advantages to being one of the pure and innocent.

Her mind churned over what Wyman might say or do this evening. As always, her thoughts fell into the same pattern. Did he think she would start feeding him information about her cases?

He can't prove anything, she told herself for the hundredth time in the past few days. But she knew there were ways. Now that Wyman had tracked down the boy, he might start to work on Kenny, and though Kenny had always been reliable, he could accidentally let something slip. Would there be enough to prove misconduct? If so, would that set Chet Belstead free?

The thought made her sick. But what else could she have done? Watch him walk away, only to meet up with him again years down the road when he was arrested for a similar crime? When another victim and her family sat on the benches with devastation in their eyes?

The nauseated feeling increased. She knew she had made her choice, and now she had to do what she could to keep Chet Belstead in jail and to protect her job and Amy. The only silver lining in any of this was that Wyman didn't want Belstead free any more than she did, so if he filed a complaint against her, he'd be risking the win he and Mace had accomplished in court. Not many attorneys she knew would do that, especially to free a man they knew was guilty.

"Come on," Caitlin said to Amy, pushing away the dark thoughts. "Let's get you over to Gloria's."

"Yippee!" Amy loved Gloria, who worked at a pastry outlet and always brought home their products. At least once a week they would find donuts or some other treat in a plastic sack on their doorknob.

Before they left the bathroom, the doorbell rang, and Amy lumbered to open it. Caitlin followed more slowly in her black high-heeled boots. "It's that one guy!" Amy called. "He has some flowers and they're so pretty. Hurry, Caitlin!"

Caitlin came into view, pulling on her dressy leather jacket. She met Wyman's eyes and was satisfied to see his admiration, though why she'd care for his approval was beyond her. "Hi," she said pleasantly, her eyes dropping to the bouquet of roses in his hands. She hadn't expected flowers.

"You ready?"

"I need to walk Amy next door."

"I can do it myself." Amy edged past Wyman and out onto the porch.

"Wait," Wyman said. "Here." He gave the flowers to Amy.

Her jaw dropped and her eyes went wide. Caitlin hadn't seen her so surprised since two years ago when Caitlin had redone her room in a princess motif for her twenty-fifth birthday. "Me?" Amy asked. "Aren't they for Caitlin?"

"They're for you," Wyman said with a smile. "Go ahead, take them."

Amy took the flowers and bounced up and down. "They're so pretty. So pretty! I never had flowers before, did I, Caitlin? I love them!" She hugged them to her chest, plastic and all.

Caitlin was laughing, feeling grateful to Wyman despite

her distaste for him. "Careful of the thorns. Come on, bring them into the kitchen. Let's get you a vase to take to Gloria's. She can help you arrange them in water."

"Okay." Amy hurried past Wyman.

"Come in," Caitlin invited. "It'll just be a moment."

Amy had already found a vase, though they were on the top shelf. There was one advantage to her being so tall. "Is this one good?"

Caitlin shook her head. "It's very pretty, but I don't think it'll hold all those flowers. Is there a bigger one?"

Amy reached for it. "I got it." She did a little dance. "I can't wait to show Gloria. And can I show them to Sarah? Will they still be alive when I go there again?"

"I'm sure they'll still be good by Monday."

Amy breezed into the living room and out the front door. By the time Caitlin and Wyman were off the front porch, she was already at Gloria's. The tall, dark-haired woman waved to them before taking Amy inside and shutting the door.

"Thank you for that," Caitlin said as they walked to Wyman's gray car—a Lexus, she noted.

He shrugged. "I didn't think you'd mind sharing your flowers."

She stifled a retort that she hadn't expected flowers at all. "Of course not."

"Truthfully, I've never seen a woman so excited about flowers before," he said as he opened her door.

"Well, Amy's not exactly a woman."

"I know."

She studied him as she walked around the car. He was different this evening, though she couldn't tell exactly why. He wore a blue plaid sport jacket and solid blue pants that were more attractive than his typical dark work suit, but his hair was still thinning and his handsome face a bit on the fleshy side. So what exactly was different about him?

He'd been nice to Amy. That had to be it. Despite the revulsion she'd clearly seen on his face earlier in the week, he'd been kind to her. Why? Was it a trick, a ploy to make her relax? She couldn't afford to relax. Wyman was her enemy both in and out of court, and she couldn't let her guard down even for a moment.

"Where are we going?" she asked.

"You'll see."

She arched a brow. "A surprise?"

"Hopefully." He smiled, ignoring the coolness of her tone.

Opera was playing in the car, and though Caitlin had developed a taste for classical music since passing the bar, she didn't want to enjoy herself. She held her body stiff and her lips together as she stared out the window in silence. She didn't want to be here with him, and there was no use pretending he hadn't forced her into this meeting.

He drove to the Avenues in Salt Lake City, pulling up in the last open parking place before a squat, two-story stucco building that looked as if it might contain three or four offices. The stucco was so faded, she couldn't tell if it was tan or gray.

"There's a restaurant here?" she asked.

He pointed to a sign over one of the double doors. "Cafe Shambala. It's Tibetan food. I hope you like it."

She'd tasted some once and hadn't hated it, so she shrugged. "Yeah. It's fine." *I'm really here only to find out what you know and what you're going to do about it.*

Inside, large colorful posters and flags lined the walls, and there were several prominent pictures of an older man with dark hair. "The Dalai Lama," Wyman explained. Besides the posters, the decorations were sparse. The clientele seemed varied, though most were relatively young. "Don't let the place fool you," Wyman told her. "They have really good food."

There seemed to be only one server, but he came to their table before Caitlin had time to completely remove her leather jacket.

"The chicken curry is excellent," Wyman suggested as the server hovered over them with a pad and pencil. "Or the chicken and broccoli, if you like broccoli."

"Okay, I'll have the chicken and broccoli."

"I'll have the curry," Wyman said. "And we'd like this momo appetizer." He lifted his eyes to Caitlin. "They don't have a liquor license here, but they have a sort of yogurt shake called a lassi that's nice."

Caitlin had tried lassi at another restaurant and hadn't been impressed, but she agreed anyway to get the evening over with as soon as possible. "I'll have that, then. And some water, please." The server hurried away with their order.

The kitchen was open to the restaurant, and they could see workers preparing the food. Caitlin wondered if it gave customers comfort when they chose some of the stranger meals. "This is really cozy," she said, settling back in her chair. "Nice." Relaxing was actually a better word since the earlier tension in her body had seemed to leak away without her consent.

"You sound surprised."

She shrugged. She *was* surprised, but she wasn't going to admit it. She'd expected a bigger show, something along the lines of Mace's restaurant choice, but not this little place, with its sparse decorations and intimate atmosphere. If the food tasted as good as it smelled, she would at least derive some enjoyment from this forced expedition.

"Something funny?" Wyman asked.

She shook her head. "I'm just wondering why we're really here."

His eyes narrowed. "Ah. Business first. I get it. Okay, I want to know if you're involved with how we found the evidence against your client."

Caitlin considered him a moment. There had been a slight hesitation before he'd spoken. She wouldn't be a good attorney if she hadn't recognized it. "Are you sure that's it? A few days ago you said something about working together." She fixed an unwavering stare on him.

He dropped his gaze first, and she had the distinct feeling he was hiding something. "You applied for my job two years ago," he said. "There may be another opening soon. You could come and work for the good guys for a change."

He couldn't possibly know how wonderful that sounded. "Strange," she said, her voice flat, "I thought you were trying to blackmail me into giving you privileged client-attorney information." Keeping the emotion from her words was the way to unnerve creeps. It worked every day with the hardened criminals she represented, as well as the hotshot attorneys she had to face in court.

"Then why are you here?"

"Maybe to gain evidence against *you*." Going on the attack was not a new ploy but one he apparently recognized.

He grinned. "I haven't done anything wrong."

"Neither have I." Her voice trembled ever so slightly, making her furious with herself.

His gaze shifted to the kitchen and then back to her. There were still a few empty tables in the restaurant, and they were relatively isolated, but more customers were coming in. They would soon risk being overheard. "Look, let's drop this for now and enjoy dinner. For what it's worth, I'm betting you're not involved in anything that could get you disbarred."

"I didn't get that impression a few days ago," she retorted icily.

He was silent for several seconds. "Look, you need to be careful of Mace."

"Mace?" This surprised her. "What does he have to do with this?" Had Wyman somehow heard of her almost date with him yesterday? She'd have to be more careful.

"I know everyone thinks Mace Keeley is God's gift to the DA's office. But I work with the guy, and I think a little caution is in order."

"He seems nice enough." Not to mention gorgeous, hot, and the focus of more than a few of her dreams, though Wyman didn't need to hear that from her.

"He is. Right up until he stabs you in the back."

"His record for winning cases is unparalleled."

"Whereas mine is at the bottom?" Wyman smirked. "Interesting. Makes you wonder how the cases are assigned."

Caitlin pondered his words. This vein of conversation was completely unexpected. She'd thought Wyman might present some evidence of her breach of ethics, not act like a jealous suitor. Could it be possible that Wyman was attracted to her on more than a casual what-will-you-do-so-I'll-keep-quiet level? The thought stunned her into complete and utter silence.

"Ah, here comes our food." Wyman's sarcasm was gone. "You're in for a treat."

They ended up sharing the meals, dishing from the serving plates to other plates the server had brought them. Caitlin, who had never really enjoyed curry because it was too hot, loved the curry chicken so much that she forgot herself and ate seconds.

They talked about the courthouse and people they knew, keeping the conversation away from current cases or anything serious. When they finally finished dinner, Caitlin was surprised to see that two hours had slipped away.

Wyman saw her looking at her watch. "It's about time, huh? You need to get back to Amy?"

"Yes." Caitlin grabbed at the excuse, not because she wasn't enjoying herself but because she was. She still hadn't decided if Wyman was out to get her disbarred, blackmail her into working with him, or woo her into a romance. Either way, he wasn't a good candidate for Amy's husband and baby scenario, and Caitlin had worked too hard to let a mediocre attorney get in the way of her career.

They talked only occasionally on the way home, but the drive was comfortable. Wyman walked her to the door when they arrived at her house. The automatic light went on, and she bent to open the door with her key.

Wyman didn't take the hint. "I had a cousin like Amy," he said, his breath turning white as it hit the cold air. "When we were young, I didn't really notice any difference, but around nine or ten I started hating it. My mom and my aunt always wanted me to take him with me when I hung out with the guys. I thought it was embarrassing, so we used to play a lot of jokes on him." He shook his head, not looking at her now. "I feel guilty every time I think of it. He never, ever caught on. He practically worshiped me for spending so much time with him."

"Did something bad happen?" Caitlin visualized a prank that went too far, something that might have scarred a younger Wyman.

He shook his head. "He's fine. Still living with my aunt. I see him only on holidays now. It's just . . . when I met your sister the other day . . . well, let's just say it wasn't what I expected. I had an entirely different concept of you. At work you're so . . . well, intent. You don't hold back any punches or seem to have any love for your clients. You're tough."

She knew what he wasn't saying. He'd thought she was the

kind of woman who might not care about ethics. "You changed your mind because of my sister?" That was a first. Usually guys headed toward the hills when they sensed that kind of responsibility. "I don't know how I feel about that," she said.

His right shoulder lifted in a half shrug. After a few more seconds of silence, his face came closer, and she could tell he was going to kiss her. A part of her ached to be kissed, to be touched, but she didn't understand anything about this man and wasn't sure if she even liked him. She stepped back, reaching for the doorknob. "Last I heard, you had a wife. Unless you're divorced now."

He nodded, his expression contrite. "We're legally separated, with a divorce in the process. It doesn't look good, but I really don't know where that's going yet." The next words came awkwardly and with a painful slowness. "So you're right. Until I, uh, know for sure, I—"

"Wyman," she interrupted, taking pity on him, "I had a good time tonight. I really did. Well, all but that first bit at the restaurant." She smiled. "But I only went tonight because of our business relationship. You and I . . ." She shook her head. "It's not going anywhere."

He leaned over and kissed her cheek. "I meant what I said earlier about Mace. I know you think he's a paragon, but consider this. Have you ever wondered why you and I try so many cases together?"

Caitlin shook her head, not understanding his implication.

"Think about it. Look at Mace's cases."

When she didn't reply, he lifted his right shoulder, turned, and sprinted to his Lexus. Caitlin watched him go, finding it difficult to reorder her previous impressions of Wyman. Was he what he appeared to be, or was he playing some game she didn't yet understand?

Chapter 13

"Grandma!" Madison shot from the doorway of the rental house and into Norma's arms. The two put their heads together and began chattering as though it was any normal Sunday at Norma's house in Mt. Pleasant.

Parker set down the boxes of clothes from his apartment and smiled. Madison's joy was worth all the subterfuge of getting his mother here. He'd packed early this morning and had driven to her house, his faithful police escort following behind. Carrying his boxes, they had gone through Norma's back fence and over a few streets to the house of a family friend, who had loaned them a car. Then Parker had driven straight here.

He'd thought about blindfolding his mother so the secret would be safer, but he might need her to check on Madison if his new plan to leave the state was delayed. Besides, she wouldn't tell. She knew as well as he did the danger Madison would be in if she was returned to her mother.

"I weel be going then," Carla said from the doorway of the kitchen. "Unteel tonight when you need me."

"Thanks, Carla. I appreciate your help." He'd given her Monday and Tuesday off in exchange for coming in this morning for two hours and for another two later that evening when he took his mother home and jogged back from his apartment. She had been only too happy to agree. He felt a momentary pang of guilt that when she returned on Wednesday, he and Madison wouldn't be there. Well, he'd leave her as much severance as he could pay.

Carla looked at him. "Eef Madeeson asleep tonight when you leave, you weel need me to come back?"

"Yes, I'll still need you." He was surprised at the question. Had Carla been raised in a home where it was okay to leave small children if they were sleeping? Or maybe she didn't understand the distance and time involved. He couldn't possibly explain his need for jogging back to the house. "She's too young to ever be alone."

"Okay." She smiled, nodded at him, and went out the back door.

Parker returned his attention to Madison and his mother. "I love your new hair," Norma was saying to Madison.

"It's like yours, Grandma." Madison twirled around to show off her new dark locks.

"Look what Grandma brought you." Norma took out bubblegum and two packs of cards from her purse. "Old Maid and Go Fish. Your favorites."

"Goody!"

Parker felt grateful. Madison could play these games forever, and that meant he might just be able to take a little nap. With all the lack of sleep, the worry, and additional exercise, he was feeling decidedly exhausted. But Madison was safe, and that was the most important thing.

He sat on the couch and was dozing before he knew it, dreaming of Dakota when they first met at a bar. She was young and pretty and flirty and had her sights on him. He'd been drinking heavily in those days, and she was just as eager to gulp down the booze. They'd gone through the next few days in a whirl of partying and semi-consciousness. She'd wanted to get married, so they did after only two months, living hand to mouth, working only when absolutely necessary. Parker had thought he was happy, but more often than not tears had wet his pillow at night. He'd been lost. Adrift in a sea. Missing his family. Seeing no sense to the world or a reason for his existence. Until Madison had come along.

And then the terrible call that changed everything.

Parker jerked awake, sweating profusely. Madison and his mother were nowhere to be seen. His heart constricted with fear that left him tingling to his fingertips. Had the police found them and taken Madison away? Why hadn't they awakened him? He shook the thoughts away. *Be sensible.*

He found Madison in the kitchen making cookies with ingredients Norma had brought from home. Parker watched his mother and daughter from the doorway, enjoying Madison's enthusiasm. They interacted in a way that went beyond the casual, and way far beyond how Madison interacted with her mother.

Norma came over to stand beside him as Madison was pouring the chocolate chips, a few at a time, into the batter, stopping to eat a few or to make the chocolate pieces talk to one another. "I liquidated one of my investments," Norma said calmly but in a painful way, as though she was barely holding everything together. "Here's my bank card if you need it, or just go into the bank and take it out, since you're on my account. That would probably be best. There's over twenty thousand so far." She held up a hand when he started to protest. "I know you have a bit saved, even with giving Dakota so much, but it won't be enough, and if they're watching you, they've probably got a finger on both our accounts. So you'd want to take it all the same day."

Could the police really be monitoring their accounts? Parker decided they probably could but only if they had a warrant, and what proof would they have for one of those? Maybe it didn't matter in a kidnapping case. He took the card.

"I'll call you on this phone when we're settled," he said, handing her a burner phone he'd bought for her yesterday on his lunch hour. It'd only work for a month, but that should be long enough.

"That reminds me. I also have your brother's passport at home. You might be able to use it for ID in a pinch. It has another year before it expires. I'll get it to you later." Before he could respond, she added, her gaze resting on Madison. "So we're really going to do this."

"You don't have to." Parker hated the idea of her selling her house and moving away from a lifetime of friends. It wasn't fair for her to start over, much less to live on the run.

"You and Madison are all the family I have, and you know how important family is to me. Make no mistake; as soon as I've wrapped up everything here, I'm going to wherever you are." She glanced at the phone. "I'll be waiting for your call."

Parker's emotions bubbled up inside him, threatening to spill over. Silence stretched out between them. Then he somehow found the courage to continue, his voice less than a whisper. "I'm sorry I haven't been the son you deserve. I'd do anything to be him."

They both knew who he was talking about. Him. Vincent, the perfect older son, the one who'd been obedient to their demanding father, the one who'd studied diligently and worked for a future he would never have. Even now, Parker felt envious of his brother and his choices. He wished they'd been his.

"I don't want you to be Vincent," Norma said softly. Her face was solemn and her brown eyes unwavering. "I never have." She put an arm around his waist and leaned into him. "And neither did your father. He didn't know how to let you be yourself or understand that you needed to find your own way. But you did find your way, after all."

Maybe. Or not really. His youthful decisions had caused so much pain, and by the time he'd finally gained the sense to put the past behind him and take responsibility for his life, it was too late to matter to either his brother or his father. The irony was that taking responsibility had ultimately led him away from Dakota and the world he'd embraced to supposedly find himself.

It was his love for Madison, the precious child who had been all his from the moment she'd taken her first breath, that had changed him. He didn't regret her existence for anything, not even to recover those useless, mindless years he'd spent as Dakota's hostage. At least now the time when she could use Madison as a weapon was over. He would take his daughter far away where she could have a normal life and keep her there until Dakota self-destructed, and they could come home again.

"All done!" Madison announced, shoving one more chocolate chip into her mouth. Her lips and fingers were streaked with chocolate.

"Good job," Norma exclaimed with the sincere-sounding admiration Parker remembered from his own childhood. "Let's get these babies in the oven."

All too soon darkness replaced the day. Madison fell asleep, a contented smile on her face from her full day of attention and love. When Carla showed up to watch Madison, Parker drove his mother to her friend's house.

They returned the borrowed car without incident, and as they crossed several streets and yards on their way home, Parker mentally went over his plans. Once his mother was safely home, he'd drive his truck to the apartment, stuff more clothes in garbage bags, and jog back with them to the house. Tomorrow he would take out a large sum of money, buy a car from a junkyard he knew where they weren't picky about records, and pack up everything he'd managed to take to the rental house. Then they would leave Utah. His mother would eventually sell his truck, and his apartment would be rented to others. Meanwhile, Norma would wrap up her own affairs and follow when she could leave without being suspected. Maybe not for a year or more. Sadness at this thought filled him as they made their way through his mother's fence and up to the back door of her house. Madison would miss her.

A heartbeat later, pandemonium set in as two uniformed policemen stepped out of the dark bushes, guns drawn. "Police!" one shouted. "Keep your hands where we can see them."

Parker stiffened. "What's this about?" he demanded over his mother's cries of protest.

Detective Sally Crumb emerged from the shadows, wearing a navy suit. "Why don't you tell me? Where have you been, Mr. Hathaway?"

"None of your business," Parker spat.

Norma put a hand on his arm to calm him. "My son and I were visiting friends. Is that a crime? Why are you on my property? We haven't done anything wrong!"

"No?" The detective tilted her head and folded her arms

over her curvy chest. "Do you want to tell us exactly where you've been? What friends? Just so we can verify."

No answer.

"I thought not."

Parker struggled to control his fury but knew his mother was right. If they were to come out of this safely, they had to remain calm.

"This is ridiculous," Norma insisted. "Now put away those guns and tell us what you want in a civilized manner."

Hesitating only a few seconds, Detective Crumb nodded at her associates, who holstered their weapons. But Parker noticed that each officer left one hand poised to pull them out again if needed.

"We'd like to take Mr. Hathaway in for questioning."

"I've answered all your questions," Parker growled.

Detective Crumb stared at him without expression. "You either come with me, or I'll arrest you."

"What?" Now that the anger was fading, numbness was creeping in. Numbness and shock. "Why?"

"Your truck has been identified as being in Salt Lake near your ex-wife's house on the night Madison went missing."

"There must be some mistake," Norma said.

Parker remembered the passing car. Whoever it was must have come forward. However, that didn't mean they could identify him or that they'd have enough proof to arrest him.

"There are hundreds of trucks that look like Parker's," Norma continued. After two heartbeats, she added, "Besides, he was here that morning."

Parker stared at her in warning, but she ignored him. "You can ask my neighbor. Parker came to fix the leak in my sink before work. There's no way he could have been in Salt Lake."

"We did talk to your neighbors," Detective Crumb said.

"They saw his truck leave, but they didn't see what time he got here. We do find it interesting that you didn't mention that when we talked to you before."

Norma shrugged. "I must have forgotten. Parker often comes here. It was nothing unusual."

The detective nodded, but her words were brittle. "Even if he'd been here all night, that doesn't preclude him from having been in Salt Lake in the middle of the night. Which is when we now believe Madison was taken."

"That's ridiculous!" Norma's calm evaporated. "If that's so, why didn't Dakota call Parker before noon? Why didn't she call the police before then? I tell you, she's the one you should be looking at. She and her drugged friends."

When Norma looked as if she planned to continue her tirade, Parker took a step toward Detective Crumb. "Let's go, then." He couldn't have his mother accidentally spilling something, which might happen while she was this upset. He put a hand on her shoulder. "Don't worry, Mom. This shouldn't take long."

"Actually, we'll need to take you and the truck to Salt Lake," said Detective Crumb. "You'll be in a lineup tonight. Might take a few hours. Or longer."

Parker exchanged glances with Norma. He hoped she remembered where Madison was so she could take care of her. "I'll go with you, just let me tell my mother goodbye."

"Go ahead." Detective Crumb wasn't moving an inch. Parker leaned down and hugged Norma. "Be careful," he whispered. "Don't lead them there."

Norma's arms tightened around him. "I love you. It'll be all right. You'll see."

Parker took out his keys and waved them in the air. "Do you want to drive, Detective? Or shall I?"

"Neither." She took the keys and tossed them to one of the officers.

"You'll need gas," Parker informed the lucky man. Since he'd planned to leave the truck in Utah when he left, there'd been no use in filling it.

"Come on, Mr. Hathaway."

With a last glance at his mother, Parker fell in between Detective Crumb and the other officer as they marched to the front of the house. There were two more plainclothes policemen waiting near the unmarked police car. Detective Crumb chatted briefly with them before opening the back door for Parker and ushering him inside. Apparently only one of the plainclothes policemen was going with them. The other went to stand with the second uniformed policeman who had followed them to the front with his mother.

"Aren't they coming?" Parker asked.

Detective Crumb nodded at the wiry man in the driver's seat, giving him permission to pull out. "Not yet," she answered. "Your mother might need to get a few things before she joins us."

Pain shot through Parker's chest. "Join us?" he managed.

Crumb smiled at him, her attractive face unmoving. "We're taking her in for questioning, too. We think she's covering for you."

Parker barely heard the words, but he understood them. No one would be around for Madison. Only Carla, who was expecting him back very soon. What would she do when he didn't return? Would she stay? Would she take Madison home with her? Would she call the police? Worse, would she just leave Madison alone sleeping, expecting him to return?

No. She wouldn't do that. He'd been clear that Madison was never to be left home alone. Ever. The generous wage he gave Carla should help her remain with Madison. But he didn't really know the Hispanic woman well, or the members of her family, at least a few of whom were in the U.S. illegally. Carla wouldn't call the police, but that was the only thing he was sure of.

Madison! he agonized. What was he going to do now?

Chapter 14

Sally Crumb could tell Parker Hathaway was anxious. He wasn't very good at hiding the emotion. He kept staring blankly out the window or looking at the time on his cell phone. She remembered the days when people wore wristwatches; now cell phones had taken their place. And a good thing, too—a watch couldn't make or receive a call, or let a detective know so clearly that a person was distressed.

Why was he so nervous? Did it mean he'd been in Salt Lake that night? Or was it for another reason altogether?

If he had been in Salt Lake the night Madison had gone missing, he was most certainly involved in the disappearance. But what had he done with the child? Everyone they'd spoken to, even the child's mother who seemed to hate Parker with as much passion as he hated her, was adamant that if he was involved, he wouldn't harm Madison.

"I hope it was him," Dakota had told Sally that morning. "Because then I'd know she was okay."

Sally didn't know what Parker was hiding, but if he'd kidnapped his own daughter, he'd lose her entirely. Which would be terrible for the child. Because she'd be left only with her mother, and Sally didn't like Dakota Allen. From their first meeting, the blond woman was evasive about the time of the disappearance and uncooperative about giving out the names of her friends. Since talking to Parker that first day, Sally had done all the checks, but though Dakota had been arrested many times for possession or for being publicly drunk, she'd never been convicted. Sally was still looking for clues, not limiting herself to the past few months. Sometimes you had to go back a few years to find solid evidence.

The mother's little boy, a son from another relationship, seemed happy enough and well cared for, but that didn't make Sally feel any better about Dakota. She had a feel for these things, and something didn't add up. Like with Parker.

She itched to get her hands on his cell phone. She'd managed to do some preliminary checking on him within the realm of her warrant, but his phone had supposedly been shut off during the time of the kidnapping. But it might hold the answers. With the recent developments on the case, she'd be sure to get a warrant before morning.

Parker met her gaze as he slipped his phone back into his pocket. "I have to get to work tomorrow. How long is this going to take?"

"As long as it takes. At least we managed to arrange things for tonight. Not easy on a Sunday. If you're cleared, you'll be free to go." He seemed more at ease then, so maybe he was only worried about his job. Sally narrowed her eyes as she studied him.

He met her stare without flinching. "I would never do anything to hurt my daughter."

She nodded. "I believe that. Not purposefully, anyway."

"Dakota lived in a meth house before I moved her to where she is now. The only time I saw Madison during that time was when she brought her to me. It was a living nightmare not knowing where she was and not seeing her regularly. When I found out what kind of place they were staying at, I rented the other house. I thought she'd change, but she hasn't."

"How do I know you're telling the truth?"

"She's doing drugs. Madison isn't safe with her."

"So you keep saying, and I promise you I'm pursuing every lead I have in that respect. But I need to know—did you take your daughter to protect her?"

He looked out the window. "I haven't done anything wrong." oaisjdf oasij dfoajs dopfij aosijdf oasodijf

A few hours later at her police precinct in Salt Lake City, Sally stood with the witness, a man who worked the night shift at a frozen food company. Dale Stewart lived in Madison's neighborhood, and on his way home each morning he almost never came across anyone.

"Could have been him," he said. "Can't tell you any better. It was dark, but I had my brights on. Didn't expect to see anyone. But it was definitely that truck I saw, or one exactly like it. I remember the dent in the front bumper and half of the license plate number."

"Thank you, Mr. Stewart. We appreciate your coming in."

Stewart inclined his head in acknowledgment. "Anything, as long as it helps bring back that little girl."

An officer led him out, and Sally stared at the lineup for a short moment. "Okay, you can tell them to go." She turned to the chief of police standing beside her. "Except for Hathaway. It's enough to hold him, I think."

"And to press initial charges. But there needs to be more proof for any kind of a legal case. You know that as well as I do." The chief was a tall, impressive man, if a little on the thin side. His suit hung on his lean frame, but his face was one you could trust. He could make hard decisions when necessary, but he was compassionate about it. Moreover, he trusted his employees to do their jobs without checking up on them constantly.

"I'll get proof." She was thinking of Hathaway's cell phone. "As long as I have enough to legally hold him and to examine his belongings, I think I'll find exactly what I'm looking for."

"What about the mother?"

"Hasn't given us a thing."

"Maybe she doesn't know anything."

"Maybe. But I want to keep her in holding a bit longer. When we do let her go, we can tail her." Sally didn't think it'd be necessary, but it paid to be careful.

The chief nodded. "Keep me informed. I'm heading back home now."

"Thanks for coming in tonight."

"Hey, we're all rooting for this girl. We need to do what it takes to find her."

Sally nodded and strode from the room, feeling sure the answer was close at hand.

Parker was waiting for her in an empty questioning room. He sat at a table, long legs sprawled, his hair mussed. "So, am I free to go? Or are you going to arrest me?"

"Your truck was positively identified as being near your daughter's house that night," Sally informed him without emotion, "so we do have reason to hold you while we investigate."

His shoulders sagged slightly. "How long?"

"Twenty-four hours unless we file charges. If you're arrested, it will be another day or so before you're arraigned."

He sat up and banged his fist on the table. "Even if my truck was there, couldn't I sometimes drive by my daughter's house to make sure everything's okay? Is that a crime? Don't you ever check on your children?"

"We'll need to see your cell phone, Mr. Hathaway. I have a warrant to search it, but it doesn't seem to be with your other belongings."

Parker blinked. "They must have misplaced it."

Sally pursed her lips at this lie. She'd had the squad car checked as well as the garbage bins he might have had access to but without result. Yet there were many other places he could have stashed the phone—in a plant, under a cushion, in a box of miscellaneous items—and if it was turned off as she suspected, there would be no ringing from incoming calls to alert them.

"Okay," she said, switching tactics. "Tell me again why you were in Salt Lake that night."

"I didn't say I was. I said it was possible." He shook his head wearily. "Look, you've already asked me a million questions tonight, and I've answered them. But I know the drill. Even if you have a reason to hold me here, I have the right to speak with a lawyer before I say anything more."

Sally stifled a curse. Those magic words meant she could no longer ask him any more questions until his attorney said so. "Do you have one?"

"No. And I can't pay one, either. Not with all my child support and bills. Maybe my mother will help. Can I see her?"

"I'm sorry. We're questioning her now."

"Are you detaining her too?"

"Unlike you, she is free to go any time she pleases. She drove her own car."

"But I bet you didn't tell her she could go, did you?" he growled.

"Where's your phone?"

"I don't know, but I already told you I'm not answering any more questions until I talk to a lawyer."

"Fine. Have it your way." Biting back frustration, Sally left the room. On her way down the hall, she took out her phone and called Tony. "Hi," she said.

"I was beginning to think you got lost."

"I wish."

"So, you coming home tonight?"

"Not yet. We found a suspect."

"Ah." He would know what that meant, but he was also familiar enough with the routine not to ask any questions. "How's Randi?"

"Fine. Just got her to bed. Don't worry about it."

"I do worry. I hate working so much."

"It's not all the time. Just when it's important. She understands. She told me she hopes you find the little girl."

"I'm closer. We're going over all his old phone records again and the pictures we took at his apartment. There has to be something more. Everyone's pulling overtime on this."

"Try not to come home too late." There was a husky note in her husband's voice. "If I'm still awake, I'll give you a back rub."

"Mmm. Sounds heavenly. I'll do my best." She spied one of her colleagues coming toward her, waving a paper and looking excited. "I gotta go, hon. See you tonight. And if not, I'll take a raincheck on that back rub."

"Deal."

Pocketing the phone, she asked, "What you got, Jim?"

Jim smiled. "Remember that unknown number we were

trying to trace from Hathaway's records? Finally got ahold of the guy, and guess what? He rented Hathaway a house on the edge of Manti, starting last week. There haven't been any more calls, so Hathaway must not have called again, or he's using another number, but I have the address."

Gotcha, Sally thought. To Jim she said, "Let's get local officers there now."

"Already on it."

Chapter 15

Though Parker was trying to maintain a calm exterior, he was beginning to feel desperate at how long he'd been separated from Madison. Too much time had gone by since Detective Crumb had told him his truck had been positively identified. He remembered the passing car that night. Why hadn't he parked on a different street?

Even if the detective came in here this minute and told him she changed her mind and he was free to leave, it would take him two hours to get back to Manti—more if he had to worry about losing a tail. How had his life deteriorated so quickly? It was like being back in a relationship with Dakota.

Meanwhile, he couldn't help worrying that Carla might have left Madison alone at the rental house. Maybe she had something important awaiting her attention and rationalized that he would only be gone a short time. They didn't really have a long-standing relationship, and he couldn't guess at her thought process or the culture in which she had been raised.

If she leaves Madison, I'll fire her, he vowed. The idea was ludicrous since he'd planned to let her go anyway.

One option was to tell Detective Crumb the truth. Maybe she really was looking into Dakota's drug use, and they could work together to make sure Madison was safe. Or maybe Dakota would be more careful now that the authorities were aware of what was going on.

Or were they? They didn't seem to be good at getting to the truth. What if nothing changed and Madison remained at risk? For all he knew, the cops didn't take his accusations seriously, and telling the truth now might only mean that he wouldn't have another chance to save his daughter. Dakota obviously wasn't changing any time soon. That was something he should have counted on, since he knew from experience how enticing her lifestyle was and how hard it was to break free. His daughter shouldn't have to deal with that, not at four or at any age.

At least he'd had the presence of mind to stash his burner phone under the window blinds in the lobby earlier when they'd arrived, pretending to stumble into the wall. In the unmarked squad car, he'd seen Detective Crumb looking at it with interest and had realized the numbers in the memory or on the phone records would lead directly to the rental house. But those numbers were safe now, and with any luck, he and Madison would be in Las Vegas before the phone was discovered.

If they let him make a phone call, maybe he could call Carla to make sure all was well. He would offer her triple the normal wage to stay until he was free. Yet what if he and his mother were arrested and held for days? And could he trust that his call wouldn't be traced? What would Carla do with Madison if she didn't hear from him?

The agony of worry ate at him, crumbling his confidence. All he wanted was to protect his daughter, but speaking up or staying quiet both seemed to have serious consequences. Except, of course, that Dakota and drugs were assured danger, while Carla was an unknown.

Better to go with the unknown. He'd have to trust Carla for a little longer, regardless of how it ripped him apart. He'd never, ever forgive himself if any harm came to Madison. But maybe his mother would get to her quickly. She knew how important it was.

With this thought, a new worry pushed to the forefront of his mind. If they allowed his mother to go free tonight, they would likely follow her to the rental house in a way she couldn't detect. After all, they were trained at what they did and would be expecting her to try to get around them now. The last thing he wanted was to see his mother in jail. He had to prevent that along with everything else. He had to get them to let him see her.

Weight pushed down on his shoulders, threatening to crush out all hope. He was so exhausted that his brain no longer seemed to be functioning. But the clock was ever ticking. His only hope was to somehow get free so he could take Madison away from Utah and the threat Dakota represented. He wished he'd done that from the beginning, instead of coming up with the crazy idea of hiding her.

Parker laid his head down on the table, trying to clear it of a sudden dizziness. If they were keeping him overnight, as it appeared they would, where would he stay? In here? Or did they have a jail cell with a bed? Or at least a bench he could stretch out on.

Sometime later the door opened, and he tried to blink away the exhaustion. How long had she left him here? At least an hour, though he could be wrong. "Where's my lawyer?" he demanded. "And are you going to give me a bed, or is this part of the torture routine?"

The detective didn't smile. "We traced your phone records, and we found the man you rented a house from in Manti. Care to tell me why you rented a house there?"

Parker swallowed, his throat dry as though he'd been drinking sand. "A lot of people move," he said carefully.

Crumb folded her long arms across her chest. "The game is up, Parker. We found the house and your daughter's clothes. She's been there very recently."

"But she's not there now." He wondered if his statement betrayed the shock he felt.

"No," Crumb said. "She's not. The house is empty."

Chapter 16

*E*arly Monday morning Caitlin McLoughlin sat at her desk, wishing she could have stayed home. Another plea deal and two more clients she would have to visit in jail. All of them guilty—that was obvious from the documentation. A robbery and an assault. Beautiful. More briefs to prepare and lies to hear.

When her phone rang, she grabbed it almost eagerly, though there was a high probability the call would mean more work. "Hello?"

"Hi, Caitlin."

"Sally?" Caitlin smiled. It was really too soon to discuss their weekly lunch date, their schedules being so unpredictable, but she was happy to hear from Sally anytime. "What's up? Nothing bad, I hope."

"No, everything's fine. Well, I was up half the night, and not for one of Tony's back rubs."

"You find the girl?"

"Not yet." Frustration laced Sally's voice. "But I think I know who took her. Only things have gone wrong, and I don't know how to fix them. The guy won't trust me, and I really don't blame him."

"Who?"

"The father."

"Ah. Do you think he's hurt her?"

"Absolutely not. This guy loves his kid, and I think he took her to protect her from the mother. We found someone who identified him as being near the girl's home the night she went missing, so we brought him in. And also his mother. Neither would tell us anything useful. With a little research, though, we discovered he'd rented a house on the edge of town, and there were little girl's clothes there, and the local officers we sent out could have sworn the bed was still warm."

"She left right before you got there?"

"I think so. I mean, I could be wrong. Maybe she wasn't there at all. Maybe he was only planning to move there and it's a coincidence. But it adds up because neither the father or the grandmother mentioned the rental house. And during the father's visits, he always brought the daughter to the grand-mother's. The rental house has to be where he was hiding her."

"Did someone warn them?"

"Hathaway didn't call anyone. Neither did the grand-mother." Sally paused while Caitlin took the information in.

"So that means—what?"

"Either the little girl got up and wandered out into the night alone, or there's an accomplice who got scared and fled with the child. Either way, she's in danger. Hathaway is pacing in the holding cell as we speak. He hasn't slept much, and anyone can see he's worried."

"But he won't talk."

"No. I'm tempted to let him loose and follow him to find out what he knows, but the higher-ups won't let me. There's too much evidence against him. And part of me agrees because he's smart. He might shake the tail and flee with the girl. So, that's where you come in."

"Me?"

"He wants a lawyer."

"Ah." Now Caitlin understood.

"He'd probably be happy with any public defender," Sally said, "but despite everything, I really think this guy loves his daughter, and I don't want to see him in the hands of just anyone."

"But if what you say is true, he kidnapped his own daughter out of her bed in the middle of the night."

"I know how it sounds, but I've met the mother, and of the two of them, I'd choose him."

"The law won't."

"I know." Sally sighed. "Look, will you come talk to him?"

"When?"

"As soon as possible. We need to find the child. Every minute that passes means more danger. We have no idea who the accomplice is, or if there even is one."

Caitlin looked at the files on her desk. She could get Jodi or one of the other paralegals to pitch in for a few hours. It wasn't like she had court proceedings this morning. "Okay, I'll be there in a bit."

"Thanks. I owe you one."

Caitlin laughed. "No, this counts as two."

"I'll watch Amy for you while you go out with the hot DA. Hmm, wonder if he's any good at back rubs."

"If only I could be so lucky." Not that she would find out

any time soon. She and Mace weren't anywhere near that level of intimacy.

Besides, Caitlin didn't want a casual fling, even if it was brag-worthy. She was looking for something permanent, something real. Something like Sally and Tony had. Disconnecting the line with a little sigh, she began dialing Jodi's extension.

Chapter 17

Things had gone from bad to worse. Parker had spent the night pacing the small holding cell where they had kept him in isolation. He'd learned that his mother had been released, but he hadn't seen her, and she didn't know anything about Carla.

Where had Carla taken Madison? In the best case scenario, he told himself that when he hadn't returned, she'd taken Madison home to her own house because she'd had to watch her siblings or nephews. Madison was safe and happy, sleeping like an angel, and would awake and begin playing with the other children. Other visions were not so nice—like Carla kidnapping Madison and selling her into slavery or something equally heinous.

He'd have to tell them everything he knew. Soon. There was simply no other option. Even if Carla planned to bring Madison back, she'd only find the police there waiting for her.

And if the worst became a reality, he had already given Carla a big head start.

There was a sound at the door, and a stocky officer he didn't recognize entered the room. They'd already come once to give him a breakfast he hadn't been able to eat, so this time surely there was news. Maybe they were letting him out.

"You have a visitor," the man said far too cheerfully for Parker's mood. "An LDA."

"A what?"

"Someone from the Legal Defenders Association—a public defender."

"Oh." Parker felt a little surge of hope.

"You want to clean up a little first?"

Parker was wearing the same jeans and T-shirt he'd been wearing when he'd been picked up. They had let him keep his coat as well, but his hair was uncombed, and he still hadn't found time to shave. But what he looked like didn't matter. Time was all important.

"No. I'm fine," he said. "Take me to him."

"Her," the officer corrected. "And I must say, you're pretty lucky. Detective Crumb must like you. I bet she had to pull a few strings to get this attorney. They say she's the best of the LDAs."

Parker didn't hold out much hope of that. From what he'd heard in the circles he'd traveled with Dakota, public defenders were overworked and underpaid. Most sent aides to do the footwork until the day of the actual trial. If Crumb liked him, she hadn't shown any sign to Parker, so it was far more likely that the detective had simply called the association, and they'd chosen one of their newest attorneys to defend him.

The woman had her back to him as the officer led him into a room he hadn't seen before, her eyes focused on the tiny, bar-covered window on the far wall several yards away. She wore a maroon suit on a figure that was a little on the full side, with curves in all the right places, though the suit seemed to do its best to hide that fact. Her bright, copper-colored hair was drawn severely into a knot at the nape of her neck, and when she turned to face him, the solemness of her pale features was broken only by the myriad of copper freckles scattered over her face. She was younger than he expected and beautiful in a slightly exotic way, though he couldn't figure out how red hair and freckles could possibly be exotic. In another setting—no, in another lifetime—he might have tried to get to know her better.

"Hello, Mr. Hathaway," she said, coming toward him, her hand outstretched. "I'm Caitlin McLoughlin, and I've been assigned to your case." She spoke perfect English, yet there was almost an Irish lilt to the tone. Like music. Her eyes were a startling blue, and her lips full and kissable despite the withdrawn formality of her expression and demeanor.

Parker suddenly felt worn and dirty. He wished he'd had time to shower and shave, though none of that was really important now. He had to concentrate on Madison, and this woman might be the means of getting him out of here.

Her hand was small but firm in his grasp. "I've been briefed, Mr. Hathaway, but I'll need more information." She glanced at the officer who'd brought Parker. "Thank you. We'll be all right." He nodded and left the room, shutting the door behind him.

"I need to get out of here as soon as possible," Parker told her forcefully.

"Unfortunately, that's not going to happen." She sat on one of the chairs at the table and indicated that he should do the same. "At least not today. Given the circumstances, I anticipate that you will be arrested before the end of the day. I will be able to have you arraigned tomorrow, but depending on the evidence the prosecution has, we may or may not get you out on bail." She sat back in her chair, watching him.

"Then why are you even here?" he growled, remaining on his feet. "I need to get out now."

"Why?" She asked it simply, as though she had no idea what was at stake. Maybe she didn't. Maybe they hadn't told her all the details.

"My daughter is missing. You know that much."

She lifted her chin slightly. "Yes, but only since last night, I believe. Or at least that's what the police believe."

So she knew more than she'd let on. "They're never going to let me out, are they?" he asked miserably.

"Not until you tell them what you know."

"No." He scanned the room, wondering if even now they were listening. "You don't understand."

"Why don't you tell me?"

"Because I'd be playing into their hands."

"Anything you say to me here stays between us. I'm your counsel."

"They aren't listening?"

For the first time, a smile curved those full lips. "Not a chance. That would be against the law."

He relaxed slightly. "I don't know where to begin."

"Begin with what happened."

"My ex-wife is doing drugs. I lived with Dakota for too long not to know that my daughter is in danger every second she's in her care. But I can't get anyone to listen to me."

"She doesn't have a record, but I do see some DUIs on yours."

"That was years ago."

"Are you still drinking?"

"I'm not an alcoholic. Alcoholics go to meetings." He'd seen that on a T-shirt once, and it would surely put her in place.

She tilted her head. "Mr. Hathaway, this is no time to joke. You're the one who asked for legal counsel. Now either you start talking to me—with respect—or I'm leaving, and you can deal with another legal defender."

Shame washed through Parker. Swallowing with difficulty, he ducked his head and lowered himself into a chair. "I'm sorry."

"That's okay. Now do you want my help, or do you want someone else?"

"Are you good?"

A twitch on one side of her mouth seemed to hint at a smile. "I'm the best at what I do." She hesitated before adding, "But while we're speaking candidly, I can also tell you that I dislike defending guilty men."

"Then why are you a public defender?"

A line appeared on her brow. "I assure you, I ask myself that question a hundred times a week, and the only answer I have besides the fact that it pays the bills is that every now and then, I actually help someone who's innocent."

There was passion in the words. This was a woman who believed in ideals and in defending the defenseless. Maybe she could understand about Dakota and Madison. In the pit of despair where he now lived, she seemed to be his best hope.

"Haven't you ever done anything you might have otherwise considered wrong to protect someone you care about?" he asked quietly.

She started shaking her head and then stopped, as though remembering something. "The end doesn't justify the means. Or so my father used to say."

Parker lifted a brow. "I believe that, or I used to. But drugs don't play fair, and my daughter's life is more important to me than my own." This woman couldn't possibly know how much it had cost him to go against the law, how every minute he'd been wracked with guilt, but he wouldn't be the one to enlighten her.

"You took her that night."

He nodded. "I thought I could keep her in Manti until the police found evidence against Dakota, but I realized on Saturday that it wouldn't work. Today we were going to disappear."

"Why didn't you run right from the beginning?"

"I should have. But I was working, and I wanted to be able to support my daughter."

"Who's helping you?"

"I acted alone."

"You left your four-year-old daughter all day in a house by herself?" There was a sharpness now to her tone, a subtle anger.

"No. I got a sitter. A Hispanic woman. A very smart and nice Hispanic woman. I knew she had relatives who are in the country illegally. Maybe she's also illegal. I didn't ask. But she wouldn't want to contact the police even if she suspected Madison was kidnapped."

"This woman was at the house last night with Madison?"

"Yes." Then he rushed on with everything he'd been thinking. "But the police can't prove Madison was there. I could have only been preparing to take her there."

"They found her fingerprints."

"She could have visited before she went missing."

"Mr. Hathaway, I know you want to get out and see if you can find your daughter, but they're not going to let you, and I can't make them."

"What if I tell *you* where she is? Could you go get her?"

The attorney shook her head. "There are rules about endangering children, and I won't cross that line. Besides, they'd have me followed. But if you do cooperate with the police, things will go a lot more smoothly for you, and we'll have a much better case. That means you'll be around to see your daughter grow up."

He sighed and stared at the table. "I'm terrified Carla has done something terrible, but if she hasn't, I don't want her mixed up in this."

"What if I can promise that?" Her hands were folded on the table, and he noticed she wore a ruby ring on her right hand but nothing on the left.

He lifted his gaze and saw those blue eyes locked onto his, almost like a touch. She was compelling, he'd give her that. No wonder she was supposedly so good at what she did. "Can you promise to save Madison from her mother?"

"Not in so many words, but I know Detective Crumb personally, and I can tell you she'll do everything in her power and then some to get to the bottom of this. For some crazy, odd reason, she seems to be on your side."

"I thought she hated me."

"She just wants Madison safe."

"So do I."

He agonized over the decision, while at the same time recognizing there was really no choice. "Okay. But I want assurances that Carla, if she didn't do anything, will be left out of this. And my mother."

"Was your mother involved?"

"No. I told her after I did it, though. She agrees with me about Madison's danger. She's already lost too—" He broke off. That was none of Caitlin McLoughlin's business.

"Okay, Mr. Hathaway, I'll go have a chat with the detective. I'll be right back."

"Call me Parker."

She gave him a slow smile that made his stomach feel warm, completely shattering his former coolness toward her. What would those lips taste like? How soft would she feel if he gathered her into his arms?

Stop. He had to keep his mind on his daughter. His social life had been neglected far too long to allow desire to start weighing in on matters now. This attorney was a means to an end. Nothing more.

"Okay," she said. "Parker it is. And you can call me Caitlin."

He felt happy at the invitation, though he sensed she made the offer more in the hope of evoking trust than from a desire to be familiar.

"Is there anything I can get you to make you more comfortable?" she added.

A bath and a week of sleep, he thought. He shook his head. "No, thanks. No one can give me what I need."

She regarded him silently for several seconds before nodding. "Maybe not yet. But sometimes we're forced to choose between the lesser of two evils."

"That's just it," he said. "I don't know which that is."

Chapter 18

Caitlin left the room feeling shaken. When she had first caught sight of the unshaven man, she had classified him immediately as one more low-life scum who was nothing but a drain on the system. A father using his child for attention—or worse. Yet when she'd looked deeper, when she stared into his honest brown eyes and saw the concern etched on the sharp angles of his jaw, all her instincts told her Sally was right about him. There was an earnestness in Parker Hathaway that called to her sense of justice. He was a desperate man, that much was true, but he believed with his whole heart that he was acting in the best interests of his daughter.

She could do a lot with such a defense, especially if she could prove even part of his accusations against his ex-wife. Drugs were a hot topic these days, and far too many children had become innocent victims. Many judges were cracking down on convictions. Parker would be put on probation and likely have only supervised visits with Madison for the foreseeable future, but she might be able to spare him jail time. Well, that is if she cleaned him up and if his record wasn't too spotty. For all she knew, there was more on him that Sally hadn't yet dug up. The prosecutor wouldn't leave anything out.

Of course, everything would hinge on whether or not they actually found Madison safe and sound. If Madison turned up dead, jail time would be a given, no matter who had been responsible.

"Well?" Sally had been down the hall but was already halfway to Caitlin's side.

"First, I want to know something. How late is he on child support?"

"As far as I can tell, he's never missed a payment. The guy's been a saint for the past few years, but I discovered he quit his job after his Saturday shift, though he kept telling me yesterday that he needed to get back to work today. With the boxes we found at the rental house, I think he was getting ready to run."

"He should have run from the beginning."

Sally smirked. "Is that your advice as an attorney?"

Caitlin ignored the comment. "I think he'll tell you what you want to know, but if he was involved with the kidnapping, and I'm not saying he was, he would like to see that the babysitter and his mother stay out of it. No legal repercussions."

"That depends. Are they accomplices or bystanders?"

"Neither of the women had any foreknowledge or were involved in anything that my client may have allegedly done." Well, provided the sitter hadn't kidnapped the child a second time, but she didn't need to bring that up now. Caitlin gave her friend a wry glance. "We'll need to get the DA involved if we're going to be able to guarantee their immunity, and that means you'll have to charge my client."

"I'll start on the paperwork and get someone over from the DA's office."

"Thanks."

As Sally hurried down the hallway, Caitlin went back inside the room where Parker waited. "It's in motion," she announced. "I'll have to talk to the DA and make sure they won't involve your mother, but for now, let's talk about what you do know, so I can advise you on exactly what to say."

"I have Carla's name and number memorized, and I know where she lives, more or less, since I went there to meet her a few weeks ago." He frowned. "Look, do you think they'd let me go with them? I don't want Madison to be scared when she sees the police."

Caitlin felt an unexpected tenderness toward him at the request. This was something she understood. There were situations that still terrified Amy, ones Caitlin worked hard to avoid, or at least made sure to be there for her sister. Like going to the hairdresser or the doctor. "I'll ask," she said. But she was sure he would be denied if the police had Carla's number and could trace it. So now was the time to make the decision—was she really going to fight for his rights? Or just do the minimum?

He smiled at her, a small smile but one full of hope. Hope that he might make his daughter feel easier at what would happen. Nothing for himself. "If we really want to go," Caitlin said, including herself in the deal, "we won't give them Carla's full name and number unless we need to. We'll just say you know where she lives. You think you can find it?"

"I can get us in the general area, and there's a big slatted barrel of flowers out in the front of the yard. I'll know it when I see it." His tone was heavy with what they didn't say—the possibility that Madison was no longer there.

"Good. This is a high-profile case, so someone from the DA's office should be here soon. We'll have a chat with them. But I do all the talking. Understand?"

"Yes. Thank you."

She shrugged. His thanks made her feel uncomfortable.

"Is there a bathroom around here?" he asked. "Maybe a razor? I could do with a shave."

She nodded. "I'll see what I can do. But make it snappy."

"I'll be finished long before the DA gets here."

True to his word, the DA was nowhere in sight when an officer led Parker Hathaway back to the room where Caitlin and Sally were waiting. He looked vastly different from the despondent, unkempt man she had met earlier. His brown, slightly wavy hair was neatly combed, reaching halfway past his ears in front, longer in back. Without the growth of beard, Caitlin could see the planes of his face, not sharp as she'd previously thought but strong and angular, his nose a little on the large side but well-suited for his handsome face. Someone had given him another T-shirt, a white one that was a bit snug for his muscular build and broad shoulders. He was nowhere near as large as Sally's Tony but on the same scale at least. Nice, and more than a little hot.

Sally bumped her arm, giving her a pointed scowl that told her she was staring. Caitlin felt herself color. What was she doing? Parker Hathaway was her client and not something to be ogled. It really had been too long since she'd had a boyfriend—or even a romantic date. She certainly couldn't count her dinner with Wyman. If prisoners were starting to look this good to her, she'd seriously have to think about getting out more.

Parker regarded her quietly, a slight quirk of his left eyebrow telling her he'd noticed her stare. She prayed he couldn't guess exactly what she'd been thinking. "I'm ready," he said. "Where is the DA?"

"Here," Mace Keeley walked in behind him through the open door.

Caitlin felt both an excitement at seeing Mace and a little resentment. He'd always brought out these feelings in her—the first because he was so gorgeous and made her knees weak, and the second she'd always chalked up to professional jealousy at his perfect case record.

Mace smiled and walked toward her, ignoring everyone else in the room. "Caitlin," he said, his voice warm and caressing. "I didn't realize you were assigned to this case. I did ask who his defense counsel was, but they didn't know."

"I just found out myself an hour ago. Is that a problem?"

"No." His voice lowered. "I was sorry about Friday."

A thrill raced up her back. "Me too."

With a private smile for her, Mace turned and sat at the table, opening a file. Caitlin felt eyes on her and glanced over to Parker. His expression was unreadable, but she felt sure he hadn't missed the exchange. No matter. She absolutely wouldn't allow her feelings for Mace to enter the equation. She had to be at her best as she had promised Parker—and herself.

She sat across from Mace and motioned Parker to sit next to her. "In exchange for information as to the whereabouts of Madison Hathaway, who was discovered missing from her home on Wednesday morning, my client would like immunity for his mother and the baby-sitter he employed, neither of whom had anything to do with the abduction."

"The mother could be charged as an accessory after the fact," protested Mace, lifting a page that held the case summary Sally must have given him.

"Who bloody cares!" Sally burst out. "A little girl's welfare is at stake here. We need to find her quickly. Prosecuting the grandmother who loves her is very much a losing proposition all around. No buts about it."

Mace regarded Caitlin. "Is that your assessment?"

"We need to find her now." Caitlin was glad she had managed to regain complete control over her face. "That's my client's price."

"Nothing for himself?"

Caitlin knew it was a trick question, and she didn't rise to the bait. There was no way they would give Parker Hathaway immunity for what he'd done. She felt Parker start to say something, but she lifted her hand and put it briefly on his to still the words.

His skin was surprisingly warm. She glanced down at their joined hands, her voice faltering ever so briefly. He was staring at their hands too. As she watched, his gaze lifted to meet hers—seemingly in slow motion, as if only the two of them were in the room. A sudden connection sprang to life, one that didn't need words. It hinted at long lazy nights full of passion. At friendship. And trust.

Startled, she withdrew her hand and forced herself to continue talking. "Nothing for himself. We already have adequate defense in that regard. His mother's involvement is negligible anyway, but my client would feel better with a signed statement absolving her from prosecution."

Mace rested his chin on the palm of his hand, his long fingers on his cheek as he studied first Caitlin and then Parker. Caitlin found herself glad Parker had shaved.

"Okay," Mace said. "It's a deal."

"Good." Sally rose from the table, satisfaction in her voice. "Then let's just hope Madison is still in Manti."

Chapter 19

Fifteen minutes after their discussion with the DA, Caitlin was sitting in the backseat of an unmarked squad car next to Parker Hathaway, with Sally and another officer in the front. Behind them drove a regular police car. Both vehicles drove at a high speed, using the police lights on top of the cars to speed up the journey.

"This drive always takes me two hours," Parker commented, the barest of smiles arcing his lips.

Sally craned her neck around and grinned. "That's the advantage to working for the law. Time is important here."

Parker's gaze shifted to the window without comment, and Caitlin was able to study him covertly. His face seemed relaxed, but there was a tautness in his body as if every muscle were straining, anxious. Just the way she'd feel if Amy were the one missing.

He was good-looking, and he probably had been even before shaving, if she could have seen past the worn jeans, rumpled and stained shirt, and the uncombed hair. Or perhaps she had seen only what she'd expected to see.

His head turned and their eyes met, sending a delicious tingle to Caitlin's stomach. She flushed. What had happened to her straight-faced attorney skills? The Irish in her seemed to be taking over where this man was concerned.

He smiled and asked in a low voice, "What are you thinking?"

How his lips might feel against hers didn't seem an appropriate answer. She shrugged, not trusting her voice for speech.

He held her stare for long seconds more, and Caitlin found she couldn't look away. *I should recuse myself from this case,* she thought suddenly. But she knew she wouldn't. She didn't want to pass him off to someone else. She was the best public defender he'd get, and she didn't want his daughter to lose her father just because Caitlin was attracted to him.

In the front, Sally laughed at something the other officer said, and the mood was broken. Yet every so often, Caitlin felt Parker's eyes contemplating her. Had he felt the connection between them, or was it only in her imagination?

In Manti they were joined by two local squad cars. Caitlin thought it was overkill, knowing Parker even as little as she did, but then she remembered the babysitter might not be what they hoped.

Sally was on the phone with the local authorities. "Still nothing new from the rental house," she informed them. Caitlin knew she'd been expecting Carla to show up there with Madison, and that she hadn't could mean the child was in serious danger.

"It's more toward the middle of town," Parker said to the officer who was driving. "Or slightly west of it, rather. I'll know it when I see it."

When they reached the right area, Parker had the man drive up and down each street, as if he really couldn't remember. "There," he said finally. "The one with the barrel in front."

The white, two-story house with red doors and shutters was as old as the other houses in this section but not particularly run-down. The lawn sported patches of snow, and it looked as though someone had tried to build a fort at one time.

"You two stay here with Jim," Sally ordered.

"Please," Parker said, steel underlying the gentle plea in his voice. "Let me go. It'll be better if I just go up and ask for her. I don't want to freak them out. In fact, it would be better to have no uniforms."

Sally regarded him silently for a long moment. "Okay. I'll go with you." She patted the gun in her shoulder holster, just visible under her cream-colored jacket.

"I'm going, too," Caitlin said.

"No, you aren't," Sally snapped. "This could be a kidnapping."

"If it is, they're long gone," Caitlin said. "And frankly, I don't trust the police alone with my client." To Parker, she added, "Don't talk to the police. Remember, anything you say can be used against you."

"Right." He didn't look as if he cared. His whole body strained toward the house.

Sighing, Sally climbed from the car and let Parker out. Caitlin was glad she'd insisted on no handcuffs. Sally made them wait by the car while she went to talk to the other officers to make sure there had been no history of trouble at the house. There hadn't been, so in the end, the two Salt Lake officers went to the front door with them, while the men from the local force went around to cover the back. Just in case.

The house had a long front porch, with cream-colored plastic chairs stained dark from the snow and rain. Freshly painted gingerbread trim swirled around the porch's solid-looking framework. Parker pushed the bell. Footsteps came almost immediately, and an older Hispanic woman answered the door. The smile that had begun on her round, weathered face faded as she saw the uniformed officers behind them.

"Is Carla here?" Parker asked. Caitlin sensed the urgency in his voice, and the woman must have as well because she tore her gaze from the officers.

"Are you father of Madeeson?" the woman asked.

"Yes. I am."

"You are very late. Carla had to go."

"But is Madison here?" asked Caitlin hurriedly.

The woman nodded her graying head, opening the door so they could see the living room and a hallway. "Stay here." She went down the hall, calling something in Spanish. Before she was out of sight, two black-haired children tumbled into view, laughing and speaking rapidly. Caitlin had learned enough Spanish to follow slow conversations, but all she understood now was the bare gist of the children begging their grandmother to let their new friend stay.

The woman shook her head and said in English, "Her father ees here."

"Madison!" called the children. "Your father! Your father is here. You have to go home."

Madison appeared at the end of the hall, looking the same and yet different from the pictures on the television. Her hair was now brown, but her brown eyes and her smooth white face were exactly the same. "Daddy!" she screamed. Grinning widely, she hurtled down the hall and into her father's arms.

"I love Carla's house!" she bubbled. "Can I come again? I really want to play here when you have to work. I like these kids! I like you best, but they're so fun to play with."

Parker buried his face in his daughter's hair, and Caitlin saw tears shimmering in his eyes. "I missed you so much, sweetheart," he said. "I'm glad you've been having fun." He glanced at Caitlin, and she could see the regret there, regret that he had agreed to show them where Carla lived. Here at least Madison had been safe.

"She ees that girl in the TV," the grandmother said, nodding vigorously. "I tell Carla, but she no believe. I tell her to call police." She looked with mistrust at the officers. "But we have nothing to do with it. Nothing." She emphasized with horizontal slicing motion of both hands.

"We know," Sally said. "Look, my associates here will just ask you a few questions. Okay?" The old woman nodded.

Parker leaned over to catch the old woman's attention. "Thank you for taking care of my daughter. Tell Carla thank you. I will send her the money I owe her. But I won't need her services anymore." Hugging Madison to him, he backed away.

"Where are we going, Daddy?" Madison asked. "Why are the policemen here? Did Carla do something wrong?"

"No. They just want to make sure you're safe. They want to take you back to your mom."

"Oh." The little girl's excitement dimmed at the prospect. "Will Mommy let me come here to play?"

"I don't know. We'll have to ask." Parker hugged her again. Madison leaned into her father, her arms curling tightly around his neck, her cheek on his shoulder with her face pointed in Caitlin's direction. Her smile faded and disappeared altogether, as though sucked away by an unseen force. "She won't let me come back. She never does." She spoke so softly, Caitlin knew she was the only one who heard.

The drive back to Salt Lake went far too quickly. For part of that time, Caitlin was on the phone with Jodi, doing as much work as she could from a distance and reorganizing her after-noon, but for most of the time, she was listening to Madison talk with her father. Caitlin had thought Amy talked a lot, but this four-year-old was incessant and would have bordered on annoying if she hadn't been so cute and precocious.

"Who are you anyway?" she asked Caitlin after she had described in detail her games with the two Hispanic children.

Caitlin wondered if Parker wanted her to know the truth, and when he gave a slight nod, she answered. "I'm your daddy's legal defender, which means I'm going to help him with some legal stuff."

Madison scrunched up her eyes in mistrust. "Legal stuff?"

"It's when the law—the police—think you've done some-thing wrong. I try to straighten everything out."

"Oh." The child turned to Parker. "Did you do something wrong?"

"No. But people think I did."

"What do they think?"

"They're mad 'cause I took you away from your mom."

"But I always come to see you."

"I know. This time it's a little different because your mom didn't know."

"You should have told her. Now she is gonna be mad. Couldn't you just give her some money? That always makes her happy."

Parker laughed. "I wish that would take care of it. Don't worry, sweetheart. Everything will be okay."

Madison nodded confidently and turned back to Caitlin. "I'm glad you're going to help my dad. What's your name?"

"Caitlin McLoughlin."

"That's pretty. Do you have kids?"

She smiled and shook her head. "No, but I do have a sister

just a little bit older than you who lives with me." That wasn't exactly true, but she didn't want to get into an explanation. Besides, it wasn't as though Parker and Madison would ever meet Amy.

"Can I play with her? Do you live near me? My mom might let me go to your house, if you could pick me up." Madison's brown eyes were eager.

"I don't know," Caitlin stalled, feeling drawn to the child but knowing that was unwise, given the circumstances.

Madison turned to Parker. "You'll take me over there, won't you, Daddy?" She smiled at Caitlin. "He always takes me. We go lots of places. One day we went to a candy place with my preschool. It was fun. They make candy there. We got to eat some." Then she was off on another tangent, and Caitlin was glad the subject of playing with Amy had been left behind—at least for now.

At the police station, Madison skipped ahead down the hall, stopping to peer in windows. Sally turned to Parker. "You'd better say goodbye. Your ex-wife is here. We have to turn Madison over to her."

Parker stiffened. "Can't you put her in state custody?"

"I'm sorry. I don't have a legal reason."

"Please try." His voice was an agonized whisper that matched the pain on his face. It was so acute and private that Caitlin had to momentarily look away.

Madison was coming back to them now, singing a song Caitlin didn't recognize.

"Mr. Hathaway," Sally said, "I gave you my word that I would do everything I could to keep Madison safe, and I mean it. But it will take time."

"Find out where her mother lived before the house they're in now. I know for sure it was a meth house. That's why I set them up in their new place. I don't even deduct the rent from my regular payments."

"I'll have a good talk with your ex-wife," Sally promised. "Threaten her if I have to. That should keep her clean. But for now, you need to say goodbye and go with Officer Clegg."

Parker knelt on the floor in front of Madison. "Sweetheart, I have to go now. I'll see you as soon as I can."

With the sudden clarity that sometimes affects small children, Madison clung to her father. "I don't want you to go. Can't I stay with you? Please?"

"Hey, it's okay, sweetheart. You're going back to Mommy's like you always do. I'll see you soon." He hugged her, his entire face drawn tight.

Caitlin didn't have the heart to tell them he wouldn't likely have visiting rights for some time. Her own eyes watered.

Madison was consoled, her trust in her father all too apparent. "Okay."

"Now remember what I told you. Don't eat anything if you don't know what it is. Like if it's in the cupboard or something. Or on the TV in a bag. Or on the couch. Only eat what Mommy gives you. Even if you find it in her purse or in her drawer, don't eat it." Parker glanced up at Caitlin and Sally in challenge, and neither woman objected, but Caitlin found it difficult to hide her shock. If Madison's mother wasn't doing drugs, this kind of talk could be damaging. If she was, the cautions, however needed, were equally horrifying.

"I know," Madison said in an aggrieved voice that she would likely perfect in her teen years. "You always tell me that."

Caitlin knew, as Parker must, that all the coaching in the world often fell apart. Studies had proven that even children rigorously taught not to handle guns did so when given the opportunity out of their parents' sight. Natural curiosity was too strong for such young children to show discipline. Which, of course, was why parents were needed to guide them through the perils of life until they had the maturity to understand and control their actions. Caitlin still had to keep all cleaners and other hazardous items out of Amy's reach, and she'd been five for twenty-two years.

Parker met Caitlin's gaze. "When will I be able to leave here?"

"Tomorrow. After the arraignment, we'll go over your case."

"Okay." He glanced at the officer who had driven them to Manti and who waited now to take him back to his cell.

Sally gave Madison the wry smile that she used when she was emotionally engaged. "It's time," she said gently. "Say goodbye to your daddy."

Parker kissed his daughter's forehead. "You go with Detective Crumb and Ms. McLoughlin."

"Her name is Caitlin, Daddy." Madison reached up and took Caitlin's hand. Surprised and a little touched, Caitlin squeezed it lightly.

"So it is," Parker said.

Caitlin shivered at the softness of his voice. *Nothing to do with me,* she thought. *He's worried about Madison, that's all.*

With his heart in his eyes and a smile Caitlin could tell was forced, Parker went with the officer. Sally started down the hall in the opposite direction, and Caitlin went with her, curious to see Madison's mother.

"Your mother is anxious to see you," Sally told Madison, "but after you give her a hug, I need to talk to her a bit by myself. I'll grab one of the officers here to sit with you."

"I'll stay with her," Caitlin volunteered, not ready to let go of Madison's hand.

"Don't you have to get back to your office?"

"They'll just think I'm taking an extra-long lunch. Which I absolutely deserve after finishing up my two cases last week. Or nearly finished, since we still have sentencing to go for one of them. But close enough. Madison and I will go see what's in the vending machine."

"There are donuts on my desk," Sally offered. "I'll have someone bring them."

"I love donuts," Madison chirped.

Caitlin laughed. "We all do. And trust me when I say you need to eat as many as possible while you're young."

"You can say that again." Sally slapped her thigh as she stopped in front of an open door. "She's in there, Madison." In a lower voice, she added to Caitlin, "Her name is Dakota Allen. She stopped using Hathaway after the divorce."

Walking into the room with Madison, Caitlin saw a woman about her height pacing the room. But any further resemblance to Caitlin was nonexistent. Dakota wore jeans with wavy script down one leg, the waistband so low and tight that though she wasn't a heavy woman, rolls of skin bunched over the top. Her chest spilled out of a tight tank top which she wore under a short camouflage jacket. Blond hair with dark roots coming in and too much makeup completed the picture. Caitlin wondered, as she always did when she saw such women, how Dakota Allen could possibly think she looked anything but cheap and trashy.

Madison did not, as Caitlin expected, pull away and race to her mother. Instead, it was Dakota Allen who sprang across the room and hugged her daughter, practically ripping her from Caitlin's grasp.

"Oh, Maddy, I've missed you so much! I was so scared!" She talked high and fast and had an odd, nervous laugh.

"I was just with Daddy." Madison's voice was petulant.

"He has no right taking you like that! He's never going to again. I promise you. Never!"

Madison had been returning her mother's hug, but now her arms dropped to her sides, and Caitlin could tell she was fighting tears. "Why are you mad at Daddy?"

"Because he stole you away. And look at your hair! He changed the color to hide you from me. What a mess."

"He didn't steal me. I just saw him like I always do. And I like my hair. It's like Grandma's." Madison began crying in earnest now. "I want my daddy!"

"I don't understand why you're acting like this," Dakota said, her brow wrinkling in confusion. "I've been so worried, not knowing where you were. It's been horrible." She tried to pull Madison to her, but the child resisted. Dakota continued to talk rapidly, trying to make Madison understand, to come around to her way of thinking.

Madison put her hands over her ears. *"No entiendo,"* she said.

Caitlin caught Sally's eye and dipped her head slightly. *Do something,* Caitlin thought.

Sally nodded. "Uh, can I talk to you for a moment, Ms. Allen?" she asked. "I know you're anxious to take Madison home, but there are a few more things we need to take care of. Caitlin and Madison can visit the vending machine while we talk."

Dakota stood, looking in confusion from Sally to Madison. "Okay," she agreed. In a high, false voice, she said to Madison, "Go with this nice lady for a minute, sweetie, and then I'll take you home."

Even with her hands over her ears, Madison understood the words. She dropped her hands and hurried over to Caitlin. "Can I have a candy bar? Chocolate." Tears stood out on her pale cheeks.

Dakota smiled. "Say please, Maddy."

"Please?" Madison repeated obediently. Without glancing at her mother, she slipped her hand into Caitlin's.

"Sure," Caitlin said. "As long as it's okay with your mom."

Dakota nodded. "It's fine. Thanks."

Madison pulled Caitlin toward the door, and gladly Caitlin escaped. After meeting Dakota Allen, her sympathy with Parker had grown. She understood, perhaps even better than he did, the danger Madison was in. Not necessarily from getting into a stash of drugs but of growing up to be like her mother—a spoiled, self-indulgent woman who lived off government aid and the largesse of others. A woman who didn't create a stable home for her children but who flitted from bad relationship to bad relationship as her hormones and opportunity allowed, her days seen only through the lens of alcohol and drugs. It was an affliction commonly passed from mother to daughter unless somewhere the cycle was broken.

From what she'd learned, Parker Hathaway had also been caught in that cycle, though his parents had not led him there. What had broken it for him? These were questions Caitlin would have to know the answer to before she could understand him well enough to defend his actions.

Or at least that's what she told herself.

Sally would have a lot of information on Parker, and as his attorney, she would have access to it all. Likely there would be more she'd have to track down. Maybe it was time to give Kenny a call. She'd been meaning to touch base with him anyway, to see if Wyman Russell had been nosing around. With all the distractions today, she'd almost forgotten that little problem.

"Haven't you ever done anything you might have otherwise considered wrong to protect someone?" Parker had asked.

She believed, as she'd told him, that the end didn't justify the means, and yet she wouldn't change her own decision any more than he'd change his. Maybe her father hadn't understood all the implications of the motto. Sometimes the possible cost of the end was so great that the means, as long as they weren't too horrible, were justified.

"Isn't that the candy machine?" Madison asked.

"Oh, yeah." They had been about to walk past it. "What do you want?"

"Can I have two?"

Caitlin laughed. "I think I have enough change. But only two."

Madison grinned up at her. "You're really nice." She pointed out the candy bars she wanted before adding, "Will you ask my mom if I can play with your sister?"

"You're sure persistent, aren't you?"

Madison giggled, her dimples showing. "Daddy says that's part of my name. But it's really not."

"I always say that about Amy, too."

"That means we'll be the bestest friends."

For a brief moment, Caitlin wished with her whole heart that such a thing could be possible.

"Okay," Madison said, once the candy bars were in her hands. "Now where are those donuts?"

Chapter 20

"Please, sit down over here," Sally told Dakota Allen, indicating a couch along the wall. She'd had them take Dakota here to this private waiting room instead of an interrogation room, but Sally still planned to get as much out of her as possible. "There are some important matters we need to discuss."

"What?" Dakota's eyes narrowed, and she held her arms stiffly to her sides as she sat.

"Well, to begin with, you should know that psychologists have counseled in kidnapping cases like this that it's probably best to play down the whole experience, and especially not to verbally attack the parent responsible."

That seemed to outrage her. "But Parker kidnapped my daughter!"

"I know that, and you have every right to be upset. But in Madison's eyes, she just went for a visit with her daddy, and she doesn't understand why you're so upset with him. When you voice your anger at Parker, Madison feels she has to choose, and that's simply not a good place for a child of that age." Sally knew she was overstepping her bounds by talking this way to Dakota, but she felt she owed it to both Parker and Madison.

"So I just ignore what happened?"

"I'm not saying that. I'm saying Madison's going to feel a lot of guilt and resentment if she has to choose."

Dakota nodded. "I guess I see that." She shook her head. "I'm never letting him come near her again. How do I know he won't take her away?"

"You don't. That will all have to be worked out in family court. Do you have a lawyer?"

"No. But I definitely want to press charges. I want him punished."

"If you're willing to compromise, a plea bargain might be better. Faster. Less stressful for your daughter."

"I don't want him to get off. I want him to pay. He took my little girl who I love more than life!" Tears watered Dakota's eyes. "And that reminds me—I really want to thank you for finding her. Thank you so much."

Sally inclined her head, trying to reconcile this sudden graciousness with the harsh woman who wanted Parker to rot in jail. "You're welcome. You should know that Parker voluntarily led us to her. As for charges, I'm sure the DA's office will be in touch, and Family Services will likely want to talk with you as well." This last would be about the drug accusations Sally planned to tell them about, but Dakota would find that out soon enough.

"Family Services? Why? I haven't done anything wrong."

"Well, they like to cover all the bases, especially when the child involved is as young as Madison."

"Oh." Dakota's gaze wandered to the door. "Is that all?"

"Well, as part of the case, we have to do a little background research on you and Madison. You've been at your house for only three months. Where were you before that?"

"At a friend's."

Sally didn't speak but nodded as though expecting more. This tactic often worked with suspects. Dakota wasn't an exception.

"Parker and I'd broken up sometime before that, and I didn't know where to go. I couldn't really afford an apartment, so I moved in with a friend."

"A man?"

Dakota bristled. "He was just a friend."

Sally knew he'd been more than that. She saw it in the way Dakota held her body, in the way her eyes slid past hers. She knew it because of the lifestyle Dakota lived. Yes, occasionally friends were just friends, but that usually wasn't the case when people of the opposite sex lived together.

"And what was his name?"

"Ron Hill."

"He lives in South Salt Lake?"

"South Jordan. But he doesn't live there anymore."

"And where is he now?"

Dakota shook her head. "I don't know. And I don't see what this has to do with anything." She stood, rubbing her hands together. "I'd better go find Madison."

Sally knew that was as far as she'd get, and legally she couldn't detain Dakota or force her to answer. She'd have to leave the questioning for Caitlin in court, if the case went that far. At least the social worker would be able to make a few check-up visits to see Madison.

Madison's voice floated into the room from the open

doorway, and seconds later Caitlin and Madison came into sight, each eating a donut. Sally had forgotten all about her promised treat, but Caitlin must have found someone to find them for her.

"That looks yummy!" Dakota cooed. "Are you ready to go?"

Madison shrugged. "I guess. Want a bite?"

"No, thanks. I'm just anxious to get you home. Your brother has missed you so much."

"Where is Ricky?" Madison scanned the room, as though expecting to see him under a chair or perhaps sleeping on the couch.

"He's with his daddy."

"Oh." Madison's smile had vanished again, and Sally felt her heart go out to the child.

Dakota took a step toward Caitlin. "Thank you so very much for everything. I'm very indebted to you. Thank you for your help in bringing back my girl."

"You're welcome." Caitlin appeared as surprised as Sally felt—not so much at the thanks but the graciousness of it.

Madison tugged on Caitlin's hand. "You forgot to ask."

"Ask?" Caitlin lifted a brow.

"If I can play at your house with your sister. The one that's five."

Ah, Sally thought. Like most young children, Madison had a good memory when it came to having fun.

Dakota blinked her surprise. "Well, uh, I'm sure this lady has a lot to do, Maddy. Maybe we can work something out another day."

Sally recognized that cop-out. She'd used it enough with Randi. Given enough time, even children with good memories forgot.

Madison stamped her foot. "I want to play with her today."

"We'll see. Right now we have to pick up your brother. And I'm sure this lady is working."

Caitlin nodded, and the excuses seemed to mollify Madison for the moment.

"She's helping Daddy," Madison stated. "I don't remember what."

Dakota hesitated, her eyes meeting Caitlin's. "Don't you work here at the police station?"

"Oh, no," Caitlin said evenly. "I thought you knew. I'm the appointed counsel for your ex-husband."

"You're his lawyer?" Dakota asked, aghast, her eyes glittering darkly.

"Appointed by the court this morning," Sally broke in. "Parker doesn't have the means to get his own attorney right now." Then an idea occurred to her, something that might help in the short term. "Caitlin here will try to get him out and working again as soon as possible so he can pay child support. I understand he's also paying for your rental house. We don't want those payments interrupted."

Dakota's eyes opened wide. Apparently, in her vengeful mood, she hadn't thought about the money. "Well, I'd better go." With a final glare at Caitlin, she grabbed Madison's hand and marched from the room.

Silently, Sally and Caitlin watched them walk down the hall, and Sally noticed for the first time the candy bars sticking out of each of Madison's back pockets. As if feeling their gaze, the child looked back at them and waved.

"I have a feeling she's not going to let Madison play with Amy," Sally mused.

Caitlin snorted. "You think? If looks could kill . . ."

"She wants him prosecuted."

"I'd feel the same way in her shoes, but"—she shook her head—"I don't like that woman."

"Maybe that's because you like a certain client just a little too much?"

Caitlin blinked, her face flushing. "That's completely uncalled for!"

Sally grinned, but she had noticed the sparks between Caitlin and Parker, even if Caitlin wasn't willing to admit to it. "For what it's worth, I agree with you, and that's why I'm going to give you copies of all my research on the case so far. The last place I want Parker Hathaway is in jail. Someone's got to keep an eye out for that child."

"Thank you. I appreciate it. I'm actually not too worried about jail time. It's the visiting rights that will be problematic. Unless I find something solid on Dakota Allen, they may never let him have unsupervised visiting rights again."

Chapter 21

Tuesday morning, Parker walked out of the courtroom feeling more humiliated than he had felt since his fifth-grade teacher caught him cheating on a test and called his father in to "discuss" the matter. It had been a stupid thing to do because he'd never failed a test, even when he hadn't read the material. He'd done it only to prove he could. Or maybe to get his father's attention. Well, he'd gotten attention all right, but only for one evening.

His arraignment on the child kidnapping charges had been held between the arraignments of other arrestees, whose alleged crimes ranged from unpaid parking tickets to drunken driving and on to robbery. He'd pleaded not guilty, though he was sure everyone knew he was lying, and though the slick DA fought against giving him reasonable bail, Caitlin had convinced the judge he was not a flight risk, and the bail was arranged. Before his decision, the judge felt it necessary to lecture Parker at length about making his child support payments, as if he were some deadbeat dad.

He hadn't yet been offered the plea deal by the DA that Caitlin thought they might expect, and in fact the DA appeared completely ready to prosecute him to the full extent of the law. Worse, Dakota had taken out a restraining order that prevented him from coming within three hundred feet of her, the house, or Madison. He'd felt sick at that, though Caitlin had warned him it was coming. She assured him that as long as they could convince a judge to allow him to see Madison, the court would amend the restraining order to permit supervised visits.

Supervised visits. The words left a horrible taste in his mouth and a gaping hole in his heart.

With rare exceptions, he'd never been separated from Madison by more than a few days since her birth. She was a large part of how he'd been able to pull his life together after the wild, uncaring months with Dakota. And now, at least temporarily, he was forbidden to see her at all.

Parker stretched his shoulders uncomfortably in the suit his mother had brought yesterday for the arraignment. It had set him apart from the other criminals, and for that he was glad, but he'd never been comfortable in dress clothes. You couldn't work or sweat or have fun in a suit—not like you could in a good pair of familiar, comfortable jeans.

He hadn't allowed his mother to attend the court proceedings. This was the day she usually got together with her women friends for brunch, and he had used that excuse to keep her away. The truth was he couldn't bear to have her see him standing before a judge. His father wouldn't have been surprised, perhaps, but his mother had always held out hope for his future.

A future that was now uncertain.

The DA had pulled Caitlin aside after the arraignment, and they were now chatting some feet away, heads close together. Parker didn't know if it was customary for the legal defender and the DA to be so chummy, but he didn't like Mace Keeley, who was as good-looking as he was smooth in the courtroom. Parker knew his type—a pretty boy who was good with people and desk work but was useless for anything truly physical. Not the kind of neighbor you'd ask to help you load a moving van or lay a bit of sod, but a guy who habitually attended the gym to make sure he didn't flab. He probably didn't even cut his own grass.

Yet Caitlin was interested in Keeley. He could tell by the way her face lit up as they talked, her smile turning her pale face beautiful. A few curling wisps of copper hair had escaped the pins at the back of her head, softening her freckled face. He felt an urge to punch Keeley.

Instead, he walked purposefully toward them. Caitlin smiled at him, but Keeley ignored his presence and said, "Saturday, then. I'll call you about the time."

"Sounds good." Caitlin's voice was light, and Parker had the feeling she was trying not to let Keeley's words be too important. Or maybe she really didn't care. Maybe she was a player like Keeley. The thought disturbed him.

"What now?" he asked.

"They'll be releasing your truck in an hour or so, and you can pick it up at the station. Meanwhile, we need to discuss your case."

"I need to see Madison."

"You can't visit yet—not even with someone there."

"I know." He wondered if she could see his anguish, if it was etched on his face as clearly as he felt it carved into his heart.

"You still might go to prison. I'll do everything I can to keep you out, but since Dakota has main custody of Madison, the law is on her side."

"I know."

"I thought money might be a factor in our favor, that maybe she'd get the DA to drop the charges to protect her child support, but just now the DA told me she's found another way of supporting herself. She's out for blood."

Probably her new boyfriend, but Parker didn't feel the need to say it aloud. Caitlin knew what kind of woman she was. She dealt with people like Dakota every day.

With people like him.

No, I'm not like Dakota anymore.

"It won't last," he said confidently. "Her plans don't usually pan out. In fact, never—at least not for very long." *Except for me,* he added silently. She'd caught him permanently, or for as long as she could hold Madison hostage. "Has Detective Crumb found anything on her yet?"

Caitlin shrugged. "I haven't heard from her today, but I'm sure if you call her later, she'll have an update. Meanwhile, it's vital for your case that we get you back working and established so if we really go to trial, we'll have a strong case to present to a jury."

"A jury?"

"It's your right, and I feel the best thing for our case. Many of them will have children and a healthy hatred of recreational drugs."

"How soon will we go to trial?"

"Not for six months at the very least. Could be several years, depending."

Parker felt a sudden urge to be sick. "But we can help Madison before that, can't we?"

She didn't reply right away, gesturing for him to walk with her. "Look, I've been appointed to represent you in the criminal case, nothing more. I'm not experienced with family court. I suggest you find someone to help you there."

"Who?" He didn't want to think about how he'd pay. He'd manage somehow.

"I'll make some calls and give you a name by the end of the day. But for now, you need to decide about going back to your job. Because whatever happens with visiting rights, that will be a big factor."

"Would closer be better? The contractor I worked for in Manti offered me a job as a foreman here in Salt Lake. I'm sure that's not still available, but he might have another position."

"Is he the contractor for the job you dumped on Saturday?"

Parker nodded, refusing to let her comment needle him. "He might not want me."

"Let's go see."

Parker blinked in surprise. "You'll take me?"

"Well, your truck isn't available yet. Besides, we have an appointment with him in fifteen minutes."

It was the first real inkling of hope he'd experienced that day. "You are good."

She shrugged. "I get up early. Now come on. I still have two briefs to work on before lunch."

He held the door open for her, and her arm brushed his chest as she passed, sending heat rushing through him. He had a strong and sudden urge to run his hand over her milky skin, to kiss her smooth neck.

Dream on, he thought. She would never look twice at a man like him. Pretty boy Keeley was far more her type.

She had come to a stop outside the door, waiting for him. Their eyes met and a jolt of attraction shot through him again.

What was wrong with him? She was completely off-limits. He needed her to help him get Madison back. He would not screw this up.

It was all he could do to look away.

Parker met Jason Rosen at the temporary office of the new building project in West Valley. The gray-haired man stood and met Parker halfway across the room, offering his hand in greeting. After that, he waited for Parker to speak, and an awkwardness fell between them. Parker wished he could flee, and in his earlier days he would have, but now there was too much at stake. Construction jobs didn't abound in the winter as they often did in the summer.

"I suppose you've heard what happened," he began hesitantly.

Rosen shrugged his narrow shoulders. "I don't believe everything I hear. I do know that you quit down in Manti, and I figured that was related to your daughter."

This was where things could get tricky. Caitlin had advised him to stick to the basics. "My ex-wife is doing drugs. I removed my daughter from my ex-wife's house because I feared she was in danger." He swallowed hard. "Turns out the law doesn't see things as I do, so now she's back with her mother, and I'm working with authorities to make sure she remains safe. Because of that, I'd like to work near Salt Lake. I promise to work hard if you give me another chance."

Rosen tilted his head, his stern expression softening. "In this business, I work with a lot of men who come and go, men who have a variety of strengths and problems and trials. Some are solid, some are even bright, some would sooner steal from me than give me a good day's work. But rarely do I see someone like you, who has the potential to excel in this business. You have worked for me an entire year, and never once have you not shown up or been lazy on the job. I can't give you the foreman job because I can't risk having your personal problems interfering with the overall construction plan, but I will gladly give you a job for as long as you're able to work. Even if it's just a week or two. We're actually shorthanded right now. When this is all behind you, we can discuss future projects."

"Thank you." Parker felt a rush of gratitude. "When do I start?"

Rosen eyed his suit. "Right now, if you have a change of clothes."

"I do. In the car."

"Then let's get to work."

Chapter 22

Parker emerged from the trailer looking decidedly happier than when he'd gone in. Caitlin climbed out of the car and into the cold morning air as he approached. He wore the suit well, though she knew he took no pleasure in dressing up. Still, he looked good—as good as any attorney or executive she had dated.

"I take it he said yes?" she asked.

"I start right now." He gestured toward the back seat at the small suitcase his mother had brought him the night before. "I'll change inside."

She stepped away so he could open the back door and reach inside the car for his suitcase. "What about your truck?"

"I forgot about that. I'll have to get it later. Maybe after work? Do you know when they close?"

"I'll ask Sally."

"Thanks."

"You don't have a lunch."

He grinned. "It won't be the first time I've worked all day without eating. Besides, the foreman always has donuts or something to share. And they have soft drinks available. I'll be fine."

Caitlin wanted to protest, but he was a grown man, and it really was none of her business. "Do you have a number where I can reach you?"

"I don't have my phone on me. I stashed it under some blinds at the police station when they brought me in. I was hoping to pick it up when I got the truck. But don't worry—I'll catch a cab. I have a bit of money in my wallet. The police were kind enough to give that back at the courthouse."

"We still need to talk strategy for your case."

"Any chance we could meet some evening or weekend? Now that I'll be in town, it won't be too far out of the way, I hope."

She could tell he was worried about messing up his chance at the new job, as he should be. Not having a job would be a definite disadvantage to their case, especially if Dakota continued to push for jail time. "Evening is fine—at least early evening. In fact, why don't I pick you up tonight, and we can get your truck and talk? I can't stay long, but I can at least outline what I think will be our best defense."

"Thank you. That's more than I expected."

And far more than she should have offered, but something about this man had her going out of her way to help him. *Because he's innocent,* she thought. Of course she had yet to prove that. But maybe Sally had uncovered more information.

Caitlin smiled. "I don't like to lose."

"Neither do I. But I've also got a feeling your pretty boy doesn't like to lose, either."

"Pretty boy?"

"That blond DA."

"He's actually quite brilliant." Caitlin wasn't sure why she felt the need to defend Mace.

Parker shrugged. "You would know, but I'm not sure how brilliant you have to be to prosecute a case like mine. After all, I'm guilty."

"Guilty of taking Madison," she retorted, "but not of kidnapping."

"Apparently the law thinks it's the same thing."

"Not if I have anything to say about it."

"I hope you do." He grinned again, this time sending a flutter of something to her stomach. "For what it's worth, I think you're a better attorney than pretty boy any day—and certainly better looking." His voice had grown husky on the last words, and Caitlin would have had to be blind and dumb not to recognize the message he was sending, whether intentionally or not. He was attracted to her. This was obvious in the way his eyes touched her face, lingering on her lips. She could feel his awareness of her, yet not in the distorted, perverse way she'd felt with many of her clients. This was . . . different.

"What time do you get off?" she asked, masking her confusion.

"Usually five, but today I'll work until whatever time you get here."

She nodded. "See you then." She turned and reached for her car door just as he tried to open it for her. Their hands collided and their faces were inches apart. She could almost taste the masculine aroma of him. Her heart thundered. Neither moved for what seemed like long seconds, then she straightened and backed away, laughing with him as he finished opening the door.

"Thank you," she said.

"You're welcome."

She drove away, feeling more than a little satisfaction that he didn't go inside but stood there and watched her leave.

Caitlin put on her Bluetooth and called Sally. "Hey, it's Caitlin. I'm in my car on my way to the office, but I wanted to know if there's any news on the Hathaway case."

"Not exactly."

"What does that mean?" Caitlin snapped, slamming on her brakes as the car in front of her stopped for a traffic light.

"Wow, who woke up on the wrong side of the bed this morning?"

"Hey, it's you I'm doing this favor for."

"It *was* originally for me, but now you're doing it for him. Not that I blame you. If I were single, I'd take a second look at him myself."

"He's *so* not my type." But Caitlin's cheeks flamed, and she was glad Sally wasn't in the car to see her face. It was one thing to feel attracted to her client but quite another to act on it—which she had no intention of doing. She had enough going on in the romance field with Mace and Wyman hanging around. "And I'm not looking for a fling."

"Whatever you want to tell yourself. But keep in mind he's not a criminal. Not like most of those others you've had to defend."

"I'm just doing my job. And just like you, I didn't get good vibes from the ex-wife. Madison doesn't deserve any of this."

"Kids with rotten parents never do."

The light ahead turned green and Caitlin started the car moving again. "That's exactly why I'm so interested in the case. I'd like to make sure Parker doesn't do prison time for this—and make sure nothing happens to that little girl. I did some research on the Internet last night. Do you know how many children die because of drug use in their homes? And not only from abuse or neglect. One toddler sucked on a plastic sack full of drugs and died. Another baby died after his mother used cocaine while nursing him. There are horrid, horrid stories. Hundreds of them, it seems. If what Parker claims is true, Madison and her little brother are in big danger."

"I've alerted Family Services, and they sent someone out, but they reported nothing out of the ordinary."

"Well, yeah, Dakota knew she'd be checked out."

"There will be more visits, surprise ones."

"That won't stop something terrible from happening in the meantime."

"I know." Sally clicked her tongue. "I did talk to a lot of her friends in the past few days. All druggy types. If you can be guilty by association, she's as guilty as sin."

"By association isn't going to get Parker off. What about that guy she said she lived with?"

"That's the 'not exactly' I was talking about. Ron Hill is nowhere to be found. Some of Dakota's friends remember hearing about a Ron but nothing of a Ron Hill. There are no public records at all for the man, and no police ones, either."

"Which means he probably doesn't exist."

"Right. He gave her a false name, or she gave us one. I hope it was her because that means she has something to hide."

Caitlin considered this. "We have to find out more."

"I know, but I've got a murder case and another missing person case that just came in today, so I'm up to my ears investigating leads. And I gotta tell you, now that Madison's back home safe, the brass aren't too excited to pursue anything more. I have Dakota's name and all the particulars tagged, though, so if anything regarding her comes up, the information will forward to me, but anything else I do on the case will be on my own time or squeezed in between official projects."

"I understand. You've been a big help so far. But maybe I'll talk to Kenny Pratt."

"He's good. Tell him if he needs info from us to call me. We've worked together before."

"Thanks, Sally."

"Good luck. And Caitlin? If the opportunity presents itself, I say go for it." She was talking about Parker again. "I know for a fact it's been years since you've even dated a man, much less been in a relationship. Maybe it's time to take a chance."

Caitlin was painfully aware of that fact. "I have Amy to think about. I have to be careful."

"That's an excuse, Caitlin. You're thirty-two years old—maybe it's time to make your opportunity and not wait for it."

"I'm going out with Mace on Saturday," Caitlin said abruptly.

"Really? When did this happen, and how come you didn't tell me?"

"I'm telling you now. We talked after the arraignment this morning. He asked. I said yes."

"Good." Sally's voice oozed satisfaction. "Talk about opportunity! Call me Sunday and tell me everything. I want to hear all the juicy details. And I mean juicy."

Caitlin groaned. "It's only a first date. Not everyone hits it off like you and Tony."

"You're right." Sally's voice sobered. "Tony's always been the only one for me."

Caitlin laughed. "At least that leaves a guy or two for me to choose from."

"And one of those choices works in construction. Believe me, they're the best."

Another jab about Parker that Caitlin decided to ignore. "Sally, I'm hanging up now. I've got to call Kenny."

"Yeah, and I have to find this missing guy. Not a fun prospect. I've met his wife, and I suspect he wants to be wherever he is at the moment."

Caitlin clicked off the phone and dialed Kenny. He didn't answer, but she left a message. He was good at returning calls. Sure enough, her phone was ringing as she rode up the elevator to her office.

"Hello?"

"Caitlin, girl, what's up?"

"I have a new case, and I need information to help my client."

"Help him? Does this mean you actually have an innocent one?"

"I think so. He was arrested for kidnapping his own child. Look, can we meet to discuss the case? I know it's lunchtime, and I'm booked solid for the next three hours or so, but I'll have a little time, say, about three-thirty."

"Why don't I stop by your office around then?" he said. "I'll be in the area anyway, and that way I can save you a few minutes."

"Great." Caitlin was relieved. After all the time she'd taken with Parker on Monday and this morning, she was running behind on her other cases. There was only so much she could delegate to paralegals and secretaries.

"Besides," Kenny added, "there's another matter we need to discuss. Remember that job you had me do a couple weeks ago? Well, someone from the DA's office has been snooping around about that. I'd like to be let in on the loop."

Caitlin closed her eyes. For a moment, she'd forgotten all about that. "Okay, Kenny. We'll talk. See you at three-thirty."

Caitlin had fifteen minutes to spare until her appointment with Kenny Pratt. She took the opportunity to file some of her completed cases. As she did, she looked over other cases she'd completed throughout the year, remembering the details and who had prosecuted her clients. Mace Keeley had been the prosecutor in only one of her recent cases—a drug-using, hit-and-run perp who had exacted sympathy from no one, least of all Caitlin.

She had seen Mace in numerous cases in the courthouse, but in the past year, she had gone up against him personally only three times. On the other hand, Wyman seemed to represent a good fourth of her cases, while the other DAs had prosecuted a fairly even number. It wasn't unusual that Wyman should have so many. Since he was the newest of the deputy district attorneys, he would likely have less choice in which cases he was assigned. She was considered tough, so some of the attorneys might pass at going up against her, especially if the case wasn't promising. Could that be why she remembered beating Wyman so often? What didn't make sense was that Mace hadn't taken his fair share against her, and the cases he had taken had been irrefutable, with little chance of losing.

No, that had to be all in her mind. Still . . .

She picked up the phone. "Jodi? Look, I know you're swamped, but when you get a moment, do you think you could do a little checking in our company files and find out which cases Mace Keeley prosecuted against our LDA attorneys?"

"Ah, so it's serious."

"Jodi!"

"I saw the way he was looking at you this morning in court, don't think I didn't. Lucky girl."

"It's nothing."

"Sure, whatever you say."

"Thank you. Let me know what you find out." Caitlin hung up, not liking what was happening. If Jodi had noticed her and Mace, it was only a matter of time until others did the same.

And what of it? asked a voice inside her head. *I deserve a chance at love as much as anyone else.* She sat back in her chair, thinking of her upcoming date with Mace, but oddly enough it was Parker's face she saw.

"Caitlin?" Kenny Pratt came into the room, startling her from her reverie. "I knocked but no one answered. The door was ajar."

Caitlin came to her feet, feeling rattled. "I left it open for you. Shut the door and have a seat." She indicated one of the chairs in front of the desk, taking the other for herself. She'd learned Kenny didn't respond well to formal discussions, so she tried to keep things as casual as possible, and eliminating the desk between them went a long way toward that goal.

Kenny was small, dark-haired, and wiry, with a bland, unassuming face that was easy to trust. His way with words caused most people to spill their darkest secrets or left them wishing they had secrets to spill. This latter group often found their neighbors' secrets almost as satisfying to share, which was fine by Kenny. Even Caitlin, knowing his profession, had to be careful she didn't get sucked in.

Before sitting, he shrugged off the thick black coat that made even his thin frame appear stocky. "So what's up?" His eyes, so dark they were almost black, glittered with anticipation.

She sighed. "First we'd better talk about the DA."

Kenny sat back in his seat. "Why are they asking questions about that case I worked for you? It's been more than a year and a half. What did you do to tick them off?"

She was glad he didn't have an idea as to what she'd done, but she had little hope of keeping it that way. Better for him to know what she was up against. Not that she would share the whole story. He didn't have to know she'd hired him not to free her client but to convict him.

"I had a client charged with rape and assault with a deadly weapon. He claimed he was innocent."

"And was he?"

Caitlin smiled dryly. "Aren't they all?"

"So he was guilty as sin."

"He claimed he was elsewhere that night, and I sent you to see if there were any witnesses that could attest to his presence."

"And I found one."

"Yes. Only what he saw was detrimental to my client."

Kenny tented his hands in his lap. "And you didn't let it die."

"A citizen has the duty to report unusual activity to the police, so that's what I told you to encourage the witness to do."

Kenny leaned forward abruptly, the jerkiness of his movement disquieting her. "I see now why the DA is snooping around. You would have won the case, and they had an apple fall into their lap. Or a bloody knife, to be exact."

"You think they'd be grateful."

Kenny shook his head. "You're not telling me everything. My guess is that you knew the knife was there. Your client must have told you at some point, and you made sure the beans were spilled."

So much for not telling him the whole story. "You're wrong, Kenny," she said lightly. "I was simply trying to defend my client."

"If that was really true, you wouldn't have told me to tell the kid to call the police. If your participation in this comes to light, your client will claim a mistrial and the evidence might be thrown out."

"Without the evidence, he'd walk." Caitlin met his gaze, and to her surprise, he was the one who dropped his eyes first.

"I've done a lot of things in my life to get information," Kenny said, his voice low, "but I've never risked as much as you did by sending me to that street. Don't get me wrong. I understand why you did it, but this is a serious breach of attorney-client confidentiality."

Caitlin shrugged. "Morality is an interesting subject. Would you want a man like him freed to stalk your daughter?"

"If I had a daughter, no. Believe it or not, I admire you for what you've done. I just don't think it was a good career move."

Caitlin didn't know how much she valued Kenny's opinion until relief flooded through her. He supported her decision, however reluctantly. He even admired her for it. "What I don't get is why the DA is so interested," she mused. "They won the case, after all."

He leaned back again and crossed his legs, the picture of relaxation. "They smell something wrong, and you know as well as I do that certain unscrupulous attorneys would enjoy the publicity they'd get from exposing this breach. Never underestimate the ambition of an attorney." He chuckled wryly. "Present company included."

Caitlin never thought of herself as hard and ambitious, but it didn't come as a surprise that others thought of her that way.

Half of success was the front you showed to the world, and the other half was what you were willing to do to win.

"They traced the boy to me, but that's as far as it went," Kenny said. "And that's as far as it will go—unless I'm called to testify. I won't lie in court."

"It won't come to that. You're the only connection."

"I don't like being in that position."

She sighed. "I know, Kenny, and I'm sorry. Short of making an anonymous call myself, I didn't know what to do. I could have planted a story, but there wasn't enough time. We were well into discovery by then."

Kenny ran his short, strong fingers through his thinning hair. "Just be careful for the next few months."

"I will." She hesitated a few seconds before asking. "The person from the DA's office—was it deputy DA Wyman Russell?"

"No. Actually, it was an aide from the DA's office. Didn't tell me who he was working for, so it could have been any of the deputies or even the DA herself." He grinned suddenly. "Sorry, I can't tell you who you'll have to bribe to make this go away. Unless you want to hire me to do a little research."

"Very funny." She made a face as she remembered her dinner with Wyman. To think she'd actually enjoyed most of that night with him. He was playing her, that much was apparent now.

"Well," she said, dismissing Wyman from her thoughts, "all unpleasantness aside, let's get down to new business." She picked up a manila folder from her desk where she had placed copies of all the information she'd gathered so far—much of it from Sally. She quickly outlined the case. "It's all here." She tapped the folder. "But in a nutshell, I need evidence against the ex-wife. Proof, if possible, that she's doing drugs and the child's in danger. Anything that reflects poorly on her."

Kenny thumbed through the documents. "Is she really that bad?" Disapproval laced his voice, and Caitlin knew he didn't like the idea of getting between a mother and her child.

"After meeting the woman, I agree with my client. He may not have gone about it the right way, but something is wrong. If I were to go by the child's reaction alone, I'd have her removed from the home. But Family Services says they can't do anything if we don't have some kind of proof. Particularly, we want to find the man the woman used to live with. We believe he may be the link we need, but we aren't sure we have his correct name."

"Not going to be easy without a name." He came to his feet slowly.

"If it was going to be easy, I wouldn't need you."

He laughed. "Touché. I'll call you as soon as I have something."

"No need to tell you we're working on a deadline here." She walked with him to the door.

"You won't go to trial for months."

"There'll be other hearings and motions before then, but the real issue is that little girl. I'll never forgive myself if something happens to her."

Chapter 23

When his fellow workers started heading home from the site, Parker borrowed Rosen's cell phone. He called Caitlin, but she didn't pick up, so he placed a call to Dakota. There was a pit of helplessness in his stomach, an ache that no one but Madison could fill. How could he be a responsible father if he wasn't allowed to see his girl?

"Hello?" Dakota's voice was bright and not upset, so she obviously wasn't expecting him.

"Hi, Dakota. It's me, Parker."

"You! How dare you call after what you did?" A string of shrill curses followed her pronouncement, and he winced as he held the phone away from his ear. Apparently, he was more vile than anything else in the world, including murderers and politicians. Great. Not a hopeful start. At least he'd had the presence of mind to go outside to the parking lot away from everyone as he made the call.

"Look, I'm sorry. I shouldn't have done it." He grimaced

because what he really meant was that he shouldn't have done it the way he had. He should have taken Madison far, far away from Dakota's clutches. "Look, I'm calling to make sure Madison is safe."

"Of course she's safe!" Dakota screamed. "You stupid man. And if you think you're getting inside my house again, it's never going to happen. I installed new locks. Big ones you can't jimmy."

"I know you're doing drugs again," he said over another tumult of curses. "You promised me that once I got you the house, you'd stop. You said you'd keep it away from Madison. For crying out loud, Dakota, I saw the bag of whatever it was on the couch last month when I picked her up." Why he hadn't called the police that day was something he'd have to live with for the rest of his life.

Her jumbled curses ceased for a moment. "Is that what you're telling the police? You realize it's your word against mine. The word of a *kidnapper*. How far's that going to take you? Besides, if there were any drugs, and I'm not saying there were, they could have been yours. You could have planted them."

"What if Madison had gotten ahold of it? Did you think of that? You know nothing's out of her reach. Not even in the cupboards. She climbs like a little monkey."

"It was a bag of sugar, that's all. We were coloring it for cookies."

"Not funny." He kicked at a mound of snow by the parked vehicles. "This is our daughter we're talking about."

"*My* daughter, and you need to back off. I'd never let anything happen to her. I love her."

"I know you wouldn't hurt her purposefully, but accidents happen. Look, all I'm asking you is to let her stay with my mom until you get on your feet."

"You just want custody. Well, I can tell you that's not going to happen. I don't need you, and I don't need your money. I have someone else to help me now. I'm on my feet, and for once you don't have control over me because of money. I'm so sick of you calling the shots. For all I care you can rot in prison!"

Gritting his teeth in frustration, he left the parking lot and walked around the huge shell that would someday be a large office building. It was good workmanship, he could see, and he was glad he worked for a man who didn't cut corners to gain additional profit. Cheated customers didn't come back for more.

"Dakota," he said, trying to remain calm. He'd learned the hard way that it never paid to meet her viciousness with anger—not when Madison was in the middle. "Please. I've forgiven you a lot over the years, haven't I? Please forgive me for this. All I want is for Madison to be happy. Please. And you too."

"We don't need you," Dakota repeated. Her voice was still hard but less vicious now.

"Can I at least talk to her? I don't want her to worry. She was stressed when I left her."

"And whose fault is that? No, you can't talk to her. You've had her all weekend. On *my* weekend, I might add. Look, I've got to go. Don't call me again. Or I'll add calling me to the restraining order. Or maybe it's already there, and you've violated it. Did you ever think of that? I'll contact you through the authorities—if you're going to be around to contact. Or should I call that cute little lawyer of yours? The way she was all over Madison, you're probably already sleeping with her."

"What are you talking about?" How could Dakota possibly be jealous of Caitlin? Dakota was the one who'd slept around while they were married, not him. Even if he'd been so inclined, he'd been too busy working and watching Madison. "Besides, what would you care if—"

She had already hung up. Parker sighed heavily. He'd only wanted to talk to his little girl, to make sure she was all right, but it seemed Dakota was out to make his life as difficult as possible. He shouldn't have expected anything else.

Slowly, he started back toward the heated trailer where Rosen would be waiting for his phone. *I should have run,* he thought. If he had, Madison would be safe right now. That was the second mistake he'd made.

It's not too late.

He contemplated this new thought. There was a court order preventing him from going near Dakota and Madison, but that didn't have to stop him, not if it meant saving Madison's life. It would take planning and preparation if he was to pull it off, but he was good at that. He would have to be. There would be no third chance.

A car honked, and he looked up to see Caitlin driving into the construction site. He pointed at the phone in his cold hand and made a motion toward the trailer. She nodded, her face smiling openly, less businesslike than she'd been that morning, making her seem relaxed and warm, and also somehow reminding him of what Dakota had said about Caitlin and Madison. Maybe this woman really did care about Madison's welfare to the extent that she'd do everything in her power to discover the proof he needed. Maybe giving her a few days wouldn't be a bad idea—provided he could get them to check regularly on Madison. Dakota was likely to be on her best behavior right now.

After returning the phone to Rosen and collecting his suitcase, he jogged to the car and climbed into the front seat next to Caitlin. Her face was no longer smiling. A tiny crease had formed between her eyebrows.

"What's wrong?" he asked.

She shook her head and sighed. "It's my sister, Amy. Just had a call from her sitter. She's missing."

"What?" He tried to remember what she'd told Madison about her sister, but nothing stood out in his mind. Just that she was young enough to play with Madison.

"I called Sally—Detective Crumb. She says she'll send someone if I want, but I think I should check the neighborhood first. The sitter is an older lady, and she hasn't searched yet."

"Better hurry. It'll be dark soon and get even colder. Where was she?"

"Here in West Valley. About ten minutes away. She wanders off sometimes, but usually only when it's warm."

"Let's go. I'll help search." He nodded toward the gearshift.

Hesitating, Caitlin blinked slowly, her lashes leaving delicate shadows under her eyes. "Your truck," she began.

"It's not going anywhere."

"I could call you a cab."

He waved the suggestion aside. "Your sister's only five, right?" he said, remembering at last what little she'd said on the trip from Manti. How horrible and terribly ironic that her sister had gone missing when she had been instrumental in making him turn over Madison. What if Amy had been kidnapped?

"Well, she's sort of five, but not exactly."

That made no sense whatsoever. "You can tell me on the way."

She put the car into reverse and didn't speak again until they were at the stoplight on the main road. "Amy is only five or six—at least in her mind. On the outside, she's twenty-seven."

She waited a moment for him to digest the information and then continued. "They don't know why it happened. Maybe the birth itself." She shook her head. "You can tell when she talks, but, well, just looking at her you might not notice anything."

Which explained why Caitlin wasn't as worried about a possible kidnapping, though there was still a lot that could go wrong with a full-grown woman who was mentally handicapped.

He sensed a waiting about Caitlin, and unsure what she wanted or needed, he said, "We'll find her." She nodded, her lips pursed and her face tight with worry.

The sitter was a sturdy older woman with white hair, who burst from the house as they pulled into the driveway. Both Caitlin and Parker jumped from the car and met her on the walkway.

"Oh, Caitlin, I'm so sorry! She heard me talking to you on the phone about being late, and she started to pout. You know how she gets. Neither Kyle nor I saw her leave. She was sneaky about it."

Caitlin patted the woman's shoulder. "It's not your fault, Sarah. I told you about last summer and how she used to disappear."

"But she hates being out in the cold. She took her coat, at least, thank goodness. And I called you the minute I knew she wasn't in the house."

"Then she can't have gone far." Caitlin scanned the street.

"I'll go that way," Parker said, motioning one way with his head. "You go the other. We'll knock on doors and ask people to search their own houses and yards. If we don't find her on this street, you'd better take Detective Crumb up on her offer. It's getting colder by the minute."

"Okay."

"I'll go inside and call everyone I know," the sitter added.

At the first two houses, Parker talked to the people living there. Everyone was extremely helpful. "If you find her on your property, please let us know," he urged.

"We'll help you after we look here," he was told at each house. Parker felt an odd lump in his throat at their concern. Caitlin had chosen a wonderful neighborhood to live in.

The next house was empty, but he searched the yard anyway. Dusk was quickly approaching, and he'd have to find a flashlight soon. He could hear people shouting Amy's name as neighbors joined the hunt. In the backyard of the fourth house, which was also empty, he spied a playhouse complete with a balcony, slide, swing, and a sandbox underneath that would probably be attractive in the summer but now looked dark, deserted, and unfriendly. Then he realized he was thinking like an adult who knew the floors would be cold, the inside dark, and the furniture dirty. But Madison wouldn't think such things. She'd be excited to have a little house all her own, and she would try to make it as comfortable as possible. Besides, though it was almost dark now, it hadn't been when Amy left the sitter's.

"Amy?" he called.

No response. It had been a long shot anyway. He was about to leave for the next house, but thoughts of Madison stopped him. Madison loved to play hide and seek; maybe Amy did, too. He'd take a peek inside and be on his way. Zipping his coat against the ever-increasing cold, he approached the little playhouse and climbed the stairs to the deck. One way led to the door of the house, the other to the slide. From his vantage point on the deck, he could see a tiny glow coming from the house.

"Amy? I'm a friend of your sister's, and we came to get you. Are you here?"

No response, but he heard a rustling inside the playhouse.

"Amy?" He peeked in and saw a woman sitting on a blanket holding a small plastic candle with a fake flame. Even in the dim light he could make out her red hair. She was bigger than Caitlin, in both height and weight, but there was an obvious family resemblance in the lines of her face. "There you are."

"I'm a bird and this is my nest," she said in a little girl voice.

He took a few steps inside, ducking his head so he wouldn't hit the ceiling. There was a second floor to the house, he saw, a loft really, and he was glad Amy hadn't climbed up there. There wasn't a safety rail and she might have fallen.

"A bird," he said conversationally. "What kind of bird?"

"One that flies. A red one like my hair." Amy hesitated. "I'm not supposed to talk to strangers."

Parker squatted down next to the woman, who regarded him with suspicion. "Then we'd better go find Caitlin. She's really worried about you."

"Good. She was late. Again." Amy stuck out her lower lip, the quintessential pouting child.

"I wasn't worried about you," Parker added.

Amy tilted her head. "You weren't?"

"Not if you can fly. If anything bad came, you'd just fly away."

She nodded vigorously. "That's right. I can fly. Are you a bird, too?"

"Sometimes. At least when my little girl wants me to be."

"You have a little girl?"

"Yes."

"Oh." She sounded disappointed.

"Is that a bad thing?"

Amy shrugged. "I want a baby for Caitlin so I can play with it. And then maybe Caitlin wouldn't work so much. But if you have a little girl, you already have a family."

"Part of one anyway. But I'm not married right now." Parker wondered why he cared that she knew. "I'm divorced."

Amy's brow gathered. "Divorced? Is that when people decide they don't love each other anymore and go live in different houses?"

When he nodded, she added, "That's sad."

"Sometimes it's necessary. But we never divorce our children. We keep on loving them and taking care of them forever and ever."

Amy laughed. "Of course. You have to."

She was so innocent. Parker was glad she didn't have a mother like Dakota. "So, should we go find Caitlin?"

"Not until we have tea." Setting down her fake candle, Amy reached for a pretend pot and poured imaginary liquid into a pretend cup. She handed it to him and poured another for herself.

Parker sat on the wood floor Indian-style and reached for the make-believe cup, sipping rather noisily.

"No," Amy said. "You have to hold out your little finger like this." She demonstrated.

"I didn't know that. I'll have to tell my daughter."

"Caitlin taught me. We always do it like this."

Parker had a hard time imagining his proper attorney sitting down to make-believe tea, but he liked the picture. It reminded him of how soft she'd been around Madison. How alive and passionate about her work. Yet once again he immediately squashed the idea of any romantic involvement. She lived in a completely different world. Besides, he wasn't ready for another relationship with a woman. Any woman. Not even one who might keep her promises. Maybe if he'd met Caitlin another way, things would be different. But this situation was what it was.

"I didn't know birds could drink tea," he said.

"I have powers. Kind of like magic."

"That's very handy."

"Yes, I have hands and feathers."

"What else can you do?"

"I can fly, and I can . . ." She paused, considering. "Well, do other stuff I don't know yet."

"See through metal? Make people tell the truth?" Madison often used these ideas in her play.

"Yes," she agreed. "Would you like some more tea?"

"Sure. Hit me again. But then I really have to go find your sister."

"Would you like to have a baby with her?"

Parker couldn't help grinning. "We'll see," he said, not wanting to upset her.

"I'm ready," Amy announced. She picked up the fake candle, clicked off the light, and set it on a shelf. "Ooh, it's dark. Scary."

"It might be lighter outside," he said, coming to his feet. "I'll help you."

"Okay." Suddenly her hand thrust into his, and she held on with a grip that was far stronger than Madison's had ever been.

He led her outside, only to find the light had faded completely. "It's dark now," Amy said with wonder. "I've been gone all day."

"It gets dark fast in the winter. And cold. That's why you should never leave without telling someone where you're going. You might get lost."

"No, I won't." But she stepped closer to him as they left the stairs. She still gripped his hand tightly. Parker felt odd walking around with this woman-child holding his hand. Yet he didn't let go or pull away. For all her twenty-seven years, Amy was still a child. He would want Caitlin to offer support to Madison in the same way, if the situation had been reversed.

They were spotted immediately as they rounded the front yard of the house. "They found her!" a teen shouted and pulled out a cell phone to begin texting others the good news.

Parker could still hear shouts of Amy's name in the distance, but gradually these ceased as the news spread. Parker and Amy were nearly back to the sitter's when Caitlin came running down the street as fast as her high heels allowed. She slowed as she reached them.

"Where have you been?" Caitlin demanded. Her eyes went to their linked hands, but Amy was already pulling away to launch herself at her sister.

"I was a bird in a nest, so I could have just flown away and not get hurt. And then we had tea." Amy pointed at him. "He drank two cups, and I had three. Then it got dark, but he saved me from monsters."

"His name is Parker," Caitlin said, hugging her sister. "And you can't leave like that. I was so scared!"

Amy looked appropriately chastened, though Parker thought he saw a mischievous smile touch her lips for the briefest of moments. "I'm sorry, Caitlin. I didn't want you to work late. I was missing you today."

"Well, I'm here now. But I still have to take Parker into Salt Lake to get his truck."

"Can I go?"

Caitlin sighed. "Yes." Her eyes went past her sister's head to meet Parker's. "Thank you."

"No problem."

"Oh, Caitlin, I just remembered something very, very important," Amy said, tugging on Caitlin's arm.

"What's that?"

"Parker isn't married anymore, so he can still have a baby with you."

Caitlin's eyes opened so wide that Parker had to grin. "Amy," she groaned. "Sorry about that," she added to Parker. "She's got a thing about babies lately."

"Well, technically, she's right," he had to say, wishing it wasn't so dark and cold so he could see if she was blushing. Her freckles did seem to be standing out more prominently.

Her mouth opened, but nothing came out. She seemed both surprised and confused. The urge to move closer took him by surprise. What was he thinking? Teasing her was one thing, touching her was another. He might not be able to stop.

People were converging upon them now, everyone happy that Amy had been found. White clouds of warm breath filled the cold air.

"Thank you," Caitlin said at least a dozen times.

Parker backed to the edge of the small crowd and watched them talk and eventually disperse. Amy enjoyed the attention, while Caitlin seemed only to endure it, though he was sure that wouldn't be obvious to anyone there. She was complete grace.

Stop, he told himself. He turned and walked back to Caitlin's car. His hands and face felt numb from the cold, and for once he was glad of it. Numb made things hurt less. There was so much he couldn't have. Madison, a normal life. He had to hope Caitlin could make it all possible for him. Maybe.

Caitlin and Amy caught up to him as he reached the door.

"I'll just call Sally," Caitlin said. "There's probably still time to get your truck."

He nodded and opened the front passenger door for Amy, who was at his elbow, looking up at him with a child's worship. She reminded him of Madison. Where was his daughter now? Was Dakota taking care of her? Was she safe?

Helpless. He hated feeling that way. It made him desperate. Caitlin was talking on the phone as he climbed into the back seat, and from the expression on her face, it wasn't good news. "Sorry," she said when she'd disconnected. "Sally says they're all closed up. We'll have to get it first thing in the morning. She can have someone get us in by seven."

That meant he was stuck without transportation, but at least he had his clothes and a bit of cash. "Is there a motel around here? Someplace with a restaurant close?"

"Oh, that's right. You didn't have lunch. You must be starving."

His stomach growled at the mention of food, though he'd eaten four donuts that afternoon. "I could eat a horse," he admitted.

"You eat horses?" Amy looked aghast.

"No, honey," Caitlin said. "That's just a way of saying you're really hungry." To Parker, she said, "Look, the least I can do is feed you."

"It's okay. You've got to take care of Amy."

"We'll go to my house. Amy will love having you."

He was curious to see where she lived, to see her in her own private environment, but surely there were rules against consorting with your clients—and for good reason. Being with her was proving both difficult and tempting. "Okay, if it's no bother," he agreed, wondering if he would regret the decision later. Maybe if he hadn't been so tired he would have been able to protest more strongly, but he was both exhausted and ravenous. Not a good combination on any day.

"Good." She gave him a smile that made heat course through his veins. He looked out the window to mask his reaction. Already he could tell this was a big mistake.

"I can show you my real tea set," Amy bubbled into the

silence. "I have the princess ones. I have Belle and Sleeping Beauty, and Snow White. I don't have Ariel, and I like her best because she has red hair like me, but I have her on my bed. I also have . . ."

Parker let the words rush over him, enjoying the babble that so reminded him of Madison. His aching heart felt lighter.

When Caitlin pulled up at her small house a few streets over, their eyes locked briefly and his confusion was back. What was he beginning to feel for this woman? Was it because he hoped she could reunite him with Madison? Because he was physically attracted to her? Or because he was fascinated with her laugh, the slight lilt in her voice, the soft look of her lips, or how her hair had escaped the mass gathered at the back of her head? The way she spoke to Amy? All of the above?

He was clearly a mess, and those thoughts weren't helping anything. What he needed was a good night's sleep so he could think clearly. Be in control. He closed his eyes for a moment, but all that got him was a vision of Caitlin looking up at him.

Chapter 24

*C*aitlin was going against all her personal rules by inviting Parker to her house. She knew attorneys who often helped their clients out with places to stay and clothes to wear. Others actually had affairs or became close friends with the people they represented. Caitlin had always been careful to keep her professional life separate from her personal one—an excellent policy, seeing as she mostly represented people guilty of very nasty crimes. Like Chet Belstead, who, thanks to her, was going to spend twenty-five years behind bars, if society had any luck at all.

"Have a seat," she offered. "This shouldn't take too long." She kept a frozen chicken casserole around for emergencies when store-bought frozen food didn't seem appropriate; it was her mother's special recipe, and she decided to use it now. The casserole would only take ten minutes to mostly thaw in the microwave and then another thirty in the oven. That would give her time to make a salad. No, scratch that because she was out of lettuce, but she had a bagged salad from Costco that had bits of blue cheese and dried cranberries. For a bagged salad, it tasted quite good.

Parker sat at the table, his dark eyes following her as she opened the freezer and cupboards. He had the air of a man who'd worked hard and was exhausted, both mentally and physically. She was glad she'd decided on the casserole instead of something less healthy and filling.

If the truth were told, she didn't invite many personal friends back to her place, either. Previously, male friends had thought it was because of Amy, and in part it was, but Caitlin also didn't like the idea of opening herself to someone by having him see her real life. It made things much easier at breakup if most of the relationship had taken place elsewhere.

"If there's someplace I can wash up," Parker said, "I'd be glad to help."

She noted there was a shadow on his face, though he'd shaven that morning, and his shirt was rumpled and probably dirty from the day's work. What he needed was a good shower, but that would have to wait until they found a motel. "I'm almost finished here," she said, "but the bathroom's down the hall."

"I'll show you." Amy jumped up from where she knelt by the hamster cage.

"You can show him but then let him have his privacy."

Amy sighed in exasperation. "He's just going to wash his hands."

"Amy," Caitlin warned.

Parker laughed. "Where is this bathroom, Amy? And just so you know, I am definitely closing the door."

Amy rolled her eyes. "Come on. It's down here." She clumped to the hall and Parker stood to follow.

He took his suitcase with him, Caitlin noted, and at the last moment she said, "You could take a shower if you have something to change into. There's time." He stopped and met her gaze with a look that sent an odd longing through her. Caitlin flushed. "I mean if you want."

"I do want. I really need a shower. I just didn't think you'd want . . . I can wait until the motel."

"No, go ahead. It's fine." It wasn't as if it was her bathroom. The hall bathroom was Amy's, filled with her toys and mermaid towels. Not personal at all. "There are extra towels in the bathroom cupboard," she added.

Caitlin busied herself gathering dishes until she was sure he was gone. Then she put her hands to her burning face. A man showering in her house. A strong, gorgeous hunk of man at that. Not something that happened every day—or ever, now that she thought about it. Not with Amy around.

This is ridiculous, she thought. Not only was Parker her client, but he seemed to have no interest in her. He hadn't even made a pass yet, which most of her male clients did within the first half hour of meeting her.

And why not? Didn't he find her attractive?

She poured out the bagged salad, thinking of the connection she'd felt between them earlier. *Imagined, more like,* she told herself. *It was nothing.*

She set the table, using her nicer dishes. For an added touch, she lit a candle. For the aroma, not for mood. After all, she wouldn't be turning off the light, and Amy would be right there with them.

She took the partially thawed casserole from the microwave and slipped it into the oven. Dumping rolls into a basket and covering them with a towel, she nodded. The only thing missing was a good dressing, and she might as well make one since she had time. As she mixed vinegar with spices, she began to hum under her breath, and the tension drained from her body. She'd forgotten how much she enjoyed puttering around the kitchen. It brought back memories of cooking with her mother while her father played cards with Amy at the table, his Irish brogue thick and musical. Those had been good days for all of them.

A noise at the doorway to the kitchen distracted her thoughts. Parker stood there in a change of clothes and his hair combed. He looked more rested. "I'll have to find a place to stay up here—an apartment or something. Someplace preferably with access to a washer and dryer. I'm going to run out of clothes soon. My mother didn't pack for more than a few days."

"You can go home and get more," Caitlin told him.

"I will. If we manage to get my truck tomorrow." Grinning, he crossed the space between them.

"We will."

"You aren't going to change into something more comfortable?" he asked, looking at her languidly.

She glanced down at her suit. "I always dress like this."

"I don't think I could stand to be in a suit all the time."

"It's a matter of what you get used to. Couldn't you imagine a time when you might be wearing a suit all day?"

"There would have to be a big incentive." He was close now, too close.

"Now that you mention it, I think I will change." She was glad to have an excuse to escape. "No use in risking a dry-cleaning bill sooner than necessary." One moment she was wondering why he wasn't attracted to her, and the next she was running away. What did she want?

Nothing, she thought. *From him I want nothing. I'm just helping his daughter.*

She chose her clothes almost without thinking: soft black

knit pants that flattered her hips, and a fitted pink and black long-sleeved top, also made of thin knit, that lay attractively over her curves without being uncomfortably revealing. She didn't want Parker to get the wrong idea. As she changed, she tried to think of Mace, tried to imagine his handsome face bending over hers, but all she saw was Parker.

She went to Amy's room to see what she was doing and found her sister curled up asleep on the floor by the dollhouse their father had made them when they were young. Her favorite Barbie was in one hand, and twin babies lay on the carpet next to her cheek.

"Amy," Caitlin said, shaking her sister softly. "Dinner's almost ready."

Amy's eyes fluttered opened, closing again immediately as she murmured, "I ate with Sarah."

She always did, but that usually didn't stop her from eating again with Caitlin. As a result, she and Sarah Burnside had worked out portion control to keep Amy's weight from becoming a problem. She already weighed so much more than Caitlin that there was no way she could lift her into bed.

"You're sure you're not hungry?"

"No."

"Okay, then let's get you to bed."

"I want to sleep here," Amy muttered, not opening her eyes.

"Okay, but don't blame me if you end up with a cricked neck tomorrow." Caitlin retrieved Amy's pillow and her Ariel blanket, tucking her in as best she could and smoothing her red hair. "You sleep then. If you need me, call me."

Amy didn't answer, having already drifted off again.

That left Caitlin alone with Parker, and she had to admit that a part of her was just the tiniest bit excited at the prospect.

He was sitting at the table, his sock-clad feet stretched out before him, looking as though he belonged. Caitlin had left her own shoes at the door when they'd entered and had taken off her nylons when she'd changed. Being barefoot seemed suddenly intimate, and she wished she'd taken time to put on socks like Parker.

"You look nice," he said, his eyes traveling the length of her. "Tell me the truth—it's a lot more comfortable than a suit."

She laughed. "You're right."

"Where's Amy?"

"Sleeping. She was playing with her dolls and dropped off. I couldn't wake her enough to get her into bed." Caitlin opened the top cupboard where she kept the slab of gray speckled granite that matched her countertop. It was handy for hot pans from the oven, but rarely did she have the opportunity to use it. She had to reach up with both hands to support its weight.

He stood. "I can help if you want."

"Oh, she'll be fine. She'll wake up before too long to use the bathroom, and then I can get her into bed."

"I meant this." He reached from behind her and took the heavy slab with one hand, his chest brushing her back.

"Thanks." She turned slowly toward him. His arm slid against hers as he brought the slab to his side. Neither of them moved, and the tension between them was suddenly so thick Caitlin could hardly breathe, the emotion both delicious and terrifying. This close she could see the details of his face, the firm line of his jaw, the slightly prominent nose, the individual hairs that made up the brows framing his eyes. She felt it again, unmistakably—the connection between them.

Her heart thumped loudly in her ears. He was going to kiss her, she was sure of it. And she was going to let him. In fact, if he didn't kiss her, she would shrivel up and die. She yearned to investigate that strange connection, to know what it meant. His face came marginally closer. Their eyes locked. It was all she could do not to grab him and hurry things along.

Then all at once he was turning away, stepping more gracefully than she would have thought, given his bulk and their awkward proximity. Disappointment throbbed in her chest. No, more than that. It was an emptiness she didn't understand.

"Don't you want . . . ?" she began. Even if she wasn't sure about what she wanted to happen, he wasn't supposed to be the one pulling away.

He set the granite slab on the table and faced her, his face carefully blank. "Want what?"

Her face burned and she turned away, wishing she'd never spoken.

He walked to her and put a firm hand on her shoulder, turning her toward him. "Want what?" he repeated, his voice gentle.

His pretense stung. No way had she misread the signs. How dare he play with her! "Nothing," she muttered. "I need to check the casserole." She pulled away and walked toward the oven.

The abrupt silence was so loud it hurt her ears. It felt wrong and awkward and lonely.

She grabbed an oven mitt, all too aware of Parker standing frozen where she'd left him. He cleared his throat. "If I'd tried to kiss you, would you have let me?" he asked softly.

She swallowed hard, drawing her hand back from the oven door. "You wanted to kiss me?" She didn't dare look his way. When had she lost control of the situation?

He let out a short laugh. "Want? Oh, Caitlin, I've been wanting to kiss you since the moment I first saw you."

She stiffened. He was making fun of her. "This isn't a game."

She could look at him now. Glare at him rather. Let him think the flushing was from anger instead of hurt.

"I know it's not a game," he said. "But you're all the hope I have right now of saving my daughter. If I scare you away . . ."

Something eased inside her. "I don't scare easily."

His left brow rose. "In court maybe not, but this is completely different."

"Well, then I guess it's good there's nothing between us. We can focus on your case."

"That depends. Are you saying there could be more?" He took three steps toward her.

She didn't know what she was saying. "I don't believe that's what either of us want." She let her gaze drop to the oven mitt in her hands, unnerved by his closeness.

"Speak for yourself."

The gruffness in his voice sent another ache of need through her. She peeked at him from beneath lowered lids. He was probably saying it so she wouldn't dump his case.

"There's a world of things I want," he continued, "but I'm learning I can't have most of them. You are so far out of my league that we might as well be in different countries."

Well, he was right about that, even if it made her a snob. But not because of his job, but because of his questionable path and his uncertain future.

"Maybe we aren't as different as you think," she said. It was as close to an invitation as she was going to give. Because she wanted to kiss him, if only to dispel this weird fascination she seemed to be having with the man.

He took another step, and his arms went around her, pulling her toward him. His eyes devoured her face as he lowered his lips to hers. His kiss was firm and questioning, with none of the initial tentativeness of her previous boyfriends.

Far from putting her emotions at rest, Caitlin found herself swaying toward him, wanting to touch him. Her hands crept up to the back of his neck, her fingers toying with his hair. He had great hair. Marvelous hair that was softer than she'd expected. As if opening a floodgate, his hands also went to her neck, his fingers warm and strong. It was all she could do not to moan with pleasure as he freed her hair from its clip and began combing his hand through her unruly waves.

"You are so beautiful," he murmured against her lips. His kiss stole her breath, making her feel as if she were flying. He angled her head back, exploring her mouth. He tasted of mint and heat. There was no fear or worry inside her, just the pleasure of the moment and the miracle of never wanting it to end. A soft groan escaped his lips.

Caitlin felt beautiful. At that moment it didn't matter that she needed to lose ten pounds, or that she often felt awkward in social situations. All that mattered were his lips on hers and the way his hands felt in her hair. All the carefully constructed walls around her were tumbling down.

He trailed kisses over her cheek to her neck. "Caitlin," he murmured, against her skin.

"Caitlin?" came a loud echo. Amy's voice from the doorway.

They broke apart self-consciously. Caitlin knew her face was redder than her hair. "Amy," she said faintly.

"What were you doing?" Amy asked, rubbing her sleep-filled eyes with one hand while the other still clutched a Barbie. "Why were you kissing?"

"I, um—"

"You told me never to let a boy kiss me." The words were accusing.

"This is different," Caitlin said.

"Why?"

"Because I'm older and because I know Parker." Caitlin glanced at him. He was watching the interaction, an amused smile on his face.

Amy leaned forward and said in a loud whisper, "So do we get a baby now?"

Caitlin felt her face flush again. "No, we do not." Turning, she picked up the oven mitt she'd dropped at some point and busied herself with the casserole.

Amy was right. She had thrust aside all propriety, and for what? For a man who was likely indulging her only for the help she could give him. She had never considered dating a client before, and Parker, for all his charm, was nothing more than a client, willing to do whatever it took to get him free of the charges against him. Even romancing his attorney, who hadn't had a decent boyfriend in two years.

Anger slowly replaced the attraction in her heart. Caitlin welcomed it, stoked it, glad for the strength it gave her. If she wanted casual intimacy, she could find that anywhere. But she wanted a real relationship, and that meant looking elsewhere.

"I thought you were sleeping," she said to Amy. "What woke you up?"

"Something," Amy said, shrugging. "I don't know. Maybe I'm hungry."

Or maybe she'd felt Caitlin's emotions clear from the bedroom. "Sit at the table then," Caitlin told her. "Dinner's ready."

Caitlin didn't look at Parker until they were safely eating. He didn't seem to have changed his attitude toward her or to be dwelling on their kiss. Instead, he concentrated on his food, wolfing it down with the air of a man who had gone a long time without a meal. She picked more slowly at her plate, her appetite gone. The food tasted like cardboard.

"Great salad," Parker commented. "I didn't think I'd like these red things."

"Cranberries."

"I like them better than raisins," Amy put in. She was wiggling a little in her seat, a sure sign she needed to use the bathroom.

"Great idea, putting them in a salad."

Caitlin didn't feel obligated to tell him it came from a bag. Parker looked over at her, still eating. "This is really great. Thanks for inviting me."

"You're welcome." Caitlin looked quickly away from his unsettling eyes.

Amy yawned. "My Barbie wants to sleep."

She hadn't eaten anything except the cranberries from the salad. Caitlin sighed. "Go to the bathroom first and then put her to bed." Amy stumbled off, muttering something to her doll.

Parker set down his fork, though his plate was still half full with his second helping. "Sorry about that."

She knew he was referring to how Amy had walked in on them. "Sorry? I got the distinct feeling you enjoyed getting caught." Caitlin let annoyance color her voice.

He grinned. "I was just thinking how I'd explain it to Madison. You know, if she'd been the one to walk in." He took a long drink of milk before picking up his fork again.

Caitlin's annoyance melted away, taking with it most of the anger she'd wanted to hold against him. "I've tried to keep Amy protected, you know, from boys who'd take advantage of her. Once when my parents were still alive, a boy in our neighborhood in Chicago got her in a field all alone. I was sent out to look for her and found her—just in time. Thankfully, he ran off when he saw me. My father was furious." She gave him a wry grin. "You've never seen an angry man until you've seen an angry Irish man."

Parker chewed his food thoughtfully. "I thought the Irish were fun-loving."

"They're as fiery as they are fun."

"Which is why you're so wicked in court, I bet. And now I know what I'm hearing in your voice. You do sound a little Irish."

Caitlin laughed. "My father was a first-generation immigrant from Ireland. My mother hated his accent. She was born in England, and even after her family moved to the States, she had a very proper English upbringing. But I was a big copycat when I was little, and I loved to make my father laugh, so I learned the accent pretty well. I guess it still comes through a little."

"Have you ever been to Ireland?"

"A few times when I was small."

"I went to Ireland once."

That surprised her. He didn't seem the type. "You did?"

"Yeah. After high school, some friends and I went backpacking in Europe for a month. I was interested in construction even then, and I convinced myself it was a good chance to look at all sorts of buildings."

"And was it?"

He laughed. "Believe it or not, it wasn't nearly as fun as we expected, though it was certainly exciting. We ended up sleeping on the roadside a lot and found ourselves in more than a few dangerous situations. I was extremely homesick after a few weeks. Looking back, I think we went more to give our parents grief than anything. We thought we were so mature."

"How long were you in Ireland?"

"Three or four days. We caught a boat over from England. What I remember most is green. It was beautiful. The girls, especially." He winked. "But it was different from what I expected—I guess because there seemed to be fewer extremists. You know, fighting in the streets or whatever. The quiet majority seemed to be regular folks, caring more about daily life rather than worrying if you were Protestant or Catholic."

"That's true—unless you happen to stray into one of the more volatile neighborhoods—especially in my dad's era. That's why he left the country in the first place. He emigrated to Chicago and met my mom. Later, he convinced her to give Ireland a try—that was before I was born—but going back didn't work out, so they returned to Chicago. Both taught history at the University of Chicago."

"How'd they end up in Utah?"

"My mom's family originally emigrated to Utah for religious purposes, so she spent a lot of time here as a child, and she always wanted to move back. She was offered a job at the University of Utah and convinced my father to come with her—after all, she'd tried Ireland. Later my father began teaching at the university too. They liked it here, especially the mountains. So they stayed."

"I love the mountains. Which, incidentally, is another place you shouldn't wear suits." He scooped up his last bite as Caitlin rolled her eyes.

"I can do anything in a suit. Even change a tire."

"Impressive."

Caitlin took a breath. "Look, about what happened earlier. . ."

He slid his chair next to hers, reaching over to touch her hand. She rose, avoiding contact that might not allow her to think properly.

"What I'm saying is that we made a mistake." She began picking up dishes, avoiding his eyes.

"A mistake. But I thought—"

"We need to focus on your case right now. Distractions are the last thing we need. Besides, we both have responsibilities." Yet Caitlin knew the real reason was that she didn't want to be used and thrown away. She had a problem with commitment, but once she was committed, she wanted the relationship to last longer than the rinse cycle. Parker might not be like most of her clients, but he was still a man whose life didn't exactly match her own. He'd said it himself. They were countries apart.

He frowned, his eyes narrowing. "Now you're the one playing games."

Caitlin recoiled. "I'm the one being professional. Look, Parker, if you want a casual relationship, you'll have to look elsewhere." She met his eyes now, her chin lifted firmly. Was that hurt in his expression? Before she could decide, the emotion was gone.

"Whatever you want." There was heat in his voice but carefully held in check. "Maybe you'd better take me to that motel."

She nodded. "I can clean this up later."

But he was already gathering the rest of the dishes from the table. "I'll help you first. It's getting late."

They worked in frosty silence, each minute a torture. When they finally finished, Caitlin said, "I'll go wake up Amy. The motel's really close, but I can't leave her."

"Okay." He dried his hands on her dish towel.

She stared at those strong hands, the ones that had so tenderly combed through her hair. Abruptly, she felt weak with indecision. She had to force herself to leave the kitchen, and when she returned with an extremely sleepy and cranky Amy, she found Parker sitting at the table, staring at a picture of Madison in his wallet.

"You're right," he said softly. "I can't ever let myself forget, not even for a moment, what I'm fighting for."

She nodded and moved away quickly before her heart could feel too much pity. If she stayed to offer comfort, things could too easily escalate to more—much more. *Why did I let it happen?* She wished desperately that the moment in the kitchen hadn't occurred. Now her heart had been awakened to him. Now she wanted more.

When they reached the motel, she pulled up outside the lobby, but he didn't get out immediately. "Caitlin." His voice came softly, sounding a bit gravelly.

She met his gaze as his hand reached out, touching her arm lightly and searing it through the cloth that separated them. "Yes?"

"I'm sorry."

She nodded. "Me too."

He glanced at the back seat where Amy was sprawled, snoring soundly, and then back to Caitlin's face. "For the record, I haven't had a casual relationship since I met Dakota."

She didn't reply. It was all she could do to prevent herself from leaning over and putting her arms around him. To kiss him again. But if she did that, tomorrow she'd regret it.

"Good night," she said firmly.

His hand slid from her arm, leaving it cold. "Good night."

Back at home inside her room, she lay awake for a long time, staring at the ceiling.

Chapter 25

Parker spent an uncomfortable night on the hard motel bed. Not that the mattress was uncomfortable but rather his thoughts were. His mind was full, not of Madison and the court case as they should have been, but of what had happened between him and Caitlin.

Caitlin was happy they'd been interrupted, so he had to be satisfied with that. He knew that on some level she was attracted to him, despite their different economic and social circumstances. But attraction hardly made a difference if she wasn't willing to see where it might take them.

He sighed as he shaved and dressed for work in the small motel bathroom. Last night in Caitlin's car, he'd dared hope she was reconsidering the possibility of a relationship, or that she might admit the connection between them was as strong as he felt it was, but she had made her intention to keep away from him clear. At least she was still helping him with his case.

Despite his attraction to her, the only reasonable thing for him to do was to pull back or risk losing her help.

He was dressed, packed, and had eaten cold cereal from the breakfast alcove in the lobby when she arrived at the motel, wearing a gray suit that was snug at the waist, showing the outline of her figure to advantage. Her hair was swept up tightly, but that didn't detract from her beautiful blue eyes or those soft lips.

"Sleep well?" she asked casually, coming up to the table where he sat in the breakfast area.

He gave her a lazy smile and said, "I couldn't sleep. I had, uh, other things on my mind." The way he said it while watching her so intently left little room to misconstrue his meaning, and he loved the way her face flushed. *Does she do that in court?* he wondered. No, because she didn't really care about those cases. Or was he just fooling himself?

"Well," she said, turning from him, her voice going cool, "sleeping in a new place is always difficult the first time."

Dragging his stare away from her was more than difficult, and he decided to give up trying. At least she couldn't fault him for inattentiveness. "I'm hoping to find an apartment today. A guy at work said he knows of a place available on a week-to-week basis. Another guy knows some people in a house who are looking for another tenant."

Caitlin met his gaze again, but this time her emotions appeared completely under control. No telltale flush. "I hope they have a washing machine."

He wanted to jump up from the table and reach out to her, to kiss her again to see if there was still a reaction. But she was the one calling the shots, and if he wanted to protect Madison, he had to follow her rules.

Detective Crumb was waiting for them at the precinct when they arrived, Parker's truck keys in hand. "I already authorized the release," she said to Parker. "Sorry it was too late yesterday. I hope you managed all right."

"We managed," Caitlin said shortly. "Thanks."

The detective looked at her closely. "What's wrong?"

"Nothing." Caitlin blinked at her. "Everything's fine."

She seemed fine to Parker, but if Sally saw something different in Caitlin, maybe she was right. The two seemed to be close.

"We had a late night," Parker volunteered, setting his suitcase on the floor next to his feet.

"Oh?" Sally reminded him of a hawk, pouncing on its prey. "How is Amy after her little escapade?"

"Same as ever." Caitlin glanced at Parker as though daring him to add anything further. Not a chance. Parker wasn't that stupid. When he didn't bite, she continued, "Well, I'd better get to work. Parker, I'll call you if I have any news. We still need to go over a few things."

"Wait." He touched her arm, felt her stiffen and pull away. "I need to find my phone, give you the number."

Detective Crumb grinned. "Oh, that's right. The missing cell phone. Well, look what housekeeping turned up." Drawing her hand from the pocket of her slacks, she held out a black mobile phone. "You're lucky it wasn't stolen. Of course, this isn't your real phone. It seems to be one of those temporary ones."

Parker shrugged without explaining that he'd left his real

phone back at his apartment while he'd been with Madison, so they couldn't be traced. "Thanks, Detective Crumb."

"Call me Sally. Seems we're going to be around each other a bit in the next month or so." As he nodded, she continued, "Good move hiding the phone—I guess. Though it made no difference in the end."

"What's the number?"

Parker recited the number as Caitlin punched it into her own phone before turning away.

"You sure everything's okay?" Sally's gaze shifted from Caitlin to Parker and back again.

"I'm fine." Caitlin clicked her tongue in irritation. "I didn't sleep well, that's all."

So she'd been awake last night too. Parker caught her gaze, and to his amusement, she flushed. He grinned. This was the Caitlin he was getting to know. The Irish part of her that burned fiery and emotional instead of the cold outer shell she normally showed the world.

"I'll call you when I have news," Caitlin said to Parker. Turning on her heel, she strode down the hall.

"I'll text you about lunch!" Detective Crumb—no, Sally—yelled after the retreating form. Caitlin waved a response but didn't turn.

"What did you do to her?" Sally asked Parker bluntly.

"Nothing."

"It had better be nothing. I'm sure I don't have to remind you that I'm a police detective and Caitlin is my friend."

A none-too-subtle warning. "I get it." He jingled the keys in his hand. "Now where's my truck?"

"I'll show you."

Once inside his truck, Parker checked his phone. One message looked like it came from Dakota's phone, though he had never given her this number. He punched in the code to retrieve his messages.

"Daddy, it's me. Where are you? Why is Mommy so mad at you? She was calling you bad words, but I plugged my ears. I miss you a lot. I wish I could go to Grandma's. Oh, Mommy's coming. Bye."

She'd left the message last night after ten. He smiled, feeling happier than he had since having to say goodbye. He had to see her somehow. Since he hadn't yet been convicted of anything, there must be a way to secure visiting rights. This was America, after all. Wasn't he supposed to be innocent until proven guilty?

Only he'd learned that sometimes it didn't work that way, especially where custody issues were concerned, even if he knew he'd acted for Madison's benefit. He'd wait until she called again, and she would call. Madison was the most persistent child he knew. Well, really the only child he knew, unless he counted Amy. The two girls would love each other.

His smile faded. Unless they never had a chance to meet. He might not be allowed that close to Caitlin's personal life again. The knowledge was hard to take, given that every time he closed his eyes he saw her face with her eyes half shuttered, her lips lifting to meet his.

Then there was the more pressing problem of the drugs Dakota was using. He had to fight back, and that meant calling Family Services—calling them every day until they made an investigation. Someone had to protect Madison, and if the authorities wouldn't do it, he would be forced to take other measures. That his mother had packed his brother's old passport in his suitcase with his clothing told him she didn't have much confidence in the system and was already considering alternatives. He hoped using it wouldn't be necessary.

Turning on his phone, he searched for the number of Family

Services in Salt Lake. He spent the entire twenty-five-minute drive to work being transferred to one person and then another until finally landing with a Mrs. Turnball in CPS—which he assumed meant Child Protective Services. It took additional conversations during his breaks and his lunch to get her to agree, not to open a case against Dakota, but to a late meeting to discuss visitation. The terse Mrs. Turnball wasn't happy about the after-hours meeting, and the child advocate assigned to Madison's case, a Mr. Reeve, seemed even more annoyed when Parker finally caught up with him. But Parker had learned that part of success in anything depended upon your ability to keep talking politely when every hope seemed lost. Eventually they agreed to meet at six, and he was to bring representation if he had any.

He didn't—at least for visitation. Not yet. But maybe Caitlin would help this once. He was sure if Mrs. Turnball and Mr. Reeve met with him, he would be able to sway them to his side regarding visitation with Madison. If they recommended him, surely no judge would deny his request.

Shortly before his last break ended, his phone rang and he answered without checking the caller ID. At this rate, he'd better go to Manti and collect his real phone because his pre-purchased minutes were going fast. "Hello?"

"Daddy?"

"Madison. Oh, sweetheart, it's so good to hear your voice."

"Are you coming to get me on Friday?"

"I'm trying to. I have a meeting with some people today to make it happen."

"Good, 'cause I'm bored. Mommy just sleeps or talks to Leo. They keep kissing and kissing. It's gross."

"Are you eating well?"

"Leo said he's gonna take us to eat. But Mommy's gonna take us to her friend's house instead."

Parker nearly growled in frustration. He would be more than willing to watch Madison, and even the boy, Ricky, but Dakota would never allow that now unless she was forced to. "I meant did you eat anything today."

"Cereal, pizza. And we had crackers and milk. You know, the brown ones."

"Graham crackers?"

"Yeah."

"Sounds good."

"Ricky is here all the time now. His daddy went away to work."

"Is that good?"

"I like him here. We play, even though he's so little."

"Is Mommy acting funny?"

"No, but Ricky fell asleep. I'm bored."

"What about your princess books? You could look at them. You could draw me a picture."

"Okay. You want purple or pink?"

"I like both. Surprise me."

"Okay."

Parker wanted to stay on the phone forever with his little girl, but he had to get back to work. The money would be what would get them to a new life if Caitlin wasn't successful.

"I love you, Madison."

"I love you, too, Daddy."

Chapter 26

Caitlin regretted last night. But what she couldn't say for sure was if she regretted that the moment between her and Parker happened at all or if she regretted pushing him away. She was still thinking about him when a knock came on her office door.

"Come in," she called, looking up from the brief she was preparing—or pretending to prepare, since every few minutes she kept stopping to reread bits of Parker's file instead. She'd have to ask Jodi to go over the brief to make sure it was comprehensible.

Mace Keeley smiled at her from the doorway. "Hi. I was in the neighborhood and thought I'd stop by."

The Legal Defenders Association wasn't exactly on his normal beat, so Caitlin knew she should be flattered, but the truth was she'd forgotten all about Mace since she'd seen him last. When had that been anyway? It seemed she and Parker had been in a world completely apart from her real life. She shivered, not appreciating the comparison. Parker was a client who needed her help. End of story.

Mace sauntered forward as she stood. "So, today's the day."

"What?"

"Chet Belstead's sentencing."

"Oh, right." She'd worked hard this weekend to put Belstead out of her mind, though she would have to appear one last time in court with him, an unpleasantness that couldn't be avoided. Caitlin walked around her desk to stand beside Mace. "Too bad I couldn't get him to accept your plea deal."

"I'm glad you couldn't." He curved his lips in that beautiful smile. "That's good for everyone. Sorry you lost the case, though."

"Thanks. But I guess it worked out well for you. I don't think you've lost a case in years." She still had the files she'd asked Jodi to pull on her desk to prove it. She'd flipped through most of them and found only good work. "At least not one I'm familiar with."

Mace shrugged, leaning against her desk. "A streak of good luck."

He was closer than casual conversation merited, but Caitlin didn't back away. "I guess," she said, and then because she was an attorney and accustomed to probing for more, she added, "Maybe it's your case assignments you've been lucky with."

He pushed away from the desk, standing at his full height. "I wish they were all easy," he said. "Wouldn't that be nice?" There was a subtle tension in him that hadn't been there before. But why? It didn't seem a big thing to be assigned cases that happened to be open and shut. Every case needed a prosecutor.

Unless he'd engineered the assignments.

Something in her mind clicked, but she tried to reject the idea almost immediately. What would be the purpose of wrangling for easy cases? Half the satisfaction of being an attorney was matching wits with other competent counsel. Besides, such a thing didn't seem like the confident Mace Keeley.

"I've watched you in the courtroom," she added. "You do good work." She was honest in saying this, but his odd tension made her want to research further. Had all the cases he'd prosecuted—at least in connection with the LDA—been those with ample evidence against the defendants? That seemed to be true for the cases she could remember reviewing in Jodi's file. Even Wyman might have been able to do justice to most of them.

Mace relaxed, but that too was subtle. If she hadn't studied people as long as she had, she might not have noticed. But his next words showed her that he hadn't appreciated her comment. "What about you? Do you often lose because of condemning evidence showing up out of nowhere?"

Caitlin laughed. "My clients are almost always guilty. Believe me, that can happen anytime."

"Ah."

Her laughter had broken the tension between them, though there was still an odd look in his eyes. Caitlin didn't know him well enough to perceive what it might mean. His hands moved toward her, touching her arms lightly, pulling her closer.

Oh, that's what it means. Though she'd dreamed of this moment for months, her inner walls were rising fast. She'd spent the last five years trying *not* to get involved with anyone she worked with or went up against in court on even a semi-regular basis, and old habits were hard to break—even if it was with someone as good-looking as Mace.

His lips touched hers, so briefly she wondered why he'd bothered. It didn't last long enough for her to decide how she felt about it, or if she wanted to react. So different from the way she'd felt last night with Parker.

"I'm looking forward to our date on Saturday," he said.

One more thing she'd forgotten. Why had last night with Parker erased everything she'd held dear?

"Me too."

"Talking about these people you represent," he said, his hands falling from her. "I don't know how you do it. Like you said, they're often guilty. Don't you sometimes just want to do something to help lock them away?"

A chill rushed through Caitlin. "Well," she said without hesitating, "I did apply to the DA's office. Anyway, it makes no difference how I feel. I have a duty to protect my client, and that's what I do. It's only when a DA doesn't do a proper job that I have to set a criminal free."

He studied her face for a long moment. "I guess you're right."

She tilted her head. "So about the Hathaway case . . . will you be prosecuting?"

"The ex-wife wants us to go as far as we can. He is guilty. Is there any reason you feel we shouldn't prosecute?"

"He was trying to protect his daughter."

"If the police hadn't picked him up when they did, that mother might never have seen her little girl again."

That was also true. Caitlin felt weariness bow her shoulders. When she was with Parker, she believed in him completely, but he *had* taken Madison. Mace obviously believed it was a case he'd easily win, and if she didn't find evidence soon, Mace was going to use his charm in the courtroom to lock Parker away. Or at least keep him from Madison until she was too old to care.

Mace took a step toward the door. "About Saturday. Is six-thirty okay?"

"Perfect."

"I'll pick you up at your house. Wear something . . ." He paused. "Wear something dressy."

She nodded, lifting a hand in farewell. But he seemed to change his mind about leaving and came toward her again. His arms went around her and this time when he kissed her, she was left with no question about how he felt or about his kissing expertise. It was promising, and there was a measure of comfort in knowing she was still in control of her actions.

He continued the kiss, and she allowed herself to respond. Not unpleasant at all. Enjoyable, in fact. Too bad it had to follow last night's experience with Parker. That kind of wild abandon was hard to live up to. But Mace was more her type. She had to remember that.

Mace drew away, smiling. "Saturday," he said, giving her his brilliant smile. "You will love it. I promise."

She watched him leave. A scene like this had been in her daydreams for months, and the reality was pleasant. Yet at the same time his confidence irritated her. She leaned on the edge of her desk, frowning at the opened door, pondering both her feelings for Mace and his involvement in Parker's case. Mace seemed so sure that he would win, and he hadn't been wrong or lost a case in a very long while. It would be so much mentally easier if she were going up against Wyman.

Wyman. She had his direct number here somewhere, and maybe he could shed some insight on her idea about Mace's cases. Within a minute, she had closed the door to her office and punched in his number.

"Wyman Russell," he answered.

"Wyman, it's Caitlin McLoughlin."

"Caitlin. Good to hear from you! Did your guy Belstead decide to take the plea deal? It's too late, you know."

"That's not why I'm calling. Look, it's about Mace." She

walked across the room to the window. It had taken her two years to earn this office, but usually she was so busy she forgot to look outside. Snow still clung to the ground in some spots, though most had melted. There was no one in the parking lot except a man in a suit who was talking on a phone.

"Oh, and I was beginning to hope you'd consider working with me."

Was he hinting again at her giving him privileged information? Since he hadn't approached her privately this week, she'd begun to hope they'd left that behind. Well, she wouldn't take that crap. "Last I checked they don't have openings in the DA's office, so what do you mean by that? Just spit it out."

"Nothing nefarious, if that's what you're implying." He sounded surprised at her vehemence. "I'm leaving to start my own practice. Well, with an uncle of mine. I would have told you at our dinner the other night, but I hadn't turned in my resignation yet. I did that on Monday. I thought you might have heard."

"I hadn't." She struggled to wrap her mind around this new idea. Attorneys as bad as Wyman didn't simply start their own practices—unless they weren't really as bad as they seemed. Unless they'd been assigned all the difficult cases. She considered the implications. She'd prided herself on being a good attorney, but apparently she didn't know as much as she thought. "Uh, congratulations," she murmured, feeling completely stupid.

"We're looking for attorneys," Wyman added. "I'd love to have you work for us. Or you could always apply to the DA's office for my old job. I did mention Saturday night that there might be an opening soon. I just didn't say it was mine. I'm sure they'd snatch you up, if that's what you want."

"Oh." Caitlin felt stunned and also a little flattered. "Well, thank you. I'll think about it."

"So what was it you wanted to ask about Mace?"

Caitlin fought to regain her equilibrium. "I've looked at his cases, at least the ones he's prosecuted against LDA attorneys, and just now connected the dots. It looks as if they all might be obvious wins."

"And?" Apparently Wyman wasn't going to launch into an explanation as she'd hoped.

"I want to know if the other cases he's prosecuted, cases not with the LDA, are the same."

Wyman chuckled without mirth. "Every single one. You can bet he didn't horn in on the Belstead case because I was losing. It was because we found the evidence to put the guy away."

"I see." She had assumed Mace was helping Wyman because he hadn't wanted him to mess up the important case. But unless Wyman was lying, which at this point she wasn't ruling out, Mace's reasons had been far more self-serving. "How can he always get those assignments?"

"Who knows? He's got pull, or someone likes him. He's ambitious. Maybe all of the above. But that's all I'm going to say. I'm still here for two more weeks."

Caitlin nodded, though he couldn't see her. She let her mind run over the facts, sifting and sorting. If Wyman was leaving and wasn't trying to get her to betray her clients' confidences, then who had sent the aide to see Kenny?

"Wyman," she asked, "did you send anyone to talk to the private detective Kenny Pratt about the Belstead case? I hired him yesterday to do some work on a case for me. He knows I'm the LDA in the Belstead case, and he mentioned someone had been to see him about it. He couldn't make sense of it, and frankly neither can I—especially since it's over now."

"You know this Kenny Pratt is the one who lost the case for

you, right? I told you at your house last week the boy who called the police about the Belstead evidence did so only because a PI was asking questions. Since you're calling me about this, I'm assuming you've guessed that man was your friend, Kenny. He encouraged the witness to come forward. If he hadn't, the police might never have found the knife."

Caitlin was glad this conversation was taking place over the phone. No risk of her face giving her away. "Isn't that what any good citizen would do?"

"Maybe. The most important question, though, is why he was there in the first place. Do you know what case he was on or who he was working for?"

She forced her voice to remain steady. "Kenny doesn't report to me about his other cases. He works for a lot of people, and he obviously did what he thought was right. But I don't understand why this matters now."

There was a long pause before Wyman said, "I didn't send anyone to talk to Kenny, but someone from my office has talked to him because there are rumors about how the police might have discovered the information. I approached you because I wanted to make sure you weren't involved before I invited you to work at my new firm. But now that I'm leaving the DA's office, all this about a witness and Kenny Pratt are frankly none of my concern anymore."

Caitlin didn't respond, her brain still puzzling over who at the DA's office was behind the Kenny investigation. If Wyman wasn't, who was? She had a sinking feeling she might already know.

"Thank you," she said slowly to Wyman.

"No problem. But I'm going to tell you one more thing. Don't waste your time with Mace. He isn't worth it. And I meant what I said about you joining me in my new practice.

I think you're the best attorney the LDA has. Last Saturday night showed we'd work well together." A warm note entered his voice, one that might or might not be related only to friendship. Caitlin didn't ask.

"I'll think about it," she said.

"You do that."

Caitlin hung up. Her thoughts raced in all directions, but she had to get this brief finished before she grabbed something to eat and headed over to the court for the Belstead sentencing hearing.

Her phone began ringing—her cell, not the office phone—and she dived for her purse in the bottom drawer of her desk. The number belonged to Kenny Pratt.

She tapped the answer symbol and sat in her chair. "Hello?"

"Hi," he said without preamble. "I have news for you, but nothing I can prove yet."

"What do you mean?" For a moment she wondered if he was talking about the Belstead case and the DA's office. Her heart pounded with dread.

"It's that guy the ex-wife was supposed to be staying with at what your client thought was a meth house."

Relief rushed over her. Of course Kenny was talking about her new case. Parker's case. "Ron Hill?" she asked, checking her notes.

"Yeah. The reason the cops can't find any record of this guy is probably because he doesn't exist, but as I chatted up her friends, the name Ron Briggs came up. It's possible he was the one Dakota was with."

"But that was what, four months ago?"

"Three," Kenny corrected, "and it's important because if we can talk with him we might be able to prove he had a meth lab and that Dakota Allen knew about it and exposed her kids to it."

"Even if she isn't convicted, that would be enough for my

case. Especially when I bring in statistics about how many children die in drug-related deaths caused directly or indirectly by their parents."

"Well, if the mother's on drugs, that child is in more danger now than of being hit by a car, even if she was sitting in the middle of the road."

"We need to find this Ron . . ."

"Briggs. I'm on it. But if you could talk to your detective buddy at the police department, she might be able to get the information faster. They might not have a file on him, but it's worth checking. I'd call myself, but I'm rather busy at the moment."

"I'll call her and let you know."

"Good. Meanwhile, I'll follow up a few leads I have on Dakota's current lifestyle. And I mean follow literally; she's in her car in front of me now. If she's doing drugs, she'll mess up soon."

"Is Madison with her?"

"Yes, and the other child, too."

"How do they seem?"

"All right. She's using a car seat for the younger one, not the girl, though. Must not know it's a law, even at that age."

"Maybe we could have her pulled over for that. It would be a strike in our favor."

"Might be worth a try. I can tell the cops where she is at any moment."

"Let's see where this Ron Briggs lead goes first. Good job on that. Thanks."

"You're welcome. She's stopping. Gotta go." The phone went dead.

Caitlin was about to dial Sally when a knock at the door stopped her. Before she could call to whoever it was to come in, the door burst open and Sally entered.

"Good, you're here," Sally said.

"I was just going to call you." Caitlin slipped her phone back inside her purse and stood, motioning Sally inside. "What brings you here?"

Sally shrugged. "You were acting weird this morning. I know you have a full afternoon at court, and that you'll probably put off eating until too late, so I thought I'd stop by with lunch. Eat your turkey sandwich and tell me about last night."

Caitlin didn't hide her exasperation as Sally set a paper bag of takeout on her desk. "There's nothing wrong. But Kenny did come up with something we need you to check out. We think we discovered the real name of the guy Dakota Allen lived with at the meth house. Any information you can give us would be nice, but it'd really help if we could talk to him. We could use his testimony about the danger Dakota put Madison in. He might even know something about Dakota's current drug use." Caitlin leaned over and wrote on a card from her desk. "Here's his name—Ron Briggs. Not Hill."

"I'll look into it." Sally fingered the card, but her gaze never left Caitlin's face. "So are you going to tell me what happened last night?"

Caitlin sighed and sank into her chair, knowing Sally was too stubborn to let this go. "I took Parker back to my place for dinner after we found Amy. I knew he hadn't eaten all day, and dinner seemed the least I could do. He'd been so nice about Amy. But then Amy fell asleep, and we were alone . . ."

"And?" Sally put her hands on the desk, her brown eyes dark and eager.

Caitlin knew her face was burning a bright red. "Well, one thing led to another, and we kissed." She remembered all too vividly the desire that had seemed to spring from nowhere.

"How was it?"

"Good," Caitlin admitted. "It was totally wrong, but it was good."

"Then what?" Sally reached for the food bag and removed a wrapped sandwich, which she tossed to Caitlin. She kept a second for herself, unwrapping it as she settled into a chair.

"Nothing. Amy woke up. We ate dinner, and then I drove Parker to a motel."

Sally blinked in disgust. "That's all? No plans for a date?"

"He's a client." Caitlin unwrapped her sandwich, which smelled good enough to make her stomach rumble. "Do you know how many clients have made passes at me?"

"Most of them, I bet." Sally gave her a flat smile. "But he's not your typical client, is he?"

"No. Yes. He's a client. That's it."

Sally's eyes narrowed. "What aren't you telling me?"

That when he looks at me, I feel alive. That I want him to kiss me so badly, I'm afraid once it's over I won't be able to let go. But she couldn't say this to Sally or anyone. Before this moment, she hadn't even admitted it to herself. "I want a solid relationship. You should know that by now. Parker can't offer that."

"I'm only saying you won't ever know what you might be missing if you don't give it a chance. Who knows? Maybe he'll be the best thing that ever happened to you."

Or the worst. Too often in her line of business Caitlin had seen it work out that way. In the beginning her clients thought something was the best opportunity they'd ever encountered, but it ended up ruining their lives.

"I want what my parents had," she said quietly. "What you and Tony have."

"You aren't falling for this guy, are you?"

"No. I'm just . . . Amy's been talking a lot about babies lately. It reminded me that I'm not getting any younger."

"Ah, the biological clock. I hear you there. But that's exactly why you should give Parker a chance before you settle down. My husband is the steadiest guy around, and he's worked in construction all his life. And Parker's got muscles, you have to admit that."

"Sally," Caitlin groaned. Normally she didn't mind having a friend who seemed to think large muscles were a necessary quality in a man, but today was an exception. "You aren't hearing me. Besides, Parker isn't my type."

"You must be holding out for that gorgeous DA. Now, *that* I can completely understand."

Caitlin took the path of least resistance. "He came by this morning."

"Lip action?"

"Yep."

"Good?"

"He certainly knows what he's doing."

Sally nodded. "What he lacks in muscle he probably makes up for in technique. Still, you may find out that a pretty face doesn't do it for you. It never did for me, though Tony is cute in his own way."

"Not only is Tony handsome, but he's the only man alive who could keep up with you."

Sally laughed. "True." She lifted the card with Ron Briggs's name. "I'll get back to you on this, but don't forget what I told you. If you change your mind about Hathaway, I say go for it." She grinned knowingly at Caitlin before escaping from the room.

Propping her elbows on her desk, Caitlin let her head drop into her hands. She suspected she hadn't fooled Sally at all. And what if Sally was right? Maybe if she let herself go out with Parker a few times, she could get him out of her system and move on to something more permanent. Maybe.

She groaned. Who was she fooling? What if she was the one who got caught and couldn't walk away? Sally was right that her biological clock had kicked in when she'd least expected it, and what she wanted now was a real relationship. Her parents had been happily married to someone in the same profession, and if she was ever going to have a family, that's what she wanted for herself—a meeting not just of minds but of lives. With all his problems, Parker obviously wasn't the man for the job. Pushing these thoughts aside, she ate her sandwich with one hand and concentrated on finishing her brief.

On her way to the courthouse with a stomach full of turkey sandwich, Caitlin was feeling better. Seeing Chet Belstead sentenced would be the highlight of her day, and if she had to do it over again, she'd probably go through the same hoops to get him there. Some cases were worth losing big.

She'd barely arrived at the courthouse when she received a text message from Parker: *I meet with Family Services at 6. Will you come?*

She wasn't technically representing him in a custody case, but when it came to social services, having her there would be better than no representation. Since she'd never given him the name of anyone else to use, it was natural for him to turn to her. Between her cases that afternoon, she'd have to call in some favors and learn some fast custody tips from her attorney acquaintances. She was willing to do that. For Madison, of course.

She typed out a brief response: *Yes. Text me the address.*

Chapter 27

C het Belstead was sentenced to thirty years to life in prison for aggravated rape and attempted murder. That meant he'd serve at least thirty years, even if he became a model prisoner, and maybe when he came out, he'd be a changed man. Caitlin always hoped for the best. Some of her clients did learn, though she didn't hold much hope for Belstead. If he ever came into the system again, she would refuse to represent him. Not that he'd want her since she'd failed him this time. The whole case made her feel dirty, though the satisfaction on the faces of the victim's family had been some recompense for her breach of ethics.

When Sally called Caitlin later that afternoon, she still had one client to represent before the judge, but there were three others ahead of them, so she excused herself from the courtroom to answer.

"Bad news," Sally said. "Ron Briggs is dead. He was picked

up three weeks ago and charged with producing meth. He managed to suicide while he was out on bail. A drug overdose, of all things."

Caitlin groaned. "Just my luck."

"Well, we're still checking his cohorts. We suspect one guy was a partner, and although the house is abandoned now, we think he might be working elsewhere. These operations aren't usually run by one person. I have some names, and I'll forward them to your email, if that's okay. Maybe your PI can make some progress."

"That reminds me. I meant to ask you this earlier when you came to my office, but it slipped my mind." Which wasn't surprising in light of Sally's grilling about Parker. "Could I have Dakota pulled over for not using a car seat? Because she's not using one for Madison."

"That's actually a good idea."

"I'm hoping I can use it when we talk to Family Services in a few hours. Parker wants to see Madison."

"Of course he does."

"I'll call Kenny and have him text you her location. Provided she's still in her car."

"Okeydokey, I'll do my best. But keep in mind I'm pulling favors for you on this one."

"Hey, you're the one who brought me in on the case. You owe me."

"All right already. As soon as you give me a location, I'll drum up some uniforms to chase down Dakota Allen. But someday you might thank me for getting you involved."

"Why would you say that?"

"I got a hunch." Sally hung up before Caitlin could protest. Caitlin found a relatively quiet corner and accessed her email with her phone, forwarding to Kenny the names Sally had sent her. Then she called him to explain and to find out Dakota's location.

"Where's Dakota now?" Caitlin asked, after she caught him up. "Because I want to have her pulled over for the missing car seat as soon as possible."

"She's at home," Kenny said in a bored tone. "Must be sleeping, 'cuz the house looks dead except for every now and then the little girl looks out the window. It's freezing out here, so I wish something would happen. If I turn on the car too much, someone's bound to notice. Wait, someone just drove up in the driveway. A man. Big guy. Looks like a football jock who's gone to a bit of fat. Receding hairline, longish in back. Dopey look."

"Probably the new boyfriend."

"License plates don't match the notes you gave me. The car screams money."

"Can't be him, then. Supposedly, he drives a piece of junk."

"Maybe he's come into some dough."

"That would explain why Dakota doesn't need my client's money all of a sudden. Well, let me know when she's on the move. And did you get those names yet?"

"Yep. Already forwarded them to a contact while we've been talking."

"Thanks."

"Caitlin, how much budget you got for this case anyway?"

Caitlin hesitated before replying. Her budget at the LDA for outside services was extremely limited. Management went over expenses with a careful eye, and they didn't smile nicely on an attorney who went too far above and beyond in their defense of a client, especially an obviously guilty one.

"Enough," she told Kenny. "As long as we prove something."

"And if we don't?"

"I have savings." She cringed as she said this, not wanting to hear Kenny's response.

He was quiet a moment. "It means that much to you?" His tone wasn't condemning or deriding but rather curious.

"I want to help Madison." And then so he didn't think her a total pushover, she added, "Her father should be able to pay some too. He's working. And there's a grandmother."

"Okay. I'll be in touch."

Caitlin hung up the phone. Never before had she considered spending her own money on a client. As a public attorney, she didn't exactly have the highest pay scale, and she guarded funds carefully because of Amy. Her parents had left them a tiny trust fund and a small lump sum that she'd put down on their house, but many months she had to be careful in order to have enough for Amy's day care, her medicines, food, and the mortgage.

I'll make Parker pay me back. She smiled because somehow, though he had fewer resources at the moment than she did, she knew he would fulfill his obligations. According to the information Sally had found, he always did.

Caitlin arrived at the Department of Child and Family Services ten minutes early. She wasn't surprised to see Parker waiting in the cold outside the building, his shoulders hunched and his hands buried in his coat pockets for warmth. His face broke into a smile as she walked toward him.

"Thanks for coming."

Warmth spread through her. This man was beautiful. Not in the way that Mace Keeley was beautiful but in a way that made her nerves hum. Maybe she should take Sally's advice and see where the attraction took them.

His eyes passed briefly over her, communicating unmistakable approval. She wore only her regular gray business suit, but she flushed all the same. *Stupid Irish coloring,* she thought. Why was it so hard to maintain her poker face with him?

He smiled and said with a bit of amusement in his voice, "Miss me?"

"Desperately," she responded airily. "I always miss my most problematic clients."

"Well, thanks for coming." His smile didn't change, but his eyes burned into hers. Who was she fooling? Not him and not herself.

"Look, I told you once before," she said as they headed inside, "I have no experience in child custody cases, so I don't know what to expect. But I really don't hold any hope of them letting you see Madison until the case is over."

He held open the door. "I have to try."

Caitlin stopped in the lobby, studying him for a full minute without speaking. She remembered how his lips had felt on hers, how close their bodies had been in her kitchen. She remembered his concern for his daughter and how careful he'd been with Amy.

She clenched her hands at her sides, steeling herself against the emotion in his face. "Okay, but here's what I don't get." She kept her voice low so the few people talking to the receptionist at the desk across the room couldn't hear. "You said you'd do anything to get custody of Madison, yet there's no record of a court battle or anything like it. You gave up custody of your daughter without a fight, and what I want to know is why."

His face had drained of color, and for a moment she regretted the question, but she had to know.

"Madison isn't my, uh, biological daughter," he said finally, his voice tense. "I mean, Dakota and I were married when she got pregnant, and I thought Madison was mine, and I've loved her all these years like she was mine. But it turns out she isn't."

Caitlin's hands relaxed. That would explain a lot. If he wasn't the biological father, he would have little standing in court. "So how did you find out she wasn't yours?"

He toed the floor with a boot-clad foot that reminded her he'd come directly from work. She would have rather had him dress up for this meeting, but it was too late now.

"A few years after Madison was born, Dakota told me she'd been with someone else and that he was the father."

The torture in his face was real, but Caitlin wasn't about to go easy on him. "And you believed her? You gave up without a fight? Without proof?"

He blinked several times. "What do you mean? You know how much I love Madison, and how much I see her. I haven't given up anything."

"I'm saying you believed a woman whom you claim has used drugs in front of her own child. You said you were married at the time of Madison's conception. So were you actually with her at the time? Living as husband and wife?"

"Of course."

A woman passed near them, and Caitlin waited until she exited the lobby before saying, "Then how do you know Madison isn't yours?"

He looked decidedly uncomfortable. "I figured women know these things."

"And when did she tell you this? Not when things were good, I bet."

His head swung back and forth. "No. It was when Madison was two, and I came home from work and found Dakota and some of her friends passed out on drugs and Madison locked in the back bedroom, crying. I was going to leave with Madison, but Dakota told me she'd never let me take Madison because she wasn't mine."

"So you stayed."

"I stayed another year—and that's when she left. Went to live in that house where they were making meth. She had her son there, and I know for sure he isn't mine. Anyway, she let me see Madison as long as I agreed to all her terms of the divorce. She'd bring Madison to me then, and it was several months before I even found out where they were living. As soon as I found out where they were, I knew it wasn't a good situation, and I got her into the house they're in now."

"I hate to break this to you, but Dakota was probably lying to you about Madison."

"Maybe." He groaned, rubbing a hand across his face. "I can't believe I let her do this. I should have called the police the day I saw the drugs on her TV, or when she was doing drugs with her friends, but because I didn't, Madison's in danger every single day. That means it's my fault."

Caitlin's heart softened against her will. It was hard to keep up indifference toward this man whose one look made her knees tremble. "Look, you're not the first man this has happened to. If we can prove she's lying, it only makes your case stronger."

"And if she's telling the truth?"

She knew what he meant. If the court ordered a paternity test and he wasn't the father, he wouldn't have much standing, despite his years of devotion.

He shook his head. "I can't risk it." The ache in his voice made her want to comfort him. "Madison couldn't be any more mine no matter what genes she has. I couldn't love her any more or be any more responsible."

"At least we can play our cards a little better now that you know it's possible she's lying. If she doesn't bring it up, then we can assume either she doesn't know for sure herself who the father is—or she knows it's you and doesn't want you to find out. In that case, she won't want the court to ask for a paternity test."

Parker gave her a half-smile. "That makes sense. If she was sure, she'd bring it up right away."

"Well, she could be reluctant because it makes her look bad."

He frowned. "Then I guess I still don't know."

"You said yourself it didn't matter."

"It doesn't, except in the legal sense." He pulled out his phone and glanced at the display. "It's time. We should find Mrs. Turnball."

"All right. But let me do the talking."

Chapter 28

Parker shrugged off his coat as they sat in two of the three chairs in front of the desk. The woman facing them was unsmiling, her blond hair cut close around her face, curling under in one long, tight curl that made Parker want to fluff to see if the curl changed shape. The style was unbecoming and decades out of date, and her reddish complexion did little to enhance the whole picture. Wrinkles gathered around her eyes, and laugh lines carved into her face. Parker had been prepared to hate this woman by the crisp, no-nonsense tone of her voice, but her face told him that if she had one fault, it was caring too much. The sternness in her voice and the careful demeanor came from fighting for children, and he couldn't fault her for that, even if she was misguided in his case.

"Thank you for seeing me, Mrs. Turnball."

"You're welcome." Her abrupt tone hadn't changed from their phone conversation, but he could see she was reevaluating him. He knew he was considered good-looking by women, and in his youth he'd used it to his advantage. But something told him if he tried to charm Mrs. Turnball, she'd see right through it. She was accustomed to people trying to fool her, much like Caitlin was in her line of work. Better to be sincere.

Caitlin opened her briefcase on her lap and took out a pen. "My client would like to see his daughter."

"Uh, if you don't mind," Mrs. Turnball said, "the child advocate should be here during our conversation. If you'll wait a moment, I think I hear him coming down the hall."

A few seconds later, a man appeared. He was round and short and sported a thick goatee. Not at all like Parker had envisioned his daughter's appointed advocate. "Sorry I'm late," he puffed, out of breath.

Parker stood and offered his hand. "Mr. Reeve?"

"Yes." Mr. Reeve shook hands and then nodded to Mrs. Turnball and Caitlin before taking the last seat with a slight sigh of relief.

"Okay, now that we're all here . . ." Mrs. Turnball nodded to Caitlin.

"My client," Caitlin began again, "is here for two primary reasons. One, he'd like to see his daughter. Two, he would like CPS to open an investigation into his ex-wife's drug use."

"We only promised to discuss visiting rights," Mrs. Turnball said quickly.

Caitlin looked thoughtful. "I understand that is a primary concern, but Mr. Hathaway has reason to believe Madison is in immediate danger. He has personally seen drugs on the premises, and before he moved Dakota Allen and her daughter to the house where they now live, Dakota was living with a man who was picked up for having a meth lab on his premises."

"Are you sure she lived with this man? Will he swear to it?" asked Mrs. Turnball.

"He was out on bail when he committed suicide last week. A drug overdose."

"I see." Mrs. Turnball made a note on the paper lying on her desk.

Mr. Reeve grunted. "Is there any solid connection? Witnesses and so forth who can attest to her being at that place?"

When Caitlin didn't immediately respond, Parker said, "Not names or addresses I can give you." Caitlin frowned at him, her eyes telling him to shut up, but Parker couldn't stop. "The meth house isn't really the issue here. What Dakota is doing now is the problem. A few weeks ago I saw a bag of drugs on the couch. That's why I did what I did. I can't risk my daughter, and Dakota obviously isn't ready to grow up and take responsibility."

"Look." Mr. Reeve crossed his legs, leaning back on his seat, plump hands folded on his stomach, "we are overloaded with cases that are more severe than your daughter's, and given the circumstances, Mrs. Turnball can't open an investigation on just your word. You kidnapped your own daughter, Mr. Hathaway, and there are some who think you are inventing a drug problem for your ex-wife to protect yourself. If you had gone through channels—"

Parker leapt to his feet. "If I'd gone through channels, Madison might be dead right now, another headliner in the newspaper! This is a child we're talking about. My child. How can you sit there and do nothing to protect her?"

Caitlin was at his side, her hand on his arm. "Parker," she said in warning. "Please. Sit down."

He knew she meant sit down and shut up, but staring into her face, he saw compassion and strength. This was her territory, and if he wanted to do Madison any good, he had to trust her. With great effort, he clenched his jaw and sat back down. So much for his plan of getting his way with calm discussion.

"Please excuse my client," Caitlin said smoothly. "As you can tell, he's very emotional about his daughter, as all good parents are about their children. Keep in mind that we are certain Dakota Allen is a danger, and that will be a large part of his defense. In fact, my department has a private investigator looking into the matter now, and we are also cooperating with Detective Sally Crumb at the police department. We strongly feel it is only a matter of time until we are able to obtain solid evidence. However, that time is what we're worried about."

Mrs. Turnball shifted uncomfortably, her lips pursed in a near scowl. "There isn't much we can do about that. As Mr. Reeve said, we have thousands of cases, and not enough manpower."

"We just want someone to have a chat with Dakota Allen so she's aware there is suspicion. Maybe make a home visit to see things personally."

Mrs. Turnball nodded. "Actually, I have talked several times with Ms. Allen, and we did visit her home. We found nothing to cause suspicion."

"Was it a surprise visit?"

"No."

Caitlin nodded solemnly as if having proven a great point, though Parker couldn't tell if the others were impressed. They should be. She was incredibly confident, and her words made it seem as if the police were inches away from charging Dakota with drug abuse.

Regret once again filled him. If only he'd called the police that day when he'd seen the drugs. But in his youth, the police had always been someone you ran from, not turned to for help. How little he'd understood then how his actions would affect his future. Madison's future. Somehow he had to make it right for her.

"I'll take this under advisement," Mrs. Turnball said. "But until the police are able to give us what we need . . ." She lifted her shoulders and hands in a delicate shrug.

Caitlin inclined her head regally. "We appreciate any attention you give this matter. You should be aware, if you aren't already, that there is a paternal grandmother who is ready and willing to look after Madison until things are cleared up."

"We are aware of that," said Mrs. Turnball.

"As for visitation—" Caitlin began.

"The judge has denied all contact for the time being," Mr. Reeve interrupted.

Parker had heard that at the arraignment, but it hit him every bit as hard the second time. His hands tightened on the armrests, and he had to swallow several times to rid himself of the sudden lump in his throat. He blinked hard to prevent tears.

Caitlin's hand was on his arm again, and slowly he was able to relax. "We understand the reasoning behind this order," Caitlin said, "but my client has not been found guilty. He is worried about his daughter and wants to make sure she's all right. Also, Madison loves her father very much. She won't be able to understand why she can't see him."

"Let me save us a little time here," Mr. Reeve said, giving them a smile that was small despite the large size of his mouth. "I met with Madison before I came here. That's why I was late. Ms. Allen was pulled over for not using a child seat on the way to our appointment, so we got a late start. Madison does miss you a great deal, Mr. Hathaway, and I personally believe it would be in her best interest to continue seeing you." He glanced over at Parker and then away again quickly, as if embarrassed to see his emotion. "If you can manage to get the case before another judge, I would be willing to recommend supervised visits." He raised a hand as though to ward off another of Parker's rants, though Parker had no intention of losing control again. "That's the best I can do. I don't know any judge who would give more, no matter how strongly anyone urged it. And in good conscience, I can't request more. Madison needs security at the moment, and for better or worse, her mother's house gives that to her."

Parker wanted to break the man's head, but Caitlin was nodding. "We would very much appreciate your recommendation."

"We're finished here, then." Mrs. Turnball stood. "We'll keep in touch."

That was it? Parker felt numb. Did these people even see Madison as a person? "Please," he said, his voice sounding gruff even to his own ears. "Please help my little girl."

"We'll do everything we can, I assure you." Mrs. Turnball led the way to the door, ushering them out. Mr. Reeve stayed behind, and Parker felt their eyes on him as he moved with Caitlin down the hallway.

"What a waste of time," he murmured as they rounded a corner and the eyes fell away.

"On the contrary," Caitlin said, slowing to a stop. "With Mr. Reeve's promise, we'll be able to see a different judge and get you temporary visitation. That's something. Then there was the car seat incident. Not a good thing in their sight, I'm sure. I hoped Sally would get to it in time."

"That was your doing?"

Caitlin shrugged. "The law in Utah says that even four-year-olds need to be in some kind of a seat. Dakota wasn't using one and got pulled over. Anyway, I think you impressed Mrs. Turnball."

"Me?" He wanted to gape at her. "I lost control."

Caitlin's hand went to his face, her fingers sliding across his cheek and up to his eye. Her fingers came away wet. "I think it's apparent you love your daughter, that's all. What you said will stick in their minds. Those kids in Mrs. Turnball's thousand other cases might not have anyone to come in and fight for them. Their parents might not have representation. Everything helps in this game."

His skin burned where she had touched him. "Madison called me today. She's all right. So far."

Caitlin smiled. "I'm glad."

"Thanks for what you did in there."

"You're welcome."

They fell silent until they were outside the building. Parker knew he should thank her again and hurry to his truck, but as they neared her car, he said, "Look, I know you've already worked late, but would you like to have dinner? My treat."

She hesitated. "There are a few things we need to discuss right away," she said, "but I have to get back to Amy. Especially after last night."

"I meant her, too. Of course. I like Amy. She reminds me a lot of Madison. In how they think and act, anyway."

Caitlin's eyes met his, her top teeth coming down on her bottom lip. He followed the gesture, remembering how soft her lips had felt on his.

"Okay," she said finally. "But I'd better choose the place. Amy can be interesting to take out. We can't go to any restaurants with play areas for children because she's too tall for the height requirement. She gets really upset when the employees kick her off the equipment." She took out her phone to check the time. "Looks like I'd better pick her up now."

"I'll follow you," he said, motioning toward his truck parked several yards down from where they stood.

"What about a place to stay?" She asked this with a hint of reluctance, as if afraid he might want to spend the night at her place. But that was far from his plans. He wasn't into frustration; he already had enough problems to keep him up at night.

"I rented a room today in an apartment, sight unseen. I paid for a week, and I can stay on a weekly basis if I want to continue. There's no lease or strings, which is great given my situation. Like a motel, only cheaper. The apartment's in West Valley. Close to the construction site. Not too far from you. Supposed to be furnished and have laundry service once a week."

"Sounds perfect. If you don't like it, you can take your time to find something better."

"I'll probably need a different place for Madison when she stays with me." The words came with difficulty, because having Madison with him seemed almost impossible at the moment. He was glad Caitlin didn't remind him just how impossible.

Darkness had fallen while they'd been in the building, and the moonlight reminded him of last night when they'd been alone in the darkness of her house.

"Caitlin," he said.

"Yes?"

He wanted to kiss her. He wanted to take her in his arms and hold her. But he couldn't make her feel the same for him. It would have to be enough that she was willing to help Madison.

"Never mind." With effort, he turned and strode toward his truck.

Chapter 29

"You're going to *what?*" Sally asked, practically yelling the words.

Caitlin had to hold the phone away from her ear because the sound threatened to break her eardrum. "Stop screeching!"

"Well, you can't be serious about taking Amy with you to dinner. You complain all the time about how she gets when she's tired, and you sound as if you're about to drop yourself."

"It's been a long day," Caitlin admitted. "Maybe I should just go home."

"No, you deserve a dinner out, and you said yourself you had things you need to discuss with Parker."

"Nothing that can't wait. Keep in mind that usually I don't even see my clients more than once before trial."

"Parker's not just anyone."

"I know."

"Ah," Sally said, her voice rife with meaning.

"I didn't mean—"

"I'm picking up Amy, and I'll take her home to play with Randi. It's been too long since they've been together. And Tony loves Amy, you know that."

"It's not necessary, Sally. I'm really worried about setting her off again."

"Nonsense. She loves coming to my house. She'd *live* there if you'd let her. Now stop worrying and go out and have a nice, quiet dinner. And if something interesting presents itself, go for it." Sally hung up.

Something interesting? Sally's suggestion was altogether too close to Caitlin's private thoughts for comfort. She glanced in her rearview mirror where she could see Parker's truck following her. She turned on her blinker and pulled out of traffic. As Parker followed her to the side of the road, she dialed his phone.

"Hello?"

"Change of plans. Sally butted in and is taking Amy to play with her daughter. So we don't have to pick her up."

"Are you still all right with having dinner?"

She should say no. "Sure."

"Great. You know what? My new apartment is just down the street and around the corner. Why don't we lose one of these vehicles at the apartment complex and go together?"

"All right." Then in case she sounded too eager, she added, "We can talk about your case on the way."

A few minutes later, they pulled into the parking lot of an apartment complex at the edge of town. It wasn't top-of-the-line, but it didn't look seedy, either. "Want to come with me in the truck?" Parker asked.

"I'd rather take my car." That gave her some power, at least. He quirked an eyebrow. "Fine."

"Aren't you going to peek inside your apartment?" She was curious, she had to admit. What about roommates? He hadn't mentioned those. "You might need something they don't have— sheets or whatever. I can lend you some until you can get down to your mother's to get your things."

"Leave it to a woman to think of that. Remind me again after dinner, and I'll run inside before you leave."

Caitlin planned to make sure she also went inside to check out the place. She told herself her interest was as his attorney— she had to make sure everything looked good when they went to court—but she was honest enough to admit that it wasn't her only interest.

"Well?" he asked as she drove from the parking lot. "Where are we heading?"

Caitlin shrugged. "I was thinking of Golden Corral, mostly because of Amy. It's one of her favorites, but if she's not with us, how about Marie Callender's? The food's decent, and I really love their pecan pie." It was also more reasonably priced than the really excellent restaurants, and if Parker insisted on paying, she didn't want to stick him with a huge bill. He'd need every asset he could gather to fight for his daughter.

"Fine. Anything sounds good to me, as long as it's edible."

She laughed. "You wouldn't say that if you ate at as many restaurants as I do."

"Hot dates?" He gave her a crooked smile.

"A lot of working lunches. It's part of the game."

He tilted his head, and as the oncoming cars passed, illuminating his face, she could tell that he was considering her words. "Do you enjoy being a lawyer?"

Her first impulse was to spout off the same platitudes she told everyone when the question came up—that she loved her work, but the hours were sometimes a challenge. And then whip into some funny story about one of her past cases that would make them laugh and forget they'd ever tried to ask her such a personal question.

"I'm good at being an attorney," she said instead. "I don't know what else I would do."

"That wasn't the question."

"I know, but that's too hard to answer."

"Why?" He seemed honestly curious.

"Because some days I love it so much I want to sing." She smiled. "There's absolutely no better high than doing a great job and seeing the law work as it's supposed to. But there are the other times, far too many of them, when you wish you never had to see another criminal again."

"I suppose it's worse being a legal defender."

"You see a lot of evil everywhere, but it does seem lately that I've been given more than my share of the really bad guys." She thought of Belstead and shivered. "I should be flattered, though, because the harder and more serious the case, the more they trust you. It might even end up reflected in my pay someday." She'd reached the restaurant now and pulled into the parking lot.

Parker didn't respond as she searched for an empty spot. "There," she said, turning the wheel and coming to a stop. She set the emergency brake and glanced at him, but he made no move to exit the car.

"I'm sorry," he said quietly.

His stare made her feel uncomfortable. "For what?"

"For being one of the criminals you have to defend."

"What are you talking about?" She made no effort to hide her surprise. "You're one of the innocent. The ones I set out to protect way back when I was in law school."

He grinned. "Well, I'm glad I've convinced you of that."

"You don't have to worry. All I need is a little evidence, and we'll not only get you free of these charges, we'll bring Madison home." She meant his home, of course, but the way it came out seemed as if she were referring to a home they shared. Feeling self-conscious, she busied herself collecting her keys and purse.

"So what about you? Do you like your work?" she asked as they walked toward the restaurant.

"I do. A lot. I like working with my hands and building things, and it's not bad pay if you work your way up. I'll be taking out my contractor's license soon, after I'm sure I have a feel for everything." He held the restaurant door for her. "Then I'll be doing my own projects."

"Did you always like to build things?" She laughed. "I mean, I was always pretending to go to court as a child. Poor Amy was accused of more wrongdoings by the time she was five than most people are in ten lifetimes."

He laughed. "I bet. I can just see you."

"Of course I always got her off."

"What about now? Do you always get them off? The innocent ones, I mean."

Their hands brushed, sending a jolt of electricity through her veins. She swallowed hard. "Always. So far."

"Good."

Yet she'd always known there would come a time in her career when she might not win the case that should be won at all costs. It was assumed that such a thing would eventually happen in every career. She and other students had held endless debates about such an event in their college days, but so far she'd been able to win any case where she honestly believed the client to be innocent. Of course, in her line of work that might not be saying much, since she mostly defended the guilty.

Mostly.

She hoped her time to fail hadn't come with Parker. She didn't know if she could live with herself if he ended up behind bars.

Stop it, she told herself. *I'll find what I need to prove he was acting in Madison's best interest. Or at least that he thought he was.*

The restaurant wasn't busy this Wednesday evening, and the hostess seated them at a small table after only a short wait.

"I did build a lot of things when I was young," Parker said, opening his menu. "Though sometimes my family didn't appreciate it when I borrowed their belongings to use in construction."

"Something tells me there's a story or two behind that statement."

"My brother wasn't too happy when I used his bike to build my two-level go-cart. Or go-bus, as my friends and I called it."

"Go-bus." She had to smile at that.

"Yeah, it fit all three of my close friends. You should have seen us cruising around town."

"What'd your brother do?"

"Vincent didn't talk to me for two weeks." He winked. "That was actually a blessing. Because when he did talk, he was always trying to get me to do something I didn't want to do."

"Like what?"

"Like my chores, my homework."

"Ah, I see."

"I had to pay for the bike. I didn't know it, but my father was teaching me responsibility." The words came out low and thoughtful, and Caitlin had the impression that something in the memory had made him sad.

Before she could decide how to respond, Parker picked up

their former conversation. "What I like best about my job is that I have a lot of time to think."

"I wish I did. Sometimes the legal field is way too hectic."

His eyebrow quirked. "Only sometimes?"

She laughed. "Okay, all the time."

"I go camping in the summers. There's this bit of land my family owns out in the middle of a small valley near Mt. Pleasant. I've always dreamed of buying up all the rest of the land and building a house there. Room to walk. No neighbors too close. You know, where you can go out in your back yard and no one's around for miles."

She had the feeling he'd shared something he didn't normally talk about. "Sounds beautiful."

"Well, building the house isn't the most important thing to me anymore. Not since Madison."

"I can understand that." She'd once had dreams that hadn't involved mothering Amy—not that she would give Amy up for all the dreams in the world. Her sister was everything.

The waitress appeared before them, a big-boned, twenty-something brunette with heavy lipstick and a ponytail. "May I take your order?"

Parker ordered turkey with cranberries and mashed potatoes with no gravy, while she ordered the chili and cornbread. Cornbread was one of her favorites, but she didn't have it often.

"So," Parker said. "What do you dream about?"

She looked at him from beneath her eyelashes, wondering that he'd thought to ask. "I want to go back to Chicago where I was born, maybe for a year or two, or longer if I could make it work. I'd look up old family friends, visit a few of my father's favorite Irish pubs. You know. There are a lot of Irish people there who would have known my parents."

"So why haven't you gone?"

"I decided it'd be too difficult with Amy, especially on my own. She's settled here. We're settled. If my parents were alive, it might be a different story." Or if she had someone to help—but that wasn't a thing to say to a man whose presence made it difficult for her to remember what food she'd ordered. She shrugged. "I really haven't thought about it much in the past few years. I'm too busy." Not quite true. Sometimes she still thought about it, even while understanding that it wasn't likely to happen. To imagine herself walking down the roads she might have walked with her father as a child, to perhaps meet a few people who still spoke with the Irish accent that filled her soul with music.

"What happened to your parents?" he asked. "If you don't mind me asking."

"My mother got really sick. It went on for months, and the doctors didn't know what it was. When she died, my father took it really hard. He followed her the next year. It was a blessing, really, for him to go. He wasn't himself without her. I've never known a man who loved a woman so much. In fact, there was never another person for either of them from the day they first met."

There was comfortable silence as Parker appeared to consider her words. "He was a lucky man."

It was exactly the right answer. "They were both lucky. They found each other late in life, but it was enough. They were happy." If she found only half her parents' contentment, she'd be fortunate, though so far her luck in love had resulted in short relationships that had ended without fanfare or even much bitterness. Probably because she wasn't willing to settle for half the happiness she'd seen in her parents' relationship. Deep down, she wanted it all.

"You could still go to Chicago," Parker said, his eyes glittering in the dim light. "Amy would probably love it. I think living in an Irish community would be enjoyable. Especially if all the women look like you."

Caitlin knew it was a compliment, and she did feel beautiful at that moment. "Thank you."

"It's true." He held her gaze for a long moment and had opened his mouth to say something more when the waitress came back with their food.

What had he been going to say?

They ate, though it seemed neither of them was really hungry. Or at least not for food. They exchanged stories until their plates were empty and it was time to leave. Caitlin felt light and happy from laughing so much. Parker had a humorous side she hadn't expected, and he seemed as content to be with her as she was to be with him. As though they belonged together. She scarcely noticed anyone around them. Only when talking about his youth was he hesitant with information, and Caitlin wondered why. He seemed to adore his mother and talked about his father with respect. What had happened? She'd read in his file that both his father and brother had died in a car accident. He didn't bring it up, so perhaps it was too painful for him to discuss.

Parker insisted on paying the bill, as she suspected, and finally there were no more excuses to stay. "Well, we'd better get going," she said. "I still need to pick up Amy." They walked out into the crisp night. The air was tingly cold and the dark sky so clear that she could see the stars. She sighed in appreciation.

"You should see the stars in my little valley," he said, smiling. "They stand out like you wouldn't believe."

"I believe it." At that moment she'd believe anything.

The drive to his apartment went all too quickly. "Thanks," he said, reaching for the door. "It was nice."

It had been more than nice. She hadn't enjoyed herself so much with a man for as long as she could remember, and she was loath to have it end. "What about checking out your apartment? You might need sheets or whatever."

"Oh, right." He dug in his coat pocket and took out a paper. "Number 21-C. That means the second floor, I think." He started walking, and Caitlin locked her car and followed.

The three-bedroom apartment was clean, if worn, and the air inside hot and dry as though someone had turned up the heat. One of the bedrooms was locked, but the others had no sign of life. There was food in the fridge, labeled with the name "Bob."

"Apparently I have a roommate named Bob," Parker said.

"Could be short for Roberta." Caitlin would never under any circumstances rent a room without knowing her roommates. Even in college she'd been particular about that.

Parker laughed. "I doubt it. I guess I pick either of these rooms. Oh, wait. There's another key here. Maybe it fits one of the other bedrooms." He shrugged off his coat and experimented while Caitlin watched. He was wearing a flannel shirt, open at the neck where it revealed a T-shirt. He wore the clothes comfortably and with grace. She watched him move, unable to take her eyes away.

"Ah, it fits this door."

She stepped closer to see that the narrow room sported a bookshelf, a dresser, a small closet, and a single bed with folded sheets and blankets at one end. That was it. Not much bigger than a college dorm room.

He turned to leave and bumped into her. "Sorry," he said, taking a half-step back. "Didn't realize you were there."

The connection she'd felt previously sprang to life in that instant. They stared at each other without speaking. Caitlin willed him to reach out to her, but he stood motionless, his hands at his sides.

"Caitlin." His voice was low, almost a plea.

Everything was up to her. She understood that without question. She could turn and lead him out of the apartment, or she could reach out and touch him. She stepped forward.

He made a noise in his throat. "Last night you said . . ."

"Forget what I said." Even to her own ears, her voice sounded as though she'd just awakened, and in a way she had. She liked Parker. She wanted to get to know him. She wanted to take a chance.

His lips were on hers a second later, his arms pulling her close. She shivered at his touch, afraid and exhilarated all at once. So different from her practiced kiss with Mace Keeley earlier that day. She could feel the beating of his heart, pounding out a rhythm that matched her own.

Sally was right. Caitlin needed this. Maybe they could simply date a while and then she'd have him out of her system. If that was possible. She'd never before met a man like Parker Hathaway.

He kissed her again, this time more tenderly, as though his lips never wanted to leave her skin. She loved the taste of him, and his smell, slightly tinged with sweat from his workday. The tremors his touch sent through her. She wondered what it would be like to see him every day, the possibility of having him become a real part of her life.

At that thought everything shifted, and the feelings became far too significant to be contained in a temporary dating situation. If she wasn't careful, she could lose herself in him entirely. Not a wise thing to do with a man who had someone else in his life. Someone innocent and small who had to come first.

This was a huge mistake.

She pulled away, struggling for breath, for composure. Parker gave her his lazy smile. "What's wrong?"

"This is." She turned her face away, blinking against threatening tears.

"Caitlin." He sounded confused, and she knew he had a right to be.

"I'm sorry. I shouldn't have . . ." She had been going to say, "led you on," but she hadn't really been leading him on. Only herself. What made her think dating him for a few weeks would free her? It would only make her more vulnerable.

His reached for her chin, drawing her face around to him. "It's okay," he said hoarsely. He kissed her once more, brushing her lips lightly, and then whispered in her ear, "Come on. We should go now." He took her hand, leading her toward the door.

Nodding, she went with him, feeling unsteady as though walking in a dream.

Chapter 30

Caitlin awoke in her bed on Thursday morning. Weak light filtered in through her blinds, making a pattern on her quilt. The angle of the light told her it was still early but time to get up. She stretched as thoughts of Parker and last night came rushing back, both the fun time they'd had at dinner and the awkward encounter at the apartment. Everything had been so right, so natural—until the fear set in. After that, it had been a relief to escape alone to her car.

Oddly enough, she'd slept rather well—after reliving the scene only a half-dozen times.

Forcing herself from the bed, Caitlin showered and dressed for the day. She planned to get Parker in to see a family judge that day, or tomorrow at the latest. Then he'd get to see Madison. Maybe that would give him the patience to trust in the system.

Her phone rang. It was Kenny. "Hey," she said. "What's up?"

"Absolutely nothing. At least not yet. Some of my contacts

caught up with Ron Briggs's friends, but they claim they don't know Dakota Allen or anything about her drug use."

"What about the new boyfriend? Where'd he get that car?"

"A car dealership. He works there now."

Caitlin's heart plunged. "She had drugs at the house a few weeks ago. That doesn't just go away."

"I'm gonna find an excuse to go inside her house today. I have a uniform that looks like the gas—"

"I don't want to know details," Caitlin said hurriedly. She hoped he wasn't doing anything illegal.

"I'll look around as much as possible, but the police covered it when the girl was missing, so I don't expect anything big. She'll be careful."

"There has to be someone who can connect her to the drugs."

"If there is, I haven't seen any sign of them. But it's early yet. I have more people to talk to. Unfortunately, that means more time."

"Whatever it takes. My case hinges on finding something. If not, my client could serve time." Not finding any sort of evidence hadn't been a thing she'd considered seriously before. People using drugs just weren't that smart.

"She'll mess up sooner or later," Kenny said, voicing her thoughts. "It's only a matter of time."

Unless it was Parker who was lying. What if he'd made everything up to get off the charges? To evoke sympathy? He could be playing her even now. She didn't want to believe that, but even his tenderness at the apartment last night could have been a ploy.

"Keep trying. I'll talk to my friend at the police station later. Maybe she's had better luck."

"Later, then." Kenny disconnected the phone.

Caitlin stared at it and sighed. Where was Parker now? Already at work? Driving there? Was he thinking of her?

She flopped onto her bed, arms outstretched and tears running down her face. Suddenly she hated her life. She hated being an attorney and working with criminals. She wanted to change her name and run away to a deserted island and lie in the sun all day, sipping something cool and fruity.

"Caitlin?" Amy was in the doorway, watching her with concern, her shirt buttoned wrong and her hair standing up on one side.

For a minute Caitlin didn't move or speak. Amy came farther into the room, sitting down on the bed. "Are you sick?"

"No," Caitlin whispered. "Maybe." How could she tell her sister that she was falling in love with a man who might turn out to be a criminal? With a man who made her want to give up everything to be with him? One thing was sure, she was certainly crazy. She had to get a grip. On herself and on reality.

She forced herself to a seated position, wiping the tears away. "I'm fine, sweetie. Just tired."

"I love you, Caitlin." Amy's worried face hadn't changed, so Caitlin knew she was still transparent. Time to put on her attorney mask—and maybe she could keep it on the next time she saw Parker.

Caitlin scooted over to Amy and began re-buttoning her blouse. "What do you want to eat today? We still have some of your favorite cereal." She hoped her sister wouldn't plead for warm oatmeal with raisins. It was nearly time to leave.

"Okay." Amy's smile was back, and the tension was leaving her body. "But there's a surprise in the kitchen. It's for you."

"What?"

"He brought them. But he didn't stay. You were in the shower."

Caitlin jumped to her feet and ran to the kitchen. Sitting on the table where Parker had eaten the other night was a vase filled with sunflowers. *Sunflowers in November,* she thought. There was a card, and she opened it hastily. In bold letters it read: *I can wait. Parker.*

Caitlin gripped the note tightly in her hand, partially crumpling it.

"What does it say?" Amy asked.

"Nothing important." Caitlin opened a drawer and threw the note inside.

Sally had nothing new to report, the judge couldn't review Parker's case until the next day, and Kenny called to say he needed a few hours to work on another case. Caitlin began to worry.

Shortly before noon, Parker called. "Any news?"

"The judge will see us tomorrow." Caitlin tried to sound upbeat. She sat back in the chair behind her desk, crossing one leg over the other.

"That means I won't be able to see Madison tomorrow, doesn't it?"

She could imagine him raking a hand through his hair. "Most likely. They usually give the caregiver a day or so to work out arrangements."

"I can't stand this."

The fact that they had no leads or evidence on Dakota was more troubling to Caitlin, but she didn't want to make his day worse. "Look," she said, "can you name any more of Dakota's friends? Or people who might know what she's up to?"

"You haven't been able to find anything, have you?"

"We're still working on it. Don't worry too much."

"What about any news from CPS? Have they called?"

"No."

He was silent. "I'm worried. Madison hasn't called me again."

She started to say that Kenny was watching the house, but he wasn't at the moment, and come to think of it, he hadn't mentioned seeing Madison that day.

"You want me to trust the system," Parker said. "But it's driving me crazy not knowing that Madison's safe. What should I do? Can you go over there and check on her?"

"I don't have a reason."

"What about on some pretense as my attorney? Please, Caitlin."

She'd meant to thank him for the flowers, but now they seemed inconsequential. She swallowed hard. "I'll see what I can do."

"Thanks." He paused, and when he spoke again his voice was lower. "Will I see you today?"

"I don't know. Maybe." There was no real reason for them to meet, except that she wanted to see him.

She worked through lunch, and finally at four she loaded herself up with files, called it an early day, and went to pick up Amy. Instead of going home, she drove back to Salt Lake City, to the south side where Madison and Dakota lived. She parked across the street, surveying the house. The neighborhood was old and run-down, though not nearly as bad as where many of her clients lived. The yard around Dakota's house in particular had been let go, and the weeds had choked out much of the grass. A battered car was in the driveway, so Dakota was probably home. By every account, she didn't have any kind of a job.

"Is this where the little girl lives?"

"Yes." Caitlin had told Amy the bare minimum about Madison to stop her endless questions.

Amy undid her safety belt and opened the door. "Come on. I want to see her."

Caitlin felt a chill. What was she doing bringing Amy here? What if there was danger? Worse, what if there wasn't danger and Parker was obsessed? What if she was falling for a crazy man?

Falling.

She closed her eyes, willing those thoughts to a far corner in her mind. She'd brought Amy as her excuse. With Amy, she hoped Dakota wouldn't simply slam the door in her face. They walked up the crumbling steps and knocked on the door. Amy hummed under her breath, unconcerned, but Caitlin's empty stomach churned with acid.

The door opened, and to Caitlin's relief, Madison stood there dressed in shorts and a T-shirt. Her brown eyes lit up. "Caitlin! You remembered! Is this your sister?" She looked up at the towering Amy without fear. "She's big."

"She's tall, but she's only just a little older than you are. I came so you two could meet." Caitlin looked beyond the child, trying to sense if someone was in the room behind her.

"I like your dad," Amy said. "We had a tea party. I told him to hold out his pinky like this." She mimicked drinking tea.

"We could have a tea party," Madison said eagerly, opening the door wider. She shivered. "Brrr. Come in. It's cold out there."

Caitlin threw out an arm to stop Amy from rushing inside. "Is your mother here?"

"She's in the bedroom with my brother. I'll get her."

Caitlin allowed Amy to step inside far enough so they could close the door behind them. That gave them relief from the cold, and it would also be harder for Dakota to kick them out. Caitlin scanned the room, her eyes snagging on the worn couch. No small plastic bag of drugs on it today. Had there ever been? She continued her inspection. There was a coffee table with a stack of magazines, an end table with a container of wipes and a rolled-up diaper balanced on top, and a small television sitting on a scratched wooden cart in the corner of the room. The furniture didn't look new or particularly clean, but even with the dirty diaper, the room didn't look overly neglected. Someone had even recently vacuumed the greenish-brown carpet.

Caitlin had the sensation of movement down the hall, and Madison came back into sight, followed by Dakota, who carried a young toddler in her arms. She was wearing tight, low-riding jeans and an oversized sweatshirt. No shoes. Her roots had been redone, and her hair looked nice, if a bit too blond for Caitlin's taste. She appeared younger and less sharp than she had at the police station. She must have been sleeping, which would explain the mascara beneath the heavy-lidded eyes, the messy hair, and the half-asleep child in her arms.

Why was she sleeping at this time of day? Was she sleeping off drugs? Was she pregnant? Or maybe she'd had a late night with her boyfriend.

The tentative smile on Dakota's face vanished when she saw Caitlin. "You're Parker's lawyer," she said accusingly.

"I'm his court-appointed representative," Caitlin returned automatically. Sometimes those words helped because they made it clear that she wasn't being paid by the client himself, and that she hadn't solicited his business. Some might also assume she didn't have a choice in representing a client, though that wasn't quite true. She could walk away at any time, recusing herself from the case. Given her obsession with Parker, she probably should.

"But he's not why I'm here," Caitlin added hurriedly. "On Monday I told Madison about my sister and promised I'd let them meet. Today seemed like a good opportunity to keep my promise."

"Caitlin picked me up early," Amy put in. "She's usually late. I hate it when she's late." She lowered her voice and added to Madison, "She's always too tired to have tea."

"My tea set's in the kitchen." Madison took a step in that direction, signaling for Amy to follow.

"Madison!" her mother said sharply. "They aren't staying."

Madison frowned. "But—"

"She's right," Caitlin interjected. "We only stopped by for a minute." Caitlin met Dakota's eyes. "Maybe we can get them together another day."

Dakota's lips pursed. "You're defending him," she hissed. "He took my baby."

Madison's eyes grew wide, and she looked ready to cry. "Mommy," she whined. The little boy in Dakota's arms lifted his head to stare into his mother's face. After a few seconds of looking, he kicked to get down and then toddled over to his sister, who put her arm around him. He was a beautiful child, Caitlin saw, as beautiful as Madison. Dakota certainly had good genes when it came to children.

Caitlin's mind searched for a way to defuse the situation. "I'm sorry we came. I thought the girls might like the company. I know what it's like being a single mother. Sort of. I have custody of Amy. She's a special girl and likes to play with girls her, uh, intellectual age."

For the first time, Dakota's attention shifted to Amy, who was squatted now on the ground, talking to the little boy and giggling like a child. "Oh," Dakota said, the anger gone from her voice.

"Well, we should be going now." Caitlin motioned to her sister. "Come on, Amy."

Dakota narrowed her eyes. "You really didn't come to talk about Parker?"

"No. In fact, we probably shouldn't talk about the case at all. The DDA is representing the state in the case against your ex-husband, not you, but I'm sure he wouldn't want you to talk to me about it." If Mace had been Dakota's attorney in the typical sense, Caitlin could be in real trouble coming here at all. She would have a chance to depose Dakota during preparation for the trial, of course, but that would be officially recorded with both her and someone from the DA's office present at the meeting.

Dakota's face brightened at the mention of Mace. "I told him everything," she said.

At a loss to know how to respond to that, Caitlin said, "He's a nice guy." Truthfully, she had barely thought of Mace since he'd kissed her the day before, but she could still remember when he'd been on her mind almost constantly. Before she'd met Parker.

"I'll say. Really nice." Dakota actually smiled. "We've spoken several times. Apparently, he's brilliant. Never loses a case."

Caitlin wondered who had told her that. "He is very good in the courtroom. Has a certain flair." *Almost like an actor.*

Dakota relaxed further, her blue eyes gleaming. "If I wasn't getting married . . ." She lifted her brow suggestively.

"I know exactly what you mean." Caitlin stifled the urge to laugh. How ludicrous to think Mace would ever consider a relationship with someone like Dakota Allen.

Yet what had Dakota been like when she and Parker had first met? It must have been about ten years ago, when they were barely out of their teens. They would have been full of youth and life, determined to enjoy themselves, doing what they saw as bucking the system. Parker was a different man now, or so the reports indicated. Something had caused him to change. Had it only been Madison's birth? Maybe.

Yet perhaps there was something more, something she'd overlooked. She'd have to go through the reports again to see if they contained a hint of what that could be.

Did it really matter?

Yes. Because if something hadn't changed him, maybe he wasn't really changed. Maybe he'd simply become better at lying.

Blocking these thoughts, Caitlin forced her mind back to the conversation. "You're getting married?"

"Yes. As soon as all this is behind me." Dakota fluttered her hands, making sure Caitlin saw the small diamond ring on her finger.

"Do you plan to sue for full custody?"

"I have full custody now. I always have. Parker only has weekend visiting rights two times a month. But soon I'll be able to make sure he doesn't keep—" Dakota broke off as though suddenly becoming aware that the children were listening. "Go to the kitchen and show her the tea set," she told Madison.

When the girls were gone, Dakota continued, her voice lowered. "Anyway, when Madison was missing, it was an awful time. I was so afraid."

So afraid that according to Sally, she'd waited several hours before calling the police.

Caitlin chose her words carefully. "I've talked a lot in the past few days with your ex-husband, Ms. Allen. I know what he did, and that it was wrong, but oddly enough he seems dedicated to his daughter."

Tears sprang to Dakota's eyes. "Everybody believes him, but you don't know him like I do. I had to live with him. He's controlling. He forces you to do what he wants. I couldn't stay with him."

Caitlin thought of how Parker had acted last night at his apartment. She thought of the flowers and the note: *I can wait.* In her book, those weren't the words of a controlling man. But if Dakota had felt half the attraction for Parker that Caitlin felt, even a suggestion from Parker might have seemed that way. Yet hadn't it been Dakota who'd walked away from the relationship? Dakota who claimed Madison wasn't Parker's child?

Dakota was watching her, but Caitlin couldn't tell if the gaze was calculating or honest. "I see," Caitlin said. "Well, we really should go."

"When this is all over, I wouldn't mind you coming by with your sister. Is she good with children?"

Caitlin had thought Dakota understood about Amy, but she didn't. Not really. "Amy loves children," she said, not bothering to explain again.

On the way home, Amy was full of conversation about her "new friend and the cute little boy." Caitlin let the sounds roll over her. She should call Parker and tell him what happened. At least he'd know that for the moment, Madison was fine.

She didn't want to call him. Despite all her blossoming doubts, she wanted to *see* him. Yet showing up at his apartment today wasn't practical or wise. Or attorney-like. Instead, she'd give him a call when she arrived home, using her best business voice. As though nothing personal existed between them.

In the end, there was no need for the call. When she pulled up at her house, Parker's blue truck was sitting in front. "You're late," he called cheerfully, lugging two grocery sacks up to the garage, where Amy ran to him excitedly.

"What are you doing here?" Amy asked.

"Bringing you dinner. I missed you last night, and you did say those pizza pie things were your favorite food, didn't you? I hope I got the right kind."

Amy delved into the grocery bag he extended toward her. "Yay!" she shouted.

Caitlin reached his side more decorously, though her heart was skipping ahead. He grinned. "For us there's steak. Do you like steak?" He hesitated, furrowing one eyebrow. "Do you know how to make it?"

She laughed. "Slap it in a pan and turn on the stove. Or I have a barbecue out back, if you want to brave the cold."

"Now that's something I can do. My coat is warm enough." Amy was already inside the house, still giggling over her treat.

Caitlin met Parker's eyes. "I just came from Dakota's." He held very still, waiting, his eyes intense.

"She wasn't very happy to see me, but Madison's fine."

"How did Dakota look?"

"Sleepy. I think I woke her up. I don't know who sleeps at this time of day. Maybe she got a new job we don't know about."

He shook his head. "She does that sometimes. Takes something in the morning and sleeps all afternoon."

"Something as in drugs?" He nodded.

Caitlin felt his worry; it poured off him as strongly as his desire for her the night before. "Well, Madison's okay for now, and we're working on the rest. Come on. Let's go fire up the grill."

Chapter 31

Out on Caitlin's tiny back deck, Parker stood before the barbecue grill, struggling to recapture the happiness he'd felt at being with Caitlin again. Yet after hearing about Dakota, his thoughts kept going to Madison. Weekends were the best party times in Dakota's view. He'd usually taken Madison during most weekends, though officially the agreement was every other week, so what would Dakota do with Madison now?

He reached for the spatula and flipped over the steaks. His breath curled white into the cold air.

"How're they coming?" Caitlin asked, slipping through the partially open glass door.

He smiled at her appearance. She'd changed from her customary suit to black pants and a snug cream-colored top. Her hair was down, and she looked so inviting that it was all he could do to remain moping at the grill.

"Nearly there. Just a bit more on the first side again."

She looked out over her small back yard, which was still an expanse of dirt, the moonlight reflecting from her blue eyes. She was beautiful. But he needed to keep his distance. After last night, he couldn't trust himself not to kiss her and scare her away. Every physical instinct told him they had something special, something he should act on immediately. But his mind knew that was not the way it worked. If he wanted more with Caitlin, more than a few weeks of casual dating, he had to wait.

Wait until what? He wasn't exactly sure. Wait until she fell in love with him? Until she was sure? Until the case was over?

Although his decision to wait had seemed so simple—even noble—last night and even this morning when he'd bought the flowers, now he was no longer sure. His hopes of proving to the world that Madison was in danger were swiftly being shot down, and that brought him closer to acting. He must save Madison one way or another, and for the moment that meant not letting things go too far with Caitlin. He didn't want to hurt her. She wasn't just a beautiful face anymore, but a woman whose every word thrilled him. A woman who tenderly took care of her sister, a woman who ferociously went after what she believed to be right. A woman with dreams that seemed as unattainable as his own. That was why he'd pulled back last night when she'd hesitated, and why he wouldn't touch her now. She deserved more, but he couldn't allow his growing feelings for her make him unwilling to do what might be necessary to save his daughter. He knew Dakota, and he knew what had happened in the past.

"Penny for your thoughts." Caitlin's arm brushed against his coat.

That if I kiss you again, I'll never be able to leave. He forced a grin. "My thoughts are worth way more than a penny, but I was thinking about your lawn. I know a guy who delivers sod. Gather a few neighbors, and in an afternoon next summer, you'll have a nice place for Amy to play."

"I'll ask you for his name then. Next summer."

It wasn't a question, not quite, but he wished more than anything that he could promise to be there to help, to arrange it all. He could lay the sod himself in a few hours. Instead he only said, "I think the meat is ready."

"Great. Let's go in."

His thoughts were jumbled. This scene—a man, a woman, and Amy acting the child—was so . . . right, and yet wrong because Madison wasn't there. Parker ate quickly, wondering what he could do to get himself away. He'd been wrong to come here, wrong to assume he could pursue a normal relationship with a woman as classy and beautiful as Caitlin. There were too many consequences for both of them. He raked a hand through his hair.

"You're going to pull all your hair out." Amy grinned at him, much in the way that Madison would have. His heart ached.

"Your phone," Caitlin said. "Isn't that your phone?"

He grabbed it quickly. "Hello?"

"Daddy?" Madison's voice came loudly across the line.

"Hi, baby. Are you okay?"

"Ricky is crying and crying and Mommy's in the bedroom. She won't answer the door."

"Okay, sweetheart, don't worry. It'll be okay. Just stay on the phone." He covered the receiver. "It's Madison. She says her brother's crying, and she can't get Dakota to answer the door to her bedroom."

"You can't go over there. We'll have to call the police." Caitlin reached for her phone. "Or at least Sally."

Madison was speaking again, and Parker tried to focus on

what she was saying, but her words were abruptly cut off. There was a brief flurry of noise, the phone dropping to the floor, and then a terse woman's voice. "Parker, is that you? I told you not to call here. You have no right!"

Parker thought quickly. He didn't want to give Madison away by admitting that she'd been the one to dial his number. "I wanted to talk to you," he lied. "But Madison said her brother was crying and that you weren't around."

"I was right here," Dakota snapped. "What did you want?"

"To let you know there's going to be a hearing tomorrow, about visitation."

"I know, and I'm going to fight you on it."

"Please, Dakota. I just want to see her. That's all."

"Leave us alone." She hung up.

Parker stared at the phone a few seconds before shoving it back into his pocket.

"I'm sorry," Caitlin said.

He shrugged. "It's okay." He looked at his nearly empty plate. "Thanks for letting me barge in, but I've got to go now." He pushed back his chair and stood.

"You don't have to go." She arose and stepped close, too close, driving his thoughts away from Madison.

"Yes, I do." He looked back and forth between Caitlin and Amy, who watched him with her wide green eyes. For a moment he wanted to weep for the woman Amy might have become. Or was it for himself and Caitlin? Definitely for Madison. She was paying for his poor choices. If only he hadn't been a rebellious idiot growing up. If only he'd been more like his big brother.

He shut his eyes briefly, pushing away thoughts of Vincent. He strode toward the door, and Caitlin hurried after him.

"Parker, you can't do anything about this. You can't go over there. If you're still worried, I'll call Sally and have her send someone, but you have to remember the restraining order. If you have any hope of gaining visitation rights tomorrow, you must not violate that. I'm speaking as your attorney, and as your friend."

"Friend?" He smiled, hoping that would take off some of the mockery he'd injected into the word.

"Yes," she said softly.

They stood staring at each other for a long moment. Parker wanted to lose himself in her. He wanted a normal life.

He forced himself to look away, to open the door. "I'll see you tomorrow." His voice was gruff. Glancing back, he saw her nod, her lips slightly parted, her tongue wetting her bottom lip. She didn't look at all like his lawyer. With a groan, he reversed his step, coming so close to her that they were almost touching. He kissed her, cutting off the kiss before she had time to respond properly. Knowing that if he held the contact a second longer, he wouldn't be able to remember that he was first and foremost a father. Within seconds he was out the door and jogging to his truck, feeling Caitlin's gaze following him.

He drove to Salt Lake and parked two blocks south of Dakota's house. He slipped out of the truck, going on foot from yard to yard. The many evergreen trees and the over-grown shrubbery with dead leaves still attached lent themselves to subterfuge. Soon he was in the back yard, careful to keep to the far side and to not make any noise that would alert the dog next door. From his vantage point, he could look into the large kitchen window, glowing with warmth in the dark night. Madison was at the table eating something. Her brother was in a high chair nearby. Dakota wasn't in view, but he sensed movement off to the side.

The air was so cold it bit into his lungs, but that wasn't what brought the tears to his eyes. He slumped against the huge trunk of a bare tree, weak with relief. *She's okay.*

The sound of a car interrupted his thoughts. Probably the boyfriend. Sure enough, the new car Caitlin had told him about turned into the driveway, pulling to the side of the house where the garage should have been, if the owner had built one. He watched as the big man walked to the side door that led into the kitchen. It hurt to know that another man could be with his daughter when Parker couldn't.

In minutes Parker was back in his truck, but he didn't start the engine. Looking out at the dirty remains of the snow on the road, he cried.

Chapter 32

On Friday morning at the courthouse, Parker smiled at Caitlin, wondering why he felt so nervous to see his daughter when doing so was what he'd been fighting for. After talking to Madison and the child advocate, the judge had agreed to allow Parker three supervised visits a week with Madison.

"No time like the present," the judge responded to Caitlin's question about when the visits could begin. Then he assigned Caitlin to be the supervisor for the first visit that would take place immediately in a room down the hall, though normal visits would occur at a different location with a regular facilitator, the cost of both to be paid by Parker.

As Madison entered the room, Parker could hear Dakota shrieking in the hall. "He steals my baby and now he gets to—" The closing door cut off her remaining words.

Madison ran to him. "Daddy!"

He'd never seen her smile so bright. "Madison." He held

her close for a long moment, her little arms wrapping tightly around his neck. He drew back to kiss her cheeks, then held her again more tightly, blinking furiously to stop the tears. He met Caitlin's gaze over Madison's shoulder. She smiled and he nodded gratefully. She was right; this was better than nothing.

Madison was talking and talking, telling him about her dream last night, about the new car she'd ridden in, and getting pulled over by the policeman for not being in a car seat. "Mommy was so mad," she confided. "But the policeman was nice to me." Then there was Ricky and how he was finally learning how to hold a cup instead of his bottle. Her voice lowered. "But most of the time, he spills it on the floor."

Parker let the words soak into him, content to hear her voice and understanding that the meaning wasn't nearly so important as their being together. At the same time, he was aware of Caitlin watching them and the fact that Dakota was outside the door, seething in fury. Well, privacy shouldn't be as important to him, either. Not now.

He hadn't counted on Madison's boredom. After ten minutes of nonstop talking, she asked, "Can we go see Grandma?"

"No, honey. We have to stay here at the courthouse today. Maybe next time we can work out something better. Maybe we could go sledding." He shouldn't have said that because the judge had been clear that he could see her only inside and closely supervised. Today Caitlin was responsible for making sure they didn't take off, and even if she let them slip away, there was still Dakota standing guard at the door. He could see her angry face periodically in the tiny rectangular window next to the door.

Well, maybe his mother could supervise the next visit. If she could get approved, she'd be far more lenient.

Staying in the room was a little like being in prison, and it made him feel guilty, as though he'd done something so terrible that Madison was forced to pay the price of visiting him. They played with his phone, told stories, and looked out the window. The minutes ticked by slowly, and though Madison started to cry when it was time to go, Parker could also sense her relief at finally being able to *do* something. For her, an hour of forced confinement in one small room with few distractions was torture. He'd have to come better prepared the next time. If they didn't put him in a real prison first.

He hugged Madison close, wiping her tears. "Look, sweetie, don't be sad. There's something more. A secret."

"What?"

Parker looked up to make sure Caitlin was out of earshot. "I might be able to come see you soon. If I do, I'll throw a little rock at your window, and you can look out and wave. Okay? Don't open the window or anything, unless you see it's really me."

Madison's smile returned. "Okay," she whispered. "And then we'll go see Grandma."

He let her think that. "Don't tell anyone."

"I won't."

"It's time to go now."

"I love you, Daddy."

"I love you too, Madison. You're my best girl. Forever." He motioned to Caitlin and she came over. "Go with Ms. McLoughlin, okay?"

"Her name is Caitlin, Daddy." Madison looked up at Caitlin. "Am I going to see your sister again?"

"I wish, but we can't today. I'm sorry. Come on." Caitlin held out her hand and Madison took it. Parker watched as they vanished through the door, feeling a sadness that sat in his stomach like a ball of lead.

Caitlin returned within minutes, walking slowly across the room to sit beside him. "She's so adorable. Gave me a big hug before she left."

"She likes you."

"I like her too." She placed a hand on his arm, obviously sensing his distress. "It'll be better somewhere else. They have toys and things. Yards, too. Or so I hear."

"It's cold outside. She wouldn't last long." He let his head drop to his hands, trying not to feel anything. "I need to have unsupervised visitation."

There was silence for long seconds and then, "If you were allowed unsupervised visits, can you honestly tell me you wouldn't disappear?"

"Are you asking for her or because of us?"

She looked away and said quietly, "Does it matter?"

He thought a moment and then shook his head once, sharply. "I guess it doesn't. But it's a fair question. She's still in danger, and leaving might be the only way to save her life. Unless you've found something we can use. Have you?" The question was tinged with hope. She'd been talking on the phone for most of this bittersweet hour. Maybe she had good news.

She shook her head. "I'm sorry. The private investigator is still coming up dry. Dakota must have really gone out of her way to clear any tracks. But don't worry, he's not giving up. Not yet. Of course, this makes our case a lot more difficult. The more time passes, the harder this is going to be to prove— especially if she really is clean."

A chill crept down his back. "She isn't. Is there a way to make her take a drug test?"

"I'll certainly try, but the motion will likely be denied without any other proof factors."

"Are you telling me I'm going to prison?"

"No." She stood, moving to stand in front of him. "I believe you, and I will find something on Dakota."

The way she said it, he knew she'd begun to have doubts. He wasn't prepared for how much that hurt him. Why should he care? A week ago, he didn't even know her name. So what if she felt right, if they felt right together? So what if she no longer believed? None of it mattered in the face of Madison's danger.

He rubbed a hand across his face. "I'd better get to work." He stood, looking past her, not wanting to see that truth in her eyes.

"Parker."

He hesitated. "Yes?"

"I'm doing my best."

He met her gaze directly. "What if your best isn't good enough?"

She bit her lip, making him vividly recall their kisses. "It will be."

He nodded and took a step toward the door.

"Parker."

He stopped again.

"When did you change? You rebelled all your teenage years. You were living with Dakota, going along with that sort of life, and then everything changed. You said once before it was because Madison was born, but that wasn't all, was it?"

At first he wasn't going to answer. She had to already know Vincent was dead, if not what it meant to him. That was his own private hell, and not any of her business. But her doubt made him want to convince her. He needed her to believe again.

"I had a brother," he began. "He was the perfect one. Always compliant, the obedient, favorite son, while I bucked against every rule my father set down. I used to time how fast I could make my father angry. Five seconds was my record." The thought made him sick now. "I was determined to be everything my brother wasn't. He earned scholarships, he could fix almost anything, he was brilliant. I was nothing compared to him. And then one day they were in a car and there was an accident, and they died. Madison had been born just before that, and I already had regrets, but suddenly all the regrets in the world didn't matter." Tears blurred her face and he looked away. "I could never tell my dad I was sorry. I could never tell my brother how proud I was of him. I'd let all the opportunities slide by. There was only my mother, and I was all she had left. It was time to grow up. So I did."

She took a tentative step toward him. "For the record, I think you turned out great."

Still, he knew she didn't trust him. Not yet. Maybe not ever. He'd been a fool to think she could. Nodding in her direction, he started again for the door.

"Call me if you need anything. I'll be home tonight." It was an invitation, one he couldn't afford to accept because he'd already made a choice.

"I'll be working late," he said. "To make up for this morning."

She nodded. Was that disappointment in her eyes? It was all he could do not to walk over and take her in his arms.

He strode quickly out of the room and down the hall, looking back only once. Caitlin had followed him into the hallway and was now talking to that pretty-faced DA, the one who wanted to put him in prison. She was smiling. The man put a hand on her back, leaning forward as though concentrating on what she was saying. Touching her.

This was a man from Caitlin's world, the kind of man

who wore suits and who worked out in a gym where there was always water and soap nearby. A man who spoke the language of depositions and briefs and arraignments.

Yet she had kissed Parker.

Stop.

It was over. After tonight there would be no reason to worry about Caitlin.

Chapter 33

"I don't know," Caitlin said to Mace, aware of how close he was. With difficulty, she forced her mind from Parker and the disappointing visit with Madison. "Tonight is hard."

"You have to work?"

"No," she said, and then immediately wished she'd lied. In a lower voice she added, "It's my sister."

"Your sister?"

He leaned forward to better hear her reply, placing a warm hand on her waist. As she stiffened with surprise at this public display, she spied Parker at the end of the hall, heading out of the courthouse. Their gazes met only briefly before he was gone.

It's not what you think, she wanted to yell after him. But wasn't it? Last week she'd dreamed of being somewhere romantic with Mace.

So what did she really want?

Two young attorneys she didn't recognize walked by, their conversation abruptly ceasing. They nodded as they passed, both ogling Caitlin and giving knowing smiles to Mace. She could have sworn one winked.

Men.

"What if we made it short tonight?" Mace said. "I really have to be at that meeting with the district attorney tomorrow evening. I hate changing our date, but it's sort of an emergency thing." He lowered his voice and added, "Rumor has it she'll be announcing the retirement of the assistant district attorney. That means his job will be open."

His excitement made it clear he was angling for the job. The assistant deputy attorney supervised the district attorney's office and answered directly to the DA. It was a significant step above Mace's current job as a deputy district attorney, but she couldn't see the purpose. Who'd want to spend more time managing than actually being in the courtroom?

"The ADA is not the only one leaving," Mace added. "Wyman put in his two weeks. Did you hear?"

"Yeah, I knew about that. He's opening his own firm, right?"

Mace snorted. "Hopefully, he doesn't go belly up. His uncle's been an attorney a long time, and he has deep pockets, but Wyman might not have quit if he'd realized the ADA position would be open. Too bad for him." He paused a moment before hurrying on. "I could pick you up right at five tonight. We can have a quick dinner and talk. There's something important we have to discuss."

Caitlin was tempted to agree, but what if Parker showed up at her house and she wasn't there? He needed her. Or was she fooling herself? "Why don't we discuss whatever it is right now? I can make time."

Mace looked momentarily flustered, his eyes darting around as though looking for some way out. "All right. I know where there's an empty room."

"Why don't we use this one? No one's here at the moment." Caitlin went inside, feeling vaguely uneasy. If she'd thought the room small when it contained a rambunctious four-year-old and her frustrated father, now it seemed microscopic.

Mace closed the door behind them, locking it. "So we're not disturbed." He came toward her, reaching out and pulling her over to the side so they couldn't be seen through the small oblong window next to the door.

"What are you doing?"

"Finally we're alone." He lowered his head and began to kiss her. "This was a great idea," he whispered against her lips. "I've been dreaming of doing this all day."

Caitlin turned her face away. "No, Mace. Stop. Not here."

He stopped trying to kiss her, but his arms tightened around her body. "I know you like me. I feel the same way." His hand began to slide down her back.

"You said we needed to talk. This isn't the time or place for . . . this."

"Why not?" He kissed her again and didn't seem the least put off when she refused to respond. His hand now cupped her backside as he pressed her to him.

She struggled to put space between them. "Because I want you to stop."

His eyes hardened as he stared down at her. "Oh, yeah? Well, I think you better start being a lot nicer to me."

A shiver ran through her at the apparent threat in his voice. *He knows,* she thought. *It's him who's investigating Kenny.* She'd suspected Mace after his visit to her office and her phone call with Wyman, but the reality still shocked her.

"That's right," Mace said, grinning at her. "I know you're responsible for the conviction against Chet Belstead, particularly how the police found the murder weapon. I can't prove it yet, but I think there's enough circumstantial evidence to destroy your career."

Her breath caught in her throat. "Is this how you're getting dates these days?" She put as much scorn as she could muster into her voice.

"Are you denying it?"

She lifted her chin to show she wasn't afraid. Their faces were inches apart. She could feel the sickening heat of his breath, taste the mint spray he must have used after their hearing with the judge. "Chet Belstead raped that girl. He stabbed her with a knife so many times she almost died. That's what's important. Any evidence the police found has no connection to me. Now take your hands off me!"

Her words had little effect. "You don't have to worry. I'll stay quiet." He leaned in to kiss her neck seductively, his lips leaving a wet trail that made her want to shudder. "All you have to do is be very, very nice to me."

Fury burst through her, fanned by the degradation she felt. She wanted to kill him. She wanted to smash him into a bloody pulp and bury his remains in an unmarked grave. Better yet, she wanted him to experience the fear and humiliation Belstead's girlfriend had felt the night she'd been attacked.

She pushed at his chest. "If you think I'm guilty of something, you should prosecute me. I'm sure my conviction would help you win the appointment with the DA. Even if it would overturn your case."

His hold on her relaxed slightly. "I think you'll be much more useful helping me win my cases. We'll be able to throw the book at a lot of dirtbags once you're giving me the inside information I need to convict your clients. Plus, you'll be doing society a favor like you did in the Belstead case." He rubbed his hand up her back, squeezing and caressing. "And there's this great side benefit of working together. Everyone knows how you feel about me, so it'll be a good cover."

His utter assurance disgusted her. Had she really been so obvious? "Whatever I felt for you walked out that door the moment you brought me in here," she retorted. "And for the record, I'd rather be disbarred than spend another minute with you."

Disbelief registered on his face and she took advantage of his surprise to break free. A second later he grabbed her again, his fingers digging cruelly into her upper arm.

"Let me go!" she demanded. She tried to recall the self-defense class that she'd taken in law school, but she couldn't seem to remember any moves.

He hesitated, anger coloring his face. "If you don't let me go this second," she said, accentuating each word, "I'm going to start screaming."

His expression went from angry to furious. "So that's the way you want to play. You're going to regret this. Mark my words." His lower lip curled. "Frankly, I don't know what I ever saw in you." He relaxed his hold just as a key turned in the lock.

Caitlin almost shouted with relief as Wyman Russell appeared in the doorway with the two young attorneys that had passed them earlier. Wyman looked concerned, the others eager. Mace tried to fake a confident smile, despite the flush of anger still covering his pretty face.

Caitlin chuckled as she walked toward the door. When she passed the young attorneys, she said, loud enough for everyone to hear, "Sorry to disappoint you guys. I don't know what he's told you, but he's definitely not my type. He kisses like a fish." She turned on her heel, leaving them gaping after her. She was nearly out of the building when Wyman caught up with her.

"You took him down a notch or two," he said, laughing.

Her anger was dissipating. "I shouldn't have embarrassed him like that." Even if Mace deserved it, she'd made him angrier. If he somehow managed to get her disbarred, how was she going to support her sister?

"Maybe, but I'm so glad you did." Wyman grinned widely. "I mean, what a shock! He hasn't lost a bet in three years."

Caitlin stopped at the door to the courthouse. "He had a bet about me?"

"Well, it's sort of understood. He hits on all the single attorneys. Like I told you before, you can't trust him. I knew he had plans for you. I also know he's still stringing along a woman in California."

She sighed internally. "Thanks for coming when you did. Things might have taken a turn for the worse."

"I saw you go in there with him and rounded up a key right away."

That was sweet. Why couldn't she fall for a man like Wyman? He might not be as hot as Mace or Parker, but he was a nice guy. A nice married guy.

"How's your wife?"

He shrugged. "We're meeting this weekend. I guess I'll find out for sure then."

"Good luck."

"I meant what I said about working with me."

She flashed him a smile. "If Mace gets me disbarred, maybe I can be your assistant."

All laughter left his face. "Does this have to do with the Belstead evidence?"

She hadn't meant to say anything. "It doesn't matter. Forget it."

"Look, it's going to be okay. There were three witnesses to what happened just now, and if Mace goes after you about the Belstead case, there won't be a judge or attorney in town who won't know he's doing it because you burned him."

Caitlin hadn't thought of it that way.

"Unless he's actually got something on you," Wyman added, cocking his head as if to study her better.

"I didn't do anything I wouldn't do again."

"Then I hope you'll only be fired, not disbarred." His eyes gleamed amusement.

She couldn't help but smile. "Thanks, Wyman." She turned and walked out into the cold streets, wrapping her arms around herself for warmth. Exhaustion fell heavily on her shoulders. She wished she could go home instead of back to work. She wished she could see Parker.

Where was he at that moment? Was he thinking about her? How odd that in this past week he'd become so large a part of her thoughts. Seeing him stuck in that small room with Madison had torn her apart, but nothing she did for his case seemed to make any difference. As it stood, he was headed toward prison, which would leave Madison to be raised by a woman who might be on drugs, and there was little she could do about it.

She'd told him to trust her, but what if she couldn't deliver? Taking out her phone, she dialed Kenny once more. "Sorry," he said without greeting. "I don't have anything except my gut that tells me she's hiding something. This woman is not good for those children, but I can't prove it."

"Yet, you mean."

"I'm looking into the boyfriend now. That might be where

I get the break. He appears to have a nice job and car, but there's something odd about him."

"Thanks, Kenny." Caitlin tried to keep disappointment from her voice. "Call me if you hear anything."

"Of course. Bye now."

It was all so frustrating. In Parker's place, she might just take Madison and run.

Caitlin stopped walking abruptly, a sinking feeling in her stomach. That, she realized, was exactly what he would do.

Unless she stopped him.

Caitlin broke into a brisk walk and reached her car, opening the doors with a click of her remote and sliding inside. She put in her Bluetooth and dialed Sally's number before starting the engine.

"Anything new?" she asked hopefully when Sally answered.

"Sorry. We did a small drug bust last night at a party in that circle—friends of Dakota's friends—but they claim Dakota has no connection to them."

"Lying?"

"Maybe. People like that lie about everything, even when they don't have to lie. It's an addiction. Most don't even know the truth anymore."

Caitlin was all too familiar with the type. "Look, I have another favor to ask."

"You name it."

"Could you take Amy home with you again tonight? There's something I have to do."

"Does this involve Parker?"

"It's just that . . ." Caitlin didn't want to continue, but she did. "I'm afraid he's going to run." With Madison, of course, but she didn't need to add that. They both knew Parker would never leave his daughter.

"Do you know that, or are you guessing? Because if you have some information, I have to act."

"No, you don't. I'm telling you this as a friend, not in your capacity as a police detective. And I'm working on making sure it doesn't happen."

Sally was silent a moment. "Fine. But think about this: maybe we've both been wrong about Parker Hathaway. Maybe he's the one lying."

"You think I haven't considered that?"

"What exactly is happening between you two?"

"I don't know. I've never felt this way before. It's like . . ." *If I think about never seeing him again, I want to shrivel up and cry.* But that was silly. She'd only known him five days.

"Like what?" Sally was still waiting for her to finish.

"We met on Monday, but it feels like much longer."

"You're falling for him, that's what's happening. I could see it coming the moment I saw you together Wednesday morning. I take it that means the gorgeous DDA is out of the picture?"

"You got that right." Caitlin couldn't help the disgust in her tone.

"That sounds bad. What happened?"

Caitlin wanted to tell her friend the whole story so they could commiserate together over what a total jerk Mace was, but Caitlin wasn't ready to let Sally share her burden, even if Sally would probably tell her Belstead got what he deserved.

"Look, I'll fill you in on that later. Just take my word for it. The man's a total moron. I don't know what I ever saw in him."

"Well, he's good-looking. I'll give him that."

"I don't care how good-looking he might be. He's an idiot. Look, I just wanted to know if you've found anything and if you'll watch Amy for a bit while I figure things out. I understand if you have plans."

"No, no. That's fine. Tony's got a bowling tournament tonight, and I was going to meet him there, but not until later— just to get in on the celebration part at the end. Bowling's boring for onlookers." She paused. "Unless it's summer and they take their shirts off."

Caitlin laughed. "Right. Thanks."

"No problem. In fact, why doesn't Amy sleep over? Randi always asks when she comes, and we keep saying next time."

"What about the tournament?"

"It'll be my excuse to stay home and spend time with the girls. I'll make dinner and popcorn for after."

Caitlin knew Amy would love that. "If you're sure," she said, hesitating. She didn't know how the evening with Parker would go, but it would take a lot off her mind not to worry about Amy.

"I'm sure. And let me know if you need anything else."

"I will."

The rest of the day dragged on. Caitlin nearly screamed in frustration as several emergencies prevented her from leaving the office until six. She broke at least two speeding laws as she hurried to pick up Amy, stopped at home for an overnight bag, and then drove over to Sally's. Home once again, Caitlin took a quick shower and changed into a red silk dress that hugged her figure and took inches off her waist. She would never have worn the outfit to work or out with someone like Wyman, though she would have worn it with Mace on Saturday. That would have been a mistake.

But she needed to feel good now. And she needed to look good enough to find the courage to give Parker a reason to stay and fight.

Now to find him before it was too late.

Chapter 34

Parker gulped a burrito he'd cooked in the microwave for dinner as he surveyed the array of items on his bed: clothing for several days for both him and Madison, snacks, toiletries, all the cash he had in the bank, and the twenty thousand he'd borrowed from his mother's account. She'd put more in, she said, but he knew he wouldn't be able to use her card. They'd be tracking her too after he was gone. It would take him years to pay her back, but he'd do it and gladly. He was a hard worker and could make good money when he put his mind to it. When he wasn't giving it all to Dakota. Maybe he'd finally start that business he'd always been thinking about. First, he had to get through the next few weeks without getting caught.

He'd signed the deed to his truck over to his mother and mailed it to her so she could sell it after he was gone, and he'd bought a junky car from someone advertising in the newspaper, paying cash. He'd planned to get a license plate from a junk yard, but the woman he'd purchased the car from had left her old one on. As he planned to abandon the car in Vegas, that suited him just fine. Somehow he'd also have to get a new ID, a new life. Until he did that, he'd be living in hiding.

A life on the run. Was it really necessary?

He slumped to the bed, thoughts of Caitlin nearly over-coming his determination. Slowly he took out his phone and dialed Dakota. Maybe she'd be reasonable. Maybe she'd give him a glimmer of hope so he could stay.

"Hello?" She sounded pleasant, not at all her normal self. He stiffened.

"Hi, Dakota. It's Parker."

"Sorry, Parker's not home. We're divorced anyway, you know."

Parker's not home? A chill spread through him. No doubt about it. She was wasted.

"Dakota, this *is* Parker. Are you alone?"

"Parker?" Amusement entered her voice. "No, of course I'm not alone. I'm with my fiancé. That's right—*my fiancé*. And we're getting married and leaving this stupid state. How's that make you feel? You may be better-looking, but he gives me what I need."

"I meant where's Madison?"

No reply except kissing noises and a throaty giggle.

"Tell me, or I'm calling the police," Parker demanded. He'd call them either way, but she didn't need to know that.

"She's fine," she said, her voice still sweet but slurring. "And you can't call the police because I'm not home. Now leave me alone."

"Where's Madison?" he insisted. "Is she okay?"

Another, deeper voice came on the phone. "Bug off. She's

mine now." *Click.* Must be the boyfriend, the one who had more muscles than he had hair—or sense, apparently.

If they were together somewhere, then where was his daughter? Probably with them, watching them get high. Or maybe in another room, tending her little brother.

Should he call the police? And tell them what? That he'd called Dakota and she was nice to him so she had to be doing drugs? That she might have left Madison at home alone?

If Dakota had even been telling the truth about not being home.

Precious minutes ticked by as Parker mentally ran over his options. But in the end, there were no options. Not really.

He began shoving clothes and toiletries into the extra suitcase he'd bought. When he was finished, he filled his smaller suitcase as well. Finished. There was nothing more to do. He grabbed his keys.

Was there time to stop and see Caitlin? But if he did that, would he have the courage to leave? Shaking his head, he opened his bedroom door, hefted the suitcases, and crossed the shared living room. His roommate still didn't appear to be home, and in fact, Parker hadn't seen him since he moved in, though there had been dirty dishes in the dishwasher. Dropping one of the suitcases, he opened the door.

And there she was, Caitlin, standing with one hand up to ring the bell. Her hand lowered, and her black coat fell open to reveal a shimmering red dress. She'd never looked lovelier, and he had difficulty forcing himself to ask, "Is there news?"

"No, but we need to talk."

"I can't right now."

She glanced down at the suitcase in his hand and at the other on the floor where he'd dropped it. "Going somewhere?"

He didn't answer as she stepped into the room. "Parker, you can't leave."

"Are you going to stop me?" He set down the other suitcase.

"No." She was so beautiful. The copper hair cascaded down her back, over her shoulders. His breath failed him, and for a moment he could do nothing but stare.

Her coat slid to the floor, and they stepped into each other's arms. Nothing in his life had ever felt so right. "It'd be better if you left now," he whispered into the hair by her ear.

She shook her head. "I'm not leaving until we talk this out."

He wanted to talk about it, to establish a base where they could go forward into the future. But there was no future for them, and living only for the moment was what had trapped him with Dakota and given Madison such a raw deal in the first place. He wouldn't do that again. He couldn't promise Caitlin what wasn't his to give.

Then it dawned on him that Caitlin had shown no surprise that he was leaving. She'd known. Did that mean she was here to say goodbye or to convince him not to leave? But he knew. The answer was in her blue eyes.

"Kiss me," she said in a soft voice, not even loud enough to be called a whisper.

That was his undoing. He kissed her deeply, relishing the feel of her in his arms. Every emotion felt new and more powerful than he'd ever experienced. He didn't know how or why, but somewhere along the line, he'd fallen in love with her. Kissing her had suddenly become as necessary as breathing.

Yet there was so much separating them, especially the fact that she'd come to convince him to stay. More than almost anything, he wanted to stay and see where these emotions would take them in the next days and months and years. Knowing the impossibility of this desire was every bit as painful as the joy of kissing her now.

"Excuse me?" A male voice came from the hallway near the still-open door.

Both he and Caitlin froze as a short, stocky man with a full beard came the rest of the way into the room, pocketing keys he'd apparently thought he'd need to open the door. In one hand he carried a large paper grocery bag.

"You must be Bob," Parker said, slowly moving away from Caitlin.

Brown eyes surveyed them without emotion. "And you must be my new roommate."

"Parker Hathaway."

"Nice to meet you." Bob offered Parker his hand. "Can I speak to you in the kitchen a minute?"

Parker glanced at Caitlin, whose pale skin was slightly flushed. "Uh, yeah." To Caitlin, Parker added, "I'll just be a minute."

Bob nodded at Caitlin and led the way to the small kitchen where he began unpacking the paper grocery bag. "Look, we need to have some ground rules about having women over."

The guy had to be kidding. "It wasn't like we were . . . she just came to see me before I left."

"You're moving out already?"

"Something came up, so I'm heading out of town." Parker thought he should shut up now. No doubt the police would be interviewing good old Bob after Parker disappeared. "Mexico," he added to confuse potential investigators. "Just a short trip. I'll be back."

Bob didn't appear to care. He tilted his head toward the kitchen doorway. "She's classy. Where'd you pick her up?"

"I didn't pick her up. She's my law—we've been working together on something. What you saw when you walked in sort of took us by surprise."

Bob snorted. "Somehow I doubt that. It's a wonder the room wasn't in flames with all the sparks between you. I'd been standing there for quite some time before you noticed me."

Parker watched an ant march across the countertop. Bob certainly had a point. There was a connection between him and Caitlin, and it was just as well the man had come in when he had. Parker had to remember to be more careful. The last thing he wanted was to hurt Caitlin—and that meant he needed to keep her at arm's length.

Bob wrote his name on a jar of mayonnaise and shut the refrigerator. He yawned. "Well, if you'll be gone for a while, I guess we can talk rules when you get back. I've worked forty hours in the past three days and I'm beat. I'm going to sit down on the couch and watch TV until I fall asleep. You two are welcome to join me if you want." He looked so smug that Parker wanted to punch his face.

"Uh, no thanks." As if staring at a television with Bob could win out over kissing Caitlin.

Except Parker couldn't kiss Caitlin anymore. Now that his mind had cleared, he had begun worrying again about Madison. Was she safe?

"Nice to meet you, Bob." Parker nodded and returned to the main room where Caitlin was standing by the couch. He pulled her into his arms and traced the freckles on her face with his fingertip, stopping on her bottom lip. So much for arm's length.

She kissed his finger before saying in a low voice, "Let's go to my place. I'll cook dinner. Amy is at Sally's, so we have the place all to ourselves."

He kissed her again, long and deep, loving the way her eyes closed contentedly. She tasted of summer skies and promises. "You're so beautiful, Caitlin." He took her hand, their fingers intertwining. "You go ahead. I'll deal with my suitcases and be right there. But don't worry about dinner. We'll go someplace nice. I'll even change into my suit."

"Okay," she whispered. Her eyes went beyond him, and Parker knew Bob had come into the room.

He walked Caitlin out into the hall, pulling her to him again and holding her far too long.

Then he did the only thing he could do. He gave her a final kiss, stepped back, and let her go.

He waited exactly three minutes before hefting his suitcases and taking them to the old car he'd hidden around the block. Caitlin's car was nowhere to be seen, and he was both grateful and disappointed. He forced himself to start the ignition and drive not to Caitlin's house but in the opposite direction.

Because there was Madison. There would always be Madison, and even if it meant closing a door, walking out on Caitlin, there was no other choice. He wouldn't ask her to share a life on the run. He wouldn't come to her empty-handed. Though every nerve in his body protested the separation, he set his jaw in determination. He was the only one who could protect his daughter, and being a father had to come first.

He drove slowly past the house he'd rented for Dakota. The place was completely dark except for a tiny glow that might be coming from a hallway light. Nearly two hours had passed since his conversation with Dakota. Was she home by now or still out with her new boyfriend?

Stopping at the house next door, Parker turned off his engine and made his way across Dakota's driveway and snow-filled lawn, not bothering to mask his approach. In the next few minutes, he would end up in jail or on his way to Vegas with Madison. He felt in his pants pocket for one of the small rocks he'd carried home from the worksite today. Would Madison be awake? Would she remember what he'd said about coming to her window? If she heard him, would she look out or bang on her mother's bedroom door in terror?

The questions nearly paralyzed him.

It was already dark but not yet ten o'clock, so Madison might still be awake. Since she stayed in bed late every morning, she would normally never sleep before midnight on his weekends.

Carefully, he aimed and threw the rock.

Nothing. He hadn't brought the glass-cutter from his old apartment, and if Dakota really had installed new locks, he wouldn't be able to get in without waking the neighborhood.

He threw another rock. And then a third.

A face appeared in the window. Fear pounded through him, but it was only Madison. Tears of relief bit at his eyes.

The window slid open. "Daddy?"

"Shhh."

Her voice lowered to a whisper. "Did you come to get me?"

"Yes."

"Wait. I have a chair. I got it from the kitchen. But I have to put it on my bed."

She vanished but reappeared within seconds, tall enough to climb onto the windowsill. There was no screen, so soon she was in his arms, and he was folding her under his coat.

"What about Ricky?" she asked as he reached up to shut the window.

"He'll be all right."

"But he was sick tonight. We were over at Leo's for dinner, and he was crying. He threw up. Then Leo got mad and drove us home."

"Is he sleeping?"

"Yes."

"I bet he'll be better in the morning." He hesitated. If Dakota wasn't home, he could still call the police. "Mommy came home with you too, right?"

She nodded. "She's sleeping. I think."

They made it to the car without being seen. At least he hoped. Now if everything went well, he might have as many as fourteen hours to put space between them and Salt Lake City before alarms went off.

"Where's the truck?" Madison asked.

"I bought a new car."

"Why?"

"Well, partly because it gets better gas mileage. You and I are going on a long trip."

Her eyes sparkled. "Goody! I love trips."

Parker tried to enjoy her enthusiasm, but his mind kept returning to Caitlin. What would she think of him when she realized he wasn't coming? Would she feel used and betrayed, or by not going to her house had he salvaged a chance to be with her after all this was over?

If it was ever over.

There was also the strong possibility that Caitlin would realize what he had done before he was safely away and call her detective friend. Parker stepped harder on the gas pedal. The more miles between him and Salt Lake City, the better.

Chapter 35

Every part of Caitlin's body felt alive. Her senses were acute. She noticed the homemade wooden turkey sitting on a neighbor's front porch, the way the melting snow sparkled in her headlights, how the stars seemed bright and the night darker. Each of her heartbeats was an individual thing, like a beat on a drum that was so big it filled the entire world.

That didn't stop the worry from setting in as she pulled into her garage. Was she doing the right thing by convincing Parker to stay? There was no pretense that he was attracted to her, but beyond that she really knew nothing. And the suitcases. He'd been about to leave.

Well, what of it? She'd do the same thing herself, wouldn't she?

He had to trust her a bit longer. She would find the information. She'd go over to Dakota's every day to check on Madison, if that's what it took.

And if he still left?

She climbed from the car, slamming the door a little too hard. She wasn't going to dwell on that thought. No, she would go inside and think about freshening her makeup and fixing her hair.

Bong! went another beat of her heart.

Sometime later, when the house smelled thoroughly of baked sugar cookies, her favorite candle aroma, she began to worry. Where was Parker? Even if his roommate had insisted on talking some more, he should have been here by now.

The headiness of the air made her feel almost drunk. Walking to her bedroom, she looked in her closet for something better to wear, but the red dress was the best she had.

To think that she'd been going to wear it on a date with Mace. A sick feeling churned in her stomach. How could she have been so very wrong about him?

Don't think about Mace, she ordered herself.

Her thoughts returned easily to Parker, to the way he'd looked at her, the huskiness in his voice when he'd said she was beautiful, the connection she felt at his touch.

She sat on the sofa and flipped on the TV. There was nothing interesting on—not that she could have paid attention anyway. Her nerves hummed, and every sense seemed tuned to waiting. Waiting for the sound of his truck. Impatient, she went into the kitchen for a glass of water, taking it back to the couch. The glass clinked on the coffee table, making a sound that brought back memories of family holidays, her first boyfriend, outings with Sally.

Yawning, she pulled a blanket over her, the red dress too thin to offer much protection against the increasing night cold. Worry began gnawing in her belly. Was she doing the right thing pursuing a relationship with Parker?

He'd leave. She was sure of it.

No, not if she could get him to trust her long enough to help Madison. There was something between them. Something powerful. He would stay.

She closed her eyes and saw herself wrapped in Parker's arms on a warm, sandy beach, Amy and Madison playing together nearby. She stretched slowly, languorously, her body soaking up the sun and Parker's nearness.

A rush of wetness caused her eyes to blink open, and she was startled to realize she'd been sleeping. Her glass lay empty on her lap, a dark stain marking where the last bit of water had run out, soaking her leg underneath the blanket. Her mouth felt like peach fuzz and tasted considerably worse.

Her eyes went to the clock, and for a moment she stared at it, unable to comprehend. It was after two. That she'd fallen asleep while waiting for Parker wasn't surprising—she was always so exhausted that at any moment of inactivity, her body threatened to shut down—but the fact that he wasn't there did worry her. Had he come while she was asleep?

No, she would have heard the door.

Then she knew, without really knowing how, that he was gone. That last moment in the hall, when he'd clung to her, had been a goodbye. Not a proper one, in her view.

I'm such an idiot.

He'd gone without explanation. He'd left her here waiting. How he must have laughed at the idea of her waiting for him to come. Blood flooded to her face. She tried to work up anger or indifference, but she was too wounded to feel either. Tears wet her face as she hugged her arms to her stomach.

After the initial hurt and shock subsided, she told herself she needed to call Sally. She had to let her know he might be running again. There was the slimmest chance that he was still in Utah, but Caitlin would bet her whole career that he wasn't.

Not that she cared in the least about her career.

She'd been such a fool. She'd thought she could convince him to stay, to trust in her. But in the end he hadn't believed in her abilities. Either that, or his story about the drugs wasn't true, and he realized that all the romance in the world wouldn't get him custody.

She pulled the blanket around her and let the tears come. She'd allow herself two minutes of tears, and then she'd call Sally.

An insistent buzzing flitted around Caitlin's head, waking her from a cold and uncomfortable dream. She blinked, looking around. She lay curled up on her couch under a single blanket. She could hear the rumble of the furnace, which probably meant it was morning, and late morning by the amount of light seeping through the blinds.

She came to an unsteady seated position, her head weighted by a dullness she knew came from too little sleep. The buzzing came again, and she traced it to the cell phone on the side table where she'd put it the night before. The thought that it might be Parker made her grab for it.

"Hello?"

"Hey, it's me," Sally said. "Weren't you coming to get Amy at eight? She's been up for hours. We're eating breakfast now. I wouldn't mind letting them keep playing, but I have to go in to work for a few hours. And you know Tony. He always works Saturdays."

"I'm so sorry! I guess I slept in." Guilt filled Caitlin as she realized she'd fallen back to sleep without calling Sally about her suspicions.

"That must have been one late date." Sally's voice exuded curiosity, but she didn't say more—probably because the girls were listening.

Caitlin flushed, not wanting to know what Sally would say if she knew how Caitlin had ended up alone. "Yeah, sort of."

"Caitlin? Are you okay? You sound funny."

"Nothing. Now stop yelling in my ear. There's something I have to tell you. It's important."

"Is this about Parker?"

Caitlin's heart plunged to her stomach, and she wished she could go back to sleep and forget everything that had happened this week. "Remember what I told you yesterday? Well, I think we might have been wrong to trust him. You'd better check on Madison. And Parker too. I'll text you his new address." The more Caitlin thought about it, the more she was becoming sure there had never been any drugs at his ex-wife's house. That Parker had played them all. An innocent man wouldn't run. He'd stay and fight.

Sally's voice instantly became crisp and businesslike. "I'll make a few calls while I wait for you. Don't worry. If he's run again, we'll find him." She didn't add that this time she'd keep him locked up, but Caitlin already knew. How far had Parker been able to get? It would be partly her fault for not calling last night if he wasn't found.

Caitlin staggered to her feet. "I could be wrong." Yet she knew she wasn't. What was it about her and men? She'd been wrong about Wyman, she'd been wrong about Mace, and now she was wrong about Parker.

"I hope so. I'll let you know."

The phone went dead, and Caitlin let it slip to her lap.

She'd done her best to convince Parker to stay, to trust in her, but in the end he hadn't given her time. This time when the police caught up with Parker, he'd go to prison, and Caitlin wouldn't represent him. No way. She didn't even want to see him again. Ever. It hurt too much.

She put on her coat, checked her pockets for keys, and drove to Sally's in a haze. When she came inside, Amy managed to tear her eyes from the Saturday morning cartoons long enough to give her a hug.

"We've been playing dress up," she told Caitlin. "But Randi didn't have stuff my size, so Sally let me use her pants. And this is Tony's shirt." The blue material dwarfed even Amy, drooping on her tall frame, but she spun around as though modeling the most beautiful dress.

Caitlin nodded and forced a smile she didn't feel as Amy plopped again onto the couch, instantly becoming reabsorbed in the cartoons.

"There was no answer at Madison's house," Sally said. "Her mother isn't picking up her phone."

Caitlin checked her watch. Nine-thirty already. "She's probably still sleeping."

"I called the precinct, and my supervisor reminded me that no crime has been committed yet, but he sent a uniform over anyway. He also sent one out to Parker's apartment."

"He's gone," Caitlin said with surety.

"How do you know?"

Caitlin lowered her voice, though Amy and Randi appeared oblivious to anything but the television. "I saw him at his place last night. I went home when his roommate showed up, but he was going to come and get me. To go out."

"Did something happen at his apartment?" Sally looked pointedly at her rumpled dress.

Caitlin pulled her coat tighter around her, knowing her face was a bright red. "Nothing happened. He kissed me, that's all. I felt like . . . I don't want to talk about it. He's just gone. I think he's been playing me all along. I don't know if I believe there ever were any drugs."

"Oh, honey. I'm so sorry." Sally hugged her.

For a suffocating moment Caitlin couldn't swallow the lump in her throat. "I-I need to go home." She made her voice louder. "Come on, Amy. We have to go."

Sally watched them leave, her eyes glittering with curiosity.

"Go find Madison!" Caitlin wanted to yell at her, but she knew Sally was already doing everything in her power. Madison's disappearance would soon be all over the news. Maybe they would find her. But it was already too late for Caitlin and Parker.

"Is something wrong?" Amy asked. "You look mad."

"I'm just a little sad." More like desperately and horribly sad. Why had she allowed herself to be so caught up by him? Why had it seemed he was the puzzle piece that fit the missing part of her? She closed her eyes for a moment, willing the hurt to leave. Everything would be okay. She would go on. She always went on. Besides, Amy needed her.

Sally called Caitlin's phone as she pulled into her driveway. "You're right," she said. "Madison's gone. There's a chair on her bed, and the window latch wasn't engaged, like it'd been shut from the outside. No fingerprints yet, except Madison's. Whoever she's with, she seemed to have gone willingly."

"Parker."

"Probably. The officers tell me Dakota's raging mad."

"Did she let them in right away?"

"Yes."

"And?"

"Nothing. It's the same as before. No drugs. They say Dakota looks like she has a hangover, but drinking isn't against the law."

"And Parker?"

"His truck is at his apartment, but he's not. The landlady said he only paid a week in advance."

"What about his mother?"

Sally heaved a sigh. "She says she knows nothing. Rumor has it she's selling the house, but as yet there's no sign in the yard."

"You think she knew he was going?"

"Yeah. But that only means she might be the one who'll lead us to him. We're getting a warrant to flag her accounts now, in case he's using her credit cards."

That sounded logical, but it made Caitlin feel even worse. The woman was probably as duped by her son as Caitlin had been. "How could I have been so wrong?"

She didn't realize the words were out until Sally responded. "I'm the one who asked you to represent him. And there is still a chance he's running to protect his daughter like he claims."

Sally, of course, didn't know the whole of it—that Caitlin had liked him so much that even the lack of proof hadn't mattered. Always before she'd paid attention to the proof.

Stupid.

"We'll find him." Sally's voice was grim. "I just hope it's in time."

Her friend's tone surprised Caitlin. Hadn't Sally said just a minute ago that Parker might still be acting for Madison? "He's not going to hurt her, if that's what you think."

Sally was quiet a moment. "Who's to say? If you're right that he made up everything about the drugs, what might he dream up next?"

A shiver of fear shot up Caitlin's spine, but she shoved it aside. "No," she insisted. "He loves Madison."

"I hope you're right. I'll talk to you later."

"Thanks." Caitlin stared at the phone for a long minute after Sally hung up. She was still sitting in the car behind the wheel, though Amy had long since bolted from the car and was inside, probably in front of the television. Caitlin couldn't bring herself to care. Why shouldn't Amy watch as much TV as she wanted? It wasn't as though it would ruin her chances of a good future.

I've done it this time, she thought, letting the tears roll down her cheeks. *Big time.* She had broken her rule about getting involved, and now her heart would have to pay.

Chapter 36

Parker stopped before exiting the Las Vegas bed and breakfast. He was sure he hadn't been followed from Utah, but he always checked to make sure no one was openly watching the outside of the building. They'd been here a week, using his brother's old passport for ID and paying cash, which had required a large deposit and prepayment. The place was small enough not to be connected to any large databases that might be searching for him, but Parker knew they'd have to move on soon. Nevada was too close to Utah, and how many fathers came to Vegas with only a young child for company?

Madison was the darling of the bed and breakfast, despite his attempts to keep her from interacting with anyone. Both the guests and the few employees loved her, and twice she'd gotten a stomachache from so many people giving her too many treats. She didn't look much like the fair-headed, light-skinned little girl she had been before his first attempt to take her.

She wore boy's clothes that didn't quite match her pretty face, and her hair was cut short and dyed black. Her skin was a deep bronze—mostly thanks to a bottled tan, though some of it was real because they spent hours each day walking through the city under the thin sun. She was loving their new life, especially being with him so much.

Parker had undergone even more of a dramatic physical change. He'd shaved his head, to look more like his brother, and grown a beard that he dyed black and kept short. It took him an hour to cut and touch up the beard every few days, but the difference was startling. He'd also traded jeans and T-shirts for dress pants and button-up shirts and wore sunglasses all the time to cover much of his face. With the ten pounds he had shed from worry, he was pretty sure he'd be able to walk past his former co-workers without them recognizing him.

But Vegas held nothing for Parker. Half of him, it seemed, had been left in Utah. He'd felt broken in this way once before, when Dakota told him Madison wasn't his child, but this was even worse somehow. There was no going back, no chance of remaking the past. At night he dreamed of Caitlin, and he regretted not showing up at her house at least to say a real goodbye, to tell her he wasn't interested in a relationship. Then Caitlin could have moved on without him under her skin. Without the what-ifs that might cripple her chance of forming another attachment. Like with that pretty-boy attorney.

A surge of jealousy roared through him at the thought, though he knew he had no right to feel that way. He could have stayed. He'd wanted to stay. Yet he'd made the only choice he felt he could as a father, and now he had to live with it. Live for Madison. And that meant making hard decisions about the future. No, the hard decision had been made before leaving

Utah. Now the decisions were just more decisions, something he had to do to create a stable, normal life for his daughter.

Caitlin was strong. She'd be okay. It wasn't as if she loved him. There hadn't been time for that kind of attachment. At least that's what he told himself. He'd done the right thing, cutting the relationship short before he did anything that could hurt her. Because the truth was that if he'd gone to her house that night, he would have never been able to leave.

Before Parker had finished surveying the outside of the bed and breakfast, an elderly man and his gray-haired wife came down the narrow front staircase—Shane and Orla O'Doherty. Madison pulled away from Parker and ran to them. This couple was a particular favorite of hers because Mr. O'Doherty always carried gum in his pocket, and Orla saved Madison the umbrellas from her drinks. Madison had quite the collection by now. Mr. O'Doherty was an investment banker in Chicago, and the couple was obviously well-off. The tans they sported were not from a bottle but from vacations to exotic places. Parker had been surprised they weren't at one of the high-rise hotels until Mrs. O'Doherty told him they'd honeymooned here as poor newlyweds and always made it a point to return whenever they were in Las Vegas.

With a last look at the street, Parker waited for the O'Dohertys to reach him. Madison was already saying her thanks for the treat and twirling her newest drink umbrella between her fingers. As usual, she was talking up a storm, and he listened to make sure she wasn't saying anything that might be viewed as suspicious. He'd reminded her time and time again to refrain from talking about personal things and to say they were from California if anyone asked. So far she'd remembered pretty well, but Parker was careful not to leave her alone with anyone in case she slipped and began talking about her real life. He'd never actually told anyone she was a boy, but the trucks and action figures he'd bought for her to play with spoke volumes. They'd been lucky so far.

"A sweet lad there," Mr. O'Doherty said, as he did every day. The fact that he'd lived in Ireland as a young boy was apparent in his speech.

Parker nodded agreement. "Thank you."

"Daddy, they're leaving tomorrow!" Madison's mouth curled downward in a frown.

"Really?" Parker felt a moment of consternation. He'd been toying with the idea of asking Mr. O'Doherty about job possibilities in Chicago. Perhaps he'd agree to introduce Parker to a few connections.

"That we are." Mrs. O'Doherty set a brown hand on Madison's head. "We'll be able to see our granddaughters. We'll tell them all about you, little one."

"I like your voice," Madison said. "You sound like my friend's sister."

Parker tensed when Madison mentioned Caitlin, but when she didn't elaborate, he relaxed. "Her parents were Irish," Parker volunteered.

Madison's head bobbed up and down. "She's got long red hair. It's curly. And blue eyes. She's so pretty, and nice too." She laughed and added, "My dad kissed her. My friend Amy told me."

Parker knew Amy had been to Madison's house, but according to Caitlin they'd only been alone in the kitchen for a short time. Apparently, it had been long enough.

"An Irish lass, eh?" Mr. O'Doherty's eyes were knowing. "You won't ever get her out of your blood. It isn't possible, I tell you. I tried many times with Orla."

His wife punched his arm playfully. "Oh, did you now? Silly man. I would never have let you get away."

Parker experience a brief memory of his mother and father joking around in a similar manner when he was very young. What would his father be like now if he'd lived? What would he say about Parker's life? Would he have mellowed enough to see the good in him? It was something Parker would never know. But he did know that he had to make a plan for his future—and fast—especially if he wanted to take care of his mother in the way his father would have. He still hoped it wouldn't be necessary for her to sell her house and go into hiding with him. Most likely, she'd have to if she wanted to be a part of Madison's life. He didn't dare hope that Caitlin would continue to look for the proof needed to free him. Not after the way he'd left things with her.

A deep and sudden yearning stole his breath, and for a moment he had to fight tears. *Get a grip,* he ordered himself.

Oblivious now to the adult conversation, Madison was crouching next to a couch in the lobby, ignoring them as she twirled her two new drink umbrellas on the shiny tile floor.

Parker dragged air into his tortured lungs. "I've been thinking about going to Chicago myself," he told Mr. O'Doherty. "You wouldn't know anyone in the construction business, would you? Someone who might need a hand?"

Mr. O'Doherty's left eyebrow rose. "Maybe. But what about your work in California?"

For an instant Parker had forgotten the fake life he'd created for himself—that he was a joint owner in a construction business in California—and he searched his mind for something plausible to say. "We're about finished with our current projects, and business is slowing because of the poor real estate market. My partner can take care of the few other projects we have coming down the pipeline, so I've been thinking about trying something new on my own." He glanced at Madison to make sure she didn't hear the next sentence. "My girlfriend was born in Chicago and has always wanted to go back."

Mr. O'Doherty exchanged a look with Mrs. O'Doherty. "I knew a woman would be behind the idea," he said. "There is always a woman behind crazy ideas."

"And a good thing," Mrs. O'Doherty said. "Our friend here is too handsome to be alone for long. He needs a woman."

"You might as well give your girlfriend what she wants." Mr. O'Doherty clasped a hand on Parker's shoulder. "I can't make guarantees, but if you decide to come to Chicago, I'll introduce you around." He handed Parker his card. "It won't be easy starting over."

"I work hard." Parker looked pointedly at Madison. "I have a lot of reasons to want to succeed."

"You do at that. I'll look forward to hearing from you."

Parker watched them go. Until this very moment, he'd been undecided about where to start. He'd known they couldn't stay in Vegas. But he had no clue which was the best state to lose themselves in. He'd met people from at least a dozen states in the past week. He'd even met a family from Iowa who owned a construction business, and their adult daughter had made no secret of the fact that she liked Parker. She'd hinted he would be welcome there. She had been so friendly that both he and Madison had started avoiding her and had been relieved when the family left for home. Not that she wasn't smart or attractive. She simply wasn't Caitlin.

Now the idea of Chicago was like a fresh breeze, blowing away the confusion. Maybe it was foolish to think he could go and make a new life there, but he was young and hardworking.

His determination would take him far. He told himself he chose Chicago because it was far from Utah, but ultimately he knew it was because of Caitlin.

What would she think of him going to Chicago? He smiled at the thought before realizing it was a strong possibility she would never even know.

Madison tugged on his hand. "Aren't we going for a walk?"

"Actually, I think we should find out about going to Chicago."

Her eyes widened. "Can we go on a plane? A big one?"

"I think we'll drive."

"In that old car? But it was hot."

"No. Not that one. Remember? I already gave that car away. We'll rent a new one. It'll be really nice." Renting a car seemed safer than an airplane, though he didn't dare use his brother's ID at either place. But he was working on that angle already.

"Can I take chips and candy?"

"Of course. And your DVD player." Investing in that portable machine had been the best thing he'd done since arriving in Vegas. "I'll buy you a new DVD too."

She gave him a hug. "You're the best daddy in the whole world!"

After that she was silent for a long while as they walked out of the hotel and aimlessly down the street. Then she said, "I wish we could tell Caitlin and Amy about Chicago."

"I do too."

"Then why don't we? Maybe they'd want to come with us. Amy and I could play tea party." A mischievous glint came to her brown eyes. "And you could kiss Caitlin."

Parker knew she said it to make him laugh, but instead the comment seemed to cut into the part of him that still hoped. He stopped walking and stared down at his daughter. How could he tell her that Caitlin would probably never forgive him for his choice? It was possible she didn't even believe Madison had been in danger. He'd seen the doubt in her eyes.

"I'm sorry," he said slowly, "but I don't think that's going to happen."

That afternoon, he took Madison to a park where he could sit on a bench and watch her play. The day was cool and she wore a jacket, but the temperature was nowhere near Utah's freezing weather.

A dark-haired man in a leather jacket and black jeans came to sit beside him. "Nice day," he commented. He was young, not more than twenty-five, and good-looking in a way that likely attracted women. His build was on the thin side, but there was steel in the set of his jaw.

"Good for moving on," Parker said. "Do you have them?" The man laid a folder on the bench between them. In the week they'd been in Vegas, Parker had cautiously checked into buying a new identity and had found this man. He charged far more than people selling stolen social security numbers and badly forged licenses, but he guaranteed that no one would ever become suspicious because of the documents. Parker assumed that meant he'd used the name of a child who had died, perhaps even a fictitious child. He didn't know and didn't care to know.

He took an envelope from his coat pocket and set it on top of the folder. It contained twenty-five hundred dollars, the second half of his initial payment. He'd pay two more installments later, after he was settled and tried out the ID. He hoped that was where it would end. If he wanted a passport down the road, it would be another ten thousand.

The younger man slipped the envelope into the folder and pulled out the documents, leaving them on the park bench. He picked up his folder. "Good luck."

Parker watched him leave before slowly scanning the park

to see if they'd attracted any attention. Two women sat talking on a far bench, and an amorous pair of teenagers on another, but none seemed interested in what Parker was doing. He moved the documents onto his lap. Two social security cards, two birth certificates, and one driver's license. Their new names were Jonathan and Jessica Hanks. Perfect. Once shortened, Madison's name could be Jess, which would go along with her boy disguise.

They left for Chicago that night. No use hanging around any longer. He'd followed Utah news as best he could from the hotel, and though the features on Madison weren't appearing as often as they had in the beginning, he knew Sally and others would still be searching. No doubt the Feds had been called in. Traveling under his own name or his brother's would have been a huge mistake. At least now he'd be able to earn a living.

He was really going to do it. Go to a city he'd never been to before and start a new life. Wild and spontaneous had been his calling card in the old days, but for the past four years, he'd lived a different sort of existence altogether. Steady, reliable, and, if the truth be told, a little boring. A man who wanted to suffer for the sins of his past. Now the adventurous man that still lived inside him was reawakening, filled with excitement at what the future might hold.

No, he wasn't the youthful Parker, who hadn't let himself care about even those who loved him most, but a blend of the new and old. A blend of fun and fatherhood, adventure and duty, love and responsibility.

His heart still ached, but that wasn't unfamiliar to any of his incarnations. Yet even there he felt a change—not significant enough to be called real hope, but perhaps if there was any chance of winning Caitlin back in the future, Chicago just might show him how.

Chapter 37

"Sorry, Caitlin," Kenny said. "Nothing yet. Do you still want me to continue?"

Caitlin thought for a moment. An entire two and a half weeks, including Thanksgiving weekend, had passed since Parker had vanished. Kenny's search seemed pointless now—and had for weeks. Only her own stubbornness had kept him on the job, though reduced to part-time.

"I guess not. There's no reason now that he's gone." No one cared if Dakota was doing drugs anymore; they only cared that Parker had kidnapped his daughter. Again.

"Well, there's my gut."

"Your gut?"

"For what it's worth, I think this Dakota character is as guilty as sin. The kid's better off away from her."

She hated the pity in his voice. Pity for her loss. Kenny hadn't been fooled by the facade she wore these days. "It's all been a lie. There's no proof. Besides, it doesn't matter. He's gone."

"Whatever you say. It's your dime."

"Send me a bill."

"I will. Call me if you change your mind."

Caitlin hung up, feeling weary. She looked numbly at the stacks of papers on her desk. More briefs to write, more criminals to move along in the system. Mechanically, she began to type out the words she knew so well. This current brief didn't really need passion or brilliance. Just another knife attack and a man destined for prison.

A knock at the door interrupted her distracted thoughts. "Come in."

Caitlin stiffened when Norma Hathaway stepped into the room. She had never met Parker's mother, though she'd seen a picture in the file Sally had put together. She was a short, sturdy woman with shoulder-length hair dyed a medium brown that did not quite match the myriad of wrinkles on her pale face. Wrinkles that seemed to have come before their time. Her brown eyes were tired, but they looked just like Parker's. Except where his exuded vitality and confidence, this woman's seemed unsure and frightened.

"I hope it's okay." She moved into the room with unmistakable grace.

"Please, sit down." Caitlin had stood as she entered and remained standing until Mrs. Hathaway had settled in one of the seats in front of her desk.

"It's about my son."

"There's nothing I can do," Caitlin said quickly. "By leaving, he's broken the conditions of his bail, and when they find him, he'll be in jail until the trial."

"They told me. That's not why I'm here. Before he left, Parker told me you were researching about Dakota. He had great hopes of you finding something that would help him keep Madison safe."

Poor deluded woman. "We didn't find anything. I'm sorry, Mrs. Hathaway, but we're beginning to think the drugs were figments of Parker's imagination."

"No!" Mrs. Hathaway's face came alive, and Caitlin could see where Parker got his looks, if not his height. "I heard them talking. I go with him to drop Madison off sometimes, and Dakota didn't deny anything when he accused her. She as much said she'd do it again, that she could do anything she wanted, and there was nothing he could do about it. They had an awful fight. You've got to believe me. Madison was in danger—I absolutely know that! Do you think I'd sell stocks and clean out my savings if I didn't know for sure?"

Caitlin didn't point out that most of the mothers of her clients did that every day. "You cleaned out your savings?"

"I gave him twenty thousand. A loan. He's good for it. But with all the work he's done at my house these past years, I owe it to him anyway. And I know he'll always take care of me. That's the sort of son he is. Besides, I have other money in stocks and the house."

Caitlin wondered if she should mention that she knew Mrs. Hathaway planned to sell her house. Did the woman know where he was? Could she get him a message? Not that Caitlin would know what to say. She thought she would have gotten over him by now, but the hurt in her chest was so big, there was no room for anything else.

Mrs. Hathaway leaned forward, her eyes holding Caitlin's. "Look, I know he had a rough beginning in life, but he was always good inside. He never teased or tormented kids or animals when he was little. He was always respectful of me and other women. He just couldn't live up to his dad's expectations, and his brother . . . Well, Parker and I have never talked about it, but his brother was awful to him. He enjoyed having his daddy all to himself, enjoyed being the successful one. He lorded it over Parker far too much. I should have stepped in earlier, but then it was too late and Parker was living his own life without us. Yet despite all that, he found his way back to me."

Caitlin pulled a few tissues from the box on her desk and handed them to Mrs. Hathaway.

"Thanks." She wiped tears from under her eyes. "I know how all this looks, but I wanted to ask if you would please keep looking for proof against Madison's mother. Something to free my boy if the police catch up to him. Like I said, I have money. I've cashed in some stocks, and I can cash in more. Parker and Madison are all I've got, and I don't want to spend any more time away from them. This could drag on for years. I'll go where I have to, but I'd rather bring them home. And there's still that other little boy, Madison's brother. He's in danger, too."

Mrs. Hathaway's eyes pleaded, and for a brief, dizzying moment, Caitlin remembered a similar intensity in Parker's eyes, shadowed with attraction for her as they had been that last night together. The night she'd tried to convince him to stay.

The woman must have sensed a softening around her. "Please?"

Caitlin sighed. "I got to know Parker pretty well during the week I represented him. I asked him to trust me. He didn't."

"I'm not surprised. There's never been anyone he could really trust, not even me, and Madison means the world to him."

"Did you know that he might not even be her father?" Caitlin said.

"That's a lie! I see Parker in Madison's face all the time. I know she's his."

"But you don't seem surprised that Dakota might claim he isn't the father."

"She's hinted at it before to me. But it's just one more way she tried to control him."

Since Dakota hadn't brought the idea up to the police, Caitlin had to agree.

Norma Hathaway seemed to take her silence as permission to proceed. "Tell me, were you close to finding anything?"

"No. It was only a feeling."

She sat up straighter. "Then you know there's something. And also why he had to leave. He had to make sure Madison would be safe."

Caitlin felt like crying on this woman's shoulder. Mrs. Hathaway might understand what that last night had meant to her, and how crushed she'd been when Parker had walked out. Instead, she asked softly, "Has your son been involved with anyone since his relationship with Dakota?" It wasn't exactly a professional question, but Mrs. Hathaway should take it as such. Caitlin had to know.

Mrs. Hathaway's head turned slowly from side to side. "He said he'd never trust another woman again. I hoped that wouldn't last, though. He's a good man and deserves to be happy." She studied Caitlin for a long moment. "You're not telling me everything, are you? Did something else happen? What did he say to you?"

For an instant Caitlin was tempted to lie, tempted to put on her attorney deadpan and deny everything. But Norma Hathaway looked at her with a mixture of pain and hope, the same feelings Caitlin had tried fruitlessly to crush for the past weeks.

"It's not what he said," Caitlin said. "It's . . . I like Parker very much, Mrs. Hathaway. More than just professionally. We were becoming friends. I tried everything to get him to stay, but against all my professional and personal advice, he left anyway. And he took Madison."

Mrs. Hathaway's tears had stopped. "Did he tell you he was going?"

Caitlin bit back the inclination to say that was none of her business, but she shook her head. "We were going to have dinner together the last night he was here. He didn't show up."

That made Parker's mother consider her, head tilted as if puzzling something out. "Maybe," she said, slowly, "if he'd shown up, it would have been too hard to leave."

So Mrs. Hathaway had read between the lines and understood there was something more than a budding friendship between Caitlin and Parker. "He could have trusted me," Caitlin insisted.

"He'll be back." Mrs. Hathaway's voice lowered as though she suspected there were listening devices in the room. "He's coming back for me. Or he'll send for me."

"Mrs. Hathaway, you shouldn't tell me that. Please don't tell me anything about Parker. I'm not your attorney, or his anymore, and I'll have to tell the police." She hesitated before adding, "And the police will be watching you to try to find him."

"I'm not telling you anything except that he doesn't make promises lightly. Now, please, will you keep looking into his ex-wife? I'll pay all that I can."

He doesn't make promises lightly, Caitlin pondered. Problem was that Parker hadn't made her any promises at all except that he could wait. Well, he'd apparently mastered that. Only now the waiting was hers, and she hadn't signed up for it.

"Please?" Mrs. Hathaway asked again.

Caitlin hesitated a few more seconds before nodding slowly. "I guess I can do that." She waited for the woman to leave and when she didn't, Caitlin reached for the phone and dialed Kenny's number. "I changed my mind, Kenny. I want you to keep looking for a while."

"I knew you'd say that. Don't worry—I'm still following her. I got a feeling. How about if I follow up all my remaining leads and see what happens? If I don't find anything in another week, we can drop it. I don't mind pulling my best on this, or giving you a discount. After all, your client might have saved his daughter, but there's still another child at that house. Cute little thing, even if he is crying all the time. The mother can't seem to do anything with him."

"I think he used to spend most of the time with his father until recently." Caitlin found she was beginning to feel sorry for Dakota. Maybe there was more to the situation than she knew. Maybe Dakota had reasons for becoming the woman she was now. Reasons that started and ended with Parker Hathaway. Look at how just five days with Parker had changed Caitlin's life.

"I'll keep you informed."

"Thanks." Caitlin set the phone on her desk.

"Thank you. I'll let you get back to work now." Mrs. Hathaway arose and took a few steps toward the door before pausing. "Look, I wanted to tell you that I heard something in my son's voice a few nights ago when he was talking about you. I didn't understand it then, but now I think it was hope. That's the only reason I dared come today. I know everything's a mess and you have no reason to trust us, but maybe you can find it in your heart to wait a bit. Give him a chance."

I can wait. That was what his note had said, arriving in a bouquet of bright, beautiful sunflowers. The flowers still stood on her kitchen counter, wilted now, though she could barely look at them.

Caitlin couldn't speak. The anger and hurt whirled around inside her, mixed up with memories of his kiss. Fortunately, Mrs. Hathaway didn't seem to expect an answer. She glided to the door with her strange grace and vanished.

Caitlin closed her eyes. A mistake because now the memories were back in full force. He'd kissed her, made her blood rush, all the while planning to leave her behind. That's what hurt the most, that he hadn't confided in her. They were good together, and she knew from past dating experience that such a connection was hard—nearly impossible—to find. If they had let it grow, could it have become similar to what her parents had felt together? Maybe she was beginning to understand, at least a little, why her father had been unable to go on after her mother's death.

She let her head drop to her hands, her fingers splaying in her hair, palms pressing against her eyes. More than anything she wanted to forget.

No, she wanted another try. She wanted Parker. To talk with him. To convince him to stay. Or maybe a chance for Parker to ask her to go with him.

"Caitlin?"

She looked up to see Jodi hovering at the door. "Sorry for barging in. I knocked but there was no answer. Your phone went to messages. Boss man's looking for you."

"Thanks, Jodi."

Caitlin made her way to Mr. Tyson's office, wondering what new case he would assign her to now. Another rapist? Another man who killed his girlfriend's baby?

I'm so tired of this.

As she reached Mr. Tyson's office, she came face-to-face

with Mace Keeley emerging from the room. "What are you doing here?" she rasped, not hiding her disgust.

Mace smiled pleasantly, looking relaxed and in control. "Just making a visit, that's all."

"Right." She pushed past him into the office, not believing him for a moment. Her being called into Mr. Tyson's office at the exact same time as Mace's visit couldn't be a coincidence.

"Ah, Caitlin, please have a seat." Mr. Tyson indicated a chair. Caitlin sat on the edge, back straight, willing her senses to stay alert.

Mr. Tyson shifted a few papers on his desk without looking at her. He was a trim man with white hair and eyebrows. His face was also pale, but his eyes were a bold blue, seemingly brighter for each year that sapped the color from the rest of him. Today he wore a white sport coat and tan slacks.

"Caitlin," he said, finally lifting his eyes. "I've had a disturbing report from the DA's office. I called you in to see what you have to say about it. I'd hoped to have them here at the time, but their representative had to leave."

"You mean Mace Keeley? I passed him on the way in."

He nodded, studying her. "Caitlin, you're an excellent attorney, and you've done a magnificent job for us, but Mr. Keeley seems to think there are some irregularities in some of your cases."

Caitlin sat even straighter and opened her mouth, but Mr. Tyson spoke again before she did. "I understand you will have a lot to say about that. It's why I brought you in here. I wouldn't even have bothered, but I have good information that says Mr. Keeley might become second in command at the DA's office, and I want to be sure where we stand."

"Well," she began, trying to keep her emotions out of it, "there's a lot more here than I'm sure he reported to you. Two weeks ago, Mace Keeley threatened me with blackmail if I didn't give him inside information and also sexually harassed me at the courthouse. There were at least three witnesses. I was going to let it go, but seeing as he's trying to bury what happened—and apparently me with it, I feel obligated to tell you now. As for my cases, I've worked hard to get every criminal on my list a fair shake, whether they deserved it or not."

A rueful smile played on his lips. "That's what I thought. Well, about the harassment anyway. I've heard a few rumors. But the blackmail . . . Look, Caitlin, these are all serious charges, both on your side and on his."

She shrugged. "Like I said, I was willing to let it go. He's the one coming in here."

"You shouldn't have let either of these things go," Mr. Tyson said. He waited a few minutes before adding, "Are you sure there's nothing else I should know about? I'll stand behind you one hundred percent because I believe in you, but if there's anything amiss, I could be putting this whole department in jeopardy."

Caitlin's indignation faded. He had no plans to throw her to the wolves, and suddenly she found that she couldn't keep up the pretense. The weight was too heavy to bear, regardless of the personal consequences. "There was something. Something you should know."

He nodded, folding his hands atop his desk and waiting. "That aggravated rape and attempted murder case I had a few weeks back. Chet Belstead."

"I remember."

"I sent a PI to question the people on Belstead's route home. I gave him a different date, so it was totally unrelated to the case. Could have been any case. He found a boy who remembered hearing something and advised him to call the police. That's what led to finding the knife."

Mr. Tyson leaned back. "On the surface it seems you did nothing wrong. You weren't directly involved in the information."

"No, but I hoped he'd find something." She didn't want to be excused so easily. It was a breach of ethics, and she knew it. "I knew about the knife from my client. He mentioned it in one of our interviews as sort of a . . . well, twisted attempt at flirting, for lack of a better word."

"I'm sorry that's something you've had to deal with."

Caitlin shrugged. They both knew it went with the territory. "Apparently Mace became suspicious at how the police were given the evidence and started sniffing around the PI—it's Kenny Pratt, by the way. As far as I know, Kenny's told him nothing about who he was working for at the time, but it's common knowledge I work a lot with Kenny. I think Mace planned to use any proof he could find about my involvement to help him get promoted, even though Belstead was as guilty as they come. That's why he waited so long after the evidence surfaced before bringing it up. But at some point, he must have changed his mind and decided it would be better to make me give him inside information about our clients—as well as offer him other side benefits."

"I get the picture." Mr. Tyson put a hand under his chin, supporting the elbow with his other arm that lay horizontally across his stomach. "It's possible when he didn't have the proof he needed, he thought the inside information was better than nothing."

He believed her. Caitlin leaned back in her chair, relief loosening her stomach muscles. "I told him to take a hike on both accounts, and I guess I'm a danger to him now, one he wants to nullify by going on the attack."

"So where do we go from here?"

She shrugged. "I don't know. I wish I could go back, but I can't."

"I think you've learned a valuable lesson. The real question is, would you do it again? In this business I can almost guarantee that you will face similar challenges in the future. Can you adhere to the standard we must maintain?"

She was silent a long moment before saying quietly, "That's just it. I don't know."

Mr. Tyson nodded. "Don't worry about Mace Keeley. I'll take care of him. But I want the names of the witnesses you mentioned, just to be sure we have backup before I wade into the fray. And if anyone asks you questions about this, refer them immediately to me. As of this moment, I'm your counsel on the matter."

Tears pricked Caitlin's eyes. "Thank you," she murmured.

But Mr. Tyson wasn't finished. "In the meantime, I want you to take the rest of this week and get where you can either finish or hand off your cases. Then I want you to take two or three weeks off while we get this mess cleared away once and for all and decide if you really want to stay here. Don't get me wrong—I want you here. I think you're the best attorney working here at the moment, the best we've had in a long time. But if you're going to stay, you have to be able to answer negatively to that question I asked you. You know as well as I do the reasons we cannot pick and choose when it comes to the fine lines of the law. No one should have that kind of power. It's too dangerous."

She nodded, blushing furiously, her English cool abruptly deserting her. "Thank you," she repeated. She stood and made her way quickly to the door.

"Oh, and Caitlin?"

She paused and turned. "Yes?"

Mr. Tyson smiled, looking more like a grandfather than

a powerful attorney. "I know how tough all this is, and how sometimes you have to follow your gut. I want you to know that if you decide not to stay, I'll still write you a glowing recommendation. There are many firms that could use your skills to protect the innocent. And you wouldn't face as many ethical dilemmas."

The tears Caitlin had been holding back fell now. "I'll keep that in mind."

How she found her way back to her office through the tears, she would never be sure. But something in her had changed. A burden had been lifted from her shoulders, a ponderous burden that had been weighing on her for a very long time. She felt so much relief and light that she vowed never to put herself in a similar situation again.

She wished she had someone to share her sudden change of fortune with, but the only person who might understand was Parker—and he was long gone.

Chapter 38

Parker rolled up the building plans and stored them with satisfaction before going to pick up Madison. The plans were every bit as good as the architect had promised. If they could pull it off, the expansive high-rise would be an accomplishment of a lifetime. And he would be a part of it, a major part—not just a crane operator but one of the planners and foremen.

After two long days of driving across Arizona, New Mexico, Texas, Oklahoma, Missouri, and, of course, Illinois, Parker and Madison had arrived in Chicago. Ten whirlwind days followed—ten very long and productive days. Mr. O'Doherty had underplayed his connections, and before Parker knew it, he was rubbing elbows with local contractors who not only were willing to put him into the trenches with their regular crews but to give him a chance as a foreman.

He'd worried there would be questions at his sudden name change from Vincent to Jonathan Hanks, even though

Shane and Orla O'Doherty weren't filling out his employment records, but he'd purposefully not given them his last name back in Vegas, and the O'Dohertys accepted his explanation that Vincent was his middle name with only an interested comment.

Every second Parker could spare from work or taking care of Madison, he was visiting sites or studying construction plans. There were some notable differences in constructing a building that was larger than he'd ever built before, and there were dozens of new city codes to learn, but the differences were not as many or as important as he'd expected. More vital to his new employers were his organizational skills and the feel he had for the project.

He was going to make it. He would have to forego sleep and work himself nearly to death in these first years, but he would give Madison the life she deserved. Of course that didn't mean everything was how he wanted it. He didn't even try to pretend that this life could make him completely happy. Despite his satisfaction at work, the growing emptiness inside him wasn't one he could easily overlook.

As he walked to where he'd parked the company truck the contractor had offered for his use while overseeing the job, his phone rang. He wasn't surprised to hear Orla O'Doherty on the other end.

"I'm calling about dinner on Friday," she said in her slight Irish lilt. "You are still planning on it, aren't you?"

He climbed into the truck and started the engine. The weather was bitterly cold in the streets now that dark had fallen. "Yes, of course. And looking forward to it very much. Thank you."

He and Madison had been invited to the O'Doherty's expensive downtown apartment already twice since their arrival in Chicago, including Thanksgiving dinner last week. So far the dinners made up his only socializing outside work, and he planned to keep it that way.

"Just the two of you, then? When's your girl coming? Soon, I hope. I'd think she'd want to spend the upcoming Christmas holidays with you. Your little Jess could use her company, and I daresay you could use the support too."

She had no idea how true that was. "I hate to say it," he finally told her after an awkward silence, "but I don't know that she's coming after all."

Mrs. O'Doherty clicked her tongue. "Well, it's hard to woo a woman properly when you're so far apart. You should go back to California to get her. Or tell her you're moving on. Maybe that'll spark a fire under her. At any rate, you can't go on this way. If she doesn't want you, I know a lot of ladies who will."

"I'll talk to her," he promised quickly. Having Orla set him up with women was the last thing he needed or wanted.

Twenty minutes later, Parker left the truck on the street near a row of apartment buildings and walked to the private residence where he left Madison each day with a middle-aged woman who also watched five other children of varying ages. Madison loved going there, and especially playing with the children, and the woman didn't seem to care in the least when she realized Jess was really a Jessica. She had already knitted Madison a pink sweater that he let her wear only to the day care.

He thanked the sitter and extended a hand to Madison. "Come on, sweetheart. Time to go home. Zip up your coat. It just started snowing again."

She was the last to be picked up tonight, so she didn't delay in grabbing her coat and backpack. It had snowed most of the ten days they'd been in Chicago, and he'd taken to carrying an umbrella to protect Madison from the wet weather. He used it now, holding it over both of them as they went out into the cold night.

Parker thought about Orla O'Doherty's comments as they walked back to the truck. He wanted to contact both his mother and Caitlin, but while he was sure of his mother's response, Caitlin was a complete wild card. What made him think she'd want him now? And if he felt guilt for ripping his mother from her comfortable life, how could he even begin to expect that Caitlin would leave her prestigious job as an attorney to accommodate his life on the run?

He supposed he could put off his decision regarding Caitlin for months, hoping for a miracle. But those were months where she might go on to build a life with some pretty-boy attorney and forget the fire between them. The more he thought about it, the more he decided that Orla was right. He needed to act. Or let go.

Maybe letting go was best for all of them. Utah already seemed like a distant dream, something no longer a part of him. Except at night he sometimes thought about his family's little valley in Mt. Pleasant and the stars shining brightly above in the sky. Would his mother sell the land? Selling would probably be a good decision since he had no idea how long he'd be in hiding, but he hoped she wouldn't. For some reason, his dreams of the valley always included Caitlin, and in those dreams it was always summer, definitely not snowing.

Logic said he should wait longer before making any decisions. He still hadn't figured out a safe way to contact his mother, much less Caitlin. He worried that the burner phone he'd given his mother might have been compromised by the police after his second disappearance, so he didn't dare contact her on it. There were only a few days left on the service, and his mother would be past anxious by now, especially after celebrating her first solitary Thanksgiving. That knowledge weighed heavily on him, but somehow leaving things the way he had with Caitlin was worse—almost as bad as it would have been leaving Madison.

He had to know where they stood.

Even if it risked everything he'd worked for? She could just as easily turn him in to the police as fall into his arms. She was an attorney, after all, part of the legal system, and he'd given her little reason to trust him.

"Daddy?" Madison tugged on his hand. He always made sure to hold her tightly, since the traffic in this part of the city was thick in the evenings, even with the snow. Around them people walked briskly to their destinations, faces hidden and bodies rounded by layers to stave off the frigid air.

"What, sweetheart?"

"Can we have macaroni and cheese tonight?"

That would be a test of his limited cooking skills, as he hadn't yet bought any boxes of mac and cheese. "We can try. We have macaroni, and we can grate some cheese. It might not taste the same."

"That's okay. I love cheese."

"I know you do."

They had reached the truck, and he opened the door and lifted her up into the air with a swoop that made her giggle. Emotion caught in his throat at how incredibly precious she was. Leaving might have split him in two, but he had to be careful never to forget or downplay the fact that Madison had been in danger every moment she'd stayed with Dakota.

Ten minutes later, as they rode up in the elevator in their apartment building, an idea occurred to him. An idea so intriguing that Caitlin might not be able to pass it up. At least not if she still held any feelings for him. And if he could be with her for a few moments, he knew he could convince her to believe in him. Maybe.

"Can I open the door with the key?"

"Sure, sweetheart."

If he was really careful, it might work. Madison finally managed to open the door, and he went inside the furnished apartment to the drawer in the kitchen where he kept the new tablet that Madison mostly used to play learning games on the Internet.

"Daddy, what about the macaroni?"

"This will only take a minute. Why don't you get out the cheese?"

The trick would be making sure nothing was traceable, not even to the debit card obtained with his new identity. But maybe, just maybe, he had enough luck, or karma, or whatever they were calling it these days, to make his idea work. The rest would be up to Caitlin.

Chapter 39

On Friday afternoon, Caitlin looked up to see Wyman Russell standing in her office doorway, looking handsome and professional in a black suit. She snapped shut her briefcase for what would be the last time in at least a few weeks and started toward him.

"So, the rumors are true," he said. "You're really doing it. Taking time off."

"People do take vacations." Though it was really a forced leave of absence, she was trying to stay positive.

"Not people who are going to work at my new firm with me."

She laughed. "So that's how it is."

"Seriously, though, I came to put in a good word for you with your boss about what happened with Mace."

"I appreciate that." Caitlin reached out to touch his arm briefly, but he put his hand over hers and held it there. For a moment they stood there in the doorway, not moving or speaking. Finally, Caitlin said, "I really appreciate everything you've done. I just don't know what my plans are yet."

"I figured that." He glanced behind him at the deserted hallway. "But I also think you've been avoiding me the past three weeks."

"Your divorce isn't final."

"Yes, it is. That's also why I stopped by. To let you know."

"Oh," she said. "That must have been tough."

He shrugged. "It's been going to happen for a long time now. It's good to be able to move forward. And that brings me to . . . well, I was thinking maybe we could have dinner again."

"Sure. That sounds good."

He was nice and she enjoyed his company, and she had every intention of going out with him again. Yet at the same time, nothing drove her to him, no heat between them made her desperate to have him near. In fact, when Wyman wasn't with her, she never even thought about him.

Truth was, she wanted what she'd felt with Parker. *I am such a fool,* she thought. In her imagination, she could still see Parker as he'd looked that last day three weeks ago. Feel his touch and how her body had reacted to his nearness.

"Who is he?" Wyman asked softly, his eyes fixed on her face. "The guy who brings that secret smile. It's not Mace, is it?" He said this last jokingly, but his comment clearly asked her if there was any hope for him. For them.

She snorted in an unladylike manner. "Not on your life. Not if Mace were the last man on earth. It's not anyone, or at least not anyone I can do something about. I just need time to sort my life out. It's been a difficult few weeks."

"Take all the time you need," Wyman said, standing aside

to let her precede him into the hallway. "My job offer will remain open for at least the next month."

"Thank you."

They rode down the elevator together and walked to the parking garage in a comfortable silence. She was thinking more and more about working with Wyman, and maybe eventually, when the memories of Parker had faded, there could be something more between them. She wanted a family, and if Wyman's kindness to Amy in giving her flowers was any indication, he'd be fine with having her around.

The ache of not knowing what might have been with Parker did at times seem to be lessening. She'd begun telling herself the separation made everything seem bigger than it had been—especially the attraction between them. How could such a connection be real? Yet several times a day something would remind her of him and the emotions would rush back, taking her breath away with their forcefulness, every bit as painful as that morning when she'd awakened at her house and discovered he'd really gone.

After opening his car door, Wyman bent and kissed her on the cheek. His lips felt warm and he smelled slightly of mint. Pleasant, comforting. Why couldn't she feel more for him? For an instant, Caitlin had the wild urge to grab him and kiss him silly to see if that would get Parker out of her mind.

Ridiculous.

She stepped away and smiled. "I have to go. I told Amy I'd be early."

"I'll call you, then."

"Sounds good." She waved as she left the parking lot.

Snow lined the streets and ice layered large portions of the road, as Utah seemed to be gearing up for record cold. Now that December had begun, Christmas lights were beginning to appear. Amy would insist on putting up lights on their house this year. Maybe Wyman would help. There would be comfort in not doing it alone.

Except why couldn't she seem to swallow that stupid lump in her throat?

She picked up Amy and had scarcely arrived home when a messenger appeared at the door. He was a red-haired, scrawny kid with the gangly awkwardness of the teen years he hadn't yet left behind.

"Caitlin McLoughlin?" he asked, extending an envelope.

"That's me." For a frightening moment, she thought he carried a subpoena that would force her to testify about what she had done in the Belstead case. With clumsy hands she opened the envelope, but inside she saw only the edge of what looked like an airline ticket. Relief flooded her. Of course this child wasn't delivering a subpoena—pizzas would be more his style. Besides, her boss was taking control of the situation.

"What's this?" she asked.

He shrugged. "I'm just a courier, ma'am. I pick up and take what they tell me to. There should be a note or something. We tried to deliver it yesterday morning, but no one was home, and the evening courier came down with the flu. Now if you'll just sign here."

Caitlin signed, all the while her hands burning to investigate the contents of the envelope. She turned from the boy as he ran out over the snowy yard, shutting the door with her hip. Slowly, she pulled out the ticket. Her name was on it.

It was a one-way ticket to Chicago. For tomorrow morning. *Chicago?*

There was no accompanying note, just the ticket. Who would have sent such a thing? She hadn't shared her dream of returning to Chicago with anyone. Except Parker.

A sudden dizziness made her reach out to steady herself on the wall. Her breath caught in her throat. It had to be him. But why? What had he to gain? He couldn't expect that she would jump on a plane at his whim. Yet even as she thought this, hope flared bright and strong, surprising her with its strength. She'd thought she was beyond that.

It was a dated ticket. Did that mean Parker would be waiting at the other end?

Just as quickly another realization fell like a dead weight on her chest, crushing the hope from her. He'd sent her a ticket. A *single* ticket. What did he think—that she'd leave her career, her home, drop all her life to go on the run with him and Madison? And what about Amy? Maybe her home and job could be replaced, but he had to know she would never desert Amy.

Of course he knew, so this obviously wasn't an invitation to enter his life. At most, it was an acknowledgement of her dream. More likely, it was a ploy to throw the police off his trail in Las Vegas where they'd tracked a vehicle they suspected he'd used to leave Utah. The ticket had probably been the cheapest available. Sobs caught in her throat. All at once the three weeks since Parker had left seemed like only three hours. Like his mother, Caitlin was apparently still waiting for him to contact her.

She opened her fingers and let the ticket fluttered to the floor. Leaving it on the carpet in the living room, she stumbled into the kitchen. She could hear the television blaring from her room where Amy was probably ensconced in the big bed, her eyes fixed on the screen.

Caitlin tried to busy herself with dinner, but her mind wouldn't let the ticket go. What if by some weird occurrence Parker was in Chicago and planned to meet her? What would make him go there?

Or maybe he hadn't intended her to use the ticket but had sent it only to let her know he was thinking about her. Maybe he meant her to feel grateful and nostalgic. But wouldn't flowers have been a better choice?

Stop, she ordered herself. She wished desperately that she hadn't shared her dream with him. The ticket was a mockery of her trust.

What hurt most of all was the knowledge that she wanted to hop on the plane and see if he was there waiting. What would it hurt? At the very least, she'd get a free trip to the city where she'd been born, even if she had to buy her own return ticket. The logical part of her mocked, saying such an idea was ludicrous. You didn't fly hundreds of miles at the whim of a man who'd left without saying goodbye, a man you'd known less than a week. Yet part of her yearned to do just that.

What was it her boss had said about going with her gut? What was her gut saying about the ticket? About Parker? And it wasn't as if she had anything else to do now that she was on leave.

Yet it really didn't matter what her gut said. There was only one ticket, and that absolutely did not translate into a future. Gut feeling or no gut feeling, she would never leave Amy to use his gift, not for any extended length of time, as the one-way ticket implied. And a day notice—or two if the ticket had been delivered yesterday, wasn't enough to plan even a short trip.

So now she was back to thinking it was meant only for a reminder of their time together. Something to put in a scrapbook and think about in her old age.

Or maybe he was mocking her. Tears started from her eyes.

Exhaustion made her mind numb and her body slow. What she needed was a good night's sleep. Maybe she should start taking sleeping pills. Ha! Not as long as she was responsible for

Amy. She tried to ignore the bitterness welling up inside her chest. Amy was her sister, and Caitlin loved her more than life. Parker was just a man. Soon she'd stop seeing him every time she shut her eyes. Soon she'd stop smelling him, remembering his kiss, how she'd laughed with him. Stop imagining lying in his arms and watching the stars in his family's little valley in Mt. Pleasant.

Caitlin dropped her head into her hands, tears leaking between her fingers, as she replayed the events of the past weeks. Could she have done something more to convince Parker to trust her? Had he only been using her all along, hoping she'd work harder on his case if her emotions were involved? The thought made Caitlin want to curl up into a ball and cry. At this rate, never dating again was beginning to look attractive.

Amy wandered into the room. "Don't you want these?" she asked, holding something out. "They were on the floor. Can I draw on them?" She was holding two airline tickets.

Two?

Caitlin grabbed them. Sure enough, there were two!

"I hope I didn't ruin them," Amy said. "They were stuck together. One's ripped a little. I didn't mean to rip it."

"That's okay."

All at once choices stretched out before Caitlin, if not in endless combinations then at least more positively than before. He hadn't sent her a single ticket; he'd thought of Amy, and that said a lot. He *wanted* her to take the trip. Should she read something into the fact that they were only one-way? Was that an invitation to stay, or had he not been able to afford return tickets?

There was still the chance he wouldn't be there, and the tickets really were a simple thank-you for her representation. Her stomach churned. If he wasn't there, it would mean there never had been anything real between them—anything besides the strongest attraction she'd ever experienced. Given that Kenny hadn't been able to turn up proof about Dakota's drug use, what did that attraction mean if Parker had been lying to her about the drugs?

Caitlin debated for several long seconds, but when it came right down to it, none of this mattered. She needed to see Parker, and if these tickets meant a chance of that, she was going. She would choose to take the risk. If things didn't work out, she'd buy her own tickets home and celebrate the fact that she hadn't let fear stop her.

"Amy," she said, her voice shaking with barely controlled excitement, "how would you like to go on a trip? We could go on a plane and everything."

"A real plane?" Amy's smile grew wide. "I *do* want to go! Yes!"

"Then let's go pack."

She'd finished Amy's suitcase and was halfway finished with her own when her phone broke her concentration. Caitlin answered it, not glancing at the number.

"Hi, beautiful." Kenny's exuberance made her smile.

"You have something?" she asked. Kenny never called her after work hours unless it was important.

"I found an old house owned by the boyfriend through some fake company. From what I observed of the comings and goings, it looks suspiciously like a meth lab."

Excitement rippled through Caitlin's stomach and spilled into her words. "You think Dakota knows about it?"

"She was there last night. Not long. An hour maybe. The little boy was screaming for some reason. That's probably why they left so fast. This afternoon, I saw two known drug dealers leaving—people who were definitely involved with the suicide guy Dakota lived with at that other meth house. I've been following them for a couple hours, but I've lost their trail. Anyway, I'll text you the address of the house when we hang up."

"Thanks. I'll let the police know."

Calling Sally meant the possibility of blabbing about the tickets, and Caitlin didn't want to tell her, even if it was best for Madison. Then again, if the information Kenny had found led them to the proof they needed, Parker would be proven right—and she wanted that more than she wanted to keep Sally in the dark about the tickets.

Quickly she dialed Sally's number. "Sally? Listen. Kenny called. He says he has something. Maybe we weren't wrong to trust Parker after all." She quickly outlined Kenny's suspicions. "I'm texting you the address he sent. Could you check it out?"

"Yes, but I want to call Kenny for the particulars and then do a bit of checking on the house's history. If I smell a rat, I'll drive by with some of the guys on my way home." Sally spoke casually, though Caitlin could sense an underlying excitement in her voice. This case had nearly driven Sally crazy, especially when Parker's trail had dried up in Nevada.

"Thanks. And Sally, double check on the little boy while you're talking to Dakota. He's been crying a lot, according to Kenny. If this turns out to be real, he's not safe any more than Madison was."

"I'll take care of it. But look, don't get your hopes up too high."

Too late for that. Caitlin was either headed for ecstasy or disaster. "Don't worry about me. I know what I'm doing."

"And what is that?"

For the first time in three weeks, Caitlin felt real joy. "I'm going on a little trip."

Chapter 40

The streets were already dark as Sally drove up to the suspected meth house with five of her fellow officers. The house was small like those in the rest of the neighborhood but not in disrepair. In fact, it looked like an ordinary house on any ordinary street.

For a moment, Sally saw what looked like a glimmer of light coming from a basement window, partially hidden by a metal window well. But no, that was most likely the reflection of the street lights.

They put on the protective gear stashed in the cars against a possible need to shield themselves from toxic chemicals that might be lurking in the air. One whiff would signal the level of toxicity.

She crunched over the unshoveled walk, praying they wouldn't have to fire their weapons. You never knew how drug dealers would react. At least Kenny's observations at the house that day had been strong enough to give them reason to conduct a search. Good thing Caitlin had kept him on the job, never mind what it must have cost her both emotionally and in cold, hard cash.

She felt distracted as she considered her last conversation with Caitlin. Where was her friend going? It wasn't like her to take off on a trip without notice. Something was going on, either at work or in her love life. Caitlin had refused to divulge more information, though Sally had at least exacted a promise that she would call later with details.

She'd better give details because Sally had a sneaking suspicion this sudden trip involved Parker, not so much because of the timing but because of the happiness she'd heard in her friend's voice, an aliveness that had been lacking the past three weeks. She encouraged Caitlin for years to get out there and find a man, but if her sudden excitement had to do with Parker, Sally was pretty sure it was a terrible idea.

Maybe I should have her followed, Sally thought.

But in the next minute, she told herself that she was jumping to conclusions. Caitlin was probably excited about the possibility of finding the meth house. And why shouldn't she turn her leave of absence into a vacation?

One of Sally's companions forced the front door open, and they spilled into the house. "Clear!" shouted first one officer and then another as they searched each room in the house. Besides random pieces of furniture and a box of old pizza, there was nothing to find.

"Do you smell smoke?" Sally asked fellow detective Jim Clegg.

He swore. "Where's the basement?"

They searched frantically for the door, hoping to save whatever evidence the basement might contain, but they barely made it down the steps before being overwhelmed by smoke.

"No can do," Sally screamed. "Get out!" That explained the light she'd seen in the basement, and judging by the swiftness of the blaze in the unfinished basement, it had an efficient fuel. Her lack of concentration had seriously cost them.

By the time they made it outside to the snow-covered ground, they could see flames in the corner bedroom on the main floor, and the scream of the fire truck one of the officers had called was only blocks away.

"Nothing," Jim muttered, taking off his protective mask, his face contorted with frustration. "From what I could see, the basement was empty. If there was anything here, they've moved it and torched the place to get rid of any evidence."

"They must have been warned."

"How? That PI was the only one who knew about this. You think he blabbed?"

Sally shook her head. "Not a chance."

"We might still be able to lift evidence if we can get that fire out soon."

"Maybe. But you're right; this doesn't add up. Let's you and me take a drive." She signaled to the other officers that she was leaving and headed to her car.

Jim jogged to keep up. "Where're we going?"

"To see Dakota Allen. And her boyfriend."

"You think they're going to fess up?" His upper lip curled slightly, but Sally didn't take offense. It was just a tick. She reminded herself to encourage him to wear a mustache. Many men with receding hairlines looked good with mustaches. Not as great as her Tony with his closely shaven head but good nonetheless.

"No. But we might catch them by surprise." Something was eating at Sally, something that first Caitlin and then Kenny had mentioned on the phone. But what had it been?

She revved the car as Jim slid into the passenger seat. "Hey, watch it." He gestured to the growing crowd of people in front of the house. "We have company. Don't want to be a bad example."

She gave Jim a flat grin. "Whatever. You're just mad because I'm driving."

The firemen had arrived and were doing their thing, and the blaze would be under control in minutes. More officers were arriving to help with the crowd. Sally knew they would evacuate the nearest houses, and normally she'd stick around to help, but her mind was still gnawing on the thought she'd had earlier. It was something Caitlin had said when she'd called with the address of the meth house. But what?

Fishing out her phone, she dialed Caitlin's number.

"Hello?" Caitlin sounded out of breath.

"Is something wrong?"

"No. Just leaving the store. I needed some things for my trip. I have to be at the airport early in the morning. What's going on?"

"The house was torched before we got there. Fire started in the basement. Someone was on to us."

"What about Dakota?" Caitlin asked. "What does she have to say?"

"I don't know. I'm heading there now."

"No one could have tipped her off. I mean, they might have seen Kenny, but that's unlikely. He's the best."

Sally had been in the business too long not to recognize trouble. "Something else must have happened—something that might have pointed to the meth house. So they torched it."

"But her house was clean. You've been over it."

"Not recently."

"She's still having visits from CFS, so I doubt there's

evidence at her house to find." Caitlin drew in a swift breath of air. "Unless one of them got sick from exposure. Maybe Madison's brother. He was at the meth house last night with Dakota."

Something clicked in Sally's brain. "And Kenny said he was crying." That was it—both Caitlin and Kenny had mentioned the boy and his tears. "Gotta go." Without saying more to Caitlin, Sally hung up, swearing under her breath.

"Kids always cry," mumbled Jim from the passenger seat. "At least mine do. Whenever they want something."

"Not kids with neglectful parents. Not as much anyway. They know there's no use." A sense of urgency mushroomed in Sally's chest, and she pushed harder on the gas. Her hunches were usually good, which was why she'd been so angry when Parker had disappeared. She couldn't understand how she'd been so wrong about him.

Maybe she hadn't been wrong.

Under the blanket of snow, Dakota's run-down neighborhood looked better somehow, the unkempt lawns and refuse covered with white snow. The street wasn't busy. In fact, for a Friday night it was far too still.

Sally was racing through the snow an instant after pulling the car to a stop, her hand reaching to ring the bell several times in rapid succession. Nothing. She rang again. Finally, Dakota appeared. She looked exhausted or hung over, her blond hair hanging straight and limp against her face.

"What do you want?" Her hand fluttered to eyes that were puffy from sleep. Or was it from tears? "Did you find Madison?" The question came as a slow afterthought, telling Sally that it hadn't been first on her mind.

"No. But I'd like to take another look at her room."

"You've already been through it."

"It'll only take a minute."

Dakota hesitated too long before saying, "My son's asleep in there. He's not feeling well."

"What's wrong with him?"

Dakota shrugged. "He threw up last night. Now he's just sleepy."

All of Sally's senses kicked into high gear. She noticed the deepening lines in Dakota's face, the eyes that seemed to be near panic, the way she kept glancing over her shoulder. Looking for someone. The boyfriend? Sally had seen his car outside, though there was no sign of the man at present. But the fear emanating from Dakota hadn't been caused solely by this supposedly friendly visit from the local police.

"I need to see your son." Sally craned her neck to see into the front room. No sign of the boyfriend here.

"You can't come in now." Dakota started to close the door.

Sally caught the door with her arm, keeping it open. "Is someone here threatening you?" she asked softly. "We can help."

Dakota stared at her dully for a few seconds, then shook her head. "I just want you to get out of here so I can take care of my son."

Sally met Jim's eyes. She gave the slightest shake of her head and pushed past Dakota.

"You can't do this!" Dakota screamed, pulling at Sally's arm.

Shaking her off, Sally strode down the hall, hand on her weapon, knowing Jim would be ready, too. She flung open the door to the children's room. Leo, the boyfriend, was kneeling by the twin bed where little Ricky lay, his bald head close to the boy's chest. One of Ricky's small hands was outstretched, hanging partially off the bed. Unmoving.

Leo jerked to his feet. "What are you doing here?"

Sally drew her gun and pointed it at him. "Step away from

the child." If she was wrong, she could be severely reprimanded, maybe even lose her job, but she'd trusted her instincts far too long to begin questioning them now.

"He's fine," Leo insisted.

"He doesn't look fine." Sally wasn't sure if the boy was even breathing.

"He was sick last night. We're going to wait a few hours and if he doesn't get better, we'll take him to the doctor."

"Go over by the crib and stand by Dakota," Sally ordered. She nodded at Jim to signal that he was to cover the pair. She holstered her own gun and knelt beside the bed. She felt for the child's pulse and found it at last, barely a flutter. *Dear Lord,* she prayed, *let him be okay.*

"Ricky," she said, gently patting the child's face. "Ricky?" she told Jim. She looked back at Dakota, who was standing across the small room near the crib, her fingers laced tightly in the bars. "How long has he been like this?"

All the fight had gone from Dakota's demeanor. "When we woke up this morning."

"You should have taken him to the emergency room!" Sally spat. She pulled out her phone and dialed 911.

"I've sat by him all day." Dakota came to the bed now, kneeling and taking her son's hand. "Please wake up, Ricky. Please."

"Why didn't you take him to the hospital?" Sally demanded.

Dakota glanced at Leo quickly and then back at her son.

"Did he tell you not to?" Sally asked.

"Don't tell 'em anything," Leo shouted.

Dakota buried her face in her hands and shook her head.

"Get him out of here," Sally growled.

Jim grabbed Leo's arm, but the heftier man shrugged him off. "I'm not leaving."

Jim pointed his gun at Leo's chest. "Yes, you are. We'll wait for the ambulance outside." Leo eyed the gun, as if calculating his chances. Sally stood up, her own gun in hand.

Leo looked between them a few times and then dived for the door. Jim was after him in an instant, and Sally knew she'd have to trust him to his job. She had to protect the child.

"Dakota, look at me," Sally said. "Did your boyfriend do something to your son?"

Dakota shook her head and sobbed, pressing her face into the mattress. "I was going to take him in. He's going to be okay. He's got to be."

Where was the ambulance? They should be hearing the sirens by now.

"Sally?" came a voice from the hallway. "Where are you?"

Sally stiffened. "Caitlin? Is that you?" What was she doing here? "In the bedroom," she called.

Caitlin came in, her coat askew and her eyes anxious. "Is he okay?"

Sally shook her head.

"Oh, no." Caitlin hurried to the bed, kneeling next to Dakota, her eyes fixed on Ricky's tiny, pale face. "I'm so sorry," she said to Dakota. "What happened?" When Dakota didn't respond, she continued, "It was the drugs, wasn't it?" Her voice was sympathetic, not accusatory. Sally had seen Caitlin break witnesses on the stand with that tone, but tonight her sorrow was real.

Dakota's sobs became louder, her shoulders convulsing violently. "Last night. He . . . drank some . . . of the water at the house," she whimpered. "The water for the meth."

Caitlin made a soft, despairing noise in her throat, her hand reaching out to stroke the child's face.

Sally tore her eyes from Caitlin, focusing back on Dakota.

She wanted to strangle the woman. "You should have taken him in last night."

"He cried and threw up. Then he went to sleep. Leo said it was all out."

"But you knew better— I can see that you did." Sally could barely speak past the rage. "Mothers are supposed to take care of their children. They aren't supposed to put them in danger. You stupid, stupid woman!" Her hand still holding the gun shook with desire to shoot Dakota. Who would really blame her?

"The ambulance. Sounds like it's here," Caitlin said, though Sally's anger had blocked out the sirens when they finally had come.

Sally holstered her gun, her eyes never leaving Dakota. "You disgust me!" With that parting shot, Sally went outside to guide the EMTs inside and warn them what they were up against. Maybe Ricky could be saved. She needed to focus on that possibility and not her urge to shoot his mother.

More police officers had arrived at the scene, and Sally spotted Leo in handcuffs. She'd let the officers deal with Dakota too. If Sally didn't stay away from the woman, she couldn't be responsible for what she might do. She gave directions to the EMTs and told them about the meth water. Pity and consternation filled their faces as they rushed into the house.

Caitlin appeared at her side moments later. "You couldn't have known this would happen," she said.

Hurt filled Sally's chest. "I knew Parker was telling the truth from the beginning. I *felt* it. That's why I asked you to help him. But I failed to find the proof we needed in time. I let both those kids down."

"I failed too. But Madison's alive. Remember that."

"Only because of Parker, not us." Sally caught sight of

Amy in Caitlin's car that was parked across the street. She was waving.

Sally turned to her friend. "Does Parker have anything to do with your sudden trip?"

A soft smile came to Caitlin's lips, accompanied by a blush that made her radiant. A woman in love. Did she know it herself? "I don't know," Caitlin said.

Sally gripped her shoulder. "Go get ready for your trip. Let this all be worth something."

Caitlin smiled and started across the street.

"You're going to Nevada, aren't you?" Sally called, her curiosity getting the best of her. "I'll bet he's still there."

Caitlin shook her head. "He could be anywhere. But I'm hoping he's in Chicago."

Sally clamped hands over her ears. "I didn't hear that. But if you happen to see him, please tell him I'm sorry."

Chapter 41

The plane was dark, and Caitlin tried futilely to read.
Beside her, dressed in bright pink cords and a pink
and orange sweater, Amy was snoring, her mouth
open wide. Amy had been remarkably content during their
time at the airport and on the plane. She'd watched planes
take off, eaten everything offered to her by Caitlin or the flight
attendants, slept when she needed to, and had taken up conversations with at least a dozen perfect strangers.

Caitlin, on the other hand, was so nervous she hadn't been
able to sleep at all, not the night before or on the plane. Would
Parker be waiting at the airport? Or were these tickets his way
of telling her thank you?

Or maybe goodbye.

A bitter taste in her mouth increased as she wavered
between surety that he would be there and certainty that he
wouldn't. One moment she was feverish with hope and the
next filled with despair at what they had lost. Parker wasn't

just any man. So what if he wasn't a high-powered, intellectual attorney? He was a smart and caring man, and hardworking to boot. Willing to do what he knew was right, despite the consequences to himself.

Caitlin pictured the limp form of Madison's little brother as she'd last seen him lying on Madison's bed. He'd died shortly after making it to the hospital, and the knowledge was unbearable to Caitlin. If Madison had been at the house that night, she might have also drunk the contaminated water. She might now be fighting for her life, instead of safe with her daddy.

"The saddest thing," Sally had told her before her flight that morning, "is the doctor said he would have lived if they'd taken him in right after he drank the water. Instead, they waited, and then when they realized they'd have to take him to the emergency room, they waited even longer so they could cover their butts by torching the house."

When she shut her eyes, Caitlin could see the still little figure. So tiny and helpless, his mother sobbing at his side. She loved him, of that Caitlin was certain, but not enough. Dakota had never loved anyone more than she loved herself.

But Madison was safe! It always came down to that. Parker had been telling the truth all along. If he wasn't waiting for her in Chicago, he might never know, or at least not for a long time. He wouldn't know that he could return home.

Then again, maybe even if he did know, he wouldn't want to come home.

Please, Caitlin thought. *Be there.*

The plane would be landing in less than an hour. Would Caitlin be on it? Parker had no way of knowing. Only after sending the tickets had he realized that he couldn't meet her openly at the airport as he'd planned. The risk to his daughter was simply too great. Yet he would be at the airport all the same. He'd leave in the next few minutes to make sure he was in place well before her possible arrival.

Just a look, he promised himself. *To see if she actually came.*

With his bald head, trim beard, new black dress coat, and dark sunglasses, he looked different enough that she might walk right past him without noticing. Maybe he'd be able to determine somehow that she hadn't told Sally about the tickets, that she'd come only because she wanted to be with him.

The daydream fell apart every time at that point, because how could he know her that well after so few days? And he couldn't risk his daughter. Maybe he could follow Caitlin and contact her later during her stay. After he was certain. Maybe.

Regardless, he would be at that airport today. Waiting.

"Rosie is my best friend," Madison said as he slipped her shirt over her head.

"Well, you be a good girl at her house today. Don't boss her around." He was leaving Madison with the neighbor for the morning because taking her to watch for Caitlin wasn't a good option.

He dragged a brush through her hair without finesse. "Ow," she said. "Give it to me. I can do it myself."

Minutes later they knocked on the neighbor's door and the mother answered. "Oh," she said, looking surprised. "I forgot you were coming. I'm sorry, but Rosie's been sick all night, throwing up everywhere. She's sleeping now, but she still has a fever. You'll have to play another day."

This was something Parker hadn't planned for. He'd under-played the importance of his appointment to both Madison and Rosie's mother, so he couldn't exactly push now. Besides, he didn't want Madison sick.

"Thanks anyway," he said with a forced smile. He'd have to hide with Madison behind a pillar or something as they watched for Caitlin.

They returned to their apartment for Madison's coat. "Where are we going?" she asked. Her sadness at not staying with her friend vanished instantly.

"I have to stop by a place for a few minutes, and then we'll go somewhere to eat."

She hugged him. "Yay! I love you, Daddy. Can we have pizza? When we go home, I'm going to tell Ricky and Grandma all about Chicago and the yummy pizza."

Parker hadn't told her they were never going home, but it did soothe him that she barely mentioned Dakota, though she talked constantly about her grandmother and Ricky.

Outside it was snowing. Not just snowing but snowing as though someone was dropping huge bucketfuls of snow directly on top of the city. Madison giggled and made to step out into the snow, but he caught her arm and opened the umbrella. "No, sweetheart. You'll be the one throwing up next if you go out in that."

Ten minutes after leaving the apartment, he could barely see through the windshield as he followed the airport directions he'd printed the day before at work. There was plenty of time, despite the sudden storm. But why was he even going? Caitlin wouldn't be there. He knew she wouldn't . . . and yet how could she not? There was something between them, something that could last more than a dozen lifetimes. Did she even understand that the message was from him? Did she understand the significance of the tickets being only one way? For all he knew, she had many grateful clients who knew she wanted to go to Chicago. There was also the strong possibility that she was in a relationship with that pretty-boy attorney or had work that wouldn't allow her to leave town.

The car in front of him slowed to a crawl, and soon he was almost at a standstill. "What's going on?" Parker asked aloud, craning his neck to see through the whiteness battering the windshield. He tried to rake a hand through his hair, finding only a bald head under his beany. It was probably too soon to let his hair grow back, but he missed it, especially when he was worried.

"Why are we stopped, Daddy?"

"Probably an accident. People forget they need to slow down when it snows. Is your seat belt tight?"

She tugged on the belt crossing her booster seat. "It's tight."

Parker stared out into the white world, unable to believe his rotten luck. He wasn't going to make it. He wouldn't be at the airport to see if Caitlin still cared. Panic filled him. He studied the map and saw that they were about a mile from the airport. A piece of cake on foot in normal weather—and without Madison. Too far away carrying her in the snow. And dangerous with the traffic.

He waited twenty more precious minutes. They were coming closer to the airport, but they might as well have been in another state. He definitely wasn't going to make it in time. But there was now a sidewalk lining the street, one that looked safe.

"Okay, let's walk." He eased the truck over to the side of the road. "You hold the umbrella," he said to Madison. "I'll carry you on my shoulders."

Madison whooped and giggled as he ran past the line of unmoving vehicles. The airport wasn't too far away now, but the snow was still coming down hard, and in a few minutes Parker was wet from the chest down. His feet were freezing. Cars were still backed up as far as he could see behind him, and ahead there was an accident involving a bus and a delivery van.

Snow pelted them as he ran past the accident and on to the airport. He let Madison down outside the airport doors, and fortunately she was nearly dry. His watch said almost noon, and the plane was to have arrived at eleven-forty. He shut his eyes a moment before opening the door. If the flight hadn't been early, she might still be at the airport, maybe collecting her luggage.

Or she could be long gone.

He checked the luggage carousels before waiting outside security, studying each passenger as they exited the gate area. No Caitlin. The probability of finding her was growing slimmer by the second.

"Daddy, can I get a drink?"

"Sure." He took her over to a machine and bought her an orange soda pop.

She settled on the bench next to the machine, sipping contentedly. "Why are we here?"

"I'm looking for someone. It'll only take a few more minutes." But they could probably leave now. If Caitlin had been on the flight, she wasn't here any longer.

Someone passed by him, bumping into his arm. "Excuse me," said a tall woman with graying hair.

"No problem." He gave her a smile he didn't feel.

She nodded and turned back to her companion. "I'm not surprised the flight wasn't allowed to land on time with all this snow," she said. "Good thing it let up enough for us to land."

Hope flooded him, and he searched the room for the huge screens that gave updated flight information. That he hadn't checked before said a lot about his state of mind. "Stay right here, Madison," he told his daughter. "I'm just walking over to that TV there. I want you here where I can see you."

"Okay." She took another sip of her drink, swinging her legs.

His soggy shoes creaked as he crossed the room and began comparing flight numbers to the one on the damp, crumpled paper in his pocket. The flight from Salt Lake City was delayed and only now arriving. He hadn't missed her! Returning to the bench with Madison, he sat back and waited. They were partially obscured by the drink machine, but he had a clear enough view.

There! His heart nearly stopped beating. She was coming through the security gate, Amy behind, her large body looking ridiculous in her bright pink and orange clothes. Caitlin was loaded down with a large purse, a pink backpack he thought might be Amy's, and a rolling carry-on suitcase. Amy pulled an identical suitcase and carried a green jacket over her shoulder. Caitlin laughed and said something to Amy. She was more beautiful than he remembered. Her copper hair was freed from its usual clasp, curling around her face. Her eyes were bright, her freckled skin perfect.

He studied the other passengers also coming through the security gate. No Detective Crumb or other official-looking person. Had she really come alone?

After passing the gate, Caitlin stopped and scanned the large room slowly. Her tongue wet her lips. Parker pulled his head back momentarily as she glanced his way, glad that Madison was standing on the bench now, near the drink machine where she couldn't be seen.

After long minutes, Caitlin's bright smile faltered and died, as though turned off by a switch. She stood there a few minutes longer as though considering her options. Finally, she took a determined breath and reached for Amy's hand, the happiness on her face replaced with resolution. She turned and began walking away.

Was he going to let her go? If only he could be sure she hadn't told anyone.

"Madison, stay here again," he said in a low voice. "Over here on the end where I can see you. Don't talk to strangers or leave."

He stood and followed Caitlin.

Caitlin's disappointment was so all-encompassing that it took every ounce of pride in her to start walking toward the baggage carousels.

He isn't here.

Which meant this was the end of any chance they'd ever had. Even when Parker learned that he had been cleared and could soon come home without facing charges, it would make no difference to their relationship. She should be thankful for his gesture with the tickets. It was still sweet, even if it didn't mean what she wanted it to mean. After all, she was finally back in Chicago where she'd always wanted to be.

"We'll get a taxi to a hotel I read about on the Internet yesterday," she told Amy brightly. "You'll love it there. It's really homey. At least it looked that way on the computer." She had addresses of her parents' friends to look up later, but for now, she desperately needed a hot bath and some sleep. Her hope must have been what had kept her going this long, because suddenly her exhaustion felt like an impossible weight.

"I'm hungry." Amy changed hands on her suitcase handle.

"They have wonderful food here. You're going to love it."

He isn't here. Her mind couldn't seem to move on from that. She had been a fool to think a few days could have created something lasting. It was just attraction. Nothing more. It hadn't meant anything real.

Yet why did she *feel* him? Why was her heart reaching out and finding . . . something?

She stopped walking. Amy continued ahead several paces before she turned and looked curiously back at Caitlin. "Why did you stop?"

Caitlin didn't answer. She released the handle of her suitcase and dropped Amy's backpack. Slowly she turned.

He was standing behind her, about twenty-five feet away. He looked different. A black beany covered his head, and his face, thinner than she remembered, sported a sexy trim black beard. Instead of his usual jeans and bulky work coat, he wore black dress pants and a long black coat. Even indoors, dark glasses covered his eyes.

One thing hadn't changed. The connection between them instantly leapt to life—no, it had already burned with life. Now the link revived and strengthened as their eyes met. He took a step and then stopped, a question on his face. But she knew the answer. She ran to him, threw herself into his arms. He hugged her tightly. There was no need for words. He kissed her, his fingers tangling in her hair. For a long moment there was no one else in the huge room. People streamed past, miraculously parting around them.

Magic.

"Is there a reason you're sopping wet?" she asked, when she could finally bring herself to speak. She was wide awake now, her every nerve buzzing with his nearness.

He grinned. "There was a traffic jam. I jumped out of the truck and ran here."

"I see." Her eyes flicked to the huge windows where, sure enough, snow still fell at a steady rate. "Ever hear of an umbrella? Unless it was too windy."

"Not much wind, but Madison had—" He broke off and glanced away. She followed his gaze to an empty bench by a soda pop machine. She felt his body tense, his head jerking around, as he searched anxiously.

"Daddy, are you finished kissing yet?" came a voice next to them. "Amy's hungry, and we want to have a tea party."

Caitlin turned to see Madison standing next to Amy, a wide smile covering her little face. Her hair had been dyed black and was as short as a boy's and the coat she wore was an ugly navy blue, but that sweet smile was unchanged.

Parker stared at her for barely a second. "No. I am definitely not through kissing Caitlin. Amy, make sure Madison doesn't run off." With that, he turned Caitlin's head and kissed her again. "I hope you came to stay," he said against her lips. "And that you didn't bring the police." This last was said only half jokingly.

She allowed herself another long kiss before replying. "No. To both questions."

"To both questions?" Hurt registered in his voice. "You won't stay?"

She took pity on him. "I've come to take you home."

"I can't. You know that. Please stay. It won't be as hard starting over as you might think. I've got good prospects here. We could have a family."

Her heart thundered in her chest. "Parker Hathaway, are you proposing?" For a moment she wished she didn't have to tell him he was free from running, that she could agree to stay here with him for a few years—or forever—hiding away from the world.

"I'm doing more than proposing." The brown eyes staring into hers were serious. "I'm offering you my whole life, Caitlin. I know it's a sacrifice leaving everything behind, but I promise I'll make it up to you. I love you."

His whole life—that was no small thing. She wanted to accept his gift, but first she had to tell him everything. "There's something you need to know. I was packing to come when Sally found the proof we've been looking for."

She thought he'd ask about the proof, but instead he said, "You came even though you weren't sure I was telling the truth?"

"The proof was in here." She put her hand to her heart.

His eyes told her what that meant to him. "What did Sally find?"

Glancing at the girls to make sure they weren't paying attention, she said quietly, "Dakota's in jail. Ricky ended up drinking water contaminated with meth chemicals. If you hadn't taken Madison away, there's no telling what might have happened."

"And Ricky?"

She shook her head, wincing at the pain in his face and at her own memory of that pale, tiny, still body. "I'm so sorry. The good news is there's not a prosecutor anywhere who would try to make kidnapping charges stick now. You'll have to jump through a few hoops when you get home, but it's just a formality."

"How am I going to tell her about Ricky?" He glanced over her shoulder at Madison. She was sitting on Amy's suitcase, showing Amy her umbrella.

"Maybe don't say anything for a while. Just love her." Caitlin drew Parker's head down and kissed him again, wanting more than anything to take away his hurt. Though their mood had turned somber, the connection between them was as strong as ever.

Sometime later he drew away long enough to say, "Might be better for Madison—for all of us—to stay here for a few years. If it's still your dream. That's why I chose Chicago. Because of you. I meant what I said when I mentioned having good prospects here. Even if I go back eventually, I have a contract I need to fulfill and people counting on me. I'm not just one of the crew anymore. I'm running the crew."

His words came to her like an answer, and all her confusion about the future faded away. Why worry about choosing between jobs in Utah when she had everything she wanted right here? While she looked for a job she didn't hate, she could visit her parents' friends, walk down streets she'd known as a child, and love Parker and Madison. Renting her house, moving their things—all of it sounded better than what awaited her back in Utah. Being with Parker sounded better.

"Okay," she said simply, watching his face for the shock and gladness she knew was coming. "Let's give it a try." He whooped and picked her up, twirling her around. Somehow his beany came off, and she couldn't help laughing at his shaved head.

They'd have to go back at some point to clear things up, but she could represent him so he could remain here except for court dates. His mother could visit and they could visit her. Maybe someday they'd go back and build a cabin in his little valley.

He kissed her again, cutting off her thoughts. Warmth flowed between them, evoking the promise of their future together. "I was so afraid you wouldn't come," he whispered in her ear.

"I was so afraid you wouldn't be waiting."

He made a noise in his throat. "As long as there's any chance you want me, Caitlin, I'll always be waiting. Always." He kissed her one last time before drawing away and putting his arm possessively around her. "Come on, girls. Let's go find some pizza."

Author's Note

Some years ago, shock radiated throughout the country when a Utah infant was found dead after ingesting methamphetamines she had found in a plastic bag on the floor of her home. What made this tragic circumstance even more notable and horrific is that weeks earlier her father had forcibly taken her from her mother and transported the baby across state lines, hoping to protect her from her mother's substance abuse. Authorities found the little girl, placed her back with her mother, and sent the father to jail for assault and burglary. A little more than a week later, the baby was dead, and the mother was charged with desecration of a corpse for moving the baby's body to cover up her own drug abuse. All charges against the father were eventually dropped.

Sadly, this is not the only real-life story of a child becoming the victim of a parent's drug use. In Tulsa, a young boy grabbed a drink of what he thought was water but which was actually lye used in making meth. He survived, but his esophagus was burned away, and he will never be the same. Other children who have ingested similar chemicals were not so fortunate.

One mother, heavily doped up on drugs, accidentally rolled over and smothered her child as they napped together on the couch. A six-year-old boy showed law enforcement officers in detail how his daddy made drugs. In meth homes throughout the country, baby bottles share sinks and refrigerators with meth containers, and the drug is often made in the same kitchen where food is prepared, which means deadly poison is only inches away from toddlers' dinner plates and glasses of milk. Law enforcement officers wear protective gear when dismantling these meth labs, but the children who live there are unprotected from toxic fumes that saturate their bodies, clothing, and toys—if they are lucky to have such things. Often these houses have no food, no toilet paper, and no sheets on the beds. The children are completely neglected, and the houses are filthy. Many of these children show developmental delays, organ injuries from the fumes, heart problems, seizures, and violent behavior.

Chief Deputy C. Philip Byers from the Rutherford County Sheriff's Office in North Carolina writes: "In 2004, over 2700 children were found in methamphetamine labs seized by law enforcement officials nationwide. Children were present in 34 percent of the total lab seizures in the United States."[1]

Some of those children were injured or killed when the labs were seized. As shocking as that is, however, experts estimate that only a small proportion of meth labs are ever found.

States seem to be losing the battle against methamphetamine addiction. Child welfare, law enforcement, substance abuse, and treatment systems are overloaded. Some estimate that more than 8.3 million children in the United States live with a parent who has a substance abuse issue. Nearly 2 million child abuse cases each year are investigated, and half a million of those have enough evidence to act on. Some 200,000 children are removed from their homes each year.[2]

But what about the cases that aren't proven? What about the children who fall through the cracks but are still at risk? To what lengths might a noncustodial parent be compelled to go to protect a child from danger?

These were the questions I thought about as I began writing *How Far.* I wanted to show one man's dilemma in balancing his need to protect his daughter against his duty to obey the law, and to depict his struggle in an overloaded system where there are no second chances for the innocent victims.

Please keep in mind that though the idea for this novel was inspired by the numerous true stories I researched, the plot, characters, and resolution in *How Far* are completely fictional. No actual experiences or interviews of real people were used in the text itself.

Could a story such as *How Far* actually happen? I believe so. The outcome for my make-believe Madison is what I wish could happen for similar little children caught in real-life tragedies. At the same time, the story is a heartfelt dedication to all those children who, like Madison's brother, Ricky, have no one to fight for them and who do not survive.

NOTES:

1. Information originally found at sheriffs.org/userfiles/file/Congressional%20Testimony/http://www.sheriffs.org/userfiles/file/CongressionalTestimony/ Deputy_Philip_Myers_Testimony_on_Fight_Against_Meth.pdf, but the PDF has since been removed.

2. Information was originally found at gu.org/documents/A0/Impact_Meth_Abuse_on_http://www.gu.org/documents/A0/Impact_Meth_Abuse_on_ Children_and_Families.pdf, but the PDF has since been removed.

Discussion Guide

1. When Parker first took Madison from her mother's house, her younger brother, Ricky, was also in the room. Given the outcome of the novel, was Parker's decision not to take the boy, either at that time or later in the story, a correct choice? Discuss how a split-second decision can change an entire future.

2. How did Parker's relationship with his father and brother influence the person he later becomes? What about his relationship with his mother? What major events in Parker's life caused the changes in his early lifestyle?

3. How do you think Parker's mother felt in wanting to protect and defend her son and granddaughter and yet not wanting to break the law? What do you think she should have done? Why?

4. Discuss Caitlin's mixed feelings about her sister. How has her choice to care for Amy affected her life?

5. Is Caitlin happy in her career? What do you think might

make her happier?

6. Discuss the different men in Caitlin's life. What are their strengths and weaknesses? Do you think Wyman would have been a good choice for a relationship? What about Parker? Do you feel he is permanently reformed? Why or why not?

7. Did Caitlin make the right choice in arranging to pass evidence to the police? What about her duty to her client? What about her duty to society? Do you think she should be disbarred for her actions?

8. What parallels do you find between Parker's taking Madison and Caitlin's choosing to pass information to the police about her client?

9. Although Parker's actions in taking Madison were against the law, do you feel the end justifies the means in this story? What mistakes do you feel Parker made? What did he do right?

10. What about Mace Keeley? Should action be taken against him for his treatment of Caitlin?

R achel Branton grew up avidly reading and watching Star Trek reruns with her large family. They lived on a little farm where she loved to visit the solitary cow and collect (and juggle) the eggs, usually making it back to the house with most of them intact. On that same farm she once owned thirty-three gerbils and eighteen cats, not a good mix, as it turns out. Rachel always had her nose in a book and daydreamed about someday creating her own worlds.

Rachel is now married, mostly grown up, and has seven kids, so life at her house can be very interesting (and loud), but writing keeps her sane. She grabs any bit of free time from her hectic life to write. She's been known to wear pajamas all day when working on a deadline, and is often distracted enough to burn dinner. (Okay, pretty much 90% of the time.)

She loves writing fiction and traveling, and she hopes to write and travel a lot more. She also loves target shooting, martial arts, Fisher Price Little People, and Hard Rock Cafe shirts. She has worked in the publishing business for over twenty years. In addition to contemporary romance, Rachel writes science fiction and fantasy and paranormal suspense under the name Teyla Branton. For more information or to join her mailing list and get a free ebook, please visit http://www.TeylaBranton.com.